TIFFANY MURRAY has published short fiction in *Pretext* and *Mslexia*, and has written for *The Times,* the *Observer Music Monthly* and the *Independent on Sunday*. She trained as an actress, then moved to New York to study Caribbean and African literature at NYU. Tiffany is now completing her PhD at the University of East Anglia, where she teaches Creative Writing.

For automatic updates on TIFFANY MURRAY visit harperperennial.co.uk and register for AuthorTracker.

From the reviews of *Happy Accidents*:

'Lively, anarchic and readable'   FAY WELDON

'Along with her whip-cracking dialogue, it is quirky images that are Murray's forte … [She] evokes a pungently recognisable time and place, capturing the Wild West feel of these rackety Border towns and lashing it to early Eighties pop references like music and recipes. The farm itself is very Stella Gibbons, but Kate's gran and the Happy clan's endless eccentricities make it Murray's own'

HEPHZIBAH ANDERSON, *Observer*

'Murray uses language that is simultaneously inventive and unobtrusive to help Kate's thoughts along as she navigates her way into adolescence … [She] writes with a lightness and sureness that is appropriate for her narrator … This discreet style means the humour is unforced, though often brutally black … Murray has shown she is a writer of singular felicity whose first novel holds out strong promise for the future'   *Independent*

'Murray manages to counterpoint beautifully the loveless, the perverse and even the wicked with all that is tender and true in human relationships. The novel is busy and alive, threaded through with odd encounters between girls and men, men and women, boys and girls, great-aunts and their sisters, mothers and their daughters. The defining characteristic of all these interactions – indeed of the book – is functional dysfunctionality; a kind of deranged but charming kookiness … [with] Murray's familial vision, the sense of humanity buzzing above Kate's narrative sings all the more sweetly'   *Time Out*

'Hysterically funny, a wonder … baroque and witty … As dark and as funny as all the best fairy tales'
TIM GUEST, author of *My Life in Orange*

'A delightfully zany coming of age black comedy'
Glasgow Herald

———————————————

By the same author

Pretext 8: Once Upon a Time …
(editor with Helon Habila)

To Mum, for being Joan

1

My mum called the combination of a red chaise-longue in a red front room a bit of posh and common. She said that was *just* like her parents.

Right now I'm lying on one, and in one; stomach down and bare bottom out.

It's freezing.

Four of my grandpa's Toby jugs sit grinning halfway up walls papered red with hunting scenes. Men in scarlet jackets blow horns, while the wet lips of a mounted stag drool above me.

My belly growls.

'Shh!'

This is a Grandpa room. It smells of cold beef fat. You have to be quiet as a mouse in a Grandpa room.

Mr Barlow, the head-vampire from *'Salem's Lot*, lurks in here. He's a big greeny thing, with a slap-bald head and very, very pointy teeth. Usually, he's behind the black oak sideboard, filled with the family silver.

He rattles it.

My favourite books are *'Salem's Lot* and *Jane Eyre*, because they're American and English, and so am I. In fact, I have dreams about Mr Barlow and Jane on outings together, but they do really dull things. Last night it was a weekly shop at Marks and Spencer: they bought lots of offal and dark chocolate liqueurs.

I shiver on the velvety chaise and wonder if the doctor will find me, our farmhouse is so huge.

There are thirty-six rooms in all, though I've only ever counted thirty. Most are locked, keys forgotten. Gran did tell me the others are hidden, 'Like those cosy priest holes, Katie, so cute! And you know what? There sure were some goddamned small priests in those days.'

My gran says 'wadder' instead of 'water' and 'yougoddamnsonsof-bitches' because Grandpa dragged her over from America, a million years ago.

One thing I do know: there are five storeys to this house. Grandpa lives on the ground floor where dark corridors smell of pee and beeswax, while the first floor is all pink and my grand-mother's ('thinks she's bloody Barbara Cartland,' Mum says). The second floor used to be Mum's and now it's mine, and the third floor is dark and cut off. There, long-gone bulbs have rusted into sockets, and rooms never lived in drip with damp.

Above us all is the attic. There are lots of groans and whispers in this farmhouse.

In the corner of Grandpa's front room the only telly sits grey and dead. I shiver some more as trees wriggle like fish in our half-English, half-Welsh garden, and November rain spits at the window like a cat. Cows thud across the backyard, ready for milking, and I can't feel my bare bottom at all.

Yum-yum bubble-gum, stick it up your mum's bum, when it's brown, pull it down, yum-yum, bubble-gum.

We sang that at my last school, knees gone to pink in the cold playground.

I've been waiting with my bum out on this chaise-longue for five mornings on the trot now. Waiting for Dr Croften to raise the boil on my backside that was once an innocent flea bite, got from spending a night with our sheepdog, Jessie 13, in his oil drum. My grandparents don't really name their animals, they count them.

Dr Croften is going to make this boil burst.

Our black telephone rings in the hall, and in the backyard, from an old-fashioned bell on a telegraph pole. I love the farm phone and the way it calls out when you're playing in the icy fields.

'Gran?!' I shout. Then I hear the clicketty-clack of her high-heeled slippers, deep in a distant corridor. Grandpa's mantelclock ticks loud above the ash-filled grate, twenty-five minutes fast, and I see myself in the big, spotted mirror by the door.

'Hello? Boldenham 5–4–7, Iris Happy talking,' she says, muffled. 'Oh yes. Sure, Doctor.'

I try and smooth down my electric hair. Gran calls it a dust-ball, and now it's speared with straw because I spent last night in the barn. I wanted to run away and join the circus, instead of going to school. It's just they don't have circuses round here, though Gerry Cottle did come to Newport in 1979.

Gran says, the problem is, I think I'm all growed up. I'm nearly eleven, so I must be. That's two years older than Tatum O' Neal, my favourite actress, when she was in *Paper Moon*, my favourite film. Trouble is, I'm as tiny as her. I stare at my four foot self in the old mirror, pull a face, but the wind doesn't change.

'C'mon trouble maker,' Gran yells from the hall. 'Clothes back on.'

'But the doctor –'

'Late. Some kinda emergency.'

'Gra-an.'

'Back on. You'll catch your death.'

She's right. That happens a lot in this house.

My bare white chest prickles cold as I sit up, but it's okay because I don't have boobs. Not like Mum and Gran, and sometimes Grandpa in a certain light. I pull up my new school uniform tights and knickers, red as ladybirds' backs. 'Gran?'

'What?'

'Can I stay at home today?'

'No.'

The silver rattles. The clock ticks.

'Pu-lease,' I point out one red leg, a skinny ballerina. 'I hate new schools.'

'Nope. Kitchen, Katie. Pronto.' I listen to her clicketty-clack away from me.

The stag's head is still drooling, then it winks at me in the mirror and I run out of Grandpa's red front room, into one of his dark stinky corridors.

This morning, after a night hiding in the barn with the rats and the rain, I decided that it's safer to give in to my gran, as she can cure anything. Even me. She's the one who gently lifts me out of bed each morning, then kills the geese at Christmas with a knife across the throat. She's the only granny I know who rides Foreo 4, her fourth in a line of black stallions, that not even the farm boys will touch. And afterwards, still in her slimming jodhpurs with her black hair and her black eyes, she'll wash and peg out Marks and Spencer carrier bags that crack in the wind. Gran is the only person I know who cries over foreign telegrams, then wipes down Grandpa's cooked chicken breast with 'just a dab' of Fairy Liquid as she's been trying to kill him for thirty-eight years. 'Slow deaths are the best, honey, and ain't that just my life?' From this moment on I'm going to do what she tells me. I think if I stick with my gran then everything will be fine.

'Right, Grandpa's breakfast,' she trills from the darkness, her breath nothing but Parma Violets.

I put out my arms like a zombie, and follow the smell. It's easy to lose each other in this house.

It's bright in the kitchen and Gran's holding a metal comb, and scissors with blades like teeth. Her housecoat is just below her knees and it's as pink as her high-heeled slippers. I've decided my gran isn't old because her favourite colour is pink. She says she's as pink as a stick of rock in slingbacks.

'Stand up properly, honey.'

'Why?'

'First day at your new school, we gotta do something about that hair.'

This close her skin smells of candy floss as well as Charlie perfume. Her nails are Maraschino cherry.

'But –'

She points at my backside. 'No buts. Straight now, shoulders back. Head down.'

I do as I'm told, and stare at her still-good legs, smooth as eggs.

Snip, and what's left of my blonde, summer hair falls on the black quarry tiles of the kitchen. I'm going to be mousy brown, or bald.

Our kitchen is the only place that's warm because a fat Aga bulges from the corner like cooking bread. That's where Gran has her coffee pot, permanently on the boil. She leans up against the Aga and starts tearing my hair into plaits.

'Ow!'

'Now Katie, did I finish telling you 'bout The Trip to The Moon at Coney Island's Luna Park?'

'Yes, Gran. Ah!'

'Well, you'd get in a tin spaceship. Land on the moon and these little silver men would take you to meet the King and the Queen. That sure was something. Because the King and the Queen would be all silver too, and he'd give you a piece of green cheese and she'd say something in moon-gobbledegook. Then you'd fly back home. My momma took that ride much as she could. Was her favourite.'

'Yeah. You said.'

'Then it was Mars. A trip to Mars.'

'Ow!'

'That was the same. 'Cept you got red cheese.' Gran ties my plaits with rubber bands. 'Then you know what happened, honey?'

'Uranus?'

She tugs at my roots, 'Don't be cute. Nope, a year after I got to this godforsaken place, the goddamned park burned down. But that's Coney Island for you. Fires and hurricanes,' she sighs. 'There. You're perfect.'

I rub my sore, mousy-brown head.

'Now for *his* breakfast. Uch!' she says, then adds salt and water to a pan of Scott's Porridge Oats.

My grandmother hates the thick salty goo that is porridge because she comes from Brooklyn, and she told me Brooklyn is full of rollercoasters, brown stones, cotton candy, and Chews; not porridge. Gran is a Chew, but Grandpa made her give up on that before they married and she ended up here; 'Just nineteen, pregnant and fat, and in Chew-killing Europe, screaming The Father, Son and goddamn Holy Ghost!'

Gran and I don't eat breakfast, because 'it's better than a tapeworm, honey'. We have coffee instead. Gran says it 'cuts the appetite', and in the evenings we drink bowls of hot water with soup spoons, as Grandpa's gravy bubbles thick as lies on the stove. The thing is, my grandmother came second in The Miss Coney Island Beauty Pageant, 1941, 'Second, because of my fat hips!' She says she's not gonna let that goddamn lardiness happen to me, so I keep to blancmange; nothing too fattening or hard to bite because I still have some baby teeth.

'Bubbles like molasses!' she cries as the porridge farts.

'Glasses like your asses!' I reply in her drawl.

'Noise! All standing!' Grandpa barks from his study.

It's really the pantry.

My grandpa sits among tinned peaches and cans with no labels, stripped in the war. I can see him inside, and it's not because I have X-ray vision, it's just he hardly moves. So, whenever I'm called for a 'pants-down-over-my-knee-Kate-my-girl' spanking, I know he'll be curled over, his one polio leg out, his long fingers wedged in the handles of scissors, carefully cutting out bits from the newspapers. There'll be a library book at his side too. Last week it was *To The Devil A Daughter* and I wouldn't go near him until he took it back to the library van.

This cutting out bits from the newspapers is part of Grandpa's Nervous Breakdown Therapy, along with the valium and the other stuff I can't pronounce. He Gloy Glues headlines onto our mirrors and floors, and if you look up, onto our ceilings too.

'TEACHERS IN LESBO LOVE-IN LESSON.'

'THATCHER SAYS "THE LADY'S NOT FOR TURNING".'

They've been on the kitchen ceiling all week.

Grandpa'll stick up anything he finds in the house: letters, ripped out diary pages, photographs. Sometimes it's like a paper trail and he calls them his *clues*.

'Stand by on deck! Stand by!' he yells.

'Oh, can it, Larry,' says Gran.

'Mother Carey's chickens!'

I see black specks in the porridge.

Grandpa talks funny because he was once Captain Lawrence St John Happy, one of the youngest Captains of His Majesty's Royal Navy, circa 1942, who went and sunk his own ship, twice. It's Navy talk when he calls stewed prunes 'black-coated workers', and kippers 'one-eyed steaks'. Grandpa was born in India, and he used to be 6 foot 8", the tallest man in the county and on his ship. Now he's coiled up like a cobra because of polio, five heart-attacks, three nervous breakdowns, and gangrene in his toes. Grandpa's hair is lard and his hugs are bones and he's so bent over he has to have shoes specially made. Last Christmas he gave me two books: *England and her Empire*, and *England: The Empire*, and he tests me on them, a lot.

Grandpa is: Bonkers!

Crazy Loco!

Muddled!

It's him who keeps the house so cold. He once told me that 'central heating's for wimps, deserters! Damned pen-pushing pansies!' And just in case I get spoilt, he keeps cold green jellies in the fridge like threats.

He turns on the World Service.

'German Byte, 4 to 6 and rising –'

'It's burning, Gran.'

'Small mercies,' she whispers.

There's a car rattling down our track, and Gran pats her Jacqueline Kennedy black bob (she says Eleanor Roosevelt is just too old and dead to idolise and even if Beloved Jackie did go marry that goddamn Greek, it's time for a little new).

'It's the doctor, Katie, honey. Tights and knickers off,' she tells me. I wish she'd make up her mind.

I drag a stool to the kitchen window to see Dr Croften parking his white Audi next to Gran's sea-blue Peugeot (because they don't do them in goddamn pink). Dr Croften is the new doctor, and he's young and clean as stainless steel. Clean and blond as a German, Gran says.

Gran's obsessed with Germans. She named my mum after one.

The doctor's having trouble walking across our shitty front yard. Gran says we should get the gypsies to tarmac, but Grandpa won't hear of it. Jessie 13 leaps out of his oil drum, barking and straining the length of his chain, and Dr Croften jumps back into a puddle of slurry. Jessie 13 is shaggier now it's winter, and mud hangs off him in dreadlocks: he looks like Stig of the Dump.

Steam from the kettle frosts the window and I hear Gran's army of geese slap-slapping across the yard. Then the doctor is stepping into the mist of the kitchen, a goose feather in his hair.

'Good morning, Kate. Has it burst?' Dr Croften is a straight-to-business man.

'No,' Gran replies for me. 'Tea, milk no sugar, Doctor?' She flicks the switch of the kettle and gets out a willow pattern cup.

Dr Croften shakes one slurry-leg and I put my cold hands in my armpits. Gran glares at me, one eye shut, my very own pirate in a pink housecoat. Then she's pushing me out of the kitchen and saying, 'What did I say now, Kate? It's the doctor. Knickers off.'

8

I run out across the flagstone hall, through the dining room and down one of our pee and beeswax corridors, until I'm back into the freeze of Grandpa's red front room.

Gran and Dr Croften are talking, blah-de-blah-de-blah. Then Gran laughs – tee-hee-hee! – and cold wind blows down the chimney. I peel off my tights, jump back on the red chaise, and think of poor Tom the chimney sweep before he fell in the river and played with the Water Babies. I'm sure being lodged up a sooty chimney is better than waiting in this room with my bare bum out.

I hear footsteps, but it's Grandpa who opens the door with a creak.

'Abandon ship!'

He hits a torn leather armchair with the steel nub of his shooting stick, gets caught up in the singed red rug, then shuffles past me and hacks a bit.

'Catch your death, Katie! Gangway!' he barks, before disappearing into the guts of the house.

'Gra-an?' I whisper, because I'm scared of Grandpa.

On cue, she walks in. This time she's got her Marigolds on – pink ones – and she's holding an enamel bowl of just-boiled water. Gran's painted her lips as cherry as her nails, and the top button of her pink dressing gown is undone: there's bosom.

Dr Croften comes in behind with his cup of tea.

'Right then, my darling,' she says, 'Are we all tip-top, what-ho?'

It never works when Gran tries to sound English. She'll watch any film with Celia Johnson in, and after she's wiped away the tears, she'll practise in the mirror.

'Ahm su awe-fully glaad to haf met chou –' she'll mouth. 'Oh, thinks moost awe-fully –'

But after a few hours her new voice crumbles and she'll be back to 'wadder' and 'goddamn' (which she says is a bad word in any accent). Anyway, my favourite actress in those old films is Ginger Rogers, and I love it that Gran sounds like that.

She lays the bowl on the floor and dips a flannel in the steaming water.

'Ready?' the doctor asks, and I hear the metal 'ding!' of his forceps as he crab claws at the now scalding flannel. Gran wrings it out then holds me down. I feel her hot Marigolds on my back.

'Don't make a fuss, honey,' she's given up on the accent already, 'you gotta do it, or the poison'll get right into your bloodstream and you'll die.'

Gran believes everything that kills must enter the bloodstream first. Everything that has happened to our family: twins; sunk ships; pneumonia; diabetes and an amputated leg, Gran said they all 'had to ride the circulation somehow'. She also knows that beef dripping and honey can cure all ills: cancer for instance. And if only her older sister in Iowa had listened, well, then Lula would be with us today.

'Brace yourself,' the doctor warns, then drops the steaming flannel on the cold skin of my bum and I'm a calf in the rodeo ring, a wee baby bit of veal, branded.

I scream. In French. 'Aiie!' (I get that from the French comic books Mum sends me.)

'Katie, calm down.'

'Fuck!' (I get this from Mum herself.)

'Katie!'

'But it fucking hurts!'

Gran uses the hot rag to 'whup' one bottom cheek while the doctor dresses the other.

Then he's tweaking my ribs and frowning. 'She *is* underweight, Mrs Happy.'

'Call me Iris, please —'

'Mrs Happy, Kate is small for her age, strangely small, but you really should get more meat on these bones. The girl needs feeding up. Oh, and get the vet in, have that dog clipped and sprayed, it's full of parasites.'

My grandmother looks away, then out of the rain-splattered window. As the family silver rattles in the black oak sideboard, her fingers reach for a pink button, the top one on her housecoat, and she threads it through the frayed eye like it's a lifesaver.

I make a run for it, out to the light of Gran's pink shagpile stairs. One of Grandpa's clues is stuck to the red room door so I tear it off, then sprint up towards my second floor.

Woman's Home Journal

5 MARCH 1943

TOP TEN TIPS ON BEING A WAR BRIDE

1) Careless talk costs lives. Your tongue is your enemy.
2) Use rations carefully. Ladies eat little. Be an example!
3) Make something out of nothing. Sausages out of bread crumbs. Mock roast goose. Learn from *Recipes For Wartime*, available from your local library.
4) Never ask your husband about his work.
5) Keep fresh and tidy, a pretty face inspires him to fight!
6) Volunteer. Above all be useful.
7) Open those spare rooms to those who need them.
8) Keep your house cheerful. If you have a garden, try your hand at Victory posies. If not, brighten your home with golden privet and cabbage leaves in a pewter pot.
9) Jams, pickles and preserves: your best friends!
10) Waste not, want not.

2

It hasn't stopped raining and Gran's black stallion, Foreo 4, squeals from his stable. The doctor's still inside, seeing to Grandpa, checking for heart attacks and gangrene I suppose. He said we should hose the front yard, before we all come down with botulism; lysteria; bubonic plague.

Orinoco, my Womble glove puppet, is sitting on my hand as I wait in the backseat of Gran's sea-blue Peugeot. The post has come and Orinoco's holding a bright, foreign postcard. He turns it round.

It's from Mum, and it's the same as all the others; a seascape with pedalos and lilos dotting the sea like Smarties. She stopped sending me kittens in baskets a while back.

POST CARD

Kate,
In Nice, ghastly place now.
Not like it was in the 60s.
V. hot. Call soon
Love Mummy

Miss K Happy
The Happy Farm
Boldenham
Herefordshire
Angleterre

'Mummy' is Marlene. Marlene like a German film star, not Marlene as in clean.

Grandpa says my mum's gone adrift.

I move to the edge of the back seat, boil and bottom sore, as one of Gran's geese pecks at the car.

I've got my whole school uniform on now, and I'm red from head to toe. This is my seventh new school since Mum left us, and every time I start a new one, she visits. That's seven visits in four years. Not bad. I glance up our muddy track: nothing yet. It took me a term and a half to get expelled from my last school. I threw pink custard at a teacher when she asked me what it was like not having a *proper* family, and Gran said bully-for-me.

My satchel's tight with *Jane Eyre* and *'Salem's Lot*. I've been mixing them up recently. I'll re-read a bit of *'Salem's Lot* when the long bits of *Jane Eyre* get boring. It's fun, and Mr Rochester's old wife Bertha is definitely a vampire. She lives in the roof, moans, and can't stand the light. They've got the same endings too: both houses go up in smoke. I used to think Grandpa might *be* Mr Barlow from *'Salem's Lot* and that I definitely must be Jane, but I changed my mind. I'm small, but I wouldn't marry a blind cripple and I'd give that brat John and his sisters all dead legs. I don't really have a reason for changing my mind about Grandpa.

Our backyard is littered with barns and barrels, and our farm-house is blurred by the rain. It's black and white and big timbers stick out of it like bones. Most houses round here are black and white. Grandpa says they're, 'as black and white as the bloody Minstrel Show'. Our house could be like Thornfield I suppose, it's old enough, except there are no battlements to throw yourself off and Gran's got a new uPVC sunlounge with double-glazed windows. That sunlounge makes me think of Mum's last visit, when we sat in there watching weak rain splatter on the glass. She didn't say a word and left three hours later.

The garage doors open and it's Iris who totters out to the car with a Marks and Spencer bag over her head. Geese scatter. Iris Tallulah Veronica Miriam Happy (née Ichmann) leaves my grand-mother at home. Iris is carefree, she has the whole day in Hereford on her own. She is wearing a body-hugging, bright pink suit, in wool, and in her suede high-heels Iris is glamorous (or impractical, as Grandpa says, which is true because she's now got cow poo all over the suede). Underneath the plastic bag, Iris is wearing a pink pillbox hat. She calls this outfit her Jacqueline Kennedy Special.

Iris Happy, late fifties (who would have won The 1941 Coney Island Beauty Pageant if it wasn't for her goddamn fat hips) would like to work with children, and animals, and bring an end to all wars.

Her measurements are 36-24-38.

'Goddamned weather!' she says, shaking the plastic bag and settling into the driver's seat. I can smell her waxy lipstick, and she's wearing the pink glass ring I won at the Hereford Mayfair. 'You staying in the back? Don't wanna sit by me in the front?'

'No.'

She frowns and wipes off her four-inch heelers with a hanky. 'Please yourself,' she sniffs and pulls on pink leather gloves. Iris flips the mirror down, checks her face, and then backs up our puddled track. I like to watch her turn the wheel like a racing driver as she stares over her shoulder and past me. The farmhouse recedes; the windscreen wipers say swish-swish, and there's still no sign of Mum.

Iris speeds through our liver-coloured mud.

'Don't want to get caught. Don't want to get trapped, Katie!' she says, then laughs, 'Hey, it's a little too late, doncha think?'

She skids onto the flooded road.

We've got two rivers circling us, and Gran told me they flood us regular as car-sick kids because our house is in a dip, 'And it ain't cream cheese and chive.' We also have quarries of underground lakes that pond our cellars and sandbag our doors. Gran says she's always called Grandpa's land 'sod' (because it's his and he's one) and because it talks as you walk on it, in little squeaks of wet. Even this hot summer when she let me eat Toffos and lie on the lawn reading about the Yorkshire Ripper in her *News of The World*, I got wet stains on my dress. Grandpa says we have owned this border-land for a squillion generations, and that land *spills* into Wales (where Gran rides her black hunter in winter, legs apart, not side-saddle, 'A damned foreign disgrace!').

I look up at St Mary's Church, small but perched safe and dry on a hill. Grandpa's prize Hereford bull is up there, and at dusk it stands out, like those sherry adverts on the plains of Spain. When Mum drove from Paris to Alicante, I thought those big, black Spanish bull signs were alive, and hid under her car seat.

Iris settles into third, and we pass the Field of Bolden. This is Grandpa's battlefield, handed down Happy to Happy, where ancient soldiers (some Happy though not all) died for something tourists now picnic and point at. There's a man in Japan who calls us regularly, wanting to rent that field for something, it's that famous. 'Over my dead body!' says Grandpa, and Gran actually agrees. Next door JCBs stand open-jawed on the almost-finished Barratt Estate. That's Beavan's land. Grandpa calls Beavan, 'A damned dirty farmer who sold his land to the Barratt bastards, Katie! Ahoy!'

Iris turns the sharp corner and we drive towards the village.

For a laugh we call Boldenham, 'Happyville', though it's just a cluster of stone houses, with one miserable telephone box and a postbox. The only pub is Borders Gate because Wales is to the left and England to the right. You can see the Black Mountains and a hill called The Sugar Loaf from here, but Gran and I don't care about that. We speed through and she peeps her horn at Mr Crabtree, who waves. Mr Crabtree walks round the village all day because his wife has The Big C. He's wet through and bent into the wind.

'Poor guy,' Iris sighs.

Mr Crabtree's from Barbados. He told me that's an island made of coral.

Iris glances up at her mirror. 'Don't lean on the door, Kate, honey. It'll happen one day, you mark my words.'

I think of her story.

Little fidget girl sits in back of car.

Little fidget girl does what she does best.

Little fidget girl fidgets –

She *leans*.

Car door opens.

Little fidget girl falls out, but her foot gets stuck and she is dragged.

Little fidget girl's mommy ignores her cries.

'I told you to stop fidgeting!' she screams.

Iris has additions: like the mother doesn't notice until they have driven fifty miles (that's Hereford to Brecon then a bit more). So when she finally stops the car, her Little Fidget Girl (the LFG) is hanging from the back door still white-socked and patent-shoed, but skinned alive. She's naked and gooey, like a baby marsupial. She's the size and colour of a red wine gum, sucked and smooth.

I inch away from the door. 'Sorry, Iris.'

Gran turns at her name, her face younger. Sometimes I wonder how she ended up here, so far from The King and Queen of the Moon; from rollercoasters, cotton candy and Chews.

I love my grandmother's stories.

It was when I was very small, 'just a goddamn pinprick', that she started me off on The Basic Facts of America. These were told as if they were Facts From The Bible and Very Holy.

1) Twice upon a time America saved your English asses, don't listen to your goddamn grandpa.

2) Americans invented everything, most importantly Marilyn Monroe, Einstein, Potato Salad and A Nice Chrysler. Americans discovered America, not the goddamn Spanish.

3) In the olden days America kicked all the English asses, with a bit of help from the French who are mostly Canadian now. So stick that in Grandpa's pipe so he can smoke it.

4) Coney Island is the Venice of The World, and don't let no one tell you different. And 4342 Oceanview Avenue, Home Sweet

Home, is on the cusp of that world: the edge of Brighton Beach and the beginning of Coney. Don't forget, honey, the cusp is the best place to be: neither here nor there, neither one thing nor the other. If you're born on a cusp, you got it made.

She whispered tales of Russia, too. Russia is where her granny came from, and they had Czars and Cossacks who murdered the Chews, like in *Fiddler on The Roof* at Christmas.

Abba are singing 'Super Trouper' on the radio, and Gran's head bobs to the music. She hasn't a single grey hair. Then I think of the packets of Clairol in her bathroom, and the Monday evenings she locks herself in there and sings, '*No* good man', just like Billie Holiday.

There's a patch of winter sun on our valley now, and I'm sure that when those tourists come in their Volvos, or even Mercedes Estates, to lay their picnic gingham cloths on Grandpa's Battlefield, they must call it 'beautiful' and 'lush' when the sun shines like that. 'As fancy as icing', they'll say, parking their sensible cars. But as soon as they sit down, they'll sink in the wet, like anchors with their chains snapped.

My mum hates Hereford. She once told me that Hereford's just a cattle-market, full of people in for the day; 'All those farmers down from the Black Mountains, darling, buying and selling while their fat wives get fatter on sponge cake at the Red Dragon. And then there's the arsing cathedral. It's where your father and I were married, you know. God help us. There's a cathedral close, cloisters, and a sodding choir. And those Vergers, Bishops, and Boy Bishops all scurry about like beetles on the bloody grass.'

Gran says Mum's not one to mince her words.

We drive down Deepmarsh Street. Three spray-can swastikas cling to the bus shelter, next to 'Pakis Go Home'. Gran told me about swastikas and Nazis and how goddamn English kids wouldn't know a Nazi if one came up and bit them on the ass. We pass the cathedral and I stare at its bird-black doors and try to imagine my parents inside.

It's not far now, Redbrook School. Gran said she chose it because, 'It's red and that's where pink comes from, honey.' But I know it's the only local school left and she has to 'goddamn pay for this one'.

She stops the car, and in the distance I see two stone pillars, either side of a long snaking drive. At the end is a building topped with turrets like traffic cones, but they're grey, not red. This school looks as boring as Grandpa's cardigans. It makes me think of Jane's school where they all died and her friend Helen Burns was religious.

Lowood.

Gran told me Helen is her favourite, because that's little Lizzie Taylor in the Orson Welles, Joan Fontaine movie.

There are three Big Girls standing at the gates, arms folded, and twice my size. They've got hair-flicks sharp as razors and pointy boots with leg warmers. Their skirts are red like mine, but skin tight, and the home-sewn stitches strain on their thighs. They're blowing Hubba-Bubba-Gum bubbles and none of them looks like a Helen Burns. It's halfway through the term. I'm probably the only New Girl. They stare at our unfamiliar car and my unfamiliar face.

Iris turns in her seat. 'Go talk to them, Kate. Make friends. They look real nice. I'm in a rush, honey.' She gets out of the Peugeot and opens my door. 'C'mon now.'

'I can't.'

'Don't be foolish, you've done this before. Come on.'

Iris has control, and her rein-tugging wrists pull the strap of my satchel until I'm standing. All I want to say is, 'No, I can't talk to those girls, they're older, and you don't do that.' Instead I cry, 'Ow, stop pulling, Gran! You're hurting!'

A Big Girl laughs.

'Don't make a scene!' Iris hisses. She pushes me away, like a soiled pup out into the rain, and yells, 'This is Kate! You'll make friends with her right? This is her first day!'

One of them takes a step forward and puts a hand on a tight hip.

I look from car to gate to Big Girls: it's a long walk. Iris shoves me, and I see there's nothing else for it: I have to run.

I bolt – gravel crunching – towards the smiling Big Girl with the hips. I'm going so fast I'm impala, cheetah, Tarzan. I'm Johnny Weissmuller on a Saturday morning jumping over the quicksand. My book-heavy satchel pulls me this way and that as it swings and slams against my body.

'Watch out Kate, you're gonna fall!' Iris yells.

But I know I'll be all right, I can zip past these Big Girls fast as Speedy Gonzales, '*Arriba! Arriba!*' Just the one with the hips has her leg out, ready to trip me. I see a flash of her laughing face as I try and jump over the obstacle, then fall.

I go down slow, like Wylie Coyote off a cliff. There's even a cloud of cartoon dust, and a pouf! as I lie splayed on the cool gravel. It doesn't hurt, yet. The stinging warmth of pee runs through my ripped tights. I hear footsteps and I close my eyes.

The Big Girls are standing over me.

'Has she?'

'Yes, look at that stain down her tights, it's disgusting.'

'She can't help it. She looks like a junior.'

'Is she unconscious?'

'Or pretending if she's pissed herself in public like that.'

One of them kicks me and I moan.

'You shouldn't have tripped her like that, Cheryl.'

'I didn't.'

'You did, I saw.'

'Shut up, slag.'

'Watch it! Here comes her mum.'

I open my eyes, but it's only Gran.

'Oh Kate, you goddamn stupid child. Come on, get up.'

'I can't.'

A Big Girl with blonde hair sniggers. She's got one badge that says 'Ska' and another that says 'Prefect'.

'Excuse me?' Gran spits. 'You think it's so goddamn funny, missy, you can just help my granddaughter up.'

'But she's dirty.'

'So?'

'It'll get on my uniform.'

'Don't be dumb. All of you, help me.'

'But –'

'But nothing. Do as you're told.'

They turn me over and there's a small gasp because my new tights are so torn on one knee that it's hard to tell red flesh from red cotton. Gran's face turns white.

'Get her to my car,' she says and I'm picked up like they're going to give me the birthday-bumps.

Whips of branches fly past as I'm carried. It still doesn't hurt.

The Big Girls lay me on the back seat of the Peugeot. They stand back and I see my blood has made darker blotches on their already red uniforms. They say, 'Poor Thing' and 'We'll look after her when she comes back', but their faces tell me, 'Stupid little cow! Look at my skirt, my nice new blouse! And I stink of pee! I'll get you when you come back, you spac!'

'Keep it up!' Gran says, pointing at my knee. She jumps into the car and backs down the street. 'I'm going to have to take you to Emergency, honey.'

And we drive towards the familiar County Hospital.

For a moment I want the excitement of an ambulance, like the one I travelled in with Dad. As I stare out at the blur of birch trees and Victorian terraces, I wonder if he felt like this, a bit numb but excited, when the ambulance men were shouting and pounding on his broken chest.

* * *

Gran squeals to a stop in an ambulance bay. It's not far, the County. She yells at an orderly who's sucking on a fag against the hospital's brick wall, 'This is a goddamn emergency, young man. I wanna wheelchair and I am not waiting.'

I don't really know why Gran's making such a fuss, she must be used to this by now. Mum always called me a Walking Disaster Fund.

The orderly flicks his cigarette into the bald flowerbed, gets a wheelchair and pushes me into Casualty. There's a smell of mince on the turn, and I make a trail of blood on the linoleum. He leaves me behind a square of white plastic curtain as a radio plays 'Don't Stand So Close To Me'.

A doctor pops his head in. 'A fall?'

I nod because it's starting to sting. Gran's yelling in the foyer now.

'That your mum?' he asks.

'My gran.'

He disappears and a young girl pulls back the curtain.

'Hello there. My name's Ange. What's yours?' Ange is holding one of those stainless steel kidney shaped dishes that I think you have to pee in. I haven't got any pee left.

'Kate.'

'Well, Kate, let's have a look here. Oh dearie me you have been in the wars.'

'I'm a Walking Disaster Fund.'

'Well, that's nice, isn't it? Now, we'll have to cut off these wet tights and get rid of that gravel and muck first. That's a very nasty gash.'

I nod and feel sick (because Ange smells of Jeyes Fluid), and my grandmother appears in time to hold me down. Ange smiles, gives me an injection, then gets to work with scissors and a big pair of tweezers.

'The painkiller should be working,' she says. 'Just think of something else. Okay?'

I am trying, but Ange's kidney dish is filling up with blood-stained cotton wool. I sneak a peek and see she's opening and closing the cut on my knee like it's a puppet's mouth. It hurts now.

'What's your name again, lovie?'

'Kate.'

'Kate, right. Now, you've got to keep still for me, darling. You're being a very brave little girl.'

'She's almost eleven,' Gran says.

'Oh.'

Ange threads a needle and I want to tell them both: I'm used to this, it's the story of my bloody life! But as the first stitch goes in I hear *her* voice like an underwater echo.

Are you sitting comfortably, Kate?

Not bloody likely.

Are you ready for story number one?

But I've heard it all before, Mum.

I look round to check she's not really here, and then I close my eyes because I can't stop her. My mum's going to whisper the stories she told me on trains, in cabs, on aeroplanes and boats, once on a small bus we got trapped on in the Alps. She's going to tell me my life story and the reasons why I have to stick so close to my grandmother: why I can't go to school like anyone normal; why I'll never reach adulthood.

Right Kate, let me begin with Accident Number One.

One day, when you weren't out of nappies, your useless father puts you on the side of the road and bam! you run out to be hit by a salmon-pink Vauxhall Cresta. I mean, my god, a bloody salmon-pink Vauxhall Cresta! It's as bad as your bloody grandmother! Couldn't it have been something a bit more poetic, like a Jag or an MG? A Beach Buggy? Fancy having to say 'yes, my poor cripple daughter was struck down by a Cresta. It was salmon-pink.' At least your father had the decency to be finished off by a Triumph Spitfire. A lovely, bang-spanking-new Triumph Spitfire. Anyway you bounced three times on the fish-coloured bonnet and were fine. Toddlers are made of rubber you know.

All I remember about that day was Mum buying me a Mini Milk and a man on the radio singing about life on Mars, as I told the Cresta driver my daddy's name was Michael and he had a dickie.

I cut Mum off like rind from bacon and open my eyes.

'Nearly done now,' says Ange.

I feel tugging and look down.

The skin on my knee is goose flesh before you put it in the oven: the blue stitches are the quill ends of the feathers, still stuck. They've made a pattern like the number '10' with a stitched line and a circle. Ten is my age, for now. The same age as Tatum O' Neal when she got that Oscar for *Paper Moon*.

'Just a few more, lovey.' Ange smiles.

This scar will join the others: on my hand (dog-bite), on both arms (stuck in a roll of barbed wire last March), on my legs (a spilt kettle of boiling water), on my stomach (appendicitis and born with a kidney back to front).

Mum's voice has gone, and I can't feel the needle anymore, though this isn't because the local anaesthetic has worked. It's because I can't take my eyes off my grandmother, in her pink Jacqueline Kennedy Special, now splashed with my blood.

She's the real thing.

Then there's her flushed face and her knuckles, pulsing rosy-pink as she makes fists in front of the plastic white curtain.

PAPER IS AMMUNITION–USE IT WISELY!

Our Woman's Weekly *Whisper*

FILM STARS RETURN

OUR beloved acting royalty, Laurence Olivier and Vivien Leigh, returned from Hollywood last week to join England in her war effort. Hurrah for them! Married in Montecito in California, Laurence Olivier has played Heathcliff and Admiral Nelson, while Vivien Leigh is most famous for her Scarlett O' Hara. Though we at Women's Weekly must say we prefer her understated performance in the wonderful Waterloo Bridge. Good luck to this sterling example of a patriotic husband and beloved wife!

AN ADMIRING SOLDIER

SHE came down to spend two days leave with her soldier fiancé. Her suit was a neat grey and white check and her head-piece a handkerchief of paisley patterned wool tied in a knot: but oh, her intriguing handbag!

All eyes turned upon her and her young man grinned with pleasure as well he might, for, as she explained, she had made it herself. It was made from two circles of rose red skiver - dinner-plate size.

I won't go into details here because if you want to make one there'll be directions in the October 'Woman and Home.'

If Some Sunbright Morning

IF some sunbright morning
  In a busy street
You should turn a corner
  And we had to meet,

I could smile and chatter
  Gaily and pass by.
All my secrets guarded.
  All my banners high.

But if it were twilight,
  With people two and two
Walking home together,
  I don't know what I'd do.

HELEN WELSHIMER

Please ladies, turn to p. 12 to read why there will be no more Lux till after the war.

3

*G*ran has a Church Meeting; 'A Protestant Potluck,' she called it, so I'm in her bed. She goes to church with Mr Crabtree most days, and they pray for Mrs Crabtree and The Big C. In the evenings they write The Holy Newsletter, though Gran doesn't believe Jesus Saves ('but that's between you and me, huh honey?'). She calls herself A Church Of England Chew, and says this is better than one of those goddamn Chews For Jesus.

Grandpa calls her a devil-dodger and Mr Crabtree a native Bible-banger, 'But at least she isn't canoodling up to her old fancy religion, eh Kate?'

The *News of The World* and the *New Yorker* are piled up, separate and sorted, against Gran's four pink walls. 'Sleaze and culture, honey. What this world is built on.' She keeps her novels under the bed: *Marathon Man*; *The Deep*; *She*, because Gran loves a page-turner.

She put on her favourite song before she left, and as Billie Holiday sang '*No* good man', I watched her slide on pink things. There was a pink corset so tight she had to force it up her legs inch by inch, while her stockings were attached by hanging clasps that looked like the teats of a baby's bottle. Her frilly silk knickers were jellyfish, and I'm sure they pulsed, in different coral shades beneath her skirt. Gran likes to look especially pink for Mr Crabtree.

This evening, she told me another story. About a girl from her street in Coney Island called Janet Fiorello. Janet travelled all the way to Italy during the war, to give donuts to soldiers, because American soldiers couldn't fight without donuts. It's the sugar and the cinnamon, Gran said.

After this she read to me; it was my baby-favourite, *Raggedy Andy and Annie and the Camel with the Wrinkled Back*. Gran won't read me *Little House on the Prairie*, because she thinks Laura Ingalls Wilder is a goddarned preachy wiseass.

My boil burst. I didn't notice until Gran pulled off the matted gauze to show me. It looked like rabbit guts: the insides of a tyre-burst bunny. Still, I can't move much. I've been in her bed since I got back from hospital, and this is a privilege. To be wrapped up in her satin eiderdown; collapsed on her feather-stuffed pillow, in this room of so many pink treasures and trinkets (including an old stick of Brighton rock, dated 1944, third drawer down, vanity chest, with a label in capitals saying DO NOT EAT ME AT ANY COST!).

Last time I was ill in her bed she had Pepto Bismol, a pink medicine, flown all the way over from America.

Jane Eyre and *'Salem's Lot* are on Gran's bedside table, next to three jars filled with sand and labelled 'Coney Island, 1940', 'Coney Island, 1941', 'Coney Island, 1942'. I can't reach my books because the painkiller is making me wuzzy so I look out the window instead. The yard is clean. This afternoon Gran hosed it down. Tomorrow, after milking, it'll be caked in shit again.

I hear a thump then the yowl of a cat; Samuel and Wilhomena are throwing books down from the third floor again.

Samuel and Wilhomena Happy are brother and sister, and they are our family ghosts. Ancient cousins of Grandpa's, they sleep in the bumps of the rugs, and are fragile as spider webs and white as new paint. They never scare anyone. All they do is unwind loo-rolls and throw books. Even our farm cats aren't scared. They sprint up there and have kittens in Wilhomena's hats. The ones that survive sprint down at five weeks and back up again, pregnant, at six months.

Samuel and Wilhomena live mostly in The Library. It smells of cat pee. Samuel's volumes are called things like *A History of The West Indies by Edward Long* while Wilhomena's are small and hard as hand-Bibles. Gran hates Wilhomena.

'Wilhomena is the reason I married your goddamned grand-father,' she once told me. 'So it's her fault. The bitch.'

Wilhomena was a writer; she wrote long and boring poems, and never cut her auburn hair. And while Grandpa was wooing Iris Tallulah Veronica Miriam Ichmann at 4342 Oceanview Avenue, he gave her a book of Wilhomena's work with an inscription.

> *To my love Iris,*
> *May my great-grandmother's great sentiments of love*
> *Reach your heart as they have mine.*
> *Yours for ever,*
> *Larry*
> *Soon to be Vice-Admiral Happy of His Majesty's Royal Navy.*

Gran told me there were a few lies in this.

1) Wilhomena Happy was a distant cousin.
2) Her poetry was not great.
3) Grandpa was never made a goddamn Vice or an Admiral, he just went crazy-loco instead.

'And you know what?' Gran said. 'He'd never even read the book. But for me, that was it. Wham-bam, thought he must be a poet too. Ha!'

I think Gran hates Wilhomena more than Grandpa now.

There's another thud, of another heavy book, followed by the hiss of a cat.

Evenings are pretty here on Happy Farm. The sky's wide and low, and there are no clouds tonight to block stars bright as lamps. This afternoon I saw the sun go red then slip behind the back field. Red spilled everywhere, into Grandpa's flooded furrows, and hedges.

Now everything's asleep, apart from the foxes; they screech like witches. The pigs in the paddock are lying flat and our fat white geese are staring up at the pinkish clouds, trying to remember how to fly, because Christmas is round the corner and Gran's sharpening her knife.

I love Christmas. I especially loved it when Dad was here. He hid things in the cold fire, then Mum lit them. Grandpa made toasts to all the Jessies down all the years (numbers 1–13), and Gran called home to speak to her other sister Rita.

She would kick back in her pink leatherette armchair in the hall, and cry, 'Oh my gawd, Reet honey? Is that really you?' her voice so young, she sounded like Frenchie from *Grease*. I would sneak beneath the hatstand, close the curtain of family macs, and eavesdrop. In the plastic-dark I thought of my Great Aunt Rita, crying back with a big 'Yes!' from America; her hair tomato sauce and her false leg a bleached bone sticking out from her skirt; 'Cos of that goddamn diabetes, sweetcakes!'

I'd shiver and wonder if the fairy lights of Coney Island were blinking; if the Cyclone was looping the loop; if the bearded lady was thinking about shaving it all off.

The last Christmas we all had together, Dad, me, and Mum spent the whole time laughing.

It began with Rita's arrival. There were no phone calls that year. Rita came all the way from 4342 Oceanview Avenue (but now Apt. 1A, as she had the good sense to turn Momma and Poppa Ichmann's three-storey home into apartments after they passed on).

Dad and Gran picked Rita up from Heathrow and the rest of us cheered from the top of the kitchen steps as she limped through the garage doors.

'Hey, honeys!' she cried.

I'd only ever seen pictures and talked to her on the phone, and now Rita was swaying towards me, a one-legged Santa bearing gifts (or rather Santa with a false leg). In fact Rita was bearing so many gifts I knew she'd topple over.

'Oh little Katie! You're like a bird, you're so small!' Rita tried to wave from underneath the packages. 'And dear Marlene, look at you, what a movie star!'

Her thin red hair was as see-through as Gran's silk stockings, and her chin wobbled as she talked. Rita was big, soft as dough, and a little moist. If you sat on her lap you weren't cuddled, you were kidnapped. The diabetes made her fat, or she had diabetes because she was fat. I never figured out which was the sugared chicken or the chocolate egg.

Rita had to have lots of wadder and shots and she said the farmhouse was 'awful cold'. She took to wearing Grandpa's socks on her hands that Christmas.

Anyway, up those four treacherous steps she came, from garage to kitchen: one false leg; presents piled, and no hands free to grip the rails. Rita stumbled (or listed as Grandpa said, like one of his god-forsaken ships).

In the end it was Grandpa himself who leant forward and caught her.

'Oh my!'

'There now, Rita.'

'Oh, Larry!' She winked and Grandpa blushed. Wrapped presents fell. 'In your arms again, eh? If it wasn't for my big sis! You've not changed a bit.'

'Rubbish. I'm an old man.'

'Oh, you always were, honey.'

'Still a card then, Rita? Starboard!'

'You bet!'

They had this conversation while Rita teetered on the brink of the top step. Grandpa, unsteady at the best of times, wobbled without his stick. Rita wobbled anyway.

'Let's get you inside,' my dad suddenly gasped. He was holding Rita up from behind.

'Get those little parcels will you, Katie dear?' she asked, pointing below her; but I didn't move. I didn't want to be crushed.

'Oh Michael, come in!' Mum cried, covering up a laugh.

'I'm trying!'

Then Aunt Rita said, 'Oh! Sweetcakes! Oh! It's going. Oh! I can feel it. Someone catch it. Katie? Iris? My leg is popping out!'

We couldn't move; we just stood motionless as this big white thing, like a baby whale, sprung – pe-dong! – out from under her skirt and plonked – one, two, three, four – down the steps.

The shiny plastic leg, with little red-painted toes, was lying on the garage floor.

Mum started first; she cried like a hyena. Then we were all in fits of laughter, we couldn't help it. Even Grandpa. All Gran could do was grab her sister's false limb, then her hand and say, 'Don't mind them. Come see the house.'

'But I can't,' Rita protested, 'I ain't no good at hopping. I need someone to buckle it back on.'

So this became Rita's party trick. When any of us looked bored, or God forbid, on the verge of a family row, kind Rita would have her leg 'pop out'. And I was allowed to buckle it back on. I loved that job. The shiny strap and the frightening sight of her little cut-off thigh. She'd wiggle it like a chicken wing just to make me laugh.

That Christmas, Dad called her Lovely Rita Meter Maid.

The leg aside, we were all excited. Not only was this the first time Gran had seen her younger sister since 1942, in the flesh (and as Grandpa pointed out there was plenty of that), but it was Rita's birthday on Christmas Day. Also, Mum was about to have two babies, the surprise twins, and Dad had a new job. He wouldn't tell anyone what, though.

'Michael, come on now –'

'No Iris, I can't say.'

'Why's that?' chimed in Rita.

'Well, it's Top Secret,' and he'd wink at them, until they giggled like girls.

Unlike everyone else, I knew what my father's new job was. I knew that on even days of the month he was a spy, and on the odd ones he performed daring feats of the imagination at the circus. It must have been exhausting, because on the 6th he'd be fighting chalk-faced Voodoo men in graveyards, then on the 7th he'd have to change into a leotard, climb the high wire, and be Burt Lancaster in that circus film Gran loved. I wasn't surprised Dad was always yawning, always disappearing for months at a time. He needed the rest.

My dad was handsome. Black hair and blue eyes. Mum said he looked like Richard Burton in *Cleopatra*, so she wore black kaftans with little mirrors on them to look like Elizabeth Taylor and complement him.

'More like *Who's Afraid of Virginia Woolf*,' Gran laughed, and then told me Richard Burton's eyes are green, 'and his goddamned hair was brown in that movie, for Pete's sake!'

Dad's hazy as London now: as dreamy as Sherlock Holmes's last opium-case. His cheeks tasted of sugar and his face was my favourite sweet: a Rolo or a Hershey's kiss.

That year, we made Christmas Day Rita's, rather than Christ's. And instead of 'Away in a Manger' she played Dusty Springfield. I made a banner that said, 'haPy biRtDae reTa', and no one corrected it because Rita said it was cute. In fact Rita said everything was cute; every cubby hole and figurine was cute, even the big male Jessie 12 we had then, who'd just gone through Gran's geese 'like a goddamn mincer', was 'cute, but in his own special way'.

Rita said she had a cockatiel back in Coney who was cute, too. This bird barked like a dog and kept her company when Zev and she split up (and before she let him rent the apartment above). She said she was awful worried about the cockatiel, called Honeybunch, because he pulled all his feathers out the last time she left him, which was to attend her big sister Lula's funeral in Iowa. When she said this, Rita gave Gran a dark look, because Gran didn't go. Gran always told me if she ever went back to America, it would have to be for good.

Mum changed the subject then, and they talked about babies. I was excited about having brothers or sisters or both. Two in one go would be fun; like having a double Shreddie, a double-yolked boiled egg or as Grandpa pointed out, a lamb with two heads.

Gran went to town on the Christmas lunch. There was the usual turkey and goose, and on the sideboard Grandpa's ham (which Rita frowned at and didn't touch), but there was also saccharine jelly, diabetic chocolate mousse, and three non-sweetened hot apple pies with whipped cream. Rita jumped straight to the puddings with a pair of Grandpa's socks on her hands.

'I don't care for savouries, sweetcakes. Never have.'

The socks looked like puppets.

'That's true, Reety. Salt-water taffy, hardballs, well candy anyhow, that was always your favourite.' Gran gave her an extra big dollop of cream on her pie, and while we mashed roast potatoes in gravy, Rita sucked up green jelly.

'You know,' she said between soft mouthfuls, 'Your gramps doesn't look a day older than when I last saw her.'

'Now Rita,' said Gran.

'No, truly, Iris, you look fresh as cream. To think, I'm your little sis!'

'Only by a year.'

'So that makes you –'

'Never you mind.'

'But Iris, you still have your figure, your lovely dark hair, and hardly a line on that cute face of yours – and look at the rest of us.'

'Well, thank you very much, Aunt Rita,' Mum said, pouting.

'Oh, not you, honey. I'm talking about us old folks. Don't you think your Iris looks great, Larry?'

Grandpa grunted.

'Come on, Larry. I remember when you caught the train from

Washington, just to see our Iris at her graduation. And you weren't her only beau.'

'I'm well aware of that.'

Gran blushed.

'A little competition never did a man any harm. Oh, Iry, you looked so cute in your prom dress, all pink and perfect with those black eyes of yours, and then this handsome British guy, as tall as the skies, comes calling, and in his English Navy uniform too! Oh, he was so pretty to see.'

'I wouldn't call a uniform of His Majesty's Royal Navy pretty, Rita.'

'Shush. You were smitten, that's all I remember. Do you know, Katie, it was me as spotted Larry first? Did I ever tell you that? I saw him at Luna Park, it was The Trip to Atlantis ride. Well, you couldn't miss him, a shoulder and head above everyone else. Like King Neptune himself!'

Gran laughed at this, and Rita joined in.

'What were you, Larry, nearly 7 foot wasn't it? Oh god, I wanted to take him to Midget City for a laugh. Could have pulled up a pitch, could have been a sideshow yourself, The Land of The Giants, right?!'

Grandpa slammed his fork down, 'It was the Lilliputian Village, Rita, and it hardly matters now. I'm bent double.'

Rita ignored him and turned to Mum.

'So, I bring him home, but it was only to get at my Zev. One year going steady at High School, and he hadn't proposed, and there he was out in the Pacific about to get shot down, so I thought why the hell not? I know I was young, but you grew up fast then. Didn't you, Iry? Who knew what was round the corner. So I figured, why not send Zev a picture of this tall, fine Englishman and say "Well, Zev Bloomfield, you may have your little hoola-moola girls out there, but just look at what I gone and got myself. A real bona-fide English Gent!" Oh, I never did send that letter, for the moment Larry walked through our door, well, crouched through our door to be truthful, he saw our Iris and that was that. Me and my cokamammie ideas, right?'

Rita sucked more sugar-free jelly from her spoon as I chewed my turkey. I loved the way Aunt Rita spoke. Everyone apart from Grandpa was laughing.

'And you know what, Katie?' I didn't because no one had ever told me anything about Gran or Grandpa or even Mum and Dad. 'Well, it only goes and takes Larry a week to propose, can you imagine. Boom! Love at first sight!'

She laughed and her top teeth fell down.

'So – hmm, 'scuse me –' she pressed them back up, 'so my sis goes to her graduation an engaged woman. Can you imagine? With this tall and very handsome English man, and all those boys just flocked to her. You loved that night, didn't you, Iry?'

'Well, I can't really remember, Rita.'

'Oh, hogwash, you lay on my pillow and cried, "Oh I love him, I love him so Rita. Oh, his poetry! And do you know who his great-grandmother was? His letters are just divine! I'm going to be an English lady!" Hmm. She always did want to be just a little English. Didn't you, Iry? Her favourite sideshow was them Hilton sisters, all the way from England. Siamese twins and played the sax. We were real young then, but Iry here had all the cuttings.'

'Rubbish.'

'Come on now. Thought you were goddarned Vivien Leigh most of the time. And he was your Larry, huh? Them green eyes of his had you scuppered all right. Remember that July? Before you got hitched? Well, me and Iris swam in the Coney Island Creek and all she did was float and cry, "Oh, Rita, he's so fine and I'm going to live in England and be a Lady and help our boys in the war!" And I said how it put me in mind of Tony The Alligator Boy and Priscilla The Monkey Girl. Cos they were opposites attracting too, right? I mean there was Tony, short and scaly, and there was

Prissy, tall and hairy, and they eloped. Loved each other crazy, and ran off.'

Sometimes Rita made my head spin.

'Yes, well, quite,' Grandpa said. 'To more important matters, your birthday, Rita, here's to it, and many Happy Returns. To absent friends.'

'Don't think that'll change the subject, Larry.'

Grandpa grunted again and shovelled more meat in his mouth.

'Happy Birthday, Aunt Rita,' my Mum said and we all made a toast to her health and happiness. I told her I wished her leg would grow back, and she laughed and stared at me.

'You know what, Katie? Look at your eyes.'

I tried but it was very difficult.

'You and your mom here are the only Ichmann Jews left with my momma's blue eyes. She had beautiful blue eyes, didn't she, Iry? Came from the Liebermans, from her daddy's side. They was Ukrainie Jews, real tall blonde people –'

'Do we really have to discuss –'

'Ah take a chill pill, Larry,' Rita said.

After more puddings and a little sherry (dry, of course) Rita told us more stories about magical Coney Island. There was a hotel built in the shape of an elephant with rooms in the head and staircases in the legs and a shopping centre in its tummy. It had red lights for eyes that shone out on the Atlantic, but someone smoked a cigar in the trunk and it burnt down. Then there was The Half Moon Hotel, which was a normal shape, and a man called Bugsy threw another man out of its window because this other man was a canary who could sing but couldn't fly. Finally she told us a story I could follow, about a fling of hers.

'He worked the sideshow by Nathan's Famous, best hotdogs in Coney.' Rita ruffled my hair, 'Actually, sweetcakes, he was one of the attractions, people said they was freaks and I hated that. He had funny little arms like flippers and called himself The Amazing

Seal-o. I didn't like the name, like it was insulting, but I didn't mind the little arms, they was just like any other arms, only shorter, and then there's me with only one leg, so what could I say? Oh, we had a lovely time that summer, me and Jeremiah, that was his name, but in the end he had to leave with the rest of them, said winter in Coney was just too damn cold and they always made good down in Florida. "The old folks," he said. "They like us. And the old folks is rich." He wanted me to go, but I ain't following no one round any country.' Rita looked at Gran. 'So Jeremiah, he ended up staying in Florida. Bought a condo in Longboat Key. Did something big in realty. I get Christmas cards, but I do miss him in the flesh something awful. Yeah, we still write. He can write, you know.'

No one laughed at this and Rita seemed sad. Mum cleared away the plates.

'My daddy's in the circus,' I said.

'Sh, Kate, you'll give the game away,' he whispered and smiled, but no one noticed. I suppose they were too occupied with the Amazing Seal-o doing back-flips down in Florida without his one true love.

Finally Rita sighed. 'You know,' she said.

'What, honey?' Gran asked, putting her small hand over Rita's big sock-covered one.

'Well. With his flippery arms and my one leg,' she grinned and looked round the table, 'well, gee, sex with Jeremiah sure was something to behold!'

That was when Mum collapsed on the floor with giggles and Dad dropped the cutlery. Even Gran was wiping away the tears and Grandpa had to cover his face with his napkin, his shoulders shaking.

But I had a serious look on my face, because I didn't understand. This made it worse because Mum pointed and said.

'Oh my godfathers, look at Kate, she's trying to picture it!'

And this time we all collapsed. Rita hit her false limb in time with her laughs and the sound echoed as if it was empty. When things were finally quiet, all I could hear was little sighs of 'oh my' and 'oh dear' and the mantelclock ticking tick-tock.

That was until Mum said, 'Michael, please will you drive me to the hospital?'

'Sorry?'

'The hospital.'

'What?'

'My water's broken. I laughed too hard.'

Gran jumped up, 'Oh Marlene, quick, let's –'

'It's okay, mother, I'll be fine.'

And they were gone, in a flurry of panic and a little leftover laughter. Then it was just me and Great Aunt Rita, with bits of green jelly buried deep in the corners of her creased mouth.

A vixen yaps in Grandpa's back field. I lift myself up because I can't turn. I often think of Jeremiah and Rita, about that summer they spent together. The Amazing Seal-o and his one-legged love. Roll-up. Roll-up! One day, I tell myself, one day I'll go and live with Rita and join that Coney Island sideshow. I'll be a freak, too. I just have to not grow anymore. Or grow too much, like Grandpa.

This morning I got another postcard from Mum.

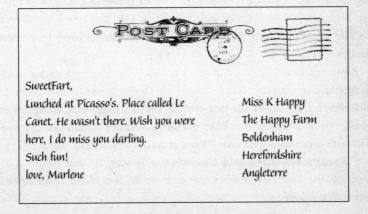

POST CARD

SweetFart,
Lunched at Picasso's. Place called Le
Canet. He wasn't there. Wish you were
here, I do miss you darling.
Such fun!
love, Marlene

Miss K Happy
The Happy Farm
Boldenham
Herefordshire
Angleterre

I keep Mum's postcards. I run out to my grandfather's slide-door barn and hide them in the top drawer of her walnut chest, because she left what remained of her stuff here at Happy Farm. 'Cheap storage,' she called it, and I suppose she was right. I might burn this one though, because the drawer in the barn's nearly full, and it must be fun to watch the seascapes shrink like crisp packets in the fire.

Marlene has a scar down her chest, because once, her heart leaked like Swiss cheese. Like my grandmother, Marlene thought the Happy surname was stupid, so she married my dad and took half of his.

'Even goddamn worse', said Gran. 'Happy-Mahoney? What kind of bull-crap is that?'

Marlene drove off one Sunday in a speed streak of a red car with a dented bonnet.

'Off to see a man about a dog, darling,' she barked. 'Going to have some bloody fun!' Her Biba scarf waved out the open window and I waved back. That's what I remember most about Mum, how she craved fun like oxygen. Everything had to be 'such' or 'bloody' fun. She told me it was the thing she was best at.

For now, Gran has propped Marlene's postcard up on her dressing table, and it's dwarfed by a battery of photographs that stand in gilt frames.

The faces in my grandmother's photographs belong to children and they're all dead.

My aunt Eva.

My two sisters.

I don't like them staring out at me, though Eva looks pretty (she's got the Lieberman blue eyes too). Apart from that, she looks just like Gran and not like Mum at all, though they were twins. It was pneumonia that killed Eva, when she was my age. Mum had it too, but she lived, even with the scar down her chest and her heart like Swiss cheese.

Some Sundays Gran takes me up to the church, and she scrubs lichen off Eva's weather-worn angel while I play with the pink glass pebbles on her grave. Gran likes to put these pebbles on the angel's head and sometimes they balance. The inscription says, 'She went to sleep in Jesus', which Grandpa liked. Millie, our cleaning lady, said it was Someone as brought pneumonia into this house (like it was a dog or a cake) and it was Someone as can Never Be Forgiven.

My two sisters don't have graves. Mum told me, 'The bloody nuns shoved them down the rubbish chute! Into the incinerator!' She said they died because Dad was a Catholic and he made her go to a hospital with nuns, who were only good for lepers and cripples, not babies. She blamed Rita too, 'Her and her bloody deadly stories!'

The photos of my sisters were taken in the hospital, as they never came home. They look like monkey-babies, small and hairy, and I often wonder if they were already dead when the camera clicked. Before she left, Rita asked for a copy but Mum said no. Sometimes Grandpa shuffles up here and hides these pictures. He shut them up in the bottom drawer of his bureau one Sunday and I think Gran was relieved; she didn't ask where they went for a month.

When we left Dad and stayed in Paris, Mum took me to an exhibition. It was a room of photographs, little black and white cards with face after face of a dead child. Most were babies, eyes gone, swaddled and huddled for pointless warmth. I threw up and Mum slapped me. 'Tu m'en merde!' she yelled, when neither of us knew what that meant. The only French Mum taught me was; *Quelle surprise! Formidable!* and something about *Baise Mon Cul*.

There are Basic Facts about Mum too.

1) Her front teeth were bashed out by Eva throwing a tin drum.
2) She went to boarding school at four with falsies, wet the bed, and didn't tell a soul.
3) She left my dad more times than she cares to remember.

4) She once slept with an entire band called Trixie; five Jamaicans with dyed green hair (though Jake the lead singer told me they came from Tottenham). Trixie stayed in our flat on the Bayswater Road and I sang 'Mary had a Little Lamb' into their microphone. Jake took me for walks in the park and when Trevor McDonald came on the news, he'd put his fist in the air and tell me *that* was Black Power.

When they left, Mum told me Black men had blue willies.
You still there then?
I blink.
Still talking about me and my outrageous past eh?
Could be.
What you don't understand is that the sixties were very draining, darling.
Oh, shut up, Mum.
I look up at Gran's black window.
I think, if my sisters ever come floating through the swirling mist and tap-tapped on the pane, like they do in *'Salem's Lot*, I'd know what to do.
I wouldn't let them in, because they'd be vampires.

Momma Ichmann's Recipe For Donuts (based on The Salvation Army's Doughboy Donut! Makes almost 50)
For her little Iry out there all alone in England

Mix one doz. eggs with four cups of sugar/three cups of
cinnamon (and Momma's little secret, one pinch of chilli powder
and the grated peel of three lemons). Add milk, and warm
kosher cooking fat.
Beat this into bowl with cups of flour until good mix, then add
big pinches of baking powder and salt.
Roll dough out and cut into hoops (with a hole!)
Heat large deep pan of 1 part oil, 1 part kosher cooking fat. Fry.
When cooked dip in pan of boiling water. Dry in oven.
Toss in paper bag with cinnamon sugar mix.

P.S could you use that powdered egg instead of real? Don't you
have chickens? I don't know what instead of sugar? Do you
keep bees on that farm Iris? And kosher? You got that? You sure
you got no conveniences? Refrigerator, electric wash machine,
and an iron, you really got none, honey? But you got a gas
mask, right? When's Larry back? They say it's real cold in
Europe right now and Rita says you got a dog. In the house?
That isn't cleanly, sweetheart. I wish we could call you, as we
got news. Did you hear? Our Janet Fiorello got a medal over in
Italy, for all that work she does with our boys. You going to take
these donuts to our boys in England, Iry?

4

I carve a notch in Gran's doorframe with my penknife; there's little difference to the last. This is my height chart and these are birthday notches. 'Buenos notches,' Gran says, 'and do you have to mark my goddamn door?' I know she doesn't really mind; she's waiting for the day I get taller than Eva.

Today I'm eleven, so maybe my mum's wrong. She always told me I'd never reach adulthood, being a Walking Disaster Fund and all.

The post has brought me:

1) A slip of lined paper with 'Many Happy Returns' written on it. That's from Great Aunt Reggie, Grandpa's twin. Reggie looks like a turtle. She has too many cats and works at the Aberystwyth Oxfam. Reggie's bent double as she had the polio too.

2) A book called *Israel and Abraham for Beginners* and three *Spiderman* comics from Great Aunt Rita. 'Sweetcakes!' she's written on one inside cover, 'Happy, Happy Day, my little ainikle, the only one I'll ever have! Give your gramps Iris a kiss too, love Reetie.'

3) A card from my only girlfriend, Jamilah. It says 'Happy Birthday Kate, see U soon'. Jamilah's two years older than me and she lives in Gloucester. Gloucester's rough. Rougher than Hereford. There's a mosque (a church with a roof like a boob) and when I stayed for a weekend last summer her mum cooked food that made the house smell gorgeous. Gran said I'd put on weight. Grandpa said I'd gone native.

4) Nothing from Mum.

I'm still off school, but I'm having my stitches out tomorrow. And because it's my birthday today, Gran's King Charles Cavalier Spaniel, Bosum 8, has a Conjugal Appointment. Bosum is her stud dog, and she keeps him chained to the downstairs bath taps. Bosum is All Balls: the sire of champions. He makes her money. In return she walks him twice a day and feeds him shellfish.

Bosum 8's morning booking is a timid tri-colour called Lara, who shook then peed when her mistress dropped her on the bathroom lino. 'Well, let's leave them to it!' Gran said, kicking the *Medical Dictionary* doorstop out the way. The mistress wept and told us it was her little Lara's first time. Gran took her thirty pounds and whispered how it was goddamned ridiculous giving a dog a name from that lovely *Dr Zhivago* movie.

Gran's as experienced as Bosum at studding. Sometimes owners change their minds and want to rescue their little Fluffy or Petal, and Gran won't let them. 'He knows what he's doing,' she tells them. 'Fifty-three champions from his essentials to date.' These are essentials she massages in avocado oil and rose water once a week. Bosum's reputation is so faultless she has a no refund policy, because, 'There's been no blanks fired in five years.'

Lara yelps and I shout, 'I'm eleven!' up at the third floor.

There's no reply from Samuel, Wilhomena, or the cats, so I stare at Eva's bedroom door. It's next to Gran's, it's called 'The Sanctuary', and it's locked. Not long ago I stole the key and snuck in. There was no bed, I suppose she didn't need one anymore, just big blown up pictures of her on the walls. She was smiling in each, her lips tinted red and her eyes tinted a blue not even a Lieberman could have. A rocking horse with flared, fire-breathing nostrils stood in the corner while piles of dusty photograph albums covered the floor. I opened one to see a younger Gran holding Eva on a pebble beach, while a woman I didn't recognise held Mum. The rest of the album had pages and pages of my grandmother's writing, each sheet stuck down with shiny laminate.

So the bombs fell and the boys were lost, that's what Gran had written, *and I met my darling Mat in Room 46. Oh, my darling. Why does Larry have to come home? Why, out of all those men on board was he saved?*

When a huge picture of Eva laughed like the witch in *The Wizard of Oz*, I ran out, and haven't been back since.

'I'm eleven today,' I whisper at her door, then limp downstairs.

I find the dog-owner, lost in a dark corridor. She's hugging her whimpering pet.

'Mummy's sorry, Mummy's sorry, Lara-kins.'

'Are you okay?'

'Who's that?'

'Me.' I wave a hand at her face. 'Do you want to know the way out?'

'Oh yes, it's just so dark.' Her King Charles squeaks in agreement.

I take her free hand, and lead them both to the back door, 'It's my birthday today,' I tell her.

'How nice.'

'And your money's my first present. Thanks. Come again.'

The woman looks frightened. She hugs Lara tighter, then runs out to her car.

On the way to the kitchen I pass the downstairs bathroom, and there he is; Bosum 8; fat and beneath the bath taps. He's asleep on my brown, crocheted baby-blanket. Millie's tidying up round him.

'Hi Mil.'

'Bludy messy animal. Wouldn't have the like in my house, mind you. Filthy.' Millie is Welsh and her voice is soured cream. It can be soft as a peach and bitter as cabbage all at the same time. 'You going to have goings on like this in your house, when you is married, Katherine?'

'What's that, Millie?'

'When you is married, you going to have dogs doing their business in a proper bathroom like this?' Millie's got ridges on her nails deep as split rock.

'I'm eleven today.'

'Is it now?' She looks up from her brush and bleach and I notice Bosum's not asleep, he's cowering. 'Eleven? That's a lucky number, in the Bible that is. And you is certainly lucky you got so far on a place like this. Not like those other little ones, mind you.' She winks and crosses herself. Millie's mysterious about most things, but especially death. A bumblebee in the house means death, and she won't do any cleaning till it's gone. Millie had a girl that died. She told me she keeps her little Bronwen on the mantelpiece in the prettiest rose-engraved urn.

She carries on scrubbing while Bosum whines.

'I mean, Katherine, your mam leaving you yere and a farm's the most lethal place in the world,' she sighs. 'I dunno lovie, you got them silos and grain stores you can drown in, had an uncle went that way, and that's just for starters.' She sits up, apron wet, tight hair peppered, and counts on her red fingers, 'Look see, on a farm we got tractor wheels, rabid bulls, them chemicals that'll turn your hair blue and your insides to boot, and plug yourself in one of those milking machines and you'll lose a finger, then there's that mud you can sink in, and the floods –' she takes a breather, 'lost three cousins in those, see, and when my Robbie was taken with the cancer there was talk it come from Beavan's farm. Bloody dirty bugger. And then there's your nana's geese, they'd bludy peck you to death soon as look at you.'

I laugh.

'I'm serious, girl. Like the curses of Moses on the Pharaoh round yere it is, and the work's slow as death himself and just as hard. *I'm* only yere by the skin of my teeth, and it's for old times' sake I stay with your nan, see. Yes, by godfathers, a farm is like the hell mouth.' Millie picks Bosum up by the scruff, and scrubs under him: he freezes, legs out, eyes bulging. Grandpa calls Millie's speeches Chapel Talk; he says she could beat the devil with her tongue alone.

Millie's been here since before I, my mum, or even Gran can remember. Gran says that when she arrived at the farm with a box of Oreo's and three suitcases of pink, there was Millie, shipped in from the valleys, not quite twelve and in charge of the empty house. Her parents were dead and her brother was off in the war, never to come back, so Millie stayed. Gran said she was a little woman on her high horse then, and thirty-eight years, a marriage, widowhood, and five children have done nothing to change that. Millie loves my gran. When she gets at the cherry brandy she talks about how they've been through thick and thin and more besides together and how everything's 'for old times' sake'.

'And there's fire.' She pauses. 'You heard about *the fire*, then, Katherine?'

'What fire?'

'The one nearly did it for your granddad? That was a real hell-mouth. I got pictures, see, my Robbie took them, for Mr Happy's insurance, isn't it? Oh it were terrible.' Her eyes brighten.

'What happened?'

'Accident it was. Your granddad was woken one night with a terrible noise.'

'What was it?' Millie's beginning to scare me; she's good at that.

'Sound of beasts, sound of terror.' She stares at me for a bit. 'So, he gets out of bed, dazed like, and walks into that backyard there, and there he sees the top barn all ablaze. Well –' she takes a breath, 'well your poor granddad, on that stick, he goes straight to the pump for water, all the while having to listen to that sound of his stock being burned alive. All his cows, his prize bull, and your nana's horse too, a gorgeous black bugger, bigger an that Foreo now. Oh, you could hear that poor thing whinny for miles.'

'That's awful, Mil.'

'Yup. And by this time your nana's got us all up, see, she come round in her very own car, and the village has a go at that fire. All in lines we were, passing buckets, buckets, buckets, anything we could get our hands on. But it was no use, and your poor grandad's there in his dressing gown wailing and gnashing and all of a sudden like, he bolts, like a horse himself, bolts right into the barn. "I got to save them, got to save them," he cries, and it was only by the quick light-ning thinking of my Robbie that we managed to pull Mr Happy from there, before it was too late. That big old barn just collapses a few minutes after, and all those beasts is put out of their misery.' Bosum moans. Millie sighs. 'Sometimes I hear them, when I'm tidying yere. I hear them scream.' She smiles. 'But Happy Birthday anyway, lovie. And have a nice day as your Yankee nana says.'

I'm a bit dazed. I grab hold of the cold bath, then turn to go.

'Hey, where you off, girl?'

'I –'

'You think your Mil didn't know it was your birthday?'

'Sorry?'

She reaches behind her bucket and hands me a parcel. I pull off the brown paper. It's a book.

'Thanks Mil,' I try and smile.

'Thought it ud come in useful, lovie.'

I stare at the cover; it's a photograph of a burnt-up armchair with a burnt-up leg in it.

'What's it about?'

'Spon-tan-eous com-bustion. You got to have your wits about you for that, mind you.'

I feel a bit sick.

'Give your Mil a kiss, then.'

I do, and she tastes of baby powder and beef dripping.

Gran's at the Belfast sink singing 'I am a Woman in Love'. She's got cobwebs in her hair. I grab an apron and she points at three packets of Digestives, so I lay them out, get the rolling pin, and crush.

On birthdays Gran and I cook, and we cook *her* way. She's told me about the wonder of bagels and lox, gefilte fish, sturgeon eggs and cream cheese. In fact she'll go on for hours about her grandpa Lieberman's deli, and the times she stole pickles from the barrels in the basement. I sometimes hold onto her fingers, to sniff out that memory of vinegar, but all I get is bleach and Oil of Ulay.

Today though, is more special than bagels. Yesterday Gran drove to Cardiff to get her extra-special food. There's a bowl for soaking and a big board over the sink that she's covered in salt. We're making chopped liver (usually my favourite, but not after Millie's story), salt beef (uch!), and on the Aga is borscht (definitely not my favourite and for Grandpa). There's also noodle kugel (which makes me laugh) and I'm making the base for the cheesecakes.

Gran's always done this on our birthdays. She says it reminds her of Oceanview Avenue and the Thursday night cook in. This morning as she warmed hot milk for my Special K (because breakfast is allowed on a birthday) she whispered her stories of those people from that other land. There was Momma and Poppa Ichmann, her parents, who were small and strong; Grandma and Pops Lieberman, her grandparents, who were taller and stronger. Then there was, Lula, Little Rita and Iry (that's her). She says these people lived on top of each other like sardines in a can, and cooked all day, 'In a three-storey wooden house, tall as a skyscraper. Bagels and lox for breakfast and tea. The Atlantic lapping at our stoop, the sounds of The Coney Island Carousel, music for our dreams.'

To me Brooklyn sounds like Narnia, like Wonderland; so fantastical I believe it all. But this morning Gran looked sad, and after breakfast I watched her put cold poached salmon, butter, and onions on a soft piece of Mother's Pride. She sighed then, whispered 'bagels and lox', and threw it in the pedal-bin.

'Kosher for the Gentiles!' she cries from her bloody joint of beef, and laughs so hard she turns the same shade of purple. The reason is that later the vicar's coming to pick most of this up, as it's going towards the Boldenham St Mary's Church Luncheon. Gran thinks this is very funny. We get to eat one cheesecake though.

She told me she has to cook like this now and again or she'd go crazy-loco. It's the same reason why she locks herself up in the attic once a month and polishes her grandmother's candlestick ('a Menora not a goddamn candlestick, Kate!'). We keep all our secrets in the attic because Grandpa can't walk that far, and it's Gran's Chewishness she stores up there. When I ask her about it, she says it's just that, *her* Chewishness, and to keep my goddamn nosey parker out. Gran's also got a stack of unused tickets to John F. Kennedy airport there. The first is dated 1969, the year I was born. The last is 1976; when I loved The Brotherhood of Man, Dad died, and Mum left us.

Grandma Lieberman's club aluminium pot is on the sideboard, greased up and ready for the oven. This pot is part of Gran's inheritance, and that's why she's got cobwebs in her hair; she's been rooting about for it in the roof space. Gran says this pot does the best kugel crust.

I crush more Digestives with the rolling pin. The beef's salted and dripping blood into the sink, and I want to ask Gran about Millie's fire, but she's locked herself in the pantry to mix curd cheese, eggs and sugar. She says it's very bad for Chewishness to mix cheese with liver and beef on our birthdays, and that's why her life is hell: because she lives on a goddamn cattle and dairy farm.

'So what are your birthday wishes?' she shouts.

'Not telling.'

'Okay, I'll guess. You want a dog, right?'

'We've got two.'

'A kitten?'

'There's five litters upstairs.'

'A bike?' She comes out of the pantry, white cheese on her hands.

'Not at the moment,' I point to my knee.

'A Sindy House?'

'I'm too old.'

This is another of Gran's rituals. We have to guess what the other person wants. Only then can they have it.

'Your ears pierced?'

'Well —'

'Ah-ha!'

'No. Guess again.'

'Books.'

'I can go to the library van.'

'A horse?'

'Not likely.'

Gran sucks her cheesy fingers as far away from the beef as she can get. I crunch a whole Digestive. Sugar and fats make us giggle.

'I got it.'

'Go on then.'

'This —' she takes Bosum's thirty pounds out from her apron pocket.

'All right.'

'We'll put it in your savings.'

'But I want to spend it.'

'No.'

'But it's *my* birthday.'

'And it's *my* money. One day you'll thank me.' She goes to the sink, pauses, then washes her hands over the beef. 'Beggars can't be choosers,' she mutters.

Putting Things By For a Rainy Day is part of Gran's plan. That's why she's got big envelopes in the attic with 'Bosum's Balls' written on the front. They're not filled with balls, they're filled with money, because Gran's decided we're *both* going back to Brooklyn on the proceeds of his many Conjugal Appointments. That's why a yelping bitch is always my first present of the day.

Millie told me Gran's got enough money to go anywhere in the world, anytime.

I watch a knob of butter melt in the pan. Birthdays with Mum were more exciting; that's for sure.

For instance:

1) On my sixth birthday we lived in Abbot Canon because Mum was pregnant with the twins. She wanted a huge party, only we'd just moved in and I didn't have any friends.

'Can't we can buy them in? From the village I mean?' she asked.

Dad laughed.

So twenty children, from two to sixteen and, 'all from the council houses darling, so mind they don't steal', came with their stay-at-home mothers. It was fifty pence a kid. They ate and pocketed the sausage rolls but wouldn't touch Mum's paella.

'Funny bloody yellow stuff, you're a fucking weirdo,' a freckled boy said as I crunched prawn heads.

Mum bought me an orange slide. A toddler got his thumb caught in the top and a stray dad had to hacksaw the handles apart. I vomited cherries into a waste paper basket, held up by one of the stay-at-home mothers, while Mum shagged the clown in the laurels. I'm sure I remember balloon dogs floating up from the biggest bush.

That night Dad gave me a record player and I thanked him for dressing up as a clown and making those animals out of balloons. He laughed and said I was a funny thing and he'd been at work in London all day.

2) On my seventh birthday Dad and my sisters were dead so Mum took me to Sardinia. We went to a mountain fair where the air smelt of burnt grass and nougat. There was a Carousel of red and yellow horses, and a donut stall, and we hitched a ride with two men in their Fiat. They were brothers. One was blond and the other dark. Mum called them Cain and Abel and they kidnapped us. Mum said they raped her.

It wasn't so bad as we stayed with their mum and all she did was moan and cook. I ate her lovely wild boar sausages and a soup called brodo, and chased chickens in the yard. We spent Christmas there (which was *very* religious) and my mum learnt more Italian than she ever had French. In fact we stayed for three months, and when Gran and Grandpa finally paid the ransom we were sad to leave.

No one ever told the police.

'That would make it so boring,' Mum said. Also, she told me

she'd moved on to enjoying sleeping with the brothers. No one really cared about the ransom money, and in the end, I think it was Mum who kept it.

There was an earthquake a few days after we got home and the village was destroyed. I read about it in the paper while there was still Sardinian dust in the creases of my feet.

'A lucky break,' said Mum, 'a damned lucky break.'

And then she disappeared, one Sunday, in her red Triumph Spitfire.

'Want some?' Gran's offering me chopped liver on Melba toast. I gobble one up as Millie comes in and we all settle next to the Aga.

Gran tells us about the time she, Lula and Rita played something called 'hookey' which isn't anything like hockey. Millie says she's wicked, so Gran laughs and cuts up the fattest cheesecake. For the first time in a year we both eat until we are full, but Millie has two Digestives because she doesn't care for that foreign muck.

'Who ever heard of making a cake from cheese?' she says. 'Scones is right, but a cake mind you?'

The borscht stinks.

'What kind of cooking do you like then, Mil?' I ask.

'Fanny Craddock. Same as your gran. All that gelatin keeps it tidy mind.'

'It sure does, Millie.' Gran smiles.

So I'm eleven and nothing out of the ordinary happens. I'm just not ten anymore and I can't get an Oscar for being in the Best Film in the World, like Tatum O' Neal. Gran says it's a small mercy *not* being a prodigy, because it never works out.

I've moved back up to my bedroom on the second floor. Millie changed my sheets and tucked them in tight as a shroud. She and Gran had a cherry brandy or two, they spoke to Rita on the phone, then Gran drove Millie home. Now there's a storm like a row outside, and a high-pitched noise that could be the wind or the echo of Jessie 13's howl in his oil drum. Rain thuds against the roof slates two storeys up; blunt nails that pop and drop to the concrete yard below.

Grandpa gave me his stuffed puffin for my birthday, then stuck a bit from the newspaper, 'Ripper 13th Victim Found', to the fridge.

The puffin is first-mate to the stuffed albatross that Grandpa hangs from his bedroom ceiling, 'As a reminder to the seafaring man! A bloody cursed albatross, Katie! All hands lost!'

I'm not sure I like the puffin: the little yellow beak and the sad teardrop eyes. It's on my bedside table, looking up at my poster of David Cassidy like it's in love. Mum bought me that poster five years ago, and somehow there are coffee stains on David's forehead. She took me to his concert in London where some girls were crushed, but I can't remember any of his songs. I like Blondie and Siouxie and the Banshees now.

Dad gave me my favourite poster. It's for *Paper Moon*, and Tatum's looking as small as me, sitting in a crescent moon by my chest of drawers. I've kept that poster, perfect.

My belly's tight with cheesecake. I feel sick and it's nice. There's still a wedge left in the pantry and it's all I can see; that one white, fluffy slice. Gran said it's for Elijah; she leaves it for him every year and he never shows up.

I creep out of my cold bed. This must be the slippery slope that Gran talks about. The, One Moment on the Lips For Ever on the Hips; The, Fatty-Fatty-Fat-Fat.

It's freezing and I want Gran's slippers, heeled pink with a fluffball on each toe. My bedroom door whines as I limp out, thunder cracks, and I hold onto the banisters just in case. It's nice that Gran leaves the downstairs light on for me, for that glass of water, that pee, or that extra piece of birthday cheesecake in the night. But right now it and the lightning are helping me see a figure creep up the stairs.

The figure's stepping onto Gran's pink shag-pile and leaving wet footprints because it's got no shoes on. Steam is rising off its wet dress that's orange and stuck tight like cling film.

It's not Mr Barlow and it's too solid for Samuel or Wilhomena.

I blink. Cheesecake rises, and then I recognise my mother.

This isn't what I wished for at all.

It's too late to shout, so I press my head between the barley-twist balcony rails and try to breathe. She puts a bare foot on the top step of Gran's pink stairs and the farmhouse shakes. I'm dizzy, and I remember how once I got my head stuck here. Gran had to get goose-grease from the larder and rub it on my ears; it smelled like Castrol GTX.

I retreat to the shadow of the ornamental dragon (the one Grandpa brought back from China as a treat, 'And don't we all hate the thing, goddamn communists!' says Gran). My mother's close now, I can hear her pant. Maybe she ran here; maybe she woke up this morning in the South of France, had breakfast with Picasso, and then ran all this way. As she turns onto my landing, I see something I've never seen her do before; not even during prayers at Dad's funeral buffet. She crosses herself; forehead-to-belly-to-shoulder-to-shoulder. Then she's tip-toeing past me and into my bedroom.

She hasn't seen me.

I suppose she could be a ghost. But that would mean she's dead and Mum doesn't look any different. Her hair is the same, though it's wet; down to her bottom and black as coal. I limp back into my room and try and clear my throat. I try and limp less so she doesn't laugh. But she's already asleep. On my bed.

Who's been sleeping in —?

I switch on the bedside light.

'Mum?' I whisper.

She doesn't wake so I lie down next to her. I notice she's not just wet, she's filthy. Her hair smells like Grandpa's, it's dusty bailer twine and lard, and the soaked orange dress is slapped to her shape, as orange as my old play-doh. I lean over and sniff her. She's vinegary, then heady like perfume. It's the smell of gone-over lilies, like the ones in that dark room where I had to kiss a dead relation called Rose, Grandpa pushing me.

I poke my mother, but her skin is warm: not dead. So maybe this mum is a zombie-mum. They're warm, aren't they? Or is that clammy? But I don't want her to be one of those living-dead who lurch about supermarkets, eating people who are stupid enough to get caught by a monster that can't run. I stare at her hands, because one thing zombies have are green hands with the flesh all hanging off. And I have to say, her nails *are* black, and the skin around them *is* brown; like she's been dipped in a cup of Grandpa's Camp coffee. She has a plaster on each thumb too, and her usually dark arm hairs are albino white. I remember that zombies have milky eyes; but Mum has hers closed.

Perhaps Mum is a vampire, then; maybe Mr Barlow got her. But if she is one, she'd have tap-tapped at my window. Vampires don't walk up the stairs.

'How are you, fish-face?' her sudden voice is loud in the half-dark room and I jump off the bed.

'Still nervous are we? Calm down, child.'

'I'm fine.'

She laughs. 'Just fine?'

'Yes.' I want her to open her eyes, just so I can check they're not all white and bright.

'I suppose you're ten now.'

'Eleven *actually*.' I sit back on the bed. Sheet-lightning flashes the land outside, she looks at me and I see her eyes are normal: blue with rusty bits in the middle and just like mine. The Lieberman-Ichmann-Chewish eyes.

'You're bloody tiny, Kate. Doesn't your grandmother ever feed you?'

'Yes.' I feel a burp of cheesecake.

'Been up to anything?

'Like what?'

'Don't know, the stuff kids do.'

'I hurt my knee,' I point at my dirty bandage. 'I'm having the stitches out tomorrow. *And* I got a boil on my bum because I picked a flea bite, but it's burst now.'

'Oh god, still a Walking Disaster Fund then? What a boring life you lead, fish-face.' She sighs and turns her back to me.

Outside, wind changes direction, rain splattering back onto Grandpa's window-panes. I look out and see the drip and wet of his fields beyond – half English, half Welsh – soon they'll be thick with crisp ice: a trap.

'So, where's the Yank?' Mum asks. She's always called Gran this, it's an inheritance from Grandpa.

'Asleep.'

'See she's still got her pink palace.'

'Yes.'

'And your grandfather. He still sectioned to the broom cupboard?'

'What?'

'Downstairs, is he still quarantined?'

'I suppose.'

'Still got that poor sperm bank dog in the bathroom?'

'Uh-huh.'

'Thought he'd be shooting blanks by now. Poor bastard. What is he, number seven?'

'Eight. He's Bosum 8.'

'Right.'

I lean closer and check Mum for tell-tale zombie or vampire signs, like bad teeth and growling.

'What *are* you doing, child?'

'Nothing.' But I'm trying to peek behind her ears for decomposition.

'Get off, Kate!'

'Sorry.'

'Wilhomena and Samuel still present and correct? Can't hear them.'

'Yes.'

'Your grandmother hasn't got an exorcist in then?'

'No. Mum?'

'Yup?'

'Where have you been?'

She sighs. 'Oh, here and there.'

'Where? Back in France? I got a postcard last week.'

'Did you?' she seems surprised.

'Where were you then?'

'Off seeing a man about a dog.'

'You always say that.'

'Well, tough.'

'You smell.'

'Hey!' She laughs and pushes me over the edge of the bed. I cling to the candlewick bed-cover as she watches me struggle; a landed minnow. She's Marlene all right – Marlene like a German film star.

'I suppose I do stink. Come on, let's run a bath, I'm bloody freezing.'

Mum strips off and I notice that she's dark all over (apart from the squiggles of stretch marks on her stomach and that familiar red line down the middle of her chest). There's no white bottom or breast: she's gone a totally different colour. I look at my own skin and it's pink, like the rims of a white rabbit's eyes.

'Do you think we'll wake up your grandmother?'

'No. She's knackered.'

'Still up to her old tricks then?'

'Sorry?'

'Who is it now?'

'What?'

'Oh, you never were very bright. Come on.'

My bathroom's steamed up and I'm sitting on the Ali-Baba laundry basket, as close to the tub as I can get. Mum's washing between her toes. I think my mother sucks in water like she is a drought herself, and she's used far too much of my Badedas.

She rubs her foot with the pumice stone and nods at the dark mould on my bathroom ceiling. 'See it's as damp and wet as ever here. God, there's a permanent fucking rain cloud above this bloody place. Surprised it hasn't been washed away.'

'Did you get back to England tonight, Mum?'

She looks blank and goes under the dirty-brown foam. Skin itches beneath my bandage and I poke my finger in.

'So, more accidents eh?' She's staring at my knee.

'Yes. I fell, I told you –'

'Still a proper casualty then?'

'I suppose.'

'You'll never reach adulthood, Kate.'

'You can't say that anymore, I'm eleven.'

'That's not an adult.'

'Nearly is.'

'Anyway, what do you think I'm doing here? It's not for my bloody health. This, my darling, *is* your birthday present.' She stretches out her arms like it's a curtain call.

'Mum?'

'Yup?'

'How did you get in? Gran always locks.'

'Used my old key. Never lost it. Funny isn't it? All this time. Hey, Grandpa will shoot me one day. The old wolf'll get his big twelve bore out, and bam!'

She mock fires in the air, foam settles on the arm of my nylon nightie, and I ask *the* question.

'How long are you going to stay?'

She pauses, then she's standing up, water dripping. 'Hand me a towel, arse-creeper.'

In my room, I watch her squeeze dirty water from her knotted hair, then put on a wooden necklace. It has small beads like peas and a disc with an old man's face, and he hangs between her breasts in line with her scar. She doesn't have a bra on and he looks quite comfy, smothered in her big boobs like that. His hair is long and white, like God's, and his eyes are velvet. She chucks her orange dress into the corner of my room.

'Who's that, Mum?'

She examines the picture upside-down. 'Oh darling, I don't really know anymore.'

'Did you meet him in France?'

'No.'

Mum sits on the end of the bed, naked.

'Actually Kate, I left France a while ago, just after my last visit here, do you remember that?'

'Yes, I'm not a retard.'

'God, you have gone as Yank as your grandmother. Anyway. I never went back, I just wrote you loads of cards and gave them to a friend to post. "At regular intervals" were his instructions. Can't quite believe he carried them out.' She stands up and circles the room. 'I just found I could simply not come back here, not to them, or to you for that matter, not for good, and I was so bored of the Continent. So I went somewhere else. I had to find myself, do you know what I mean?'

I watch her stare out of the sash window like some stupid heroine in one of Gran's library books, except Mum's got no blinking clothes on. She turns round, dramatic and loud, and her boobs shake.

'Darling, I had a *revelation*, do you know what that is?'

I frown.

'Everything in the past became nothing, all the mistakes I'd made. And I had to find like-minded people, not come back here to all this damned *history*. And d'you know the wonderful thing? I found them, for a while at least. Oh, you'd have loved it there, Kate. A commune they call it. And it's only down the road, about forty-five minutes from here, just over those mountains, in Wales.

I've been there for quite a while now. And I really have found myself.'

I stare at her.

Forty-five minutes. That's less than old children's telly at lunch, less than *Play School* to *Fingerbobs* to *Pipkins*. Mum is telling me she's just been a few lunchtime children's programmes down the road and now she's smiling like it's all a pretty secret.

I hear a door creak open downstairs.

'Noise!' Grandpa shouts. 'No compass!'

Mum's smiling at me: arms open, breasts sagging.

'And now Kate, at the end of this wonderful year, at the very end of this very wonderful and awful decade, I just had to come back to you, my child. Isn't that wonderful? We'll be together, we'll say goodbye to the seventies together, darling. Come here. Please. Mummy's back.'

She's practised this stupid speech. I can tell. Behind her David Cassidy's laughing.

'Mum?'

'Yes.'

'It's 1980 already.'

She frowns for a second.

'Oh darling, numbers, numbers, you were always such a stickler for stuff like that. A pedantic little woman!'

'I –' but I can't speak anymore, instead I walk up to my mother and I spit in her face.

I don't care about my knee. I run down two flights of stairs and slip on Gran's reminder notes that yell 'Stamps!' and 'Gelatin!' from her pink steps. The storm's still howling outside, and so is Jess. I open the back door, and limp over sandbags. In the yard wind's pushing the rain in waves, and it rattles through me as I hop ankle deep towards the slide of my grandfather's black-ice fields.

It's freezing and I'm crying as if I have a bad cough. It's like being sick. Then I see arcs of light and all the deep puddles in the yard are mirrors.

'Kate? Katie? Where are you?'

I hear my grandmother behind me, she's shining her torch and her voice is being swallowed and spat out by the wind.

'Kate, come back inside. Katie, please!'

MILLIE'S FIRE

5

I'm sitting in Gran's pink chair in the hall reading *Spiderman*. I want to look busy: not at all interested in what's going on upstairs. A bowl of Shreddies balances on my lap and I eat them dry, no milk, as Peter Parker gets bitten by a nuclear spider.

'Look, just leave me alone Mr Quack, or whoever you are,' Mum says. 'Don't you understand English? I'm *fine*.'

I hear mutters from Dr Croften, then my Gran's higher pitch. 'Please honey, you just need a little help. The doctor thinks –'

'Fuck the doctor!'

'Really Marlene!'

I'm a hamster: Shreddies lodge in my cheeks.

'You know what? I don't give a shit. My daughter fucking hates me, I'm back in this hellhole and you can all fuck off. So come on Dr Wonderful, bring it on, what have you got? I'll take everything –'

Then she's quiet.

Mum's been back two days and she's driving us mad with her middle-of-the-night music, though Gran did say that '"My Sweet Lord" has a certain numbing quality.' The Beach Boys and 'Wouldn't It Be Nice' remind me of the flat Mum and I shared on the Bayswater Road, so I put the pillow over my head. I haven't been back to school. No one tells me to go, so I don't.

It's because of the music that Gran thinks Mum's been brainwashed, by those goddamn orange hippies up that mountain in

Wales. She said that if Mum were a dog she'd put her down, but as she's a human she called the doctor.

'Please, Marlene.'

'Yes, Miss Happy, it's to make you relax.'

'I'm a Happy-Mahoney!'

'Good. Good. Now tell me the year, Miss Happy.'

'Nineteen–bloody–eighty according to you lot.'

'Good. Good.'

And they're all quiet again.

I listen to the grandfather clock next to me, tick–tock, then all I can hear are my grandmother's whispers.

'How long, Doctor?'

Tick–tock.

'Do you think?'

Tick–tock.

'Some kind of shock?'

Tick–tock.

'Just everything coming back to her? She was with the hippies you know –'

Tick–tock.

'It's not like her father, is it? Not permanent?'

Tick–tock

'Oh, I see. Some time. It'll take some time. Yes. I understand.'

Tick–tock.

'Then everything's back to normal?'

I've never heard of that.

This morning I had another postcard from Mum.

K.
Cannes.
Will call.
M.

Happy Ferme
Boldenham
Herefordshire,
Angleterre

It wasn't even her writing.

I munch a Shreddie that tastes like hay. The comic falls from my lap. Peter Parker's climbing up a wall and being American, like my gran. The phone rings, and I look up to see her hopping down the stairs to answer it.

'Boldenham home 5–4–7?' she says, then frowns. 'No, and again no, I have told you countless times, Mr Iwase. Mr Happy is not willing to rent the Boldenham field to you or your country, thank you and goodbye.' She hangs up.

'That that Japanese man again, Gran?'

'Goddamn –'

'What does he want the field for anyway?'

'Filming a goddamned battle. The Battle of Boldenham, and we got enough battles going on in here, honey. Come on, out you go.' She starts shooing me like one of her geese. 'It's a great day out there, Katie.'

'It's pissing down.'

'Don't be ridiculous. And language.'

'But my leg.'

'Now you know the doctor's made that all better again. Stitched it up real good.'

'But –'

Gran's already grabbed my yellow mac from the hatstand and she's helping me on with it.

'You'll be fine and dandy if you use that crutch.'

'I don't want to go outside, Gran.'

'Well, I'm telling you that's where you're going.' She opens the back door, and shivers. 'And in an hour or so when your mom's all settled, I'll take you out. How does that sound?'

'Where?'

'The Red Dragon. We'll have lunch. Now give me that cereal bowl and scat.'

She closes the door. Then the opening twang of 'My Sweet Lord' blasts out from the second storey. I'm getting to like that tune.

The backyard's still a battleground after the storm. No one's bothered to clean it up. There are mad things strewn across it: a tree, a milk crate, what looks like a dead goose, and a pair of maroon trousers. It's like a clown's done the milk round in a tornado.

The tree's just missed Mum's car.

It's strange to see it again, her Triumph Spitfire; still red, and the bonnet still dented.

I swing across Grandpa's yard on crutches. Cows bellow from the lower field, udders full, as Stan Ruck circles them in our tractor. Stan works for my grandpa. He's got hands like walnuts, and he told me he does the milking so the cows won't burst.

Brian Ruck, Stan's son, is at the mouth of the hay barn. Brian's big for fourteen and he's got his Parka on: he's got everything in that coat. He used to keep a pet rat and live chicks in one pocket: 'They just eats when they's hungry,' he told me. Gran says he's feral, and calls him Heathcliff, but I think Brian's love bites are sherbet Dip–Dabs, and in the summer, his brown legs are polished floors.

'What chu done to yourself?' he shouts down at me.

I limp up the incline, and sit on a damp bale near him. Brian's eating an apple. He calls eating 'chucking it down your neck'. Sometimes he *shoves* it and *pushes* it, too.

'I said, what chu done to yourself, Kate?' He talks at the same time as he eats and there's bits of pith on his fleshy lips. Brian's hair is black as Gran's and he's got big blue eyes that make him look soft. I once overheard Millie tell Gran that he got Sam Morris pregnant, 'under the willow'.

'I fell,' I tell him.

'Stupid.'

'No I'm not. I was chased. By a wolf.'

'Dun't talk rubbish, ent no wolves round 'ere. A fox m'be.'

Brian once warned me not to chew grass blades from the

hedgerows, as a fox could have peed on them and according to him, fox pee kills. Brian hardly goes to school.

'Well, I was chased, so there.'

'Says who?'

'Says me.'

'Yeah, and you're bonkers.'

'What?'

'The whole lot of you, my da said.' Brian wipes his mouth. 'He said your mum's come back too. That right?'

'Could be.'

'That's her car ennit? I remember it. It was in the papers, they took pictures –'

'Brian, what are you doing here?'

'Had to get the bull in from the hill. He's next door.'

On cue Grandpa's big prize Hereford makes a foghorn noise, like those ships the Queen throws bottles at. Grandpa studs his prize bull in competition with Bosum 8, and he thinks he's won hands down. 'It's the bloody size of the balls, Katie. Doesn't compare with that dog's chocolate drops. The ones on my beast, like two heads in a sack. Magnificent!'

Brian knows everything about bulls. That's his job. He let me watch bull-mating once and he had to hold the bull's willy. 'Goddamn, that's as heavy as a ham hock,' Gran said and made me go inside. Once, Stan Ruck and my grandpa lifted a whole bull in a sling hung on a crane, but the rope snapped and the bull fell and crushed the cow to death. I didn't see that, Mum told me it happened when she was a girl.

Brian sits down next to me. 'Happy Birthday for the other day, Kate.' He hands me a brown paper package tied with string, and I know it's another penknife. I put it straight in my pocket.

'Thanks.'

He's eating the apple core now. It's disgusting. Pips appear then disappear, mulched by his tongue. Brian's only handsome when he doesn't move or speak.

I watch water shimmer down our yard and into Grandpa's drain. There's a warm touch to the air, like being in a greenhouse.

'Wanna see my willy?' says Brian.

'Pardon?'

He's grinning at me. 'My willy, wanna see it?' He gestures at his crotch and goes for the top button of his Lee jeans.

'Not really.'

Brian usually shows me leverets, and buried crocus bulbs.

'Ah go on, you'll like it, really you will, it's right nice.'

I stare at the tides of water.

'Give it a look, Kate. See, here.'

He stands in front of me, blocking my view. I shiver with damp, and wonder what the doctor's doing to my mum.

It was nice to have Gran pick me up the other night, and carry me into the house like a baby. She's strong and I could feel her bed-warmth, caught beneath her quilt dressing gown. She put me straight into her pink bath and filled it with luke-warm water (Mum had used all the hot). I remember the bath water turning red with the blood from my re-split knee. 'Is she upstairs?' was all Gran said to me as she sponged my cold face with red water.

'Go on, Kate, let me get it out. My willy.'

I'd forgotten about Brian. I glance up at him. He's taken off his Parka and he looks excited, like he's got a new Scalectrix or something. I once saw his mam whack him with a track of his Scalectrix, until it broke.

It was Mum who first told me about willies. She called them 'cocks' and 'pricks' and told me what to do with them. 'Nice to give a good blowjob, darling!' she'd say. 'Handjobs? No problem!'

It sounded like a lot of hard work to me.

I saw Dad's willy, but I didn't think it was interesting or unusual, and I doubt if Brian's can be any different.

Sharp shafts of straw dig into my bum, but I don't move. Wind blows across the yard, cooling the sweat on my face. 'Go on then,' I tell him.

He fumbles, his fingers dirty, his nails nibbled to the quick. His y-fronts drop and I'm surprised at the big, red marks his tight jeans have made round his belly.

'What chu think then?'

It looks like it could smell. It looks like Millie should give it a nice soak in Domestos. He has a lot of black hair there (which *is* a bit frightening), but the willy itself is long and thin. There's a big bag behind it, that doesn't look like Bosum's balls or the prize bull's two-heads-in-a-sack. It's more like turkey neck.

'Go on, touch it, Kate.'

I've never touched one. You just don't. Not as your dad's running past you into the bathroom, looking funny and bent double to cover himself up.

'Will I catch anything?'

'Don't be stupid, can't get pregnant by touching.'

'I know that, Brian, I'm not a kid.'

'Yes you are, you ent even got tits yet.'

I look down at my chest. When I was seven Mum used to pinch my nipples and say, 'Not long now, Kate!' But it's been ages.

'Touch it, please.' Brian's gone red in the face.

'Okay.'

I hold out my hand, then stop: I'm worried about getting dirty. It must be the same as putting your fingers up a cow's bum, like James Herriot.

'I'll touch it if you get me a bucket of water.'

'What?'

'You heard.'

'But why?'

'To wash my hands, after.'

'I ent dirty, I told you!'

'Then I won't touch it.'

I know I'm being what Mum called 'a prick-tease.' She'd use that phrase in conversation, even when it made no sense, like, 'That fucking car, it's going to the scrap heap – nothing but a prick-tease!' One day when we were driving round London with the radio on (she liked doing that) I asked her what it meant and she told me, 'It's playing with a cock, darling. Never giving it what it wants.'

I had images of chickens, so I had to ask her again.

'It's never doing what you said you'd do, Kate, sweetheart. What you promised to do. Don't ever be a prick-tease, darling. It's the worst thing in the world.'

In front of me is a black bucket, water lapping over its edges. Brian's standing next to it, out of breath. His willy is standing up now, which does look funny but not ha-ha, and it's wet on the end like he's just had a wee. It's solid as a pig's trotter, so I grab it, and pull.

Brian squeals. That sounds like a pig, too. He knocks over the bucket as he falls. I watch him wriggle on the wet, straw-covered ground, and I think about the last time I hid in this barn. Just a few weeks ago. I think about all the times I've hidden in this barn, just waiting for my mother to come back.

Brian's gone white. He's pulling up his y-fronts, and his willy has gone small and wrinkled. He takes a deep breath. 'Dunt cry, Kate,' he whispers, 'I didn't mean t'scare you.'

I touch my face. I didn't even know I was.

He does up his denims, carefully, before he sits down with a sharp gasp on the bale. He tells me he feels like throwing up and that I shouldn't yank at a man's business like that. Then he puts his arm round me and it feels nice, much nicer than his willy.

'There now,' he says, holding my shaking shoulders tight, 'dunt cry. Let's tek you in, get your nan to mek us some tea. She meks nice tea your nan, though she's foreign.'

I hear the steady thud of dairy cows walking to the milking shed.

'Did I hurt you?' I ask.

'Nah. Not really. But you dunt have to touch it again, mind.'

I'm glad.

It starts to rain, hard. I can just see the blur of Dr Croften's Audi back down our long drive. The milking machines suck next door and Gran is standing under the awning, with a big, pink umbrella. Bosum 8 sits obedient at her side, while Jessie 13 runs in circles round them, wagging his filthy tail. She waves at us and I swallow.

'Come on then,' says Brian.

I wipe my face and snotty nose on my cardigan sleeve. 'Okay, but I'll make you a cup of tea, Brian, and I'm sure Gran'll let you have it in the kitchen with me. Instead of in the sheds I mean.'

He smiles and laughs at this, though I don't know why.

The Brooklyn Daily Eagle

April 15, 1944

NATIONAL TRAGEDY OF LOCAL PATRIOT

By Frankie Wright

Local girl Janet Fiorello was officially 'missing in action' last night. A brave member of our own Coney Island Division, Janet enrolled to help her fellow countrymen battle for Allied freedom.

Janet and Mabel Linton (an English girl) were the 'donut gals' in Northern Italy, where many of our soldiers have been posted. They would drive out to the battlefields early morning and provide much needed succor to our US soldiers in the form of donuts, and allegedly, tea (coffee is on strict rationing). This patriotic action had won Janet the Medal of Bravery, and Mabel Linton the English equivalent.

Yesterday morning Janet and Mabel made their usual run at 0400 hours. They never returned, and it is reported that their route was ambushed at 0430 hours.

Their shelled jeep has been recovered, but at going to press they are still officially classed as 'missing.'

Our thoughts and prayers are with their families during this time.

6

They're playing 'Silver Lady', that song by Starsky or Hutch, as red dragons spit fire from the wallpaper. The carpet's red too, and the leather armchairs we're sitting in. 'Overkill,' Gran said as she walked to her usual seat by a bay window. Then she nudged me and whispered, 'Hey, road kill more like, right, honey?'

It's taken a week for Gran to bring me to the Red Dragon Hotel for lunch. She's been looking after my mother. Still, it *is* a treat, even if the dining room looks like Satan's house. Gran calls this place 'goddamn tea and scones at Tiffin and Long Live The Empire', but she secretly loves it. We come to the Red Dragon Hotel after the funerals and weddings of people she knows, and people she doesn't. We came here to celebrate when Jacqueline Kennedy divorced a Greek man and to be sad when that singer Elvis Presley died. Gran told me, 'Picture him young, honey, then you'll be sad.'

There's a great gaping mouth of a fire. Logs topple out and singe the carpet that looks like Jessie 13's back when he's got the mange. I'm wearing yellow wellies and my Redbrook School summer dress: it's red gingham. 'Goddamn paid for it, got to get some mileage out of it,' Gran said.

I've got seafood pancake and Gran has her usual breaded plaice. We're allowed to pig out at restaurants. Gran says that if you pay for something you've got to goddamn eat every last morsel: 'Think of the starving Africans, Katie. And those Boat People.'

The room echoes with the stabs of our cutlery. We're the only ones in for lunch. A handwritten sign on the wall says; 'New Wine Bar, The 1-9-8-1, Coming Soon!'

'Katie, I want to talk about your mom.' Gran's already finished her plaice; she's quick with fish. She can filet and swallow a Dover sole in two minutes.

A cheesy prawn gets stuck in my throat, I cough and it flies back into the white dish.

''Cos you know she's got problems, don't you, sweetheart?'

I think how Mum makes a racket all night and sleeps all day, like she's bonkers Bertha Rochester, only instead of cackling and setting our beds on fire, she plays George Harrison. I take another bite of pancake and my eyes water because it's hot.

'Now come on, don't get upset. Not here,' says Gran.

'I'm not upset,' I cough.

'Well anyway. I don't know what those goddamn hippies did to her, but I figure your mom is going to take a long time to come back to us.' She pauses, 'Because I think someone's done something to her brain. I think somebody's *washed* it.'

Gran leans in but I've stopped listening. I'm bored of Mum and her stupid stuff. It's like she never left now. I stare at the waitress. She can't be much older than me, and she's cleaning under her nails with the prong of a fork. I like her eye make-up; it's thick and black, and she's got a line of stud earrings up one ear. She wipes down the plastic covers of the menus as an old couple walk in. It's then I recognise her; it's Sam Morris, the one Brian got pregnant under the willow. Her hair used to be blonde, now it's black, and she's got on a tight pencil-skirt and no sign of a belly. I wonder if she had the baby, or got rid of it, or if the nuns chucked it down the rubbish chute.

'– and your mom's going to need a lot of help, from all of us.'

I look up at my grandmother. Gran knows Sam, but she didn't say hello.

'Is that Sam Morris?' I whisper.

'What?'

'Sam Morris, who used to go with Brian?'

'Have you been listening to a word I've said, Kate Happy?'

'I just wondered –'

'Well stop it. Yes, that is Samantha but the less you know about her the better, young lady, how they let her work here I just don't know. Now, about your mother. She's been through, well, things.'

I stare at my cooling pancake and try and remember what Mum says she's been through.

1) There's, the ringer
2) Hell on earth
3) A living hell
4) And finally; a house on fire (as in her bringing a new boyfriend home and saying, 'Oh! You'll both get on like a house on fire, darling!')

To my mind she's been through a couple of years tanning herself in the South of France, then being a smelly orange hippie up a mountain in Wales. I put down my knife and fork. Sam's explaining the sweet specials to the old couple. She looks bored too.

'Profiteroles. Black Forest Gâteau, Sherry –'

I wonder if Sam likes Siouxie and The Banshees.

'– and that's why Marlene went away, Kate.'

'What?'

'Your mother. Don't you care?' Gran tilts her head to one side. '*Things* happened to her. She went a little crazy. Do you remember anything about that, honey? About before your mom went away? What we *all* went through?'

Sam's past 'Knickerbockerglory' and now she's listing the plain ice-creams. 'Vanilla, Strawberry –'

'Why's the doctor with Mum every morning?' I ask.

Gran's reapplying her lipstick; it goes with the crimson drapes.

'Has she got cancer?'

'What?'

'Cancer. You know, Gran, like Mrs Crabtree.'

'No, she has not. What a stupid thing to say.'

'Is she pregnant?'

'Kate! Sh!' she looks round at Sam, who's dragging a huge log to the fire. Gran presses her napkin to one side of her mouth, then the other. She folds the napkin in half and pops it into her mouth, puts her lips together, then takes it out: she's made a perfect red cupid kiss on the white linen. She smiles. 'Honey, your mom'll be fine. Just leave her alone, that's all I'm saying. Just stick by me and you'll be all right. Okay?'

I shrug because I've known that all along.

'So, how was your pancake?'

Sam comes over and clears our plates, but none of us say 'hello' or 'how have you been?' or 'what exactly did you do with that baby, leave it under a tree?' I stare at the black ribbons she's got tied round her wrists. Sam's trendy. I bet she likes Blondie and hates bloody Barbara Streisand and Starsky (or Hutch). For a treat, Gran orders sherry trifle, and then says we must skip supper for a month.

I eat the cream topping first, and stare through the glass doors of the Red Dragon dining room, to the plush corridor and the first step of the stairs that lead up, up. Four flights up must be room forty-six. That was once Gran's favourite room. The one she wrote about in the book she locked in Eva's Sanctuary.

So the bombs fell and the boys were lost, and I met my darling Mat in Room 46. Oh, my darling. Why does Larry have to come home? Why, out of all those men on board was he saved?

It's still raining but we've got umbrellas. I limp across the High Street as water rushes into the kerb grates. Gran's wearing one of those plastic caps over her hair; the ones that fold up to the size of a stamp. Her flesh-coloured stockings are splashed and she smiles at a few people. One man takes off his cap and bows.

We pass a pregnant woman who slaps her tight belly and yells, 'Stop fucking turning me around! Stop fucking putting me off, you bugger!'

Gran takes a sharp left and dives into the back of Marks and Spencer.

There's a gasp of heat and the comforting noise of tills. Marks is as bright as a hospital.

I make a puddle of rain as I wait for my grandmother, because she takes ages arranging herself for an afternoon here. She has to shake her pink umbrella, neatly fold up her plastic cap, then smooth down her damp pink suit (it's linen and a cerise shade today). She smiles at a passing assistant who's got a big hairy wart on her chin.

'Hello, dearie. How are the boys?' Gran asks this in her Celia Johnson voice.

Mrs Hairy Wart smiles. 'All right, Mrs Happy, all right. They got over them measles in no time. Cheers for the recipe. Didn't take to it first, mind, not used to foreign stuff but in the end that chicken macaroni soup was a godsend.' The wart wobbles as she talks.

'Chicken *noodle* soup,' Gran corrects her, 'a little penicillin.'

Grandpa calls it pipes and chicken stew.

'Now, dear, would you mind, this old mac and our umbrellas, could you take them while we shop?'

'I'm not really s'pose to, but seeing as it's you, Mrs Happy. Go on.' Mrs Hairy Wart takes my yellow mac too. I stare at her chin until she disappears with our bundle of wet plastic.

'She's an okay girl,' Gran says, back to American, 'not too bright though. Lord no. Interbreeding, Katie. That's the goddamn English all over.'

She pulls out a trolley and heads towards the food hall.

For the past ten years (ever since it came to Hereford in a blaze of trumpets and bunting) Marks has been my grandmother's supermarket kingdom. She visits every day. At home, there's one room on the third floor that's full of folded Marks and Spencer bags; floor to ceiling. She keeps the big carriers *and* the little ones they give you for packets of frozen meats.

Gran's headed straight to the potato salad. She calls them her Little Tubs of Wonder because they remind her of home. I watch her inspect each one. It takes her ten minutes to select five and lay them in our trolley.

'For the week,' she tells me: that's pretty much all she eats.

Gran sorts through everything; she'll examine every package until she finds the best, because, 'If I can't do that with a husband I'm gonna goddamn do it with produce.'

She moves on, stopping sharp at Frozen Poultry.

I know what's to come, so I step back and count. One. Two. Three. Then my grandmother gives a little skip and a jump, and dives into a freezer. Her legs wriggle as a boy points and his mother shoos him. But for those regular shoppers who pass, this is just the everyday ritual of Mrs Iris Tallulah Veronica Miriam Happy (née Ichmann) launching herself into frozen foods.

Inside, she's leafing through every blue Styrofoam packet of chicken breast, leg and wing; until she finds the very best.

'She knows what she likes, that one,' a woman laughs.

Gran pops up; hair brushed with ice.

'That's a nice piece, isn't it, Katie?' She holds up chicken thighs, skin puckered.

'I suppose.'

But she's not content. She throws it back and dives in again, legs jerking like one thick limb. My gran's a bloody earthworm.

And she doesn't even eat chicken.

I shuffle on the spot, bare feet sweaty in wellies. I try and pull down the short sleeves of my gingham summer dress; try and disappear into the bright white lino.

I want to be back in the Red Dragon, staring at Sam Morris.

'Okay, honey! Action stations!' (sometimes Gran talks like Grandpa). 'Whadaya think? This the one?'

She's emerged from her burrow and she's holding out a packet that doesn't look any different from the last, but then Gran says I haven't got *the eye*. She grabs the trolley and chucks it in.

'Right, now fish for your mother, it's good for the brain, and beef for your Grandpa too.'

Grandpa doesn't eat the meat, just the dripping, and Gran gives the joint to the dogs. Millie calls us 'terrible wasteful'. 'Think we never did have rations the way your gran goes on,' she says, 'and while them lepers in Africa is starving. Come Judgment day!' Millie thinks everyone in Africa is a leper because of The Mission at her Church. She brings in red, plastic towers for me and Gran to fill with two pence pieces. 'This one'll stop their hands dropping off,' she tells us as she puts the towers on the kitchen table. 'And that one there's for their ears and their feet, mind you.'

I follow Gran, dragging my wellies till they squeak on the floor, and I think about Sam Morris. Sam has big breasts. I could see them beneath her thin, white, waitress-blouse; the strap of her bra was as thick as a bandage. I quite fancy the idea of boobs now.

Gran's prodding beef with her ridged nails. Once she took a selection of cuts out into the street, 'To see them in the light'. They let her and she squatted in the pedestrian zone of Hereford High Street, five purple meat cuts round her. 'Like a bloody native,' Grandpa said.

Blood oozes from one packet as she presses down. I turn and walk to Lingerie before it can get any worse.

Lingerie is a funny word. You hear it on *Are You Being Served?*.
Lawn-ger-ie.

Two men are curled on chairs behind the aisles of knickers and bras. I pass a fat woman who's holding up a nylon slip and shouting, 'What do you think, Harold?' at them.

The men ignore her as she giggles.

I don't know what I'm after, something that'll make me look like Sam Morris I suppose; some big bra with hooks and lace and padding. I stare at the nursing bras and a woman tut-tuts behind me; I touch a long line of lacy blue bras and they feel hard as ice.

'Can I help, love?'

I look up and it's Mrs Hairy Wart.

'Where's your nan then?'

'In meats.'

'You lost, duckie?' she's talking to me like I'm six.

'No. Actually I'm after a bra. A sexy one.'

She looks like I've punched her in the throat and she's gasping for breath. The wart wobbles. 'Sorry, love?'

'I said I want a sexy bra. One to turn my boyfriend on. You know what men like, don't you?' I wink at her and she looks like she's going to be sick.

'*You* got a boyfriend?'

'Yeah. What of it?' I feel sulky and annoyed. I feel like Sam Morris.

'What size are you, love?' She's got me there. I don't think I have one.

'Small,' I tell her.

She looks like she's changing her mind about something, then says, 'Tell you what, come with me and we can measure you up. That okay?'

I think about the showers after games at my last school, how most of the girls with breasts and hairy bits would hide under their towels, while the rest of us jumped and skipped about.

It smells of M&S lattice pork pies in the changing room. The assistant at the entrance has got flakes of pastry round her fat mouth.

'Right then, love,' Mrs Hairy Wart says. 'You just take your top off and when you're ready I'll come in and measure you up.'

I slip off my dress and stand in front of the mirror. I'm just a skinny kid in stupid yellow wellies *and* I forgot to put on knickers this morning.

'Come in,' I tell her.

She flicks the curtain back and looks at me like I'm the ugliest thing she's ever seen. I wonder if I'm fat. Maybe it's the combination of birthday cheesecake and seafood pancake. Two cakes in two days. Mrs Hairy Wart loops a measuring tape behind my back and it's cold.

'Think what we need here is a training bra. Shelley! Shelley love! Can you get one of those – er 'scuse me, my bab.' I hear her whisper outside. 'Shell, get me one of those kiddies' bras. In white. That'll keep her going.' Then she's back, holding a small, string-like thing. 'So what's your boyfriend called, love?'

'Brian.'

She does up the clasp; the cups wrinkle on my flat chest like forgotten party balloons.

'He at school with you?'

'Nope. He's left school. He's nearly fifteen.'

She tries to tighten the straps but the cups are still empty.

'Your nan know?'

'About what?'

''Bout you having a boyfriend his age, and you at yours.'

'She might. Might not.' I feel powerful in my new white bra and yellow wellies. Then Mrs Hairy Wart grabs hold of my shoulders and turns me round.

'Look, love. You should tell her. She's a nice lady. An' you should be careful. You're never too young to get caught, mind. I had a cousin had one at thirteen and I'm not proud. Dunt look like it, but you had the curse?'

I thrill at this word. No one's ever asked me before, except for Mum when I was seven. I shake my head.

'Well, that's summat.'

The bra is scratchy; it's like wearing a first pair of winter shoes after a summer in bare feet. I pull the straps down, but I don't know how to undo the rest.

'Oh you're making a right bugger's muddle of that, love, come here.' Mrs Hairy Wart unhooks it, and it falls to the floor.

'You having it then?'

For a moment I can't move. I just stare at myself. Then I pull my red gingham dress over my head, and run out; past the smell of pork pies, and back to meats and my grandmother.

She's at the till.

'Can we go now, Gran?'

She takes out her Parker fountain pen, ready to write a cheque. 'Where have you been, stranger?' She's gone Celia Johnson again.

'Just about. Can we go?'

'In one minute, Katherine.'

'Hurry up.'

The woman on the till gives me a look.

'Pu-lease.'

'In my own good time, Katherine. What *is* the matter with you?' Gran glares at me then smiles at the woman. 'Children, what can one do?' she laughs, and hands over the cheque. 'Do you need my card?'

'No, Mrs Happy, this is perfectly fine.'

'You are a dear.' Gran presses fifty pence into the woman's palm. The people queuing behind us stare. I pick up a full carrier and wait for my grandmother at the exit.

Mrs Hairy Wart is there with our coats and umbrellas. I let her put mine on. I wonder if she'll say something to Gran.

'So kind, so thoughtful,' Gran tells her, then she's pressing another fifty pence into Mrs Hairy Wart's chubby hand.

'Say goodbye, Kate. Say thank you to Tina.'

'Goodbye Tina. Thanks.' I smile but she doesn't smile back.

It's still raining on the way home and Gran skids a bit. She's always been a pretty awful driver. I do love the splash of rain on her windscreen though; the fan pumping too much heat and her indicator blinking and clicking as she makes turn after turn in the dark. It's only five o'clock but it's pitch black. Gran's going on about the *QE2*. She always goes on about ways to get back to America when it's night. It's her wistful time, she says.

'You know one day you and I'll go back to Brooklyn on that goddamn ship. Do it in style, huh? Carve through that wadder. Once, just after the war, when we visited your Grandpa in Southbourne we sneaked onto it. The *QE2*. Be-oo-tiful. Only docked for a minute and already there were workmen, painters, and polishers climbing all over it like roaches. Cleaning, cleaning. It's the sea, they said, rots it so quick. Yup, that sure is the sea, honey. I mean look at your Grandpa.'

I stare out of the passenger window, which is a bit like staring out at a dark sea, and I wonder what 'we' Gran is on about. Her and Mum and Eva? Maybe Millie too? She turns the radio on and Jona Lewie sings 'Stop The Cavalry'.

My Darling Iris,   8th June, 1944

The days pass and all I can think of is you. I have my
men, my ship, and secrets of war so great they would
dominate the mind of any man. But there is still a
space for you. I hate to think what I have done to
you, how you have been left stranded on the farm in
such a condition, parted from your loved ones. I know
I have abandoned you in an unknown place and feel I
must rectify this. Therefore, please will you
reconsider her offer and stay with my sister Regina
during this last month of your confinement? Now the
farmland has been given over to Beavan, and you are
left alone, I feel I must insist. For your and both our
babies' sakes. Is the doctor still sure you are expecting twins? I am overjoyed and shall write to Regina
directly to say you are expected.

    You are for ever in my thoughts and for ever my
love,
    Your loving husband,
    Larry
    (Captain Lawrence St John Happy)

7

It's still raining. The sandbags are at the doors and Gran's out. I told her that if the water rises, me and Mum won't be able to escape, and she laughed.

'Well, we all drown somehow, sweetie, in love, in bitterness, in wadder, it don't matter which.' She drew on her lipstick. 'Even Eva, honey, she drowned, in a sense.'

Gran was right. I've looked up pneumonia, like I've looked up gangrene and polio, anthrax and thorax (and now bubonic plague, lysteria and botulism). It's all in the *Medical Dictionary* in Bosum's bathroom. Eva's lungs filled with water as sure as if she'd dived and died in a swimming pool. I wonder if I'll see Eva when I next swim in the river. She'd probably be a Water Baby by now, rosy-cheeked, all giggles and fun.

It's Wednesday night and like every Wednesday night Gran has her Poker evening with Mr Crabtree, so I'm alone in the house with Grandpa. What's not like every Wednesday night is that my mum is in my bed upstairs: brainwashed.

It got worse this morning because one of The Beatles got shot. Gran was hysterical as she thought the man on the radio said, 'Jack Lemmon's been shot'. She calmed down when she realised her mistake, then Mum started screaming upstairs.

I think Dave Lee Travis spoke more clearly.

Tonight at least, she's quiet: the doctor gave her an injection. All I can hear is Grandpa in his front room, shouting at the telly.

'Up the Boche! Listing to starboard!' he barks and Bosum howls.

Before his hips (and knees and feet and toes) gave out, it was Grandpa who put me to bed whenever I stayed here. 'Snug as a bug in a rug,' he'd say, then read his favourite story, the one his nanny, his ayah, his mammy told him. It was *Little Black Sambo, the Mongoose and the Eggs*.

'And Little Black Sambo paddled across the river as fast as his little black arms could go –'

Afterwards, Grandpa would switch the light off and whisper, 'If you make a fuss, Kate, the Bogeyman beneath your bed shall get you!' and he'd limp across our oak landing. Gran called him Old Ahab on his deck. Footsteps in time with the grandfather clock in the hall. Tick-Tock. Tick-Tock.

Tick-Tock.

Like Captain Hook's crocodile.

Tick-Tock.

'Damned dirty Hun! Avast!' Grandpa yells. I hear the clatter of his supper tray as he throws it at the wall.

'She's going down! She's going down! Mother Carey's chickens!'

I glance at Gran's bedside clock: it's seven p.m. exactly.

Seven p.m. Wednesday night. That means *Dad's Army*.

Dad's Army is Grandpa's favourite programme, but when Clive Dunn sings 'Who do you think you are kidding Mr Hitler?' Grandpa has what Gran calls 'a goddamn episode', which is something to do with the war. So every Wednesday night she gives Grandpa his bottle of valium, some cheese and port, and leaves the house to play poker with Mr Crabtree. The supper always ends mashed up against the wall, and I always go to bed.

I wonder if he's woken up Mum, then I wonder if he did this when she was my age.

There's canned laughter coming from the telly, so I get out of Gran's bed. I notice she's put a new photograph on her dressing table.

It's a picture of Mum and Eva hugging a woman in the backyard. The woman isn't Millie. She has freckles and overlapping front teeth.

I walk downstairs, and sit on Gran's pink armchair by the phone. I can see Grandpa past the half-open door of the red front room. He's in the big leather armchair, his thin, polio leg straight out. There's a glimpse of a polio ankle beneath his faded pyjamas, and it's withered and white as a pipe cleaner. I've never seen the whole leg, but when I was smaller he'd balance me on his thin thighbone, and bounce me until I cried.

'Caught the sugar-lump disease on a Banana Boat, Kate! Off the coast of New Zealand, Zanzibar, Timbuktu!' he'd laugh, and bounce me again. 'Go on, love, don't cry, touch it!'

I thought it was going to snap.

There's a triangle of Camembert stuck to the hunting-scene wallpaper above his head. The blue light of the telly reflects off his skin and I stare.

Grandpa once told me his laughs were history, 'They're all the bloody Gordons and Khartoums and Indian Mutinies, Kate my girl! All the Hindu bullets greased with cow fat, all the Muslims hanged in pig-skin!' I didn't know what he was on about, but I'm glad he's not laughing now. Grandpa was in something called a Sanatorium after the war. It was in Southbourne, and Millie said they'd go down there for their holidays, and visit. She said he was locked up for years and years, but they always had a lovely break.

It was Grandpa who gave me my first nightmare. The first I can remember, before Mr Barlow and Jane Eyre started shopping for offal and liqueurs at M&S.

I dreamt I was in a four poster bed, smothered by a red satin eiderdown. Thirsty, I called out. The door creaked open and I saw a paw, then a big wolf's face, and it was Grandpa.

'Want some water, my dear?' he said in a sharp whine, then padded closer, until his wet mouth dripped on my face and his long finger-paws caressed me: it was nice and I fell asleep.

While I dozed off, my Grandpa-wolf took me from the red bed and laid me down on a yellow mattress. When I woke he was rolling me up in it like I was the meat in a sausage-roll. I looked down at my feet, but they were so far away. I was stretched and rolled out like Tom Kitten in *The Tale of Samuel Whiskers*, though it wasn't pastry as my yellow roll cuddled and scratched at the same time. Grandpa had wrapped me up in loft insulation.

I never could wake up until Gran shook me, yelling, 'What is it, Katie? What is it?'

Who's Afraid of The Big Bad Wolf?

I am.

I look up and see Grandpa's face, and this time, it isn't a dream.

'What in God's name are you doing in this cold hall, Kate?'

'I —'

'Fancy a bit of telly? Aft!'

'I —'

'Well, come in then, must be chilled to the bone.'

I'm thinking -*all the better to eat you with, my dear*- as he takes my hand, but I can't call for my mum as she's a loony too.

The grate is full of red coals, Grandpa's mantelclock is still twenty-five minutes fast, but it's actually warm in his red front room. I don't mind it in here when the telly's on. Gran doesn't watch much TV, apart from *Agony* and *Dallas* (she's sure she knows who shot J.R.). Grandpa, on the other hand, is a big telly watcher and he likes the old repeats best: *Dad's Army*, *Basil Brush*, and *Some Mother's Do 'Ave 'Em*. He likes a good laugh does my grandpa. Boom Boom! He also thinks Bruce Forsythe is a Chew: 'Talks like one, damned poodle faker. Is he a Chew, Katie love? Look it up in *The Radio Times* there's a good girl.'

I'm on the leather chair next to him, and I want to flick away the bits of Digestives in his hair. Bosum is curled by the fire, his nostrils so small he snores.

'Poor bugger,' Grandpa says. 'Poor bloody milked gigolo. Full ahead!'

We've ignored the broken crockery on the tiled hearth. *Dad's Army* is over and it's time for a Frank Spencer repeat. Frank makes me laugh so much I wet myself.

'Amazing chap,' says Grandpa. 'Does all those stunts himself, you know,' and he stabs a lump of cheddar with the metal end of his shooting stick. 'Not just some pansy actor that one, no,' Grandpa smiles and pops the cheddar in his open mouth. 'Waste not want not, eh Katie? But I've no taste buds left. Pity. Scarlet fever as a child. Though I *can* remember the taste of my dear mother's Dundee Cake. *Dreadful*. Made it with curry powder, y'know. Only way in Madras. Flood cue!'

He smacks his lips, cheese coating his teeth. Cheddar lodges in the corners of his thin mouth as he laughs.

Tonight Frank and Betty are trying to get to Australia, which I thought could only be done by digging on the beach. Betty's voice is the same wavy pitch as Millie's.

Frank's making a mess of his interview at the Australian Embassy. My father's sister lives in Australia. She came to his funeral and told me about her daughter who's my age and called 'Lulu Dingo'. She said I should come and live with her and be called 'Kate Kangaroo', so Mum crawled over the buffet table and slapped her; she dragged her heels through the pâté and they had a fight on the crudités. Grandpa had to break it up by firing his twelve-bore at the ceiling. That was when my aunt called us mad, then called the police.

There's still a hole in the drawing room ceiling, and sometimes sections of plaster will drop on your head as you walk under.

I look at my grandfather. I've seen pictures of 'Him in His Youth', when he had black wavy hair and eyes so green they looked like an ocean. He doesn't look like that now.

Grandpa showed me his feet once. He undid his size fifteen specially made shoes and asked, 'Ever shown you these have I, Katie?

Take a look. Yellow as a Chinaman's, eh?'

They didn't look like feet. They were twisted, scarred, and all of his toes (except for half a big one on the left foot) were missing.

'Uh —' Grandpa wakes, shaking his head like a foal. 'What's this, what's this?'

'*Some Mother's Do 'Ave 'Em*, Grandpa.'

He doesn't look wolfish anymore, though I'm still on my guard. His eyes are small and covered in a yellow film.

'Good programme this. Does all the stunts himself, you know —'

'Yes.'

'Not one of those pansy actors.'

'No.'

'News now. What are you doing up, Kate? Should be in bed long ago. Time to get down to thirty fathoms, young lady.'

I don't move. I don't want to go back upstairs. Mum's playing 'Imagine' by that Beatle that was shot.

'Come along now, you've got rivets to count.' Grandpa stands above me and tries to pull me up. 'There now. Can't be that bad. Slow Ahead! Come along, Kate. Don't shirk!'

'I can't.'

'Katie —'

'I can't, Grandpa, please —' I'm about to cry and Grandpa smiles.

'There now, don't fret. I'll get you back to bed. I'll come with you. It'll all be all right. Bear up!'

And Grandpa, with his polio leg, twisted back and half-a-toe, picks me up with a fireman's lift. It takes ages to get to Gran's first floor, because he gets lost in a pee and beeswax corridor and has to shout 'Port!' to get his bearings. I'm light as any midget eleven-year-old who eats nothing, but I can still feel his arm shake around me like it does when he holds a soup spoon too long. All the blood's gone to my head by the time he's climbing the pink stairs, then he has to stop for breath after each step. When he lays me down on my grandmother's bed we're both dizzy.

Grandpa puts his head between his legs.

'Are you okay, Grandpa?'

He lifts his head and puts up a hand, asking me to be quiet. Mum's still blasting out that song, and I think of the way Grandpa shouts, 'Noise!' at every sound in his big house. He stares at Gran's gilt frame photographs: the pictures of the dead Happy girls.

When he got drunk on sloe gin last Christmas, Grandpa told me my mum and her dead sister were the last time he and Gran touched. 'Ah, when my fresh bride Iris gave in! Periscope down! And what do I get? Twins. Lene and Eva, my little girls. Sight cargoes! Then a few years later, Hitler shoots himself. Three momentous events in one decade, eh Kate? Too much for one man to bear. Full ahead crash dive! Damn it all to hell.'

Now he looks like he might cry.

'A proper potmess. Shouldn't have all those up, not with Lene back. Damned –' and he gasps a word I've never heard before '*macabre!*' He looks back at me and pats my head with his big hand.

That's the one thing about Grandpa, he has very beautiful hands, long and elegant; not like a farmer at all. Then he parts his legs, finds balance, and heaves himself up. He walks over to Gran's dressing table, opens the top drawer and, one by one, places the pictures of our dead-child relatives on top of her pink slips. He does it ever so neatly, like he's putting them to sleep, patting them all on the head, too.

'Goodnight, Kate,' he says, 'don't let the bedbugs bite.' And he fumbles in his stuffed pocket, picks out a small battered roll of Sellotape and a crumpled bit from the newspaper. He sticks it to Gran's mirror.

At least he's skipped *Little Black Sambo, the Mongoose and the Eggs*, as well as the Bogeyman under my bed. And because Gran's had pink shag-pile laid on the landing, I don't hear him limp Tick-Tock, like Ahab on his deck. Anyway, now I know that's just the clock in the hall making that noise.

I close my eyes.

Still up are we?

Oh Mum, get some bloody sleep.

Can't.

Please. And turn that blinking music off.

Don't think you can get away that lightly, because let's not forget Accident Number Two, darling, when you, the why-are-you-still-living-child? ate blue rat-poison in your grandfather's barn on Christmas Day. You spoilt that, didn't you? Pissing me off, and vomiting blue in the boot-seat of my lovely new Triumph Spitfire before I could get your stomach pumped.

You're just like your sodding father.

21 JULY 1943

WARTIME SELF-MAINTENANCE FOR WOMEN:

Chair, Wobbly.

If a chair wobbles badly, one of the two legs on which it wobbles needs shortening. To find out which should be dealt with, cut four blocks out of the same piece of board, and stand the chair on them. Remove the block from under one of the longer legs and put a weight near the other to keep it down. Note how level the chair now is. Having decided on which three legs the chair is most stable, scribe a mark round the fourth using the block as gauge, and cut off to the mark. Wobbly tables are treated in the same manner.

8

I don't know whose idea it was, West Midlands Safari Park. Did Mum creep down and wake Gran in the early hours last night to mutter, 'A trip, the animal park, I'll do the sandwiches,' then hop off back upstairs to her comatose life?

Whoever came up with it, I'm now sitting in the back of the Peugeot with my mother. She's sleeping with her eyes open and looks vague as our farm cats. Her cheek's gone white against the cold window and I want to reach over and lock her door, just in case.

Grandpa's cramped into the front seat reading Zane Grey. I think Cowboys and Indians are the only Yankee things he likes. Gran's driving, in her pink Jacqueline Kennedy Special (a good soak in Dreft got my blood out) and she's turned on the radio; no conversations allowed. We speed up the M5, through fog and rain, listening to an afternoon play, and I can smell the sandwiches Millie has made. They're on the back shelf, corned beef and mustard.

By the time we drive through The Park's jungly gates, we're past excitement. Grandpa says all the bloody animals will be in hibernation anyway.

'Oh good god,' says Mum as a crowd of children spill around the car like baboons.

'Don't be a party pooper,' Gran scolds and peeps the horn. 'This will be fun. Won't it, Katie?'

A boy flicks the V-sign and Grandpa hits the car door with his shooting stick.

'Abandon ship!'

'Okay, okay, hold on to your pants, Larry.'

We park in a disabled zone and watch Grandpa haul himself out of the car. It takes five false starts for him to finally make it.

'Bloody thrombosis!' he barks, then shuffles across the car park to the lavatories, back horizontal, face down at the tarmac.

Mum sighs.

'Please Marlene, for the child.'

'Did Mr Prisoner-Poisoner Doctor suggest all this then?'

'He said it would be good for you. A family day out.'

'Ha! Don't make me laugh, some chance the drugs he's got me on. I feel like shit.'

'Shh! Marlene!'

'Well, I come back and you dope me up.' Mum pinches my arm and tap-taps her head, 'She's a crazy lady, Kate, your grandmother, you better watch out.'

Gran gets out and opens my door; she's trying to avert disaster so I let her drag me away. We leave Mum lighting up a blue Sobranie in the back of the car.

'What's the doctor giving Mum?'

'Something to make her better. It's complicated, Kate. Your mother is not ill in the body. It's just, well you know how Grandpa can be? It's almost the same thing.'

'So she caught it from Grandpa? Could I get it too?'

'No, honey. You know it was that place she was at, that *commune*. We don't know exactly what they did to her, but Dr Croften's read up on brainwashing and I know about the Moonies. They give you fudge. It was in the *Readers' Digest*.' Gran pulls me between two coaches, their exhausts spluttering. She shouts over the noise, 'Or was that the Hari whatstheirnames? Well anyway, fudge with drugs in it. They get you at airports and *now* they're over here. Don't ever eat fudge, Katie. It's the devil's work.'

Kids crammed in the coaches above us stick out their heads and blow raspberries. I think about fudge and how to wash a brain. Would you do it in Fairy Liquid, like Gran does with Grandpa's cooked chicken breasts? And how would you put the brain back in?

I'll check Mum for Frankenstein scars later.

Two school kids vomit on the crushed-chip tarmac beyond. Gran stares, 'Well let's just have a nice day. Together.'

We jump over the puke and I wonder if animals do come out in the cold. I wonder if Mum will wake up and be her old self.

I'm not sure which one scares me most.

I've got six bags of nuts; *keep you occupied*, said Grandpa. He also bought my mother coffee in a Styrofoam cup, but his hands were so shaky most of it spilled on its journey to the car.

'Thanks, Dad,' she said and smiled.

'A pleasure, poppet.'

Gran stared at them, her face dark as a cloudburst, and we were silent as she started the car and the radio came back on.

Now Mum's chewing the edge of her cup as a monkey chews our aerial. The monkey's shivering; rain hugs it like a blanket.

'Poor blighter,' says Grandpa.

'Goddamnit, why didn't you put that down, Larry? The creature's going to snap it.'

The voice on the radio fizzes and hisses, Gran blasts the horn and the monkey jumps off. Fearless, she unwinds her window, reaches out and grabs the aerial. 'Little goddamn monkeys!' she yells, fist in the air. A group of them stare at our car, arses up, tails like question marks.

'This is nice, isn't it?' Gran tries. 'What does it say about these monkeys, Katie, you read it.'

I've got The Safari Park brochure, and it's filled with useless facts like 'The African Baboon has deep hair follicles' and 'The Asian Tiger can go three months without food'. All it says about these monkeys is that they live in a troop and are very sociable. Their babies take ages to be independent. They eat nuts (in captivity). They get a lot of viruses.

One jumps up to Mum's window and she laughs; its hands are delicate, baby-like, and it pulls off the rubber round the window. She sighs as it nibbles at the rubber then spits it out.

'Well, they're certainly cute,' says Gran.

Grandpa's snoring.

Another huddle of monkeys have retired under a tree, away from the spitting wind. A magpie pecks at the road.

'It's not natural,' Mum says. 'They're hot creatures.'

Gran looks in her mirror. 'We better get on, Marlene. Before your father wakes up and wants to go pee.'

It's slow, waiting for each gate to open. Most of the fences have signs saying, 'Winter Hibernation. Closed'.

I've fed a woolly camel all the food: he ate the paper bags too, his bottom lip sulky, his teeth goofy. I just wanted to see his wrinkled back, but his hump was more like Aunt Rita's belly: floppy fat.

A huge goat's been following our crawling car for ten minutes now, bleating. Its ears have been pierced with yellow tags, and they've frayed: the goat's eyes are green and a diamond shape, and it's giving Gran the willies.

'What does it goddamn want?'

'Wants to follow us to the lion pen, Mother.' Mum's smoking and we're trying to breathe. I unwind my window and the goat leaps up; it smells like a chicken coup.

'Bloody hell!'

'Katie, language.'

'It nearly butted me.'

'Give it a corned beef sandwich,' Mum says. 'That's almost canni-balism. Isn't it, Pa?'

'Bovine.' He points at the devil-eyed goat, 'That's ovine, darling. Permission to proceed!'

I chuck out Millie's Mother's Pride specials and the goat curls its lips over mustard and corned beef. It has little black hooves, shiny as patent leather.

'Is this meant to be therapeutic, Mother?'

'Don't be difficult, Marlene.'

'Should have put me in a room with a paint pot instead.'

'Oh, Marlene.' Gran checks her hair in the mirror and Mum flicks out a gold-tipped Sobranie stub.

'The goat'll eat that and die, Marlene.'

Mum shrugs.

'I need a stop,' says Grandpa.

'Oh, not again, Larry.'

'Don't embarrass him, Mother. Look there, Dad, by the giraffe pens, it says "conveniences".'

We park on a verge and Gran takes Grandpa to the loos. The goat rushes after them.

'Torpedo! Attack!' Grandpa shouts and a warden has to fend it off. Highland cattle bolt.

'It liked the sandwiches then,' says Mum.

'Yes.'

She lights another Sobranie; green this time. 'It's a dangerous place, a Safari Park, you know.'

'Is it?'

We watch a single rhino, bored behind an electric fence.

'Yup. People come to these places to top themselves.'

'What, stick their heads in an oven in the middle of a field?'

'You're such a little smart arse aren't you? No, darling, something far more dramatic than that. People have been known to leave notes at home, come to a zoo and run into the lion pen, or jump in with the crocodiles. I read about a woman who walked under a giraffe one morning and just stood there waiting for it to sit down. She was there until teatime. Someone filmed it. In the end she *was* crushed.'

'Sounds mad.'

'Yes, and looks like the best you could do here is to get butted to death by a Brummie, corned-beef loving goat.'

'Are you okay, Mum?'

'Okay? Ha! Please, don't question me, darling. Anyway, thought you hated me.'

I look out for my grandparents.

'Well never mind, never mind. Let *them* have their way for a while. Then we'll be off.'

'Where?'

'The bloody jungle. Do it properly. Get strangled by a snake. You know in his darker moments, and by god there were enough of them, that's how your father wanted to go.'

'A snake?'

'No. In the mouth of a lion.'

'Oh.'

'And then the poor sod gets run over. How *ordinary*.'

She inhales, deep, and seems to consider a large ox, moulting in the field below. 'He took me to a zoo once, Michael. He cried at the monkeys because they were surrounded by water. He thought that so cruel because monkeys are scared shitless of water. "A life of terror," he said, "Look at that, Marlene, a life of unrelenting terror. I should bring a gun and shoot them, they'd be better off." That's what your father said, and he threw his nuts away. No pun intended.'

'Where is he, Mum?'

'Hmm?'

'Dad.'

'What d'you —? Oh, you mean his *remains*.'

'Of course, I'm not stupid.'

'No you're not. Not a retard at all. Oh, god knows where he is, Kate, I might have left his ashes in that shabby hotel in Nice. Yeah, he's probably in a poubelle in the Côte D'Azur, poor bastard.'

I want to slap her, but Grandpa's hitting the door with his shooting stick. Mum gets out and opens it for him. I'd forgotten how much she loves Grandpa.

In the distance I see my smart, pink grandmother help three wardens load the big goat into the back of a black truck.

A lion is crouching in the grass because that's what lions do. It yawns and I wonder if my Dad could have fitted into that mouth. The guidebook tells me he'd have been better off with a hyena because they have the most powerful jaws in the animal kingdom. 'A hyena will sniff out the breath, and bite through a human head like a Cantaloupe melon' it says. It's very graphic this guide. It also has a pencil drawing of a female hyena that reminds me of those drawings in Mum's book, *The Joy of Sex*, with that hairy hippie man with a beard and too many bits. The female hyena also has too many bits. She's got girl bits *and* boy bits. She's got balls like Bosum 8 and a false willy, which looks too large to to be false.

'Great beast,' Grandpa says and I look up. He's talking about the lion.

'Did you ever bag one in India, Pa?'

'No lions, darling. Tigers. Several. Not proud of it though. It was youth.'

Grandpa doesn't shoot anymore (apart from ceilings). One day he even set his pheasants free. He fired his beaters and the game-keeper, and our roads were splattered with pheasants for ages. 'Stupid birds,' Brian told me, 'them can't get on on their own, they needs shooting.' Grandpa's tiger skins are up in the attic, and in the summer they smell of curry. The stink creeps down each flight of stairs like a spicy predator.

Mum's drumming her fingers on the doorhandle and staring at the lion. I can't stop watching, because she could do it. When my mum's with Gran and Grandpa she's like a sulky kid.

Mum isn't a grown up at all.

I'm suddenly scared, not just because she might jump into the lion pen, but by the other things she could do in a public place; it's a scary thing.

Like the time she left Dad and me at our favourite table at our favourite Italian restaurant in Bayswater, and I found her doing it to the waiter in the loos.

Or the time she left me on the ski-slopes in France, and didn't come back until the evening, smelling of peach schnapps and telling me how everyone at the hotel had seen her and my ski-instructor doing it in the snow. 'Nearly froze my arse off,' she said.

And the time –

'Marlene, stop it!'

I look across: Mum's got the door half open and she's winking at me. The lion yawns. I think of the headline Grandpa could cut out: 'Brainwashed Mother In Mouth of A Lion. Daughter Saves Her.'

'Lene, no!' says Grandpa.

She closes it. 'I was only kidding everyone. Calm down.'

'You don't kid around with beasts like that,' Grandpa shouts, hitting the door with his stick. 'Drive on Iris! Scuttle!'

'Yes, Larry.'

Mum looks suddenly tearful. The lion didn't even move.

We're starving on the way home, but we don't stop. Our stomachs grumble as Gran's wipers work overtime; the drizzle's turned to thick rain.

I think we all want to get home; back to our moat-circled castle, back to our own floors. This 'family day out' the doctor ordered isn't natural for us because The Happys aren't communal creatures. I open my Safari guide and under the flickering lights of the motorway try and find the animal we're most like.

Leopards, I think.

'Solitary, aloof and secretive. Long after other large carnivores have been eliminated from the area, the leopard will remain.

They take their kills to respective branches of the same tree and devour them.'

That's us, locked up on our separate floors, in our separate rooms, doing our own very private things.

Big white flakes hit Gran's windscreen.

Snow leopards, that's what we are.

My Darling Mat,   *May 5th, 1945*

Miss you. I'm locked in my bedroom, thinking of you, and I just want to drive off, with my best lipstick and you in that old pick-up. Read Martha Gelhorn today. That place. That camp. I didn't listen to my poppa, thought he was crazy in his letters, but he was right all along. Feel sick.

Those people. My people, right? How can I bring these babies up in a world with that?

How can I do it, Mat?

I got the coupons. Let's meet Friday, The Red Dragon, our usual room. 46. Millie's having the babies overnight. Feel okay now Marlene's getting better, my poor little darling. Guess you can get time off? We'll spoil each other, okay? Forget about all this, and spoil each other like we always do.

It's got to end soon, you'll get out of the factory and I'll get out of here. It's got to.

Then what'll we do? Haven't heard from Larry in forever. Lost at sea, right?

Your Iris.

9

'You see an elephant, then?' Brian yells.
  'No.' I shout back.
  'A hippo?'
  'Don't think so.'
  'A bear?'
  'Not really.'
  'It's sounds bloody crap then.'
  'It was.'

The trailer's bouncing in and out of white furrows, and so am I.
Brian's collie, Sid Vicious, is in the trailer with me, barking at the red
cows huddled under Grandpa's oaks. The fields are patchy with snow.

Millie says we've had a cold snap that could kill.

Brian and I haven't been to the huts since September when he
dropped Sid Vicious down a well. The huts are just that: long, black
wood sheds with corrugated tops that litter a field. Grandpa said
they used to be for POW's, who were people on the wrong side in
the war. Grandpa told me, 'There were only two Germans. Launch!
And they were from Devon. Rest were Poles. Good workers. Hands
like paddles. Great with beets. Faces like seaboots.'

After the war Brian's dad turned the huts into chicken coups, but
the fox and a disease got them. Now Brian and I have made a special den in one. We play mummies and daddies, and sometimes *Star
Wars* and *The Empire Strikes Back*.

I make Brian be Yoda.

The tractor shudders to a stop. Sid Vicious jumps out and tunnels into the hoops of leafless brambles. It's cold, and I bite my lips before the frost does.

Gran said she never went near the POW's during the war, though she said she hated the Poles much more than the Germans from Devon. 'Those Poles, honey. They'd wave at the trains from the fields. Wave.'

I don't think that's such a crime. Waving. Perhaps they knew someone on the train and were just saying goodbye.

I limp behind our hut and undo myself.

'What chu doing?' Brian asks.

'Baking a cake.'

'That's disgusting.'

'No it's not. Better than peeing in your pants.'

'Let's have a look then.'

'Fuck off.'

'Go on.'

I grin because I love to pee outside. I rest my back against the hut where train-waving Polish, two Germans and a load of chickens have slept. There are benches to lie on inside, but not much room for a man to turn on his side, or a chicken to stretch up on his scaly legs and crow. There aren't any windows either. I touch old graffiti carved into the wood wall above me. The words are foreign and gone black.

We've found knives, razors and a dentist's chair in these huts. Three boots, a trumpet, and a Bible, too.

'What chu want to play?' Brian asks. He takes out his torch and opens our hut door, checking for rats.

I pull up my pants.

'I said, what chu want to play, Kate?'

I kick a Tiny Tears and I lie down on our damp mattress. 'Mummies and daddies. But let's do it properly.'

'What chu mean?'

'You've got to show me your willy again.'

Brian looks scared. He picks up one of our dishcloths and pretends to wipe an invisible cup. 'What about "House"?' he asks. 'I like "House".'

He's a bit old for tidying up imaginary things, and I laugh when he puts on the floral pinny I nicked from Gran.

'Brian!'

'What?'

'You can do it to me if you like.' I look at the wood walls and think the hut is a bit like a sauna. Mum took me into one once and told me sex was slippery in a sauna.

Brian puts the imaginary cup on an imaginary table. 'A woman's work is never done!' he says, squeaky.

'What's the matter with you? You did it to Sam Morris, didn't you? I saw her at The Red Dragon –'

Brian throws the dishcloth on the rat-dropping floor and runs out.

'Bri-an!'

I watch him walk fast up the overgrown path, past the white-topped evergreens, and towards the big abandoned building on the other side of the track. I hate that place, but I kiss my bald Tiny Tears and run after him.

It's tall and black and it doesn't look like it ever had windows. Grass grows on the roof slates and crows top the crumbling chimneys. People round here call this building, The Happy Home. There's a playground at the front, with a blue roundabout rusted so tight it won't turn, and two swings with their chains broken. I like the green slide with no steps.

It's silent here, not even birdsong.

Brian's kneeling on the ground by the boarded up front door.

'What are you doing?' I ask him.

'Making a fire.'

'Why?'

'Burn a hole in this chipboard here, then we can get in.'

'But that'll make the whole place catch.'

'Nah.'

There's a stone inscription above the door.

'To Serve in Thy Honour'
This Orphanage was Established 1822
by the Honorable Samuel Edward Lawrence Happy and his beloved
sister, Wilhomena Lucia Happy, Philanthropist and Poetess.
'May our hearts be as sealed as our lips.'

I often wonder why Samuel and Wilhomena don't haunt here instead. I can imagine her trailing her scarves in the undergrowth, and writing long, boring poems with a quill pen in the shade of that awning. She'd take off her hat, too, and let the sun lighten her endless auburn hair. And Samuel, he'd be in his frilly white shirt, coughing up some tropical disease by the locked-tight roundabout.

Maybe they don't haunt here because there's someone else inside.

'It's creepy in there, Brian. Let's go back to the huts. We'll play house.'

'No.'

'Why?'

'Dunt wanna.'

'Brian —'

'Grab hold of this, Kate.' He hands me a box of matches and runs into the shelter of thick green trees. Then he's back with a handful of twigs and old copper fern.

'These uns are dry, this'll do it.'

'Have you been in there before?'

'Aye. Ent nothing to it. I get in through that hole in the roof but you won't make that. Too high. This'll be better.'

I watch him crouch over, strike the match, and blow until smoke comes, then a few bright flames. Fire cracks.

'There, that's him. Stand back, Kate.'

Little curls of orange lick up the board covering the door and I wonder if the whole place will go up, and if anyone would care. Mum told me Wilhomena and Samuel had things called plantations in the West Indies (that's where Bertha Rochester comes from) to build this place. She even took me to Liverpool Art Gallery and showed me a painting called *The Happy Family and Slaves, 1755*. She pointed at some ugly distant relatives in wigs and big dresses. They had servants holding plates of fruit, and a monkey, and Mum said the fruit and the monkey and the servants were from Africa. She started crying then, and grabbed me by the collar and told me that that was what the Happy family was built on, and that was why she drove round Hereford in a white Rolls-Royce shagging Trixie, the band from Jamaica and Tottenham with dyed green hair. She said *that* was rebellion, *that* was making up for it all. She also said that Grandpa told her she was a bloody idiot and wouldn't speak to her for a year.

Grandpa gave this place to the council, years and years ago, and Millie said they put funny kids in it.

'Brian, stop it. I don't want to go in.'

He kicks the burning board and sparks fly up: he kicks it again and a bit comes off. Then he's stamping on the flames until they're out.

'You coming in?'

'No.'

There's a red and charred gap, just big enough if we crawl. The edges smoke.

'Get in, Kate, go on.'

Sid dives in and Brian follows. Embers catch on his Parka and it smells of burnt feathers. His hand comes out and I take it.

It's pitch black inside, apart from slits of light coming from the edges of boarded-up doors and windows. It smells of wet, dirty sheets. Brian lights a match and I see scary faces, big, and leering at me from the wall. I squeeze Brian's arm, and he turns his torch on.

It's a mural of Snow White and the Seven Dwarves.

'That's good, innit?'

Sid barks from somewhere in the house.

'Come here boy! Hey Kate, you reckon there's tramps in here? Helloo!'

I stare at Snow White. She's got an evil look on her face. I think of Millie's stories. She used to do the beds here when the council had it, and she said it was a terrible place. 'Well, see, poor mites, couldn't hold themselves, could they? Not like us. They'd be locked up in their rooms all night, then I come in. Council said it was my job to clean them down. Take off them plastic knickers and plastic sheets and deal with all that muck, isn't it? Oh, that was a terrible job, and the smell. Some of them didn't know themselves, and they'd put that stuff all over, and some of them would eat it. Poor babs. Not bad mites, mind you, just better if God had taken them to his bosom, see.'

I think I can smell it now, that stench. I think I can hear them playing too; on the roundabout; on the broken swings and the slide with no steps, their screams muffled like they've been stuffed inside a pillow.

Poor mites.

Brian walks down a corridor.

'Wait for me!' I yell at him.

Brian lights the way with his torch and I see that all the doors are open, as if the children have just run out to play. In one room there are five iron beds. They've got funny straps hanging off them like the clasps on Gran's corset, and there's a mural of Mowgli from *The Jungle Book* in here. He's dancing with King Louis and Baloo, who's got coconut boobs, and he's not as scary as Snow White. Brian turns his torch off.

'One Step Beyond!' he shouts in the dark and I scream.

'You're a bloody scaredy cat ent cha?' He switches his light back on, and in the middle of the room is a pair of plastic knickers.

They look big, too big for a baby.

'Creepy innit, Kate?'

I'm cold.

'You hear bout that story then?'

'What story?'

'Bout that kiddie was here back in the olden days, you know, the Happy one. He died right in there.' Brian points at a cupboard door: it's blue, with a big Deputy Dawg painted on it. The door is smeared with dirt.

'What are you going on about?'

'Ent your grandad told you?'

'No. There weren't any Happys here. There were just orphans and mongies.'

'My mam told me, it was them famous Happys of yours. The ones with a tomb in the church, with her writing all them verses and him galavanting. That's what my mam says. Well they had a babbie together see, brother and sister, and so they didn't get found out they had this place done and put the babbie in it. That was in the olden days.'

'Don't talk stupid, Brian.'

'It's all true, you ask Mil. But the babbie see, he was all wrong, cos he come from the same family twice over. He couldn't speak, deaf and dumb, and in those days deaf and dumb meant you was a Joey. So one day them olden day nurses here go an lock him in the cupboard, and they forgot all about him till he started to smell and they did never hear the banging, cos all them kiddies banged and bashed all day and night, and he couldn't make no other noise so it was only when the smell came that they found him.'

'What do you mean, they found him?' I stare at the filthy cupboard door.

'He was dead mind, and rotten.'

'That's disgusting, Brian, and a lie.'

'No it ent.'

'Don't be stupid.'

'You go and check, he's in the churchyard now. He's "Little Boy." My mam showed it me and I'll show you. He's your great-great-great-great-times-a-zillion-dad!'

'Shut up, Brian!'

'Joey in the cupboard! Joey in the cupboard!'

I run into the darkness of the corridor; I don't want to breathe in the stench of rotting relations and dirty pants. The walls are wet, and I stop in the only bathroom. My eyes are used to the dark now and I can just about see a line of low, small sinks and loos, and a single big bath.

Brian comes up behind me. 'Think they all got in that bath then?' He puts a hand on my shoulder.

'I don't know.'

'Be a squeeze eh?'

'So?'

'Didn't mean to upset you.'

Sid tries to dig through the lino; his long nails making a noise like rats in a cage.

'Brian, did you ever come here when it was open?'

'Yup. My mam worked here weekends with Mil. Got good pay from the council, too. She'd bring me. I was a babbie then. They was all Joeys but they was nice, she said. I dunt remember it but Mam told me she'd take em for walks in the woods w'me.'

'What were their names?'

'Mam called one of em Brian after me, he didn't have no family.'

'When it closed, where did they all go?'

He shines the torch on the floor of the bathroom and there's a towel, stained and torn. 'Dunno.'

I think about the two Brians playing in the wood, as he picks up the towel and I see there's blood on it.

'It's good for animals in here,' he says. 'They have their babbies. Good shelter. I found fox cubs in that cupboard of yours once.'

'It's not *my* cupboard.'

'Well, the same one your Happy died in, anyways. I played with the cubs when the mother was gone.'

'And he's not *my* Happy either,' I mutter.

Brian chucks the towel into the big bath and walks out into the corridor.

'And that was a mistake mind, Kate. I should a known. You got to never touch wild babbies, no matter how nice they look.' He sighs and cuts the torch light. I can see his teeth in the dark. 'Cos when I come back the next day, the vixen'd killed em all. They had my scent on em see. A wild animal'll do that when she's scared, Kate, she'll kill her young, easy as nurse em.'

Wind blows down the chimneys, or maybe it's moaning from that distant cupboard. Now I know why Samuel and Wilhomena don't haunt here. I concentrate on the big chink of daylight coming from the burnt hole in the front door board, and try not to think of Little Boy. Setting this place on fire wouldn't be a bad idea after all.

Sid's howling in the yard. I crawl back out and breathe.

Woman's Home Journal

5 FEBRUARY 1944

TOP TEN TIPS ON
GOOD MOTHERHOOD

1) Regimen is all.

2) Do not fuss baby every time he cries.

3) Put baby down at the same strict hour each afternoon and night.

4) Until baby can sit up alone he should not be allowed in water longer than three minutes. When he is able to sit up he can have five to seven minutes.

5) Bottle is best.

6) Bleach for nappies.

7) Spoil Daddy too!

8) Keep up your house and yourself.

9) Manners, even in baby, are everything. No thumb-sucking.

10) You are a mother now, but your wifely duties must come first.

10

'*Wake* up, you sleepy head.'

I can smell my mother; it's a mix of patchouli oil and Chanel No. 5.

'Hmm?' I rub my eyes against white morning light and see she's sitting at Gran's dressing table, staring at dead Happys in gilt frames. Lids of bright snow are stuck to the windows.

Mum's wearing a mangy fur coat that makes her look like Grizzly Adams. She turns to me. 'Get out of bed. We're off.'

'Where?'

'London. Five minutes. Pack some things.' She suddenly shoves each framed photograph face down amongst Gran's hairbrushes and pots of make-up. A lipstick falls into the shagpile and Mum is gone; like the pink in this room is catching.

Gran's side of the bed is cold. I pull the blankets off and shrink back. Downstairs, Grandpa has the Farm Report on, so it must be early.

'Kate! Get a move on!' Mum shouts from the hall.

I flannel my face in Gran's bathroom and wonder if we're leaving for good. Was Mum's 'London. Five minutes,' a 'we're going back to the Bayswater Road, like it or lump it'? I borrow a bit of Gran's blusher for my cheeks but I won't pack any clothes, I just grab my satchel and my books because I don't believe in tempting fate.

Mum's at the foot of the stairs.

'Do you have to wear that?'

I'm in my Redbrook school uniform, blazer and all.

'It's the nicest I've got.'

'Well, if you want breakfast grab some bread or something. No time for anything else.'

'Where's Gran?'

'Off on a horse.'

'What?'

'Went off on that mad stallion this morning.'

'But there's snow. Does she know we're going?'

'Don't ask questions.'

In the kitchen I stuff two slices of Mother's Pride in my blazer pocket, slip into my yellow wellies and kick over my Just in Case, a giant Haig whisky bottle I won in a raffle, Grandpa drank, and Gran filled with change. Ten pence pieces scatter and I pick them up. They smell of Grandpa's breath.

'Oh do get a move on, child!' Mum yells from outside.

The ground's thick with dirty ice, and I think about Gran on that black horse who's not Beauty with his hoofs pawing the air to save you from the baddie. I bite into dry bread as Mum's Triumph Spitfire skids across the yard. She's got black sunglasses on and a long purple scarf: she looks like Penelope Pitstop.

Mum throws a blue Sobranie into the frozen snow.

'Get in, Kate. Don't be difficult.'

She revs the Spitfire and I feel sick.

'Do–not–cause–a–scene. Get in.'

I suppose I should be excited; a trip to London with my mum, it's my adventure.

Maybe it's Christmas shopping. Maybe she's taking me to Madame Tussaud's.

All the same, my heels dig into ice.

She opens the door. Creak. It smells of smoke.

'Come along, sweetheart.'

My mum's a loony, like Grandpa.

'Please, darling.'

And I hate this fucking car. It's all this fucking car's fault.

I get in.

We drive past the Barratt Estate in silence. It's bloody freezing but Mum has the soft top down. She gives me a scarf for my head and I stare out at the white fields, looking for a black horse and my grandmother. I'll call her with a ten pence when we get to London.

'So,' Mum shouts (you have to in the open Spitfire), 'how's school?'

'I only –'

'What?'

'I only went once!'

'Oh, yes. Fell over, right?'

'Yes.'

She changes gear.

'Do you have lots of friends, Kate?'

'What?'

'Friends!'

'Two.'

'Who?'

'You don't know –'

'Names?'

'Brian and Jamilah!'

'Funny name.'

'She's from Gloucester.'

'What?'

'Gloucester!'

Mum checks her reflection in the mirror. 'Anything else?'

'Eh?'

'Have-you-done-anything-else? Your grandmother taken you anywhere? Have you gone to America yet?'

I shake my head.

'Didn't think so. Did you like your new school? You like the bloody uniform.'

'What?'

'New school? Did-you-like-it?'

'It was okay!'

'What?'

I open my satchel, and get out my books. My throat hurts from shouting.

'Well, if you're not joining in, light me a cigarette.'

'Sorry?'

'Oh bloody hell. A cigarette, Kate, light one for me!'

She points at her Sobranies. I don't know how she's going to smoke in all this wind, but I press in the familiar lighter button, choose a green fag and suck. She snatches it from my mouth.

'And don't read in the car, Kate, you'll throw up.'

I've packed a *Spiderman* comic, *Jane Eyre,* and *'Salem's Lot,* and I try and flick through each one as white Herefordshire whizzes past. It's difficult with the comic because the pages snap back and forth. The books are easier. Icy wind numbs my cheeks as I read small print and come to these conclusions:

1) It's better to get bitten by a radioactive spider than a vampire (though even better is a flea as the bite just turns into a boil).
2) Families aren't always a good thing. See Mr Barlow's 'family' of vampires and Jane's Aunt Reed who's an old cow (see also Mum).
3) And if they're nice, they die. See Helen Burns (though boring), Peter Parker's uncle and aunt, and my dad.
4) Crimes will always be discovered. See Mr Rochester/The Green Goblin (and Mum).
5) Adventures always happen when you go to London.

Mum jerks the gear stick, and we fly onto the dual carriageway, but it's not *Chitty-Chitty Bang-Bang;* laughing in the clouds and singing 'Truly Scrumptious'. I press my face back down into the pages of *Jane Eyre*.

'I said you'll throw up if you read that, Kate.'

'What?'

'Oh don't bloody start.'

'Sorry?'

'Look, I am taking you to London. You should be grateful. I am your mother you know. Want a pee?'

'Eh?'

'I need petrol! Do-you-need-to-piss?'

She turns into the slow lane and the nearest garage.

I don't sit.

'Catch a disease, darling, listen to your mother! There are crabs on the seat! V.D. on the porcelain! Any ghastly person's arse!'

I'd prefer to let my legs dangle, but *she's* waiting outside.

'Save Your Kisses For Me' is playing. It's just the music, no words, piped into the cubicle, so I fill them in as I splash pee on the seat.

'Kisses for me, save all your kisses for me. Bye bye baby, bye bye. Don't cry honey –'

Splash-splash.

Dad held my hand as we watched Eurovision that night, snuggled on Grandpa's torn leather armchair. Dad had driven down specially. Mum was in London; it was the final time she left him because the twins were dead. Dad and me cheered and screamed when The Brotherhood of Man came first.

'They bloody won! God this is awful!' he laughed.

But I thought it was the best thing ever.

Gran and Grandpa were asleep ('Foreigners? Singing? Pah!'). It was just me and my dad. We made sandwiches with chicken leftovers and Hellmann's mayonnaise, and he frothed up my first milkshake. He'd brought the syrup with him; Strawberry Sundae and it was creamy and sweet as blancmange.

'How's your mother?' Dad asked, but I didn't know either. I did know that Dad's hands were toasty bonfires and his chipped front tooth made his smile a lovely crooked one. No one knew why Dad had a chipped front tooth; Mum called it charming, Gran called it cute. I liked to imagine him younger than me, jumping out of a tree, landing badly on tarmac, and chip! his handsome feature was carved. When The Brotherhood of Man sang their winning song again, Dad gave me a piggyback round the room.

'We won! We won!' he cried, and my wellies hung off my feet.

After The Momentous Result, we sat out in the front yard, on the stoop Gran had built. Big Jessie 12 was alive then, and Dad let him out of his oil drum. We watched him chase his tail as I slurped pink milkshake and Dad smoked the tobacco he kept in a tin that said 'Franklins' Fine Shag, Always Good Till The End'.

That was our joke: A Shag Always Good Till The End Ha! Ha! Dad had to explain what a shag was, as I didn't know then, but it was funny all the same.

Dad's orange-stained, bonfire fingers, made him warm all over. Dad's face scrunched up like clean paper and made you smile.

I sing at the lavatory tiles. 'Kisses for me, Save all your kisses for me –'

Mum hits the cubicle door. 'Get a bloody move on, child! And stop singing that dreadful song!'

I dribble my last bit of wee, wipe, but forget about the seat.

'For godsakes. I'll be out in the car,' then the stomp-stomp of her knee-high boots as she leaves.

I wash my hands and walk out.

There are dirty magazines and sweets in the bright garage. Mum calls these places *fucking perverts' paradises*. I can see her in the Spitfire by the petrol pumps; she's brushing on more eyeliner that makes her look like a panda. I'll do anything to never get into that car again.

I stare at the sweets, and then grab a packet of Spangles, some Love Hearts, a Marathon and a Curly-Wurly; but what I really want is some Reese's Pieces (Great Aunt Rita sends them at Chewish Christmas, smashed and yummy in a brown envelope).

'All that?' a man with a big belly says. His yellow fingers drum the counter.

Dad. Dad. Dad. Except this man has a greasy face and a packet of Silk Cut in his breast pocket, not Franklins' Fine Shag Always Good To The End Ha! Ha!

I add Toffos, beef and onion crisps, a Sherbet Dip-Dab and two cans of Vimto to my pile.

'Could I have a bag?'

I use up my ten pence pieces: all my Just in Cases.

Outside I breathe in petrol, as the heavy plastic bag hits against my leg.

'What the fuck's all that?' Mum asks as I get in. She's put the soft-top up and the car's tiny and too warm inside.

'Nothing.'

'You'll get fat.'

She revs out of the station and I start to eat.

I decide it's fun reading the small, tight writing in *Jane Eyre* and crunching a Spangle while Sherbet Dip-Dab fizzes on my tongue. Though it is starting to hurt behind my eyes. I flush hot and think about the colour. What colour do beef and onion crisps, Spangles, some sherbet and Love Hearts make (washed down with purple Vimto)?

Mum hasn't bothered to stop me.

I carry on reading. It's the bit where Miss Oity-Toity Blanche Ingram arrives at Thornfield. I bite into my Marathon and here she comes, snotty Blanche, walking over Mr Rochester's threshold, all loud and blousy as Jane's small and mousey upstairs. Squeak, squeak. I crunch a handful of beef crisps, which taste weird with chocolate, and take a swig of sherbet. A gulp of Vimto makes it all fizz up, purple, and I turn to the bit where Jane's just heard a blood curdling scream from the attic. All the Ingrams run out.

'Oh, what's that?' they cry.

'Back to your rooms!' shouts Rochester, angry and half dressed. And I throw up.

I mostly vomit on the wood-looking gear stick. It trickles underneath the seats.

Mum swerves onto the hard-shoulder.

'You little sodding —!'

She leaps out of the driver's side. Lorries squeal.

'Out! Out! Out!'

I'm retching as she yanks me out of the car and onto the verge. The roadside smells of crows. Mum pulls up my red school skirt and slaps my left leg like I'm a toddler. She does it in time with her words.

'You-little-shit. You-had-to-go-and-spoil-it-didn't-you!'

Wind blows patches of her fur coat bald. Mum hasn't hit me in four years. She slaps me on the other leg, then out of breath, sits down on the wet grass. Lorry-spray hits us.

'What *is* the matter with you, Kate?'

My head's thumping.

'You're behaving like a child. Answer me.'

'I hate that car and I don't want to go to London.' A kestrel shivers over a splattered rabbit. 'Why did you keep it, Mum?'

'What?'

'The car.'

'A sodding trophy, whadaya think?'

I wipe sherbet drool from my red school blazer and she hands me a balled-up Kleenex. 'Here. Clean up that mess in the car. That's all I've got,' she stares at the small, white tissue; 'Sorry,' she says for the first time, 'but you know I can't go near sick. Allergic.'

I do remember that Dad was the one for illnesses. Small ones at least.

In the end, I use my *Spiderman* comic to get most of it up. The car smells sharp and eggy, but we get back in: soft-top down.

'Bit of wind will be good, and at least we won't notice Slough, right?' says Mum.

'Yeah.'

She pulls out, not looking.

Gale-force wind presses my cheeks cold, and I try to remember the Bayswater Road. The memory is a haze, but I can see white pillars and double deckers (which is odd as Mum always took black cabs). I know a girl called Annie looked after me then. Mum called her Cockney Annie. She'd take me out of the flat and into the park to fly kites. I'd watch her kiss her boyfriend, and when Mum left us for a week together, Annie tried to strangle me.

I came back and there you were in a Peter Pan collar with blue bruises round your neck. Had to send her back to the ghastly place she came from. Fiddled with by her father. That's where it stems from, Kate. All that. Don't, whatever you do, take it personally.

I went to live with my grandparents after that.

Mum's hands are red-cold on the wheel. Her face is set. Concrete blocks graph the horizon as we drive up, up, onto a fly-over, and it's like taking off, to somewhere great, because adventures always start in London.

It's the same rule as People Die in Paris. Though that didn't stop Mum leaving Dad for the Grands Boulevards. *Oscar Wilde, Jim Morrison – they all bought it in gay Pay-ree*, Mum said.

'Where are we going first?' I ask, hair blown hard with sick.

'Shopping,' Mum shouts.

We're landing now: past the big old black church, diving down off the fly-over. Traffic slows us, and men with hairy faces walk past. We shake like dogs from the cold.

'We're going to Harrods, Kate.'

Mum takes a small brown bottle from her fur-coat pocket. She drops a white pill in her open mouth and glares at me. I think she's back to wanting to slap me, just to get some warmth into those fingers: they twitch, and a car honks behind her as she swerves.

* * *

It's the revolving door I love. It's my very own Tardis. I could twirl round in it for hours, until it spat me out into The Other Dimension of the Perfume Department.

I'm glad to be out of that car.

We walk among the counters. Mum squirting herself at each station.

'Got to get this sodding smell of sick off,' she says, as the over made-up women coo into life.

In the lift on the way up to the Toy Department, Top Floor, I think Mum smells worse. There's been a reaction and it's chemical.

We walk through Linen. I get butterflies, and it's not the thought of Egyptian cotton sheets. There's a rush of noise: children scream.

'Are you going to cheer up, fish-face?' Mum asks.

'I'm fine.'

'Doesn't look like it. God, take you to London for some bloody Christmas shopping and all I get is puke and a long face.'

'I'm fine, Mum.'

Her eyes film over and I follow her towards the noise of children.

She flushes as we walk into the hot room of toys. Families cram the aisles. Children older than me are yelling, faces pig-red.

'But I want this one!'

'Daddy, tell him!'

I can't believe the racket.

Mum laughs and walks down the steps. She stops at cuddly toys and picks up a huge stuffed owl.

'What do you think of this?' The owl's bead eyes shake. 'Make your mind up. I haven't got all day. Got other things to do, you know,' she pulls up her fur coat sleeve and scratches her arm.

I walk into the throng.

'What other things, Mum?' I have to shout.

'For me to know and you to find out.'

'That's why I'm asking.'

'Don't be a smart-arse.' She chucks the owl back with the other owls. A boy runs past us crying.

'Mum?'

'Yes.'

'Are we going back to the Bayswater Road?'

'Hmm?'

'Back to our flat?'

'What are you talking about? That was years ago.' She picks up a chemistry set. 'What about this?'

I frown.

'Oh don't be so bloody picky, Kate.'

Her face has gone from red to white. Blisters of sweat bead her top lip. Children jostle her.

'Are you okay, Mum?'

'I told you, don't ask questions. Look, do you want this or not?'

'Not.'

'Well, I've had enough. Here –'

She takes two ten pound notes from her pelt pocket.

'That's from your grandfather and me. I'll pick you up later. Be exactly here at three, right? I'm off to see a man about a dog.' She ties her coat belt tight as a snare. 'Have fun,' she tells me, and walks off.

'Mum?'

I see her raise a hand from Linen.

'Mum!'

But she's gone.

I look out at the Toy Department. It's so loud in here: I haven't heard this much noise for years. I never realised how quiet the farm was till now.

'I wanted the *blue* one!' a big boy yells. 'You said I could. *You said*!'

At least people look different here; a woman in a black sari in the Sindy aisle has got a something silvery that looks like a mole trap over her face. That's different.

I feel like putting cotton wool in my ears, though.

Mum always called Harrods 'the babysitter', because she'd leave me up here for whole afternoons while she 'lunched'. Mum always 'lunched', because Grandpa gave her lots of money. Harrods was Dad's favourite place, too. On our Saturdays together he'd bring me here with some of Mum's money and make me buy an Action Man. We played commandos in the aisles, and afterwards he took me to the Natural History Museum to tell me about dinosaurs and where I came from. 'Those films are rubbish you know, Kate,' he said, 'Raquel Welch in a fur bikini fighting a Tyrannosaurus Rex? Give me a break! There was no Man when dinosaurs ruled the earth. That was the point – it was just the bloody dinosaurs.'

There were only a handful of Saturday visits like these. Dad was busy. He was up mountains catching snow leopards for his act; he was jumping into volcanoes and saving the world. Once though, in the pet department two floors below, we did share a packet of cheese and onion crisps with a Shitzu puppy. In the end the assistant asked us to leave. 'You could kill it, you know,' she said. 'There's chemicals in that!' Dad told her that death wouldn't be such a bad thing as the puppies had no real Mums and Dads and were grown on puppy farms. Like in my book of *Nonsense Rhymes*, with ink drawings of babies growing in the vegetable patch, still attached like a courgette.

Tall shelves shadow me and I don't know where to start. Signs say: 'Sindy', 'Rubiks Cube', 'The Empire Strikes Back'. Brian said he wanted a Matchbox Starsky and Hutch car for Christmas. Brian likes jumping off the wall and onto the front of his Dad's tractor.

But is that Starsky? Or Hutch?

I walk to the boys' section, where shelves of Navy ships and fix-it planes remind me of Grandpa, but they've also got the new trans-former things that change from a car into a robot, then shoot plastic spears.

'Give me that!' a small boy with a white eye-patch shouts.

'No!' another boy yells.

'I'll tell the nanny on you!'

I buy a Starsky and Hutch car, red with a white stripe, and it's only ninety-nine pence. A girl in a sparkly tutu dances past the till and four boys hiss; she pokes out her tongue. She's holding one of those Make-up Heads; the heads on a plinth that are always blonde and have a clump of hair at the back which you pull until more hair comes. It's coiled up in the brain like a tape-worm, and it's disgusting.

The ballerina with the Make-up Head is screaming now, because the boy with the eye patch punched her. No one looks happy.

'Heinz! Heinz, come here!' a woman screams.

A big-nappied toddler crashes into me.

'Oh Heinz, my little darling!' The mother waddles over and frowns at me, like it's my fault her child's named after baked beans.

It's so hot I'm sweating in my red blazer; the ballerina girl kicks eye-patch boy and they're both howling now.

I think about the revolving door below, and the cold breeze from it as pop! you're spat out like a sweet onto the street.

'Are you okay?' an assistant asks me. 'Have you lost your mummy?'

'No, I haven't.'

I hate looking younger than I am.

'Are you sure?'

'Yes, cos she's off fucking a man about a dog.'

The assistant steps back. Maybe it's the smell of sick. Her face has the same expression as Mrs Hairy Wart's at Marks and Spencer.

'Thanks anyway,' I tell her, and push through a puddle of children, up the steps, and back to the crisp coolness of the Linen department. I say 'Ground Floor' to the man pressing the gold buttons in the lift, and sink.

I think I've grown out of the Toy Department.

In Perfume, I sprint, sick-caked hair hitting my cheeks, because I don't want to see Mum. Ladies behind a bright make-up counter laugh like clowns, their eyelids too blue with shadow, their cheeks rosy red. I dive into my Tardis and am spun out into the lovely cold.

'Taxi, Miss?'

I listen to the familiar shud-shudder of the black cab. I smile at the driver and jump into the back. It smells of rubber-rings and armbands.

'All right, my darlin'?'

'Yes.'

'Where you off then, young laydee?'

'Natural History Museum, please.'

'All right then, petal.'

The fairy-tale turrets of Harrods recede and I'm Cinderella, escaped for the night. I'm Rapunzel or one of those stupid Make-up Heads, and I've damn-well thrown down my sicky hair.

The Western Daily Press

22 February 1946

OUR BRAVE GIRLS RETURN HOME!

What remains of the invaluable force of female volunteers who have worked so hard during the war years are to return home this weekend. The TNT factory in Rotherwas was closed soon after Armistice, but many stayed on as paid landgirls in an effort to rebuild our local community.

Also, many from as far away as London and Manchester have decided to stay in Herefordshire for good, thanks to the lure of our local lads! Mrs James Biddlington, formerly Miss Lucy Grey, said, 'Oh yes, I much prefer the country now! I couldn't really go back to London as my street was bombed by the Jerrys. It was nice to help with the war effort here, but I'm glad to be away from that factory with all that yellow powder!'

A Miss Mathilda Greene has even set up her own cottage industry down here, working with our own American, Mrs Iris Happy, and catering for weddings and other occasions. They are called 'Something Out of Nothing' and are sure to be a hit in these rationed times! What the modern woman does these days! 'It's a banquet at cut-price prices,' says Mrs Happy. 'The war years made us use our imaginations in the kitchen, and Mat and I intend to carry on!'

Captain Lawrence St John Happy, Mrs Happy's husband, is at present resident at The Shineways Sanatorium, Southbourne. Captain Happy was decorated, and left the Forces with an honourable discharge. During the years of its operation there were two explosions at the TNT factory based just outside Hereford, where fifteen workers were killed, including eight girls from London, six of our own and a nightwatchman.

11

I could stare at the gargoyles forever, waiting for a twitch, a blink. Stone pterodactyls. Tapirs, lizards, and bears. Fish with jagged teeth eating other fish, and iguanas wrapped round each other in a bow.

Dad once told me the Natural History Museum gargoyles come to life at night. He even put on a funny posh voice.

'Now listen, dear one. The sabre-toothed tigers, beaked griffins and creatures with no name jump from terrace to turret so nimbly no one ever sees!'

Then he got bored and went back to normal.

'And they eat the pigeons. Good thing too, flying rats with no toes, that's what pigeons are.'

Dad told me the story of this building but I've forgotten it. All I get is a picture like one of Gran's old cine films. Dad's in black and white, pointing up at turrets while I'm much smaller, though still in yellow wellies, holding his hand and staring up. I think it was like that.

'Come inside, Kate,' he said (in his posh made-up voice again). 'Come and see what you come from. Roll up! Roll up! It's all in there! Evolution. Survival of the Fittest, and that's you, my darling, because you're the only one who lived after all.'

If Harrods was Mum's babysitter, the Natural History Museum was Dad's.

Now I think it looks like Mr Barlow's house, pretty but frightening, and you could get holed up in there for ever while the millions of bricks make patterns in black and brown around you. One thing I never understood, though, if this is the Natural History Museum, what's Unnatural History?

'Your mother,' Dad said.

A man is heaving a pushchair up the big steps as a school party spills past. I join the children, my red at odds with their striped blue and gold uniforms. They run like soldier ants, all following the same path. A teacher at the door tries to tell me off for being red, but I slip past her into the vague warmth of the huge hall and my big, black-boned dinosaur winks. I haven't seen him in years. The blue and gold kids scatter round him, pointing and squealing, while I stand crimson beneath.

I'd forgotten about my skeleton dinosaur; how his ribs are the hull of one of Grandpa's model boats, and his face is a shoe. His tail is my favourite: the little locks of bones like Meccano; the tip that could stab through a queue of children if he lashed it, moody as a cat. Once, when he was in a chatty mood, he told me how he's coming to life one day, kicking off the splints that hold him down and grabbing the nearest child. Then he's going to thrash them round the room like a dog with a rag (and he's got feet like a whippet's, too). 'Fair enough,' I said, 'but I'll be able to see your stomach fill with their bits, and then they'll drop out, because you'll be like a skeleton drinking a glass of water in the cartoons.'

And he laughed.

But he's quiet today, my dinosaur. He just winks at me and whispers, 'So, where's your dad?'

I don't have the heart to tell him.

Stained-glass windows light the spotted marble floor like they do at Boldenham's St Mary's Church, and I remember Dad told me this hall has arches like a cloister (which he said was a very holy place). I climb the wide staircase, where carved stone rabbits and pheasants curl up and twitter. My footsteps echo. One last glance down at the columns with patterns like those on ice-cream cones, and I'm up to the glass cases of stuffed things.

This is where Dad brought me.

'The Victorian Gentleman,' he said, 'was an avid collector. Even of things not yet born.' He was standing in front of a case of eggs, and they were so pretty; some spotted, some blue or yellow. The Bee Hummingbird had the tiniest egg and I wanted to take it home and hatch it, but Dad told me the insides had been blown out. He put on his funny-posh accent again, and squinted one eye, 'The Victorian Gentleman was a proper bounder! He was the murderer of all things!'

I didn't laugh, because Dad was pointing at a stuffed Dodo. Extinct. Gone for ever. In fact, I started to cry, so he had to yell, 'Bear bum!' at the back of a red grizzly on display.

The dead animals haven't changed. The same monkeys cling to the same branch, mid-scratch. The Giant Lemur's still Gone! Extinct! (probably because the poor thing's just a skeleton, climbing up a branch). But the Mandrill with the bald arse has had his blue and red face-colours freshly painted. I once asked Dad how the stuffer got their dead faces so alive.

'Taxidermist,' he said.

'What?'

'Not stuffer. Taxidermist. That's what they're called. People who stuff animals.'

I thought of Grandpa's shed then, stacked with a lifetime of Jessies, numbers one to twelve, all stuffed and sitting to attention; all with the same brown, glass eyes.

But how do you stuff an octopus? A slug?

At the back of the dark and chilled room, a marble Charles Darwin sits like a stone cold Father Christmas, and I wonder if he cut up all these animals himself. I wonder if he chose the decor too; the red, embossed wallpaper, and the burgundy, electric carpet. It smells of sawdust and leather and I stop at a Pyrennean Mountain

Dog because Mum had one of those, when she was pregnant with me. She called it Faceache and it bit her in the tummy. 'That's why you're so bloody feral,' she told me.

I try growling at the dog in the glass cabinet, and a red-headed boy laughs.

'Weirdo,' he says, and turns to the wolf next door. 'Can't catch me, can't catch me, can't catch me for a toffee flea!' he shouts at it, his big raspberry tongue out.

I hope the wolf has the same plan as my dinosaur.

They have those ice-cream cone columns in here too, except at the top of these a stone owl or a curly-horned ram stares down: it's creepy. In fact this room makes my skin prickle. Signs say; 'The Struggle to Survive', and 'Death from Natural Causes'. I wander past the display cases, and it's like the taxi-whatstheirnames have stuffed every animal to look vicious, even the vole seems threatening; clinging to a reed, his mini-teeth bared. All these dead creatures remind me of that *Planet of The Apes* film I saw with Dad, with Charlton Heston running about a human museum, staring gog-eyed at stuffed people. I wonder if Mr Darwin stuffed some humans too? Because if it's survival of the fittest, we're the fittest, aren't we? Maybe they're all hidden, in the basement, or the attic. Grandpa told me Americans shot Pygmy people in Africa just before the war, and stuffed them. He said the Dutch put the live Pygmies in safari parks, and now they're called Bushmen.

So maybe Dad *is* behind one of these thin-glass displays?

Nah. He was cremated.

My head hurts with thinking and being sick. I leave the dark room; and walk back downstairs to the brightness of the Bird Room and The Birdcall Listening Station.

This is where Dad used to leave me.

'I'll be back in a minute, Tippi. Just have to make some phone calls,' he'd say, and in seconds I'd be hovering over the North Sea, listening to Arctic Terns.

The Bird Room is brown and light, though the carpet's still electric. It smells of sawdust and feathers this time, and it doesn't make my skin prickle. I lie down and put on a pair of big head-phones, like I did years ago, and the first thing I hear is a chainsaw.

'The Minah Bird,' a voice says, 'is an Amazonian mimic, and will copy the modern noises of the disappearing rainforests, its natural habitat. It can imitate a car starting; a chainsaw; human conversation –'

I close my eyes, breathe in the smell of sawdust, and try to remember.

'I'm going to be sick, Dad!'

'Just one more!' he said and turned up the radio. Marc Bolan sang 'Metal Guru'; it was Dad's favourite song. This was our fifth trip round the roundabout and I squealed each time we passed the exit I wanted, the one for Betinna's Circus.

'Dad!'

'What?'

'Please!'

'We'll be late for your mother.'

'Call her! I've got 2p!'

And he swerved and took the turn. We parked in mud and the radio died.

'Can we go in? Can we go in, Dad?'

'It's the middle of the night, Kate. The animals are sleeping. What about your mother?'

Mum was in mourning for the twins.

'Please!'

Dad giggled like a milkshake as he carried me over elephant poo, towards the silent Big Top.

'We'll get arrested,' he whispered, making it sound like fun.

Tigers moaned like the old women in our church; a chimpanzee shrieked like them too. Ropes warned us not to trip, and tents flapped open, inviting.

We crawled inside the Big Top.

It was everything I could hope for in sawdust. The ring was empty and dark, but I could imagine Palominos high trotting and men on the tightrope dressed in a single white tight; the crowd roaring.

'I'll take you one day, darling, to a show,' Dad said.

'It doesn't matter.'

'Yes it does. You should be spoilt. You should see clowns and men swinging up there.'

'Yeah.'

'Tell you what, watch this. I'll fly for you.'

And I heard the slaps of his bonfire hands on the red and white swirled pole. He was climbing up to the trapeze.

'Dad!'

Was there a safety net, ready to catch him like a knob of butter falling into flour?

'Dad! Don't be silly!'

I couldn't see a thing.

Then the lights slammed on and a stranger's voice boomed, 'What are you doing here, little girl? Show's over, this is trespassing you know.'

I looked up to see a man bigger than even I could imagine. His forehead protruded like a rhino's, and his eyes were so deep set I thought he must be blind. He looked tired and his shoes made Grandpa's look small.

'Are you a giant?' I asked.

He smiled, 'Now where's your mum and dad?'

'I don't know.' At least I wasn't lying. Dad really had disappeared, up a candy pole.

'What? And left you here on your own? Weren't you scared?'

'Not really.'

The giant reached out a hand, big as a bicycle wheel. 'Tell you what, kid, come with me. You can call your poppa on the telephone, and for phones you'll have to talk to my wife, Betty.'

Outside, I sank in the deep mud. The giant had to pick me up and I felt sick at the height.

'Vertigo' he told me. 'My wife gets it too. By the way, the name's Norman.'

He said he was eight foot tall in a pair of good shoes and that his wife, Betty, was just four foot. 'Four feet four inches in her gold stilettos,' he laughed. He said circus folk were always like that, touched his nose and said, 'Opposites attract, eh?'

I thought of Gran and Grandpa.

Betty was taller than me though, and she was French. She had on bright orange lipstick and she made me sweet tea in a very small cup. She and Norman lived in a tent as Norman couldn't fit in a caravan and they'd been married for twelve years with no children.

'Ze thought!' said Betty, as if we were scorpions. She held her round belly and looked up at Norman as she said this. He was quiet.

Betty was the owner of the circus. She said she didn't dress in a top hat and tails, she paid a man with mustachios to do that.

'Chérie, come. Call your mère et père.'

Her face was podgy and her voice squeaked. Yet her 'r's rolled like waves. Norman sat in a big chair, and she made him tea in a huge cup she had to hold with both hands. I held the receiver of their phone and asked them what their act was.

'You did not see?' Betty said.

'I had to go to the loo,' I lied.

'Hmm, les enfants.'

'Betty plays my baby daughter, who's a pain in the you-know-where.'

'Norr-man! In front of the child! La langue!' But Betty laughed and Norman hoisted her up on his knee. He rocked her and she disappeared into his big arms.

'It's a bit like this,' he told me, 'but everyone laughs.'

Betty rested her head on his breast and they both looked a bit sad. It really was like Gran and Grandpa, but times a zillion-billion.

I put the phone down, and confessed. 'I want to join the circus,' I told them.

'Zats what zey all say.'

'But I really, really do.'

Norman sighed. 'It's a hard life.'

'But I'm small too.'

'Ah!' Betty waggled her stumpy finger, 'but you will grow. Eh bien.'

'I don't have to, do I?'

They both laughed, and then my dad walked in.

'Oh my little girl!' he cried. 'There you are. Me and Mummy have been looking for you everywhere!' He winked.

Betty slid off her husband's lap and bit at Dad's heels. 'Leafing un enfant in zis place. We haf tigers you know. Wolves even. An elephant can trample one so petite az her! I own ze place, je le sais!'

Norman stood up too, head brushing the roof of the tent. 'You really should be more careful, sir. A child is a precious thing.' His hand reached down for the top of Betty's head and he stroked her hair.

Dad stared at Betty and Norman, then he laughed at them, as if they really were freaks.

'Come here, Kate,' he said, but I didn't move. So he hollered like a baboon, grabbed my hand and ran out. All I had time to shout back was 'Thank you' and 'Goodbye!'

That was the only time I went to the circus, and the second to last time I saw Dad.

And that's how I remember it.

There's a man kneeling above me, his lips moving, but I can't hear him over 'The Thrush'. I take the headphones off.

'Are you okay?'

I sit up.

'You here with your mummy and daddy?'

Not this again, I take a deep breath, ready to be rude.

'Are you crying because you're lost?'

I touch my cheeks and feel embarrassed.

'Do you want me to find your parents?' He reaches down and pulls me up off the carpet as a blond toddler giggles next to him; it's the man with the pushchair I saw struggling up the front steps.

He has lovely ice-blue eyes, and shaggy, sandy hair; and he sounds posh, like Dad's put on voice.

'Sorry?' I say.

'Or your teacher? Do you want me to find your teacher?'

'I'm on my own.'

'Oh.' He smiles. 'Listen, Harry and I are going down to have lunch, would you like a lemonade or something?'

I think; Don't Talk to Strangers!

'Do you have any sweets?' I ask him.

'Pardon?'

'Sweets, do you have any?'

'No.'

'That's okay then.'

He's wearing a long tweed, Dr Who coat, and he pulls out a big hanky that smells of Persil from the pocket. 'Here, wipe your face,' he tells me, and puts Harry the toddler into his pushchair. 'I think you should come with us, a lemonade would be nice, wouldn't it? Cheer you up?'

I nod and he walks off. I decide to follow.

On the way to the café, I try and remember Mum's list of tricks.

1) Kick them in the balls.
2) Stab them in the eye.
3) Scream as loud as you can.
4) Get a bloody policeman.

I could always ask my dinosaur friend to tail-stab him through the chest.

Dad never took me to the café. 'We'll make sandwiches,' he said, 'take a beaker of juice', and the juice would be warm, half of it leaked away into the plastic bag.

There's a rush of noise as we join the queue. People are clanking knives and forks. The man turns round.

'I'm Jeremy by the way, and this is Harry.' Harry looks as fat and strong as the Superman baby.

'I'm Kate. Kate Happy.'

'That's a brilliant name.'

'It's stupid.'

'No, it's wonderful. Must be an advantage going through life with a name like that. You could be, well, I don't know, Kate Gristle or something.'

'What?'

'Well, that's pretty awful isn't it?'

I laugh because Jeremy has a pretty smile and he doesn't look much older than Brian.

'Lemonade, Kate?'

'Soup please.'

Jeremy smells like tobacco. His eyes have gold bits in with the blue.

'Soup. All right.'

'And a beef sandwich, I've got twenty pounds.' I don't want him to think I'm a starving beggar, an orphan girl alone in the world with crusty-sick hair and no Mummy and Daddy to wash it clean.

'Well, that's quite a sum, but it's all right, Kate. My treat.'

He picks up the full tray and we sit down at a pine table. Jeremy rolls a cigarette from a tin.

'What kind is that?'

'Sorry?'

'The tobacco.'

'Golden Virginia.'

'Oh.'

Not Franklins' Fine Shag Always Good Till The End Ha! Ha!
I drink my minestrone. I'm starving since I threw up.

'So, Kate Happy, how old are you?'

'Guess.'

'Gosh, I don't know, anything from six to sixteen I'd say.'

'Eleven.'

'Well –'

'I'm small.'

'Is this a school trip? You're the only one in red, and, er, yellow.'
He nods at my wellies.

'I'm Christmas shopping,' I tell him. 'My mum's at Harrods
buying me stuff. I came here because my dad used to bring me.'

'And where's he?'

'Dead.'

He looks me in the eyes and his eyebrows go up. 'I'm sorry,' he
says and hands Harry a sticky bun. 'Do you live in London,
Kate?'

'No. Herefordshire.'

'That's a nice place.'

'I prefer London. I used to live on the Bayswater Road.'

'Really?' Jeremy lights his fag. Yellow has tinged his fingers like it
did Dad's. The warm soup's woken me up, and I want to talk.

'This is like a grown-up conversation,' I tell him. 'Why don't you
talk to the women here instead of me?'

He laughs and coughs at the same time. His teeth are very
straight. 'Sorry?'

'A woman, why don't you chat one up instead of talking to me?'

'I'm not chatting you up, Kate.' He looks upset.

'Are you a homo?'

'What?' His eyebrows are up again.

'My mum had an affair with a homo called Andy. He sold
antiques.' I start in on the sandwich; the beef's chewy.

Jeremy inhales. 'Are you sure about that?'

'Well she said he was a homo. My mum's had loads of affairs.'
I think the beef's gone to my head too.

'All with homos?'

'Nah,' I smile. 'Have you ever seen *Paper Moon*?'

'What?'

'The film, *Paper Moon*?'

'Think I missed that one.'

'It's got this girl in it called Addie Pray, and Tatum O' Neal is her
and she's amazing. You look like my dad, a bit.'

'What bit?'

'Your hair, it's wavy and long, though his was black and his eyes
were like yours too, only a darker blue.'

'So not really like him at all then?'

I swallow a ball of beef and Jeremy flicks his hair like a girl. He
actually looks like Ryan O'Neal: Tatum's dad. Beautiful Ryan with
a killer smile and crystal blue eyes.

'So, what do you want to do when you grow up, Kate?'

'Join the circus,' I tell him. 'I could be, I don't know, The
Miraculous Miss Midget.'

He laughs. 'Oh come on, you're not that small, anyway you'll grow.'

'That's what they all say.'

'And they only have acts like that at freak shows.'

'Yes, I know! Have you ever been to one, because my aunt Rita
had an affair with a guy called The Amazing Seal-o at the sideshow
in Coney Island, it was by Nathan's Famous Hotdogs, and my gran's
family's all from there, and he had flippers for arms –' my jaw aches,
unused to movement, and I have to stop.

'All the women in your family have affairs then, Kate?'

'Probably.' Not Gran, I think. Not My Gran.

He stubs his cigarette out in my empty soup bowl. 'Why were
you crying?'

'What?'

'In the Bird Section. You were crying with headphones on.'

'Some of them are extinct.'

'Well, yes, that is very sad.'

'Actually I was thinking about my dad.'

Jeremy rolls another cigarette. His nails are nibbled.

'My dad was in the circus,' I tell him.

'Ah, that's where it comes from then is it? What did he do?'

'Everything. Tamed lions and jumped from burning buildings like Dumbo.'

'Gosh. That's cool.' I can tell he doesn't believe me. 'So why did your dad bring you here?'

'Dunno.'

'Do you think he wanted to teach you things?'

'Maybe.'

Harry has a baby-spasm and throws his sticky bun. It lands at the feet of a man at the next table.

I have an idea.

'Jeremy?' I whisper.

'What?' he whispers back.

'Would you help me steal an egg?'

'Sorry?'

'An egg, from one of the cases. I want the Bee Hummingbird one.'

'Why?'

Because it's an Addie and Moses Pray thing; a Ryan and Tatum O'Neal thing; a father and daughter *thing* to do.

'It's so tiny no one would miss it,' I tell him.

'We'd get into trouble.'

'Don't be a chicken.'

'Or an egg.' He laughs, but I don't. 'You're a bit serious for a child aren't you, Kate?'

The man next door hands Jeremy the sticky bun. 'I think this is yours,' he says, gruff.

Jeremy smiles, 'Thank you, sir,' and makes a silly face at me. I giggle.

'Ah, you do laugh then? Thought you were quite a sad little thing.'

'Well everything's dead here.'

'That's certainly true. But why do you want an egg?'

I think about the eggs I take from Gran's fridge and stick in the airing cupboard to hatch, until they break under a pile of towels, all yolky. I think about the little blue eggs that fall from our rafters to the yard below.

'It's my dad. He said he'd steal one for me, then he died.'

Jeremy's eyes look sad. He gets up and holds out his hand. I take it.

'Come on then, Kate,' he says.

There are rare ones in the first case: Ostrich, Emu, the extinct Elephant bird (and blowing out those insides must have been a job). The boring ones are next: Hen, Canadian Goose, Pheasant. Canadian Geese make my gran sigh. When they fly over the farmhouse she points up and sings, 'Fly home, fly home to Jesus,' then whispers; 'They're going home, Katie honey. If only I was a goose.' I reckon that's why she keeps the fat, white ones, and clips their wings; and kills them.

Harry is sleeping, sugar gone shiny on his lips, and we're alone. There's a case of albino birds and a sign above them that says; 'Individuals with disadvantageous characteristics do not tend to survive.'

Jeremy moves to a case of coloured stones and eggs. He tries it.

'It's locked, Kate. They all are.'

School kids yell from the hall; it sounds like the noise from inside a swimming pool.

'We could smash one open,' I offer. 'Just one of the little panes of glass on the side, no one would notice.'

'No. We'd get arrested.' Jeremy's a bit flushed. Harry squeals.

'Let's check them all,' I whisper.

This is more fun than trying to steal the Pink Panther. I start at the end of the room and press my hands on each section of glass, but every one is solid. Jeremy and I meet up in the middle.

'Anything?' he asks.

My hands feel the sides of the last case, and I look and smile, because my fingers are poking into the display. There's a tiny gap, a piece of missing glass so small, even I've only just managed to slip my miniature fingers through.

'Kate, you'll cut yourself, careful.'

It's a case full of stones, not eggs, but they're bright and pretty as jewels.

'We better not, they look valuable.'

'Don't be a scaredy cat, anyway, the only one I can reach is that one, and there's two of them. No one will miss it.' I point at the tiny purple stone; it has a sister, small and paler. Florite, the hand-written sign says. Jeremy does a 'quick or don't do it at all!' face because footsteps are coming closer.

I poke at the stone, it's hard to reach. The footsteps get louder. As I tease the purple gem towards the gap, I bite my lip, then I've got it. I tear back the wrapper from my packet of Love Hearts and lay the stone on top, just as the gruff old man from the café turns the corner.

'Hello sir,' Jeremy says.

'Hmf!' says the man.

We run out, pushing Harry, and our laughter echoes in the big hall. It's so loud it touches the glass cages, and maybe the stuffed creatures shake like it's all been a long nap. Maybe the hyena giggles and the monkeys screech, or my dinosaur chooses this moment to gobble up a laughing child, as the wolf says, 'All the better to eat you with my dear' to the ginger-nut boy.

I haven't had so much fun since Dad. Jeremy and I struggle down the frosty outside steps with the pushchair and I feel a wet patch in my pants. Too much excitement: too much soup.

The purple stone is warm in my pocket but everything else is cold, even the bread I'm rolling into little balls for the sparrows and pigeons. There's a park area at the side of the museum, and we're the only ones in it. It's dark now, and double deckers yawn down the wide street behind us. Harry is sleeping, cheeks pink as pigs' ears.

'Actually, the museum's more like Mr Rochester's house than Mr Barlow's,' I tell Jeremy, and throw some more bread.

'Who are they?'

'Mr Rochester's the bloke in *Jane Eyre* and he's sexy. His mad wife sets his house on fire and jumps off the top of it. Mr Barlow's a head vampire in a different book.'

'Oh.' Jeremy lights another cigarette. 'You're very literary. I was more into Sven Hassel at your age.'

'Who?'

'Nazis and war stuff.'

'Like *Anne Frank*? I've read that.'

'Not quite.'

I throw a whole slice of bread at a one-footed pigeon. 'I wish you could come home with me, Jeremy, but my Mum would probably shag you.'

He laughs. 'You know, you're an exceptional child, Kate.'

'I know. I don't have brothers or sisters.'

He scrunches his face up in a smile, and I look up at the huge building. 'My dad said those gargoyles come to life at night. Shall we watch?'

It's hard to see in the dusk; flocks of starlings spill about the sky but I can't make a single gargoyle out.

'So what happened to him?' Jeremy asks. 'If you don't mind me asking?'

'No.' I hit a cold pigeon with more bread. 'My mum ran him over in her Triumph Spitfire and he died. It was Eurovision night. She didn't go to prison though. They said it wasn't her fault.'

'Are you telling the truth, Kate?'

'Brownies' honour.' I hold up three fingers: I think that's right.

'Because that's a terrible thing to lie about.'

'I'm not.'

'And did your dad really work for the circus?'

'No.' I shiver; my legs are cold. 'I don't think he ever had a job. How old are you, Jeremy?'

'Twenty-three.'

'Is that young to have kids?'

'Not really. Anyway, I wanted them.' He stands up, probably because Harry's nose is as pink as his ears. 'Come on now, Kate, let's share a taxi. I'll drop you off at Harrods. Are you sure your mum will be there?'

'No.'

'I'll wait with you then.'

'You'd better not.'

'Think she'll shag me there and then?'

'Probably.'

He doesn't laugh this time. 'I'll give you my phone number and address, just in case. Don't want you lost in London.'

That sounds nice, better than being Lost in France like Bonnie Tyler. Jeremy holds my hand and it feels warm. We walk to the road where black cabs glow yellow.

On the way to Harrods I give Jeremy my address. I want a Christmas card from Jeremy, I want a Valentine's too. He waves goodbye from the back of the cab, Harry in his arms, and I feel like Gran when she watches *Brief Encounter*. I feel happy and sad at the same time.

Of course Mum isn't here. The revolving door spits people out, but not her. Then the doormen say goodnight and Harrods is closed. I sit beneath a window display of four mannequins in fur coats, standing round a pear tree that's chiming out 'The Twelve Days of Christmas'.

I hear the thud of her high-heeled boots first. It's in time with 'On the se-venth day of Christ-mas', and the light from the shop window shows me Mum has a new coat. It's a copy of one in the window. Also, she's holding a mini Chinese house made out of matchsticks; it has a pointed roof. It's only when she comes close that I see it's a cage, filled with little black birds.

She drops it on the pavement and the birds scatter, perch to perch, wings purring. Mum makes a strange gurgling noise, and then pulls me up by the arm and slaps my legs again. Her breath is sour with wine and she's silent. It doesn't hurt because she's wobbly. Then she sways and stops, and the birds twitter. They've got yellow beaks and coloured stripes under their eyes; it's like a magician has shrunk a load of those Amazonian Minah birds and sold them on the cheap.

I wonder if they'll sound like chainsaws.

A Pagoda. That's what Mum said. Not a bloody Chinese house. We're sliding back down the M4 in the pitch black, soft-top up. The Spitfire splutters and the birds tweet-tweet in the box seat behind me. They are my Christmas present and at least they're not stuffed. I throw my red blazer over the cage and they're quiet.

My cheek's pressed against the cold window so I lock my door. Mum hasn't said a word. There's just the shudder of the Spitfire's soft-top in the wind. On long journeys it was Dad who used to sing; 'Three maids a-ri-i-i-sing!' Dad liked to sing in the car.

He must have really belted one out the night of the Eurovision, because he travelled all the way up from Portsmouth. Dad went to live in Portsmouth, and none of us really knew why; he didn't have a job. Mum was locked up on the Bayswater Road, ignoring me, and I was doing the usual: living with Gran and Grandpa. I think, that night, Dad drove all that way because he liked to watch foreign singers who were crap, and he didn't have a telly.

I remember the Norwegians singing 'Mata Hari'.

He arrived at dusk and my grandparents went to bed. Dad held my hand and kissed me on the forehead, then he switched on Terry

Wogan. The Brotherhood of Man were on first, they sang 'Save Your Kisses For Me', and they were fantastic. They had the biggest flares I'd ever seen.

'My god! Look at them!' Dad cried and hit the arm of Grandpa's armchair.

He was drinking Gran's Gordons gin. I made cocktails for him, and he liked 'more gin than tonic and squeeze the lemon in there, Kate.' When The Brotherhood of Man came first with a whopping 164 *pwants*, Dad dropped a splash of gin in my strawberry milk-shake and hugged me.

'A moment to remember,' he said. 'This is definitely a moment to remember, my darling.' That was when he gave me a piggyback and started whooping round the room like an Indian Brave and all the hunters and the foxes on Grandpa's wallpaper woke up. Bosum 7 did too, and Jessie 12. They howled so much, I had to drag Dad outside.

We sat on Gran's stoop. The one she'd built when she first got here. Dad hugged me a bit more and sang 'Save Your Kisses For Me', though he couldn't remember many words. I sipped my ginny milkshake as we held hands in the moonlight, listening to the snorts of Grandpa's bull and the whinnying of Foreo.

'Will you marry me, Dad?'

'Sorry?'

'When I'm grown up I mean.'

'Not sure that's legal, pumpkin.'

'Will you?'

'You'll meet a boy much nicer than me.'

'No I won't. I'd never –'

'Oh come on now, don't be a silly billy.'

I nestled into him and he smelt of Dad. 'Can you come and see me more often?'

'I'll try.'

'I get lonely.'

'Oh don't say that, pumpkin.'

'Pu-lease.'

'Of course I will.'

'And will you marry me?'

'Tell you what, if you don't get any other offers, yes. I'd love to. But don't tell your mother.'

'Okay.'

It was a lovely night and I was so young I wished we could fly away on a magic carpet and have adventures for the rest of our lives. Then we'd come back with special powers, bring my sisters back from the dead, wake Mum up from her Sleeping Beauty sleep she was having on the Bayswater Road, and everything would be like Christmas.

I wished all this until the headlights of a small, speeding car turned down my grandparents' track, and both Dad and me knew it was Mum.

'What the fuck is she doing here?' he spat. I put down my ginny-milkshake and shivered.

They started the row before she turned off the engine, before he even stood up. They were like ratting terriers.

In seconds Gran was running down her stoop in a pink nightie; she must have been awake all the time, waiting by the door. She just grabbed me, she didn't try and shut my parents up, because Gran said that was The Way They Were, like Barbara Streisand and Robert Redford. But when Grandpa appeared, we knew it was serious. Gran said it was his war-sense, his battle-premonition, because he came limping out of the house, yelling, 'Stop this nonsense! Abandon ship!'

But they didn't.

Mum got back into her sportscar. Her Triumph Spitfire. Her special red baby. She revved the car, headlights on, and the wheels spun in our muck. Dad jumped into her pathway. I remember he put up his hands, shielding his eyes from the headlights as she sped towards him.

'Watch this, Kate!' he yelled, and leapt out of the way at the very last minute.

He was still laughing as he brushed himself down, but his laugh was hollow and sad. Like opening a nut at Christmas and finding there's nothing inside.

Mum turned a tight circle in the yard and the bullfight began again. The problem was Dad was a crap matador. Or maybe he was the best, because this time he called Mum's bluff. This time he didn't jump.

In the hospital Mum was surprised.

'He can't be dead,' she said. 'It's a tiny bloody car. It couldn't crush a flea.'

But he'd stood there, eyes shut and laughing, and the wheels had caught his softest part. It was a freak, an accident.

The police escorted us back from the hospital, and we sipped cherry brandy in Gran's lounge. None of us were crying. Or maybe I was. I can't remember.

Mum was given bail because she had to cook the food for the funeral. There was a trial, a quiet one, and Marlene Ginger Celia Martha Mathilda Happy-Mahoney was released on charges of manslaughter. A suspended sentence for reckless driving, and banned for two years.

A national paper wrote; 'An End to an un-Happy Chapter.' Bad pun, Grandpa said, and he didn't cut it out. Gran told me Grandpa had got Mum off, as he was a magistrate, a respected member of the community, of our village, with its red post and telephone box.

It's amazing what you don't remember, and what you do.

The car bounces. Mum pulls in. The hazard lights are on and we're at the top of Grandpa's driveway. There's more snow. The Spitfire's yellow light flashes across his white land, tick-tick-tick.

'Are we stuck, Mum?'

'I just can't cope, Kate.'

'What?'

'I'm not as strong as you. I can't do this anymore.'

'Do what?'

'Go back there. Go anywhere.' Mum sniffles in the flashing dark.
'We can go back to London if you like.'

'No. You don't understand, Kate. They died. It's all fucked up.'

She snots into her pelt collar as I watch Grandpa's hazard-lit
snow. Then Mum hits the confines of the tiny driver's space with her
fists. She's having a freak out, that's what she calls them. Sometimes I
wonder if her running over Dad was just a freak out. Gone wrong.

I can't hold her hand or kiss her better because it's hard to touch
Mum; she jumps. So I let her take it out on the car.

Out on the hard land I see flickers of light that aren't ours,
they're white and long beamed and look like those search lights in
the war films on the telly. I expect a siren and Alsatian dogs. Then I
see two figures; both small. It's Gran and bent-over Grandpa, followed by a neat line of geese. They're coming to our rescue, slowly.
As they get closer, I notice my grandparents still have slippers on
and snow is caked to their legs like cream.

The geese honk.

'Oh god,' says Mum, and she stops hitting the dashboard. 'We're
being rescued by poultry and fucking geriatrics.'

Of course, they die, the mini-Minah birds. Gran hangs them above
our bed and before I snuggle up next to her for a quiet sleep, I watch
them fall from their perches one by one as if they've been gassed.

'Oh my,' Gran squeals. 'Oh my!' as the fifth and final one flops
dead on the Pagoda floor.

The reason? Me. I filled their mini-troughs with water, except I
carried it from the bathroom in Gran's cup; the one she uses to
soak her few false teeth in. I didn't notice the three pearly whites
and the little strip of her false gum, pink as candy floss, as I poured
it into the birds' drinking bowls. I didn't see the cloudy and lethal
dose of Steradent, not even as my little shrunken Minah birds drank
and sank and never made a single sound.

No rainforest chainsaws, no car horns; not even a tweet.

Gran puts the cage out on the landing, hoping the cats on the third floor will gobble the dead birds up before dawn. I don't cry because we don't cry about things like this. It's like the time I found a baby bird and Gran put it into the Aga to warm it up: we both forgot about it and Millie had to scrape it off the hot plate a few days later. Then there was the time Grandpa shot a rabbit. I didn't cry for it; I picked it up and played with it like a doll, in my towelling, yellow knickers. Grandpa said I'd get fleas and ticks and more besides, but I was just pretending it was still alive.

In the dark I listen to my grandmother's high-pitched snore, and make up a rhyme in honour of my Minah's short, birdy lives. I whisper it at Mr Barlow, crouched by the wardrobe.

> *Steradent, every day,*
> *kills little birds in every way.*
> *The refreshing smile of their dead feeling.*
> *In Steradent, every day,*
> *kills little birds in every way!*

'Accidental Death by Happy Misadventure', the local paper said, but Grandpa didn't cut that out either.

December 11th, 1946, Southbourne

My Dearest Mat,
Saw that film, A Matter of Life and Death with
handsome David Niven, and Kim Hunter, what a gal.
Had a line in it made me laugh. 'Can an American girl
be left in cold, drafty English houses?' Ha! Ha! Wish
you could be with us. Larry OK, crackers, but nurses
treating him good. Marlene and Eva just fine. Come
down for Christmas, I'm counting on it. We can drive
back to the farm together.
   Love, Your Iris

Miss Mathilda Greene
The Happy Farm
Boldenham
Herefordshire

12

*T*ime has stood still since we came back from London. It's stalemate and even our ghosts are quiet. Gran goes to Marks every day. Grandpa stays in his pantry with the wireless. Bosum has his Conjugal Appointments and no one mentions School. All I sense from Mum on the second floor is a smell, musty and forgotten.

It's freezing and Gran's snoring. Before bed she knelt at the pink linen box in the bathroom, elbows resting on its cork top, and prayed for half an hour. I sat on the loo shivering, watching her red lips move over whispers I'd never decipher. I wondered if she was praying to Jesus or the Chews. She took two pink pills, and hasn't stirred since.

There's a full moon and shadows play on her pink embossed wallpaper. Three oaks are down in the West field and the corrugated barn roof has been ripped off like a scab. A white Christmas, the forecast says. I fidget beneath Gran's Wolsey wool blankets and wonder if she's ever shared her bed with anyone apart from me.

Floorboards creak. I stare at the ceiling, and then hear bath water running. I feel under the bed for my torch and cardigan.

Tonight I'm going to find my dad.

Out on the pink landing I stumble into the Pagoda cage; the cats *did* take the birdy bodies. I can hear a high-pitched voice, singing. It's Mum.

"'If you go down to the woods today –'"

'The Teddy Bears' Picnic' has always scared me. I switch on my torch.

"'You're sure of a big surprise –'"

I tip-toe across Gran's landing and climb the stairs up to the second floor, feet numb with the cold.

"'If you go down to the woods today –'"

Steam from my open bathroom door swirls out in the moonlight. It's dark inside, but I can hear splashing and giggling.

'Mum?'

"'You'll never believe your eyes –'"

The air smells of my Badedas. I stand on the threshold and shine my torch in. 'Mum, are you okay?'

'Lions and tigers and bears oh-my!' she says and goes under the foamy water. Her new fur coat is on the floor. I step down into the bathroom and the lino is wet, so I grab hold of the towel rail: no more accidents. She bobs up. "'If you go down to the woods today, you're sure of a big surprise.'"

'Mum?'

'Do you remember that rhyme I taught you up in Scotland, Kate?'

'Sorry?'

'You know. It was really filthy.'

'No.'

"'Mary had a little lamb, she thought it rather silly. She grabbed it by its little leg and pulled it by its willy –'"

'What are you going on about?'

"'– was a watchdog, lying in the grass, along came a bumblebee and stung him on his arse no questions, tell no lies, have you ever seen a Chinaman –'"

I switch on the main light. Mum looks small in the over-bubbled bath. The hot tap is running and she has the plug out. I stand on the loo seat and open the window; cold air sucks the steam away.

'Mum, can I ask you something?'

She splashes again. 'Bombs away!'

'Where's Dad?'

For a moment she looks at me, confused, then she paddles her feet in the water. 'He's down the pan! Down the rubbish chute! Into the incinerator with the bloody penguin nuns. Holy Mary Mother of God. Ha!' Then she starts singing again; '"John Brown's body lies a-mouldering in the grave, mouldering in the grave, mouldering in the grave!"'

Mum's gone very bonkers. It's like she's drunk, but I can't smell it.

'Never mind,' I say, close the window and walk back to my old room, feet wet.

There's a taste of too much sleep in here. I turn the light on and David Cassidy's still smiling. Tatum's still in her crescent moon too, but on my dressing table is a record player, and a yellow plastic tray with two bottles of pills on it. My mother's name is printed on both.

MARLENE GINGER CELIA MARTHA

MATHILDA HAPPY-MAHONEY

VALIUM

TWICE DAILY

BEFORE FOOD

MARLENE GINGER CELIA MARTHA

MATHILDA HAPPY-MAHONEY

DIAZEPAM

TWICE DAILY

AFTER FOOD

I open the bottles, sniff, and they smell like sherbet, but neither of them says 'Eat Me', so I empty them into my cardigan pockets (one lot look like Gran's Parma Violets, the others like Jessie's worm pills). Mum's old rabbit coat is on the floor and I put it on, along with two pairs of her socks. The coat is huge and it drags behind me like a train as I scan my old bedroom, looking for Dad.

He's not hard to find because he's still in the Hellmann's mayonnaise jar Mum poured him into after the funeral. She said an urn was too heavy for cabin baggage, and she'd used four jars of Hellmann's for the potato salad at the buffet, so why not? I knew she'd never leave him in a poubelle in the South of France. I pick my father up from the bedside table, and shake him.

'Hi.'

My dad: more burnt than pork scratchings. I don't believe it's really him.

'How have you been, then?'

I put him in the fur coat's deep pocket, and walk up to the top of the house. On the third floor landing, cats brush against my bare legs and I'm sure I hear Wilhomena whisper, 'What in heaven's name do you think you are doing, Katherine?' as Samuel coughs into his handkerchief. Wilhomena smells of aniseed and cloves.

Mum's still splashing as I run on up to the attic.

Tomorrow morning I'm going to untie Jessie 13 and set him on Dr Croften. That man is evil and he's sending my mother mad.

Two chimney breasts, warm from afternoon fires, lurch into the attic, but there's frost on the underside of the roof slates. The rest of the place is shadows, a darkness the single lightbulb can't touch. I do up Mum's coat, and put a pair of socks on my hands, just like Aunt Rita did.

Gran's Chewishness is in here somewhere. And bits of Mum. She told me this was where she hid from Gran and Grandpa when she was the same age as me. Mum said she pretended to be Anne Frank up here, 'Apart from the last bit.'

This is also where I hide my scrapbook.

I open the roof of a dolls' house (and that's where Anne would be, right up there in the attic). I pick out a lightbulb, and push the steel end of it into the socket. Light glares. Once, I stuck my finger in that socket and got a shock that was like melting from the inside out.

Dad's still in Mum's fur-coat pocket, so I take him out and sit his Hellmann's jar on the floor next to me.

My scrapbook lives in the cubby hole (behind three loose stones in the left chimney breast) and the cover is warm as I blow on it. It smells of smoke and spice; the leather's dark red and ripped, and it's filled with the photographs and letters I find posted on our ceilings and floors; under our rugs and in our airing cupboards too.

Gran thinks it's Grandpa who steals her stuff, but it's me.

I lie down on my tummy and watch the light glare off the first laminated page.

It's a picture of Grandpa and Gran: their Wedding picture. No one's missed it. They're walking through a tunnel of men in Naval uniforms who are holding up swords. Grandpa's breast pocket is covered in medals and little squares of colours like building blocks: he's huge and very handsome, and they're both laughing. He's got his big hand over Gran's and it nearly covers her whole arm. On the white border is Grandpa's pencil-scrawl that says: '*Iris and Larry, City Hall, New York. A Happy Day! August 12 1942*'. Grandpa sellotaped this to the telly three Christmases ago as we watched *The Morecambe and Wise Christmas Special*. It covered up Glenda Jackson.

I take down one of Gran's pink ball gowns that hang from the rafters. There's graffiti underneath that says:

I. I.

+

M.G.

Gran's other gowns swing like criminals on a gibbet as I lay the dress between me and the cold floor. I quickly flick through my scrapbook, because I know what I'm looking for: it's the last page filled in. I smooth down the hard newspaper, yellow as my father's fingers.

'This is it, Dad,' I tell him.

The Hereford Times

MANSLAUGHTER VERDICT FOR LOCAL WOMAN

Marlene Happy-Mahoney was released on charges of manslaughter through reckless driving, at Hereford Crown Court today. She received a suspended sentence and was banned from driving for two years. Her father, local magistrate Naval Captain Lawrence Happy Esq. spoke through his solicitor, Mr James Hall, in a prepared statement. 'Today justice has been done and we can close this terrible chapter of our lives. What happened to our beloved son-in-law Michael Mahoney was a dreadful and tragic accident. That my daughter Marlene was behind the wheel of this tragedy simply doubles the pain for us. Michael was a treasured son to us and to his dear departed parents David and Katherine Mahoney, and through his many prob-lems we have supported him. What we seek now is peace and solitude, to come to terms with this great loss.'

The Crown prosecution were disappointed with this verdict and had been seeking a murder conviction. This was quashed when Mr Mahoney's suicidal nature was made clear by Mrs Happy-Mahoney's defence. Michael Mahoney's only living close relative, an older sister who lives in Brisbane, Australia was unavailable for comment.

Michael Mahoney leaves one daughter, Katherine Alouicious Jemima Happy-Mahoney, who is currently living with her grandparents at Happy Farm, Herefordshire. Katherine was at the scene of the accident at 12.30 a.m. on 23 April 1976. She told the prosecution at the trial that she and her father had been watching the Eurovision Song Contest and the victory of The Brotherhood of Man.

I'd forgotten Dad called me Jemima Puddleduck, but I remember the courtroom smelled of sweat and Pledge; almost the same mix as Grandpa's dark corridors. An angry man who was on Mum's side asked me how much my dad had drunk that night.

Not much. A ginny milkshake. Or was that me?

'That's not much, is it, Dad?' I ask the jar, but he's in a quiet mood.

There was a bumblebee in that courtroom too; it crashed against the high, thin-paned windows as Millie twitched in the front row. But she wouldn't leave me, not even for that omen of death.

I turn to the empty back pages of my scrapbook. I never put anything in after this, because nothing seemed right; but now Dad's here, he could help.

'Couldn't you?' (still quiet as the grave).

'What do you reckon? What shall I put in, Dad?'

Truth is, there's so much in this attic, I'm spoilt for choice. I don't need a Ouija board to bring the lives up here back to life: there are boxes and boxes of Gran and Mum's stuff. Even Eva has her own aquamarine trunk. I suppose I could tear out bits from Gran's High School Year Books because I love the old pictures: Gran at the Prom wearing the pink dress I'm now lying on; Gran with her Beau; her Corsage, with all those American words she shares with me.

'Oh Brad, of course I'll be your girl,' she'd say, 'I'll wear your friendship ring. Are you at the game, Saturday? Go Cougars, go!'

And in the end something supernatural or extra-terrestrial happens, like in *The Blob* with Steve McQueen.

Such as:

1) Gran's dress grows tentacles that eat up Brad.
2) Gran shoots webs from her wrists and climbs up the High School wall dressed as a cheerleader.
3) She flies away in a convertible ('Fly home, fly home to Jesus').

I often wonder how different I would be if I was American. Would things be peachy and cool? Would Mum cook meatloaf and give me peanut and jelly sandwiches for High School? Would I pledge to a Sorority? Would I pledge Allegiance? Would my mum have bumped off my dad?

'Sorry,' I whisper.

There's always Eva's trunk, covered with paintings of mermaids, and King Neptune himself on the lid. There are treasures inside.

I pull a sock off my cold hand and open it: hinges creak. Eva's schoolbooks are on top, and I take one. Pressed daisies fall out and a picture postcard of someone called Margaret Lockwood. On the very first page Eva has written, 'The Rules of Etiquette by Eva Regina Mathilda Poppy Happy'.

How to Take Tea With a Close Friend
1) Do not ring the bell for tea, this is OSTENTATIOUS
2) Do not make the tea yourself as a servant has his/her job to do (must instruct Millie)
3) Pour the tea first, never the milk. Do not be a MIF ('milk in first')

Eva makes me laugh.

In the trunk are some of her clothes, folded neat and in plastic. Gran embroidered Eva's name in big letters on the hems of her flared skirts, and on the breast pockets of the small blouses. Mum told me Eva 'thought she was bloody Elizabeth II and I was poor little Princess Margaret', but I think they'd be more *Laverne and Shirley* in these get-ups.

I choose another exercise book. This time it's filled with writing, in two different hands.

Hello M.
Am leaving this in our place, hope you escaped the pirates. Beware the third floor and the moan of prisoners! My clue is 'early to bed, early to rise, found on a penny stamp, beautiful eyes'.
E.

Eva,
I can't get that one, and the pyrates nearly got me. I have the cabin boy up here, and he keeps licking my face and he's made a mess on the floor. I stole keys to the living room as Mummy's fruit cake is in there. I'm lonely up here waiting for you. It is cold. I'm leaving this in our cubby hole and going downstairs.
Marlene

First Mate M.
Never use our real names! We will be discovered! And must you always think of your stomach? We have greater things to which we

must attend. We must help Papa in this dreadful sea war so he can come home from the faraway land of Southbourne. Please get cabin boy out of ship before PIRATES find him and eat him for tea, and he messes on the carpet again. I'm in the smallest room. Come and find me. I will then give you an easier clue.

E.

Eva,
I am in the kitchen with Millie as I fell over looking for the smallest room. Don't be cross. Come down and have tea. My knee hurts a very lot. She's leaving our book for you in our secret place (sorry I had to tell her where it is) as we're shouting and shouting but you won't come out. I don't like this game anymore. Let's play horses.
Marlene

I wonder if Eva ever did come out for fruitcake?

I look at Dad.

'I could rip these out? What do you think?'

He doesn't say a word.

On the underside of the lid of Eva's trunk is a photo of her and Mum on a beach. They're almost grown up and in proper swimming cosies. They look so different for twins: Mum is small and mousey like me, Eva is tall and dark. Next to them, Gran and a lady are sitting on the pebbles. They're both wearing flowery dresses with waist belts and the lady is waving at the camera, a cigarette smoking in her mouth. My grandmother's tiny writing on the border tells me: *'Us and Mathilda. Southbourne. 1953.'* I've seen this photograph before, it used to be in the glove compartment of Gran's Peugeot, at least it was the last time I looked.

I close the trunk, and lift the top off the record player Dad bought me for my sixth birthday. My records are still piled up on the stem, dusty. There's:

1) 'Me and You and a Dog Named Boo'
2) 'You're so Vain'
3) 'In the Ghetto'

I always liked the last one best; about cold and frosty morns, and baby children being born. I think ghettos must be like mangers. Special Christmas places. I click play, but it doesn't work.

'Typical eh?'

Dad doesn't reply.

'I said that's bloody typical, isn't it, Dad?'

Silence.

'What's the matter?'

I grab the Hellmann's jar and undo the lid: it's surprisingly easy. Dust puffs a bit, but I put my nose in and breathe all the same. There's no smell of bonfires; of milkshakes. Dad doesn't smell of anything now, not even ash. I sneeze, three times for good luck, and screw the top back on, tighter than before.

I wasn't allowed in the crematorium when they burnt him up. After the church service I had to go back to the farm and eat devils on horseback with Mum.

'Silly billy,' I say, and lift up the seat of Gran's old piano stool. She's got her real goodies in there; the unused plane tickets to JFK; the envelopes bulging with Bosum's ball money.

I put Dad inside.

'Do you think you'll like it up here, Dad?'

Stop asking me so many bloody questions.

'Oh. Sorry'

I burrow out a place and push him down to the bottom. 'You'll be safe there,' I tell him. 'Nice and quiet.'

About bloody time.

Dad's hidden by a big brown envelope I don't recognise, so I take it out and empty the contents on my lap. It's just a boring bundle of letters tied with a pale pink ribbon, and a few loose black and white photographs.

I pick the photographs up.

They're of the seaside, but I'm sure it's not Coney Island as it's too grey and empty, though there is a pier and big lit signs that say

'Regents' and 'The Brighton Dome'. There's no Mum and Eva grinning in swimming costumes in these pictures, it's just Gran, dolled up and really, really young. She doesn't look much older than Sam Morris. She's smiling in front of the long pier, and then in front of a big, white hotel. There are crowds of old-fashioned people. In one photo she's in the driving seat of the old pickup that's now rusting in our barn. She's blowing a kiss with dark lips, and wearing a headscarf and sunglasses that make her look like an olden-day film star, except she's pregnant. It's obvious. In the last picture she's pointing at her big belly.

There's a note paperclipped to this photograph.

My Iris,

Right my duck, Mussolini shot by us and Hitler shot himself, the bloody coward, so it's all over damn soon. Never mind your President Roosevelt, he's looking down from heaven and cheering. Me and the girls at the factory got tight as ticks with the news last night, but I think of all the bombs we made here, and all that yellow bloody dust, and I just want to get back to you. So, what now if I'm out of this place? Too many questions to ask, I think. How is little Marlene? Hope Millie's looking after her well. Maybe we can get to room 46 this weekend? Or I might bike over and give you a hand with it all. You said Larry's been sent to a different hospital? Where is it? Is he worse? That's a wicked thing to ask (and hope for), I know. Poor old Larry. But I just want us to die old maids, making love in that attic of yours all day. Us two old maids of Boldenham up in the bleeding roof space. But I won't tempt fate, my duck. Who knows, it might just all work out for the best. Love to you and the little girls, with a special get well kiss for my little Marlene.

Your, Mathilda.

P.S Look what I found! Pics of our trip last year. I'll never forget that, duck, it was the best. Still makes me blush like a bloody schoolgirl. Don't you look gorgeous?

Mathilda. That sounds like a doll's name. Like Hambel from *Play School*. I wonder if she really lived in this attic, that many years ago, but how did she make love to my gran?

I shift on the ground, and reopen Eva's trunk.

There she is again, '*Us and Mathilda. Southbourne. 1953.*' She's sitting next to Gran, and Mum, and Eva. I wonder who took the picture.

Freckles: her two front teeth overlap. I've seen that smiling face somewhere before. I turn back to the beginning pages of my scrapbook, past the prize bulls and parties, to one picture of lots of girls lined up like in a school photograph. They've all got curled hair and dark lipstick, and the ones on the end of the rows are leaning up against big shiny bombs shaped like Flash Gordon's space ship. Some of the girls are smiling, some are laughing, and one's blowing a kiss to her bomb. It's this girl who has a circle round her head, and *For You Iris, Love, Love Mat x x x x* is written underneath.

Mat is the same as Mathilda as she has the same freckled face. At the bottom of this photograph, someone has written '*The Girls from The TNT Munitions Factory, Rotherwas, Hereford, May 12th 1945. Long Live The King and God Bless England!*' I found this photo under Gran's mattress.

Roadrunner cartoons have TNT in them. Roadrunner and Wylie Coyote and his big box of TNT that goes boom!

Mathilda was around for ages. And she lived up here in the attic all that time?

So the bombs fell and the boys were lost, and I met my darling Mat in Room 46. Oh, my darling. Why does Larry have to come home? Why, out of all those men on board was he saved?

My Darling Mat.

My Darling Mathilda.

I'll go a-waltzing, Mathilda.

I pull the pink ribbon holding the bundle of letters together, and they uncurl, like hair coming undone. At first, they're hard to separate as the feather-thin sheets are clasped together.

I close the lid on Gran's piano stool and my dad.

'Night, night. Sleep tight,' I tell him.

Or tight as a tick, as Mathilda says.

Dear Mrs Happy   20th July, 1943

I'm covered in yellow again, so pardon me if I mark this nice paper you sent. It's the factory, see. Covered in TNT dust morning noon and night. Yellow as chickens, that's what Mabel says, it's even in our knickers! But I'm running away with myself. I'm writing to thank you first for the paper and second to say it was so nice to meet you at the dance and third to ask a question. You see Mabel's put me up to this and what with your Mr Happy being so far up in things, I was wondering if he'd have any sway with them at the ministry as me and Mabel, well, we're so desperate to get out of this factory and was hoping for work as land girls instead? Do you have many on your farm? I can't remember you saying. Anyway, I am so sorry for asking when you've been so kind and all, but anything to shut Mabel up! It was nice to meet you at the dance, and you were very grand. Lady of the Manor, and all, and your stories about America were just lovely. It was nice to see you with such a grand chap as Mr Happy. Is he still on leave? You haven't been married long have you? You said about a year? You seem so young to be left alone. Sorry I'm being nosey, it's just my nature.

Yours,

Mathilda Greene.

My Dear Friend Iris,   14th November, 1943

Well, that was quite a night wasn't it, duck! I still can't believe we rode our bikes all that way from Rotherwas to yours after the dance. The bloody landlady had my guts for garters when I got back this morning. Said those who stay in her house have to be respectable, not out all night with soldiers! Ha! If only she knew it was you and me and a bottle of your Mr Happy's Navy rum. Oh, but we did have a laugh, didn't we? You're too young not to have a laugh my girl, stuck all alone in that place. As I said, you should take some kiddies in, evacuees, something to keep you busy, now your land has been given over to that neighbour chap. Anyway must dash, the horn's gone and it's back to the yellow dust. See you at the next dance a week Saturday, maybe we can get some fellas this time? (Opps, forgot about Mr Happy – I know he's back next weekend – no news I suppose about getting my job changed?)

All the best, Mathilda

Dear Iris,   24th January, 1944

Thank you for the writing paper, the stockings and that lovely food parcel for Christmas, duck – my folks back in Hastings think you're a Queen! Now look lovie – sorry if I'm going to use this lovely paper to give you a lecture, but it can't be a surprise, expecting – can it? Unless you know something I don't? Mr Happy will have his shore leave and you got your marriage duties. How far along are you? Please don't drink like you said in your letter dearie, it won't do any good. The old gin and a hot bath never works. You'll just ruin yourself. What you need is a proper doctor for all that, and if you want it to go that way please talk to me. Mabel had the same trouble last year, by one of your boys in the camp next door (a real handsome bugger though black as the ace of spades). Now she had it done and I went with her and she said it wasn't so bad, expensive like, but clean. So I'll look after you Iris, don't you fret. I'll even look after the baby for godsakes if you want to keep him. I love them I do and don't think I'll ever have them myself. So don't be sad. You should be glad, girl. Have you told him?

Now – let me tell you something to cheer you up. You know that every night when us girls get back to the boarding house we scrub ourselves with carbolic, three or four in a cold bath – because the water heater has been on the blink for the past for ever – well this evening, guess what happened? We got stuck! Can you believe it! All four of us, Queenie, me, Mabel and Lotty, all yellow and soaped up and stuck in the iron tub. We had to call the landlady (Mrs BattleAxe) but her bloody husband (Mr Peeping Tom) comes in! Oh, the riot we had. (And when I brush my teeth I spit yellow Iris, that bloody evil stuff gets everywhere.)

You know, deep down I'm jealous of you in that big house with your important husband, walking round all day in your Wellington god blimey Boots and now a little one on the way. I'd take yours anyday, duck. So don't sit in that big old house and drink yourself away. You can drive – by god you got Mr Happy's pickup don't you? and more petrol than any other rationed bugger – so get out there, do something. You're always going on about that blinking Janet whatshername girl next door to you in America, her and her bloody donuts out in France or Italy or wherever you Yanks are. So get your bleeding arse over to that Yankee camp up in Shrewsbury, and make these lads some of them donuts you go on about. You know I'm only being cruel to be kind, love. You know I am. Your, Matty.

PS any news on getting me out of this place yet?

Dear Iris,   22nd February, 1944

I will be there Saturday a.m. Taking the milk train. If you could pick me up from the station I would be ever so grateful. I got three days off and I can't leave you on your own anymore girl, your letters are awful. When do you get your phone?

Matty.

My Dear Mat,   *March 1st, 1944*

Thanks for your letters, honey. They really do cheer me up. Stop me thinking about home so much, you know? We're both lonely, I figure. You know what I do most afternoons? (Lazy kid that I am.) I lie in bed, close my eyes and try and hear Coney. I listen out for that jingle of the Carousel, the rumble of the Cyclone, then I get out all the boxes from under my bed and cry a little. Stupid, right? Me, fat and bawling and Bergdorf boxes of underwear I can't fit into. Stupid kid, my poppa would say, 'Think about our boys out there dying! Think about someone other than yourself, little Iris!' But it's hard, on your own. I always was kind of selfish and now I can't figure out why I left the best place in the world for this. I miss Rita. Lula. Momma and Poppa. But you're right, Mat, so, guess what? I volunteered today. Nothing crazy, no getting shipped out to France, no donuts and coffee. Just the Women's Institute, doing collections and making woollens and all. It's got to be cold out there, right? They say it's awful cold. I go with Millie and it's real nice. Rather be in a factory like you, feeling real useful, but I'm getting fat as a pregnant sow so what can I do? Don't give up on me yet. I just wish Larry would get that goddamn phone. Then I'd be in heaven.

It's dark outside now, and the ghosts on the third floor are up, but I'm not scared of them anymore. The Jerrys are bombing that Severn River again. Love, Iris.

P.S Got nylons for you from Chadds.

TELEGRAM FROM MRS IRIS HAPPY TO MISS MATHILDA GREENE TNT
FACTORY ROTHERWAS HEREFORD 15/3/1944

BE READY BY EIGHT AM STOP GOT PETROL AND COUPONS STOP
LETS DRIVE ANYWHERE THE SEASIDE STOP FOUND A PLACE
BRIGHTON ON MAP STOP IS IT HOME STOP US YANKS LOVE
TO DRIVE STOP ITS AN ADVENTURE STOP
IRIS

The Slipway Guesthouse
Brighton
Sussex

My Darling

I don't really know what to write. I feel like it's a hot summer's day in Coney, and I'm dying from the heat but it's so nice dying. Before you, Matty, I've only ever had beaus. Even Larry. How could I fall out of love with him so quick? But I don't want to think about that right now. I just want to write this at this funny old desk and watch you sleep. The sheet's fallen off you, Mat, and I can see you. You're beautiful, you know. Why didn't I meet you years ago? Why didn't you come to Luna Park instead of here as a kid?

It was a beautiful day yesterday. All those crazy photos we took. Felt like a real bonafide model. I'll always remember this. Always. I'm twenty years old and in love.

I remember my first time with Larry, I just thought 'is that it?' Is it? Will it be? You seem to know more than me, honey. You said you've always been like this. Who with? Mabel? See, I'm jealous already.

I'm going for a walk out there. Meet me by the Carousel. What do you call them anyways? Merry-go-around?

Your Iris

p.s. when you find this, don't laugh at me

13

*T*he green van in the Rucks' icy yard is filled with ladies in bright saris, while Brian and I are in black.

Mrs Crabtree died from the Big C.

Mrs Shah waves from the front seat, but she won't come out, she hates Mrs Ruck. I overheard Mrs Shah calling the Rucks, 'poor backwards people who sleep with family'.

No one takes any notice of Mrs Ruck when she locks her house up because the Shahs are visiting. She even puts a chain on the outside loo. 'Dunt want their Paki muck in my bog,' she says. Mrs Ruck smells of biscuits and B.O.

Mrs Shah's got pink silk over her head. I want to ask her where she got it from, because Gran would love it, but Jamilah's running towards me. Jamilah's not as beautiful as her mum. She's got a beautiful name but hair like bat fur on her face, and she's a tomboy. Jam's wearing a long shirt with baggy trousers in dull blue beneath her Parka.

'All right Kate?' Her breath blows white in the cold; there's still snow on the ground.

'Yeah.'

'Brian says your mum's back.'

'Yeah.'

'That's good isn't it?'

'Suppose. What you been doing?'

'Not much, just school. Bor-ring!'

'Yeah. Bor-ring!'

And we laugh. Jam's gold bangles clang on her wrist as she hits my arm. It's sad I only see her once a month when her brothers, her dad and Mr Ruck kill a sheep.

'I went to West Midlands Safari Park,' I tell her.

'Cool. Been there loads.'

'And London.'

'Brilliant. Look what I got, Kate.'

'What's that?'

'A Stereo Headphones. Brilliant eh?'

'A what?'

'You can listen to music on these little things and walk round. Dad got it from a cousin in Singapore. Here.'

It's like the Bird Listening Station, except smaller. I put the foamy bits in my ears.

'Ow!'

It's loud and sounds like Showaddywaddy; Jamilah loves rock and roll. She pulls the headphones out.

'It's The Stray Cats, they're brill. I really fancy the lead singer, he's got the biggest quiff ever *and* he's called Brian.'

'Oh yeah.'

'Yeah.'

We watch the other Brian as he slips behind the shed with Jam's brother Najid.

Jamilah sighs, 'Bugger, I wanted to go first, I'm bursting.'

Behind the shed is where we all go to pee because of Mrs Ruck locking the bog.

Jam's three little brothers and an old man are following Stan and Mr Shah into the slaughtering shed. The sheep starts bellowing, because they tie it up first, and Jam and I share the Stereo Headphones. The singer yells, 'Runaway boys!' over the sheep's squeals.

'I fucking hate this,' Jam says.

'The music?'

'No stupid, the bloody sheep.'

'Why'd they make so much noise?'

'I've told you Kate, it's Halal. It has to be bred proper and you have to cut its throat. It's holy and stuff.'

'Oh right.'

('Runaway boys!')

'And that Mr Ruck makes a killing out of us, that's what my dad says. Anyway, after Christmas, I'm being vegetarian.'

She switches the music off. The sheep must be dead.

'Why are you in black, Kate?'

'Funeral.'

'Whose?'

'A woman from the village. Mrs Crabtree. My gran's making me go.'

'Bloody hell.'

I can smell rusty-blood in the air.

'When's it our turn? I'm bursting!' Jamilah yells at the shed.

'We can go in the field.'

'Nah. Bulls and bloody nettles, and up to your knees in mud. Wish that stupid cow wouldn't lock her outhouse, though. Haven't they got a toilet inside anyway?'

'No.'

Jamilah puts her hand between her legs and bites her lip. 'So who was this Mrs Crabtree then?'

'She was posh and retired. She used to teach at that Cheltenham Ladies College. The one your sister goes to.'

'Yeah, Pearl's a bloody snob. She's only been there a term and Mum says she's got a chip on her shoulder size of a potato field. She won't come home at weekends now and I think she's going skiing or something this Christmas with some posh plonker from Hong Kong. Silly cow. She calls it "H.K." as well. Oh, shit, look at that!' Jam punches me again and points to the Rucks' open kitchen window. Mrs Ruck is balancing a big radio there. She waves her fist at us and suddenly Kenny Rogers booms 'The Coward of The County' across the yard.

Jamilah giggles.

'Shut that bloody racket up, mother!' Stan yells.

Mrs Ruck once caught a coach all the way to London to see Kenny Rogers. She turns it up.

'Woman, I said shut it off!'

'Get them Pakis frum here!' she shouts back. Then the music goes dead because Stan's turned the generator off.

'Stupid bloody woman,' says Jam.

'Finished!' Najid runs out from the side of the shed, doing up his flies. Najid is the most beautiful boy I've ever seen; he's tall for fourteen and he's got eyes big as puddles, and just as brown. He sprints over.

'Go on then, Jam,' he says, 'but watch out for Brian, he'll cop a look. All right, Kate?'

'Yeah.'

'You seen *Friday The 13th*?'

'Eh?'

'*Friday The 13th*. It's an X but my cousin got me in, it's murders and stuff and it's brilliant. I've seen it five times. Made me sick.'

'Brill.'

'Yeah.'

'I've seen —' but I can't think. I hardly ever go to the pictures.

'Come on Bri!' he yells. 'You still got your air-rifle? Let's do bottles!'

Brian joins him as Mrs Shah calls, 'Play nicely boys!' from the mini-van. It's getting steamed up, but I can still see the pretty-sari ladies sipping from plastic cups.

I lean up against the slaughtering shed and pee next to Jamilah in the freezing cold. Our arms touch as hacking and sawing comes from inside; Jam's got that soft bat fur on her arms, too. We listen to

Stan and Mr Shah talking about a bet at Haydock Park. Jam told me they met at a betting shop, and that's where they hatched The Halal Butchery Scheme. Mr Shah has all his friends getting meat from Mr Ruck, and I heard Stan say he's 'making a pretty packet from the wogs'.

One of Jam's younger brothers is being sick inside.

'Do you ever get used to it, Jam?'

'What?'

'Killing sheep.'

'Well, do you? You live on a bloody farm. Bloody meat factory.'

'We're cows. And it's dairy.'

'Rubbish you are. Anyway that's just as bad, making cow's boobs so big they're fit to burst. That's oppression that is.'

Jamilah is the cleverest person in the world. If she was prettier and didn't have the bat fur Gran says she could be President.

'Can I come with you?' she asks.

'Where?'

'To the funeral.'

'Why?'

'Dunno. See what it's like I suppose. My nan's funeral lasted about a week. Is she being cremated, this Mrs Crabtree?'

'Dunno.'

Jamilah finishes before me. She pulls up her shirt and her brown skin is goose pimpled. As she wipes herself with a dock leaf I see she's got hair down there. I'm jealous.

'I'm going to ask my mum. I'll say I'm going to play with you. She won't mind. They can pick me up on the way back, and I hate our bloody picnics in the Black Mountains anyway. Wait here.'

She runs off, her long blue trousers trailing in muck.

Me, Jam and Brian are sitting up in the churchyard on the hill, playing *Operation!* The ground is freezing and I wonder how they'll dig a hole for Mrs Crabtree. Patches of hard snow blotch the graves.

'Brian?' I ask.

'Yeah.'

'Do you think opposites attract?'

'Eh?'

'Like my gran and grandpa.'

'They bludy hate each other.'

'Okay, like – um – Marilyn Monroe and Joe DiMaggio.'

'Who's he when he's at home?'

'He played baseball, he's American,' says Jamilah. She really does know everything. She's got her Stereo Headphones in her ears, but the music's off.

'What's baseball?' Brian asks.

'Like rounders,' I tell him.

'That's a bludy girls' game.'

'Bri–an!'

'Well, give us another opposite, then.'

'Okay, like you and Jamilah,' I try, losing patience.

'Or you and Najid,' Jamilah barks back.

'Yeah. All right.'

'Racist,' she says.

'What?'

UH-HA! The board game buzzes and the man's red nose lights up.

'Operation!' Brain yells.

I drop the little plastic heart.

'Right that's five-three to me,' he says and snatches the tiny metal tweezers.

Jam is sitting on Hester Pines. I'm on Eva because she's family. We're both blowing into our hands for warmth.

Hester's got a lovely name, and a lovely grave, and Jamilah took a fancy to her the first time she came up here. Hester's son is buried with her and they both died in 1774 when people had wooden teeth and didn't know what a banana was. Hester was seventeen and Jamilah said that was oppression. She tells me a lot of things are oppression, and she's going to be a solicitor when she gets older to help people with it. Jamilah says her dad's an oppressor, but she loves him anyway.

Brian's got a lung. I play with the pink pebbles on Eva's grave, balance one on her angel's head, and give one to Jam.

'When are they all going to get here?' Jam asks.

Brian's got the kidney now and he's going for a fibia.

'Don't know, suppose they have to pick up the coffin,' I say.

'Will it be open?'

'That's Catholic, isn't it?'

'Well, I saw my gran and I'm not one of them.'

Brian nicked a black dress for Jamilah, from his sister Joanne's wardrobe. It's a black disco dress, with sparkles and a slit up the back; so she's keeping her Parka on top.

'You look nice in black, Jam,' I tell her.

'Yeah, I'm Siouxie bloody Sioux.' She chucks the pink pebble at the yew tree, then gets up and wanders among the gravestones, looking moody.

I never feel moody here. I like it. In summer Brian and me cut the grass on the graves with Gran's nail scissors. We swap flowers and wreaths around. Last summer Millie and I scrubbed Eva's angel with Daz; it gave her a blue rinse and Gran went mad. Little Boy is somewhere here and Samuel and Wilhomena have a tomb inside the church. That sonnet by Wilhomena, 'Shall I whisper to thee of Summer Days?' is hacked into stone by the font. Jamilah copied it down last year and then told me my great–great–great–great–great second cousin was a plagiarist. That sounded really bad.

Jamilah's staring at our famous gargoyle. It's a stone woman with her legs spread so wide tourists take pictures. The gargoyle makes Brian laugh and he always goes up to the black wall and pretends to shag her. Jam never laughs at that. Things like that make her *very serious.*

I'm bored of *Operation!* so I join Jamilah under the fanny-gargoyle, and look up at her stone spread legs. Jamilah's reaching up like she wants to touch *it*.

'Yeah!' Brian shouts from the yew. 'Got it! My go again.'

'Do you like having your mum back, Kate?' Jam asks.

'Suppose, she's a bit mad though, she's on pills. She bought me birds for Christmas and I killed them by accident.'

She makes a face. 'You can always come and stay with me.'

'Thanks.'

'Do you think she'll stay? For good I mean?'

'Dunno.'

'It must be really weird.'

'What?'

'Having a mad mum.'

'Yeah.'

Brian pushes into us and stares up at the fanny-gargoyle like he's never set eyes on her before.

'Oh Brian, give it a rest,' Jamilah tells him.

'What?'

'Haven't you ever seen a woman's vagina?'

He's goes red and looks at the ground. 'A what?'

'A va–gin–a.'

'Don't say that Jamilah, that's rude that is. My mam said –'

Jamilah and I giggle, but Brian squirms. Jamilah looks lovely when she laughs (which isn't often). She grabs my hand and we run back to the board game.

'Hey, Brian!' She picks up the tweezers and has a go at the head. 'If I get this, you have to kiss Kate!'

'Yeah and if you don't get it, you have to,' he shouts.

Jam smiles at me; 'All right then.'

I watch the tweezers poke round the little plastic brain. Jam's got it: she lifts it out.

UH-HA! The man's red nose lights up and she's lost. Jamilah

leans across and kisses me. Her bat-fur top lip tickles, but it's soft and I don't want her to stop. I think of Mathilda up in the attic with Gran, being old maids and making love.

Was this the kind of making love she meant?

Brian is standing above us. 'Now I kiss you, Jamilah,' he says.

Jam pulls back and stops smiling, while Brian squats and crawls over Hester Pines, flattening rye grass. He sticks his tongue in Jamilah's mouth. It takes ages to finish and they're like cows, chewing.

'Does everyone kiss like that?' I ask him.

'Was a matter with it?'

'It's very messy. What about just the lips?'

Jamilah's wiping her mouth and frowning. 'How many girls have you kissed, Brian?'

'Millions.'

'Who?'

'None a your business.'

I think of Sam Morris in The Red Dragon and brush drizzle from my face. I hope Brian doesn't get Jam pregnant. Then I see a trickle of bodies in black walking up the hill to the church, and it starts to hail.

We sit at the back, breathing in church dust (I've decided that's mouldy pollen, vicar's breath and hats). The hail's still coming down as Gran walks in with Mr Crabtree, he's taken his brown hat off and his hair is speckled white. He looks very smart though, in a black suit with a silver-tipped cane. It tap-taps as he walks down the aisle with Gran. She calls Mr Crabtree a tall cup of coffee with cream, and she looks good next to him, in pink. Mum and Grandpa haven't come.

The coffin comes in last, it's tiny, and I watch Mr Crabtree's head fall onto my gran's pink shoulder.

I'm dying for Jamilah to kiss me again: I liked the fuzzy feeling of her top lip.

'Jam?' I ask.

'Sh!' says Brian, and gives the coffin at the altar (just a table with a doily on top) a look.

'It's okay, Brian. No one's going to get you,' I whisper. I'm sure of this because the only things out there are ghosts, zombies and vampires. Gran says I'm an agnostic, which sounds like a stew.

The vicar coughs. 'Would you all please rise for hymn number three hundred and fifty-one.'

Jam lets go of my hand and sings 'All Things Bright And Beautiful'. We've still got our coats on and melted hail from my mac drips on the blue carpet.

Sun shafts light the aisle.

This is the first time I've been inside St Mary's since Dad's funeral, and I don't remember much about it because I couldn't see a thing. I was plonked behind his sister from Australia, who was enormous. Mum didn't come to that either; 'Too busy being on bail and making the buffet, darling. I refuse to have bloody pineapple and cheese on a stick. Not on Michael's day!'

And that's what it was: Michael's day, like it was a treat or a celebration.

Grandpa called Mum's spread, the funeral-baked meats. 'Bloody Niobe, eh? Midships!' he yelled, but Gran said my mum had suffered enough.

'Look at her eyes, Larry. Look at those lovely Lieberman eyes. The life's gone. Let her be, honey, please.'

We sit as Mr Crabtree reads aloud from the pulpit; something about spring and new life and fly away home to Jesus. I listen out for geese, but it's quiet; even the hail's done. Mr Crabtree has glasses that go dark in sunlight, and his voice is like lotion. Jamilah leans up against me and I put my head on her shoulder. I wonder what I might write to Jamilah: a letter or a wartime telegram?

TELEGRAM FROM MISS KATE HAPPY TO MISS JAMILAH SHAH

II DECEMBER I980

JAM MY DUCK

I LIKED KISSING YOU STOP YOU HAVE A FUZZY LIP STOP IT

MADE ME FEEL VERY NICE STOP DO YOU WANT TO DO IT AGAIN

DONT STOP SEE YOU JANUARY LOVE KATE

'You two gonna get married then?' Brian whispers.

A woman turns round to hiss, 'Sh!'

I try and forget about Jamilah's top lip and Mathilda in the attic at home, and I stare at Mr Crabtree.

Mr Crabtree is from Barbados, a coral island, and he's trying not to cry.

The tractor got stuck so Brian's giving me a piggy because I've got my posh funeral shoes on. It's my first piggy in four years. We're still in black, apart from his Parka and my yellow mac, and we're filled with Gran's lockshen pudding and something Mr Crabtree called salt fish and okra. He told me his favourite was flying fish, and Brian and I laughed because fish can't fly. Gran pushed us out of the kitchen.

Jamilah's gone home. She invited me to stay in the New Year. I'd like to stay with Jamilah for ever, especially if she's got an attic.

Brian grabs hold of my arms because I'm slipping. I'm resting my head on his shoulder now, listening to his heavy breathing as frosted brambles catch on my black tights.

'Are we nearly there?'

'Yeah, sleepy. Lucky you don't weigh a bludy thing.'

I tighten myself round him and shiver; it's the coldest it's been in ages. 'Where are we going anyway?'

'The bull.'

Sid Vicious jumps over white bracken.

'Bor-ing.'

'Well, you think of summat. I got to tek him in, didn't last night. Your granddad'll have me for it, mind.'

I kick Brian in the sides. 'Gee-up then! Gee-up donkey!'

Brian once said that if I was going to pretend I was riding him, at least he could be a racehorse. I kick him again. He stops.

'Quit, you bloody lezzie.'

'What?'

'You heard.'

'What's a lezzie?'

'You.'

'How do you mean?'

He shifts beneath me. 'You kissed Jamilah.'

'So did you.'

'That ent the same.'

'Why?'

'Bludy hell Kate, you thick or what? A girl kissing a girl is like being a homo and you know what a homo is dunt cha?'

'Course I do.'

'Well then. You're one.'

'Because I kissed a girl?'

'Well bludy done, got it in one. Brains of bludy Britain you are.'

'Brian?'

'What?'

'Is making love the same as sex?'

'Yeah.'

'So if a girl made love to another girl, in an attic or anywhere, would that make them a lezzie too?'

He drops me, 'Course it fucking would!'

'Ow! Brian.'

'And that's disgusting that is.'

It doesn't sound disgusting. Not if my gran did it. Not as disgusting as looking at Brian's willy.

I get up and walk.

The air smells fresh as Mr Sheen, but it's so cold it makes me cough. There's a white mist above the ground like in the Dracula films and Brian's footsteps crunch. It's nearly dark and I can see the few lights of Boldenham in the valley as we walk through the graveyard.

The yew is like a white-sprayed Christmas tree now, but the church is blacker. Hester's grave's gone frosty, and Eva's angel is iced to death. There's no trodden-in confetti like after a wedding; just a smell of vinegar. 'That's the formaldehyde,' Jamilah said, 'or maybe the cancer drugs.'

Mrs Crabtree's got a fresh hill to the right of the yew tree and the red earth's crusted white. It looks *very* Dracula. I wonder if Dad would like to be buried up here instead of in Gran's piano stool.

Brian turns round. 'Kate, why don't you kiss me?'

'What?'

'You kiss Jam, but you ent never kissed me.'

'Well, you never asked, you just give me love bites and show me your willy.'

'You should kiss me, you kiss her.'

'Okay. I will. But not now. I'm cold and it's scary up here.'

'You scared of the graveyard then?'

'Yes.'

'You're a right little girl, ent cha?'

'Suppose.'

He walks on, out the kissing gate, and across the brow of Grandpa's hill to the bull's field. I look back at the yew; they protect you from witches, yew trees.

'You coming, Kate?' he yells.

'Yeah.' I run after him.

It's difficult jumping over molehills in the dusk, and it's even harder to see Brian in the mist. Then I hear him.

'Buggering hell!'

Sid Vicious is barking at something.

'Get out, Kate, go back!'

'Is the bull chasing you?' I shout into the blank.

He doesn't reply; so I don't move. Instead I think about getting crushed, like Dad. It must be better than Mrs Crabtree's Big C. I wonder, if I just stand here, will I get run over by the bull? And will it have eyes like headlights?

I could be a crap matador too.

Instead of a big beast, though, Brian's running towards me.

'Dunt – dunt go over there, Kate. I got to – got to get my dad.'

'Is it coming? Is the gate open?'

'Just – stay here.' He sprints back to the kissing gate, and through the churchyard, then he's gone.

Sid's still barking. I can't hear anything else, so I stumble towards the noise, and only trip once. The five-bar gate to the bull's field is freezing to touch. I check I'm not wearing any red and climb over.

Like Brian, the bull is hard to spot in the mist. I can hear it though, panting heavily as if it's been on a run. I walk forward, arms out like a sleepwalker, and then it's right in front of me.

Grandpa's bull is bloody enormous. I pull down the hood of my mac; I've never got this close to Grandpa's bull.

Fat rolls off him in waves. There's steam rising too, in the cold, and he's the colour of fresh soil. The thick brass ring pinned through his fleshy nose looks painful, and he is making a terrible noise: like the sheep do in Mr Ruck's slaughtering shed.

'Are you okay?' I ask him.

His eyes roll back like a doll's.

He's wet with sweat, and as I walk in closer, cold puddles crack.

The bull's lying on his side, and I finally see what Brian was yelling about. The bull is stuck because his legs are frozen, knee deep, in the hard mud. There's a puddle of bright red blood round him too because they are broken. I know this as the bones have burst through his skin. They stick out like the timbers do on our farmhouse. He must have sunk in the mud and got iced in overnight: he must have struggled so much his legs snapped like toothpicks.

But you can't die from broken legs can you?

'There, there,' I say, like he's a kitten with the flu in one of Wilhomena's hats. 'There, there, silly billy.'

I touch him and he's wet-hot, like a horse when you take off the saddle.

Sid snaps and the bull lifts its head. Then Sid bites its ear and the bull roars, red foam flying. I grab a rock and throw, and it gets Sid on the muzzle.

'There,' I tell the bull, 'that's better.' I take off my yellow mac and lay it on his fatty hump.

He smells of silage and sweat. I pat his twitching skin.

Sid's circling me and the bull like we're both game now, and I wish I had a bucket of water to throw at him. I wish I had Grandpa's gun.

Then I hear the pickup.

'Grandpa!' I yell. 'Grandpa!' I leave the bull and jump back over the gate with blood on my hands.

He drives past me. Stan and Brian are in there with him. Gran's Peugeot is struggling up the track behind and I see she's got Mum in the front.

Brian opens the gate.

'Get that dog from here,' Grandpa yells, 'before I damn well shoot it! Avast!' He's got his twelve-bore cocked on his arm.

Brian kicks Sid and I stand by the hedge and watch.

'Tie that bludy animal up, Brian Ruck,' his dad tells him.

Grandpa walks up to the bull, he's balancing on his shooting stick and trying to hold the heavy gun.

'You want me to do that, Mr Happy?' Stan says.

Grandpa pushes him away, drops his stick in the frozen mud, cracks the gun closed and holds it to eye level. The bull looks strange in my yellow mac; it looks as big as a handkerchief on him. Grandpa wobbles a bit, then he shoots.

I fall into the hedge.

* * *

It's pitch black outside, but the engine's running. The radio is on and Toto sing 'Africa'. Over it I hear bellowing coming from the field, and for a moment I think the bull is still alive, then I recognise the noise: it's Grandpa. He makes that sound at home when he's having one of his 'episodes'.

My mother shouts, 'Leave him, leave him to me. Pa? Pa?'

'Mother Carey's chickens! Sound the disperse! Smoke! Smoke!'

'Pa?'

There's a tap on the window, but it's just Brian and he's doing the 'wind down your window' sign-language.

I open the door.

'Are you okay, Kate?'

'Yes.'

'It had to be put out of its misery.'

'I suppose.'

'You faint then?'

'I think so.'

'You coming back to mine?'

'What?'

'To mine?'

'No. I want to go home.'

'Oh.'

'I'll be over soon enough.'

'When?'

'Oh sometime, Brian, can't you just leave me alone?'

He looks at me strangely, as if I've whacked *him* in the face with a rock, not his stupid dog. Then he slams the door and I'm glad because the air was cold. I can see Gran walking towards me: she's still in pink from the funeral. But there's no Grandpa, no Mum; only the flood of lights from the Peugeot and the pickup.

The Times

15th May, 1951

WAR DEPARTMENT ADMITS TO ERROR

Referring to the disaster on the Naval ship, *HMS Guinivere*, three months before Armistice, Vice-Admiral Getes revealed that 'human error in this case can not be ruled out.' The disaster, where one hundred and twenty-three British hands were lost after an Allied torpedo attack, gripped the nation at a time when celebration should have been uppermost. The controversy arose when it was claimed the charge was their own, ordered to fire by Captain Lawrence ('Larry') Happy, against the wishes of Commander Richard Bylaw.

The internal inquiry has been in operation since 1945. The Captain, who is still recuperating under the terms of an honourable discharge, at Shineways Sanitarium, Southbourne, was unavailable for comment, as was his American wife, currently resident at their farm in Herefordshire. It is understood that Captain Happy was previously under investigation due to a similar incident, though exact details of this have been kept strictly confidential.

14

'Dramas, nothing but goddamn dramas this family.'

Gran's putting on cold cream (it really is, I put my finger in it once).

'We could win Oscars the way we go on. Je-sus. You wouldn't think it was Alice Crabtree's day today, no sir. We have to go one better. Goddamnit.' She slams the white pot down.

Through the window I can still see Grandpa's pickup lights beaming across the top field. They're slowly fading, yellow as the moon.

'Think she can come back here, act like a crazy girl then take over? After everything. Everything her father and I did for her?'

Gran's palm slaps her cheeks with more white cream. She looks like a wedding cake. 'Goddamnsonsofbitches.'

The headlights are moving across the field now, they disappear over the furrowed brow of the hill.

Gran fidgets next to me in the dark. Tonight all I want to think of are her stories. Chicken Licken and the sky falling down. Raggedy Andy and Annie. Green cheese and The King and The Queen of the Moon.

'Honey, get up.'

I look up at the bedroom's bright bulb and my grandmother's face; the cream wiped off.

'Honey, we've got to go. C'mon now Katie, you can sleep in the car.' She pulls me out of bed and my dungarees feel cold as she dresses me because I'm still asleep.

'Please, honey. Gimme a break here.'

She's crying and her hair's still in rollers, so I put my socks on and follow her downstairs to the garage. Gran revs her Peugeot as I find my wellies in the mess of old shoes and buckets of bleach-soaked rags.

'Hurry it up, Katie!'

The plastic car seat is cold, and I shiver as I settle and she backs down the drive. The doors of the garage are left open; the lights on. We turn onto the road and the car skids.

'Buckle up.'

I click my seat-belt and stare out at the horizon; the darkness is tinged with pink, like a puppy's belly. 'Where are we going?' I ask.

She turns on the radio and it's Cat Stevens. I listen to his silky voice and go back to sleep.

I wake up in the hospital car park. The car's empty and I'm cold. There are lights on inside the building, so I climb out and wander in. In the foyer I stand in front of a fat lady who's mopping the floor. It sounds like the suck of Grandpa's milking machines – slop-slop-slurp.

'Visiting's over, my bab,' she says.

'Have you seen my gran?'

'What she look like?'

'Tall, black hair, in pink, not old really.'

'Lady come in not long back and run to the lifts.' She points down her cleaned corridor, but the only person I can see is my mother. She's walking towards me, holding two plastic cups that spill brown on the newly cleaned floor. The fat woman tut-tuts.

'Kate. Take this, it's hot.' Mum turns to the woman; 'Do you know where I can buy cigarettes? Sobranie?'

The woman frowns.

'Oh never mind. Kate, sit down and drink this soup. I can get you some crisps if you like? You like animal flavour, don't you?' Her hands are shaking. 'Soup's foul, from a machine.' She sits next to me, on one of the three plastic chairs in the waiting area.

'Mum, what's going on?'

She sips from her cup and grimaces, 'It's your grandfather. Had a heart episode, up in that field.' Her face goes red but she doesn't cry.

I hold onto my soup. It's the same beef soup you get in swimming pool foyers.

'Is he going to die?'

Mum takes out a half-smoked yellow Sobranie from her coat pocket. 'Don't be dramatic. Of course not. He's had loads. Heart attacks I mean.'

'I thought it was a heart *episode*.'

'Do you have a light?' she asks the cleaning lady. The woman picks up her bucket and walks off and Mum plays with her empty cigarette packet. 'I think he had his second after Eva died. Births and deaths and shocks in general. Had one after that ghastly fire. Poor Daddy.' She crushes the packet and throws it on the floor. 'And I remember we took so many photos of you propped up in the bed with him. Something to remember him by. Thought he wouldn't make it. Don't know where those pictures are now.'

'Does he always get better?'

'Always.'

'How old is Grandpa?'

'Not as old as everyone thinks.'

'Mum?'

'Yes, darling.'

'Are you better now?'

'What do you mean?'

'Are you still going to be bonkers?'

She cough-laughs into her soup and it spills. The light above us buzzes.

'Mum?'

'Oh, what is it now, Kate?'

'Who's Mathilda?'

We both look up at the sound of Gran's high heels on the hard linoleum floor. She's taken the big rollers out of her hair and it's perfectly bobbed. She comes towards us clean and neat. The fat lady nods at her and she nods back.

'Katie. You okay, honey?'

'Yes.'

'Good.' Gran stares at Mum and her lips go small; she doesn't sit down.

'I see you're better, Marlene.'

'Yes.'

'It's amazing what a bit of excitement'll do. Then again, you've always risen to the occasion.'

Mum bites her cup's edge. 'Don't start, Mother.'

'If I did, I wouldn't stop.'

'Then don't.'

'Okay. Just one question. Your performance since you've been back. Why?'

'It was your quack who drugged me.'

'We thought you were ill!' Gran's tight bob unsettles.

'Thought I was brainwashed, I mean how ridiculous.'

'Well, looking at you now honey, it ain't such a bad idea.'

'Shut up, Mother, you've always resented me, always.'

'What do you mean?'

'Oh, never mind.'

'Are you going to go back to being a crazy lady once we get your father home?'

'No.'

'And how can I be sure of that?'

'*I* am going to look after him.'

My grandmother clicks. That's what it sounds like; it's a movement in her throat. She grabs hold of my arm and pulls me up.

'Listen here, girlie. This child here is your daughter. That man in there is my husband. Let's get our roles right. Okay? I will be dealing with him, as I have for the past thirty-eight years.'

'Yes and look at him.'

'What's that supposed to mean?'

'The man's a wreck.'

'Oh and that's me and not the goddamn war, huh? But why am I even defending myself to you? Who are you? Nobody. A stranger who waltzes in and out of our lives whenever she goddamn pleases.'

'I am Kate's mother!'

'Right, and an unfit one –'

'Hah! Oh you can talk about unfit.'

'What's that supposed to mean?'

'Do you know what Kate just asked me?'

'Don't you bring her into this.'

'Your granddaughter just asked "who's Mathilda?"' Mum puts on a baby voice, and Gran goes a bit whiter.

'Listen Marlene, I don't know what you've told the girl, but the past is the past. Please leave it and leave me to deal with my own husband.'

Gran lets go of me. Then she's sailing back up the corridor, and all Mum can get out is 'bitch' before she spills her soup down her dress.

A radio comes on.

'"Time for the morning quiz. Quack-Quack-Ooops!"'

Mum throws her half-empty cup in a plastic bin. 'What were you doing in that field with that boy, Kate?'

'Pardon?'

'That mess of a boy who caused all this, Stan's son, can't remember his name. Thick as pig-shit. Looks like a gypsy. What where you doing with him alone in a field?'

'He's my friend, and he's not thick. We were coming back from Mr Crabtree's.'

'Well I don't want you playing with him anymore.'

'Why?'

'He's trouble. And common. Get yourself some nice friends.'

I feel like clicking, like my grandmother, but I don't know how. Instead I chuck my soup in the bin too, and run down the corridor after her.

3rd June 1953

Dear Papa,

Yesterday was such a wonderful day and I hope you saw it in Southborne. Here at school the prefects of each class (and that is me) were allowed to watch Queen Elizabeth being crowned on the television box in the Headmistresses very own house. It was so beautiful and holy. We had lovely biscuits. Marlene isn't a prefect so she didn't see it. I hope you are not too hot by the sea. I keep asking Mama and Mathilda when we are going to visit you next, but they say you will be home soon for good. I do prefer visiting you because we can play on the beach. I like Southborne and Bournemouth a lot. I love school too but Marlene doesn't. We are in different classes and I am best in my year at writing.

It is our birthday soon so don't forget Papa. We will be nine.

fondest love

your Eva

p.s Can a commoner be a Queen when she grows up? Also one that is half American? Mrs Herald, our Headmistress, says that Mrs Simpson was never a Queen and never could be.

15

Grandpa doesn't dribble and he can move his arms and legs. 'It's not that sort of heart attack,' Gran said, and I wondered how many different ones there are. Gran brings him his favourite meal in bed, 'floaters in the snow' (which is sausage and mash), and Mum reads him the *Western Daily Press*. I tried with *'Salem's Lot* the first afternoon he was back, but he waved me away. It was the bit in the morgue when the bodies start shaking back into vampire-life.

Grandpa's sad he couldn't mount the bull's head, not after he shot it there, but Stan's bought him lots of catalogues filled with more pictures of bulls and he's circled them with my felt-tip pens.

This morning Rita phoned, and for the first time she sounded muffled and a million miles away. She still told me a story, about how someone had found a racoon living in the Astrotower at Coney and some terrible gang of kids had smoked it out. She cried a bit then.

Now I'm running round the house in my socks and Addie Pray dungarees. I'm sliding up and down dark corridors. Mum and Gran are in with Grandpa and all I have to do is keep upright.

Don't fall over, Kate!

Don't drink anything from a funny bottle! (even if Alice did).

I slam into the wainscoting, turn, run, and slide back into darkness: except this time I hit something soft.

'Hello.'

I squeal a bit, and fall over. Something's leaning over me; all I can make out are the whites of eyes, and teeth.

'Are you the famous Katherine?'

So our house *is* infested with vampires. I pull up my collar.

'Is your mother around?'

I squint in the darkness and can smell sweet flowers.

'Is she back? I heard she was. Katherine?'

I back down the corridor, towards the light.

'Katherine?'

Then I see that it can't be Mr Barlow because this vampire's got blond hair. Winter sunlight blasts through the window by the phone, and I pray he follows me into it. I shield my eyes, waiting for screams and singed edges. Nothing happens.

'Katherine? Are you all right?'

I peek out through my fingers. This maybe-vampire's got ruddy cheeks and he's holding a bunch of roses. He's much too healthy looking to be the living-dead. I knock on Grandpa's door, but don't turn my back, just in case.

'Mum? Someone to see you.'

'Your grandfather's sleeping, Kate, go away.'

'It's a man.'

I hear a scurrying noise from inside and she opens the door. Then my mum squeals a bit, like I did, and jumps into the man's arms.

'Francis!'

So that's his name, and it's a girl's.

He spins her round, 'When did you get back?'

'Not long ago.'

'Well, I wasn't going to wait for *you* to call, Marlene!' He puts her down on the parquet floor. 'I heard about your father, is he all right?'

Gran's pokes her head out of Grandpa's room, 'No he is not. Please, be quiet.'

'Hello, Mrs Happy.'

'Hello, Francis. Now if you two will just take your shenanigans someplace else?' She closes the door.

'Oh, don't mind her Francis, darling, she never liked you.'

'Ha! I suppose you are forthright as ever, Marlene.'

'But of course.'

I skulk behind and follow them.

The lounge is Gran's favourite room, it has wallpaper with bluebirds on it and is always locked. It's the only room with booze in, so Mum has the key.

She's pouring two huge gin and tonics and it's like I'm invisible. Francis is sitting on Gran's best cream sofa and I'm on the patch-leather pouf in the corner. I don't think they can see me.

Did I drink a magic potion this morning?

Have I got bitten by a radioactive spider like Peter Parker? I check my arms for fang marks.

Francis is big and he sounds posh. He looks like Toad of Toad Hall in his tweed suit, and he and Mum talk in hums and sighs.

'So, where have you been, Marlene Happy?'

'Here, There, and Everywhere, my dear.'

'Are you back for good?'

'Oh really, please, don't ask me crazy things like that.'

I rest my head on the body of Gran's mahogany piano and glance out at the steady litter of clean snow recoating our yard.

'You're looking good anyway, Lene.' He's calling her Lene like Grandpa does. Mum pouts out her lips. She's wearing a white kaftan, and it's so loose and low cut you can see her boobs when she reaches for her glass.

'Don't look so bad yourself, Francis'

He pulls her to him, and she sits in his big lap. 'Did you ever think of me, Lene?'

'No.'

'I didn't think you would.' He giggles, burying his head in her neck. Then they start kissing, with tongues.

'Can I have a sip of gin?' I ask.

They both jump and Mum crawls off his lap. She knocks over one of Gran's Queen's Coronation display plates.

'What the fuck are you doing here?'

'Can I have a sip of your gin?'

'No you bloody well cannot. Arse off.'

Francis looks uncomfortable, he picks the plate up off the carpet. 'Look Marlene, let me take you to lunch.'

'I'll come too,' I tell him.

'No you bloody well will not,' says Mum.

'She won't do any harm. She can come can't she, Lene?'

Mum turns on him. 'Don't you tell me about my daughter.'

'Shall we go to the pub?' I suggest. 'I want scampi.'

'I'm sorry, Marlene, I didn't mean —'

'Or cottage pie, I like cottage pie.'

'I only meant for us to —' he stutters.

'Well, don't interfere, it's none of your business. Kate, you can't come, your uncle Francis and I need some time alone.'

'He's not my uncle and I am coming. That your car out there, Francis? The big brown one?'

'The Range Rover? Yes.'

'Right. See you there then.' I walk out of the bluebird room and don't hear anything else.

Borders Gate is Grandpa's favourite pub. He comes here to read and underline the obituaries in red pen. The walls of Borders Gate are covered with horseshoes and bits of ploughs, and it smells of sticky drinks and bacon.

'God, this place hasn't changed,' Mum says as we walk in.

Francis closes the latch door, but it's not much warmer in here. Mum's got her new Harrods fur coat on, and she looks odd in this place. Three old farmers in suits are standing at the bar; they stare at her. She flicks her hair and sits in a corner while Francis buys the drinks. I follow her.

'Why the hell did I come here?' she whispers. 'Bloody place.'

A woman behind the bar is rubbing a glass with a tea towel and looking daggers at Mum.

'Grandpa likes it.' I sit down.

'Big fucking deal,' Mum hisses, then smiles sweetly as Francis bounds towards us.

'There you go, girls.' He looks huge in this low room. I take my coke and crisps and sip through the pink-swirled straw as he snuggles next to Mum.

'So, Marlene, tell me everything.'

'Ah, my adventures,' she laughs. 'Well, it hasn't been easy, Francis. In fact I'd go so far as to say it's been hard. Very hard.'

The barwoman is about to drop the glass now, because Mum has her hand on Francis's crotch.

'It really has been so very, very hard.' She giggles, and Francis's face goes even more red. Mum opens a packet of Sobranie with her other hand and I stare at the gold tips.

Marlene you're so glamorous, so ethereal, so beautiful, so outrageous.

That's what Antique Andy said to her when they did it in our flat in London. Mum said Andy was a homo and when Dad came back that night I told him, 'Mummy and Andy slept in the same bed all afternoon, I think they were very tired.'

Marlene, you're such an almighty fucking bitch.

'But never mind about me, what about you, Francis. Have you just been waiting here? For me?'

'Ah,' he laughs, 'think I've been standing to attention by the phone do you?'

'Well –'

'Actually, I've been in Canada.'

'Oh.' She takes her hand off him.

'Yes, great farming opportunities out there.'

'What the hell do they farm? Ice and bears?'

'No, Marlene, it's more complicated than that.'

Francis tells her about farming in a cold country and I watch my mother's eyes glaze over. 'Living on an Island' comes onto the juke-box and I look over to see Brian leaning on it. He loves Status Quo.

I take my coke and crisps and wander over.

'Hi.'

He stares down at the jukebox.

'You okay?'

'S'pose.'

'What you been doing?'

'Nuthing.'

'Did my Grandpa fire you?'

He doesn't reply.

'I haven't seen you.'

'I got other jobs you know.'

'Only asking.' I look over at Mum and she's mixed up with Francis, limbs and arms twisted together. They look like a ball of stoats, coiled round each other like that. Brian showed me five stoats tumble down his garden in a ball like that once. 'What else have you been up to then?' I ask him.

'Not much.' He smiles.

'Don't you want to come and play anymore?'

'You sound like a kid.'

I take a mouthful of animal flavoured crisps and talk through them. 'I found out my Gran was a lezzie, once.'

'What?'

'Never mind.'

'You're bonkers, you are. The whole lot of you. My mam says you're snobs.' Brian drains his pint and frowns. 'He going to die then, your grandad?'

'No.'

'Good.'

'Brian?'

'What?'

'Was it your fault?'

'What?'

'Leaving the bull in the field that night.'

He looks like he's going to cry. Mum screams with laughter and the whole pub stares.

'Who's that with your mam?'

'Oh, some plonker.'

'He's that Wyn-Franks bloke from Sugwas, that's who he is. He's got a bludy huge farm. Soft fruits.'

'Oh this is boring, Brian, let's go.'

'Okay. I got summat to show you anyways, Kate.'

We walk straight past Mum and Francis, but they don't notice.

I listen to the crunch of my boots. Snow pushes over the tops of my wellies as we trudge through one of Grandpa's fields. My head's hot in my knitting-by-the-blind hat, and Brian's holding my hand so I keep up.

I stop, because I've always loved sinking in the snow.

'You set?' Brian asks.

Flakes settle and melt on my lips and I don't feel like talking; snow makes you quiet. I just want to hear the sound of my cold breath, smarting my front teeth.

'C'mon Kate,' and Brian helps me over a barbed-wire fence. I look up and see we're near the Happy Home. Crows stand out in the white sky above it, like back to front pirate flags.

'I don't want to go in there again.' I wipe my hot face.

'We ent.'

He pulls me down the drive, away from it and towards the huts. A pair of robins jerk on the five-bar gate and don't fly off till we're so close we could snatch them. Robins are the souls of the dead, so

Millie says. 'My Robbie, he come back as one, mind you, down at the bottom of the garden he lives. Comes to my bedroom window every morn and wakes me. "For old times' sake, eh Mil" he chirps! Ah, my Robert!'

I jump off the gate and land softly. Covered in snow, the huts look like long igloos. Brian runs to ours and opens the door. Snow catches my eyelashes and everything blurs.

'Come on, Kate!' he says.

Inside, I stamp my feet and stare. Brian lights an oil lamp on a new table, and I see he's made the best den ever. The table's got a yellow cloth with two of his mother's biscuit tins on top (and I hope they're full because I missed my scampi). There's one of those big gas heaters in the corner, and Brian's hung up lacy curtains even though there are no windows. He's even pinned an old Lena Zavaroni poster to the wall.

It smells different too. It smells of Shake n' Vac.

'What d'you reckon then, Kate? I used all the stuff Mam was chucking.'

'It's great.'

There's a chair, and our mattress now has a sleeping bag on top, and pillows. Our hut is like Calamity Jane's cabin after she goes all girly and in love with Wild Bill Hickock. I wonder if Brian will start singing about golden daffodils and secret loves, like Doris Day.

Instead, he lights a candle that's stuck in a jam jar and switches on the gas fire. 'Let's get you ready, eh Kate?' He comes over and takes my mac off; he's very neat, Brian, and he hangs it behind the door on a new nail. Then he's kneeling at my feet and pulling off my wellies. The snow inside them has melted and my socks are wet. I put my hands on his back to balance, and he feels hard and warm.

'Want some cake?'

'Yeah.'

He opens a tin and sticks a big piece of fruit cake on a plate for me. Brian unlocks the straps of my dungarees.

'I got pillows too,' he says.

'I can see.'

'Mam's best covers on them.'

My dungarees fall and Brian's at my feet again, taking off my wet socks as I bite into Mrs Ruck's cake. He kisses the scar on my knee.

'Let's get you under the covers Kate, you're frozen.'

The buttons on my Vyella blouse are undone, and he hangs it on the back of a chair. I've only got my knickers on now: I'm glad I remembered them.

Brian touches the marks on my belly.

'What's that from?'

'Appendix.'

'And that?'

'Had a kidney back to front.'

'Oh.'

He kisses these scars too, then takes my hand and opens the sleeping bag. I get in and the mattress smells clean as an airing cupboard.

Brian's right; the pillowcases are Mrs Ruck's best, he'll get a thrashing with a Scalectrix track for this.

I eat cake and watch him take off his shirt in the yellow light. His back's still brown from a summer in the fields and he's got black hair round his nipples which are big and soft. The light from the oil lamp looks nice on his skin, and his jeans drop, but he keeps his y-fronts on. I'm glad as he climbs in next to me.

It's tight in the sleeping bag together. Brian smells of Old Spice and condensed milk. I'm on my back and he's on his side.

'Kate?'

'Yes.'

'Would you like me to do it to you?'

Light flickers on the walls.

'Not really.'

He takes the fruitcake from my hand and puts his arms round me, then he rests his head on my chest and it's heavy.

'You've made this really nice,' I tell him.

His big hand lies on my stomach, turning.

'Thanks. You warmer?'

'Yeah.'

He kisses my chest.

'Brian?'

'Aye.'

'Did you do it to Sam Morris?'

He tightens against me.

'Yeah.'

'Why?'

'She made me.'

'What do you mean?'

'She dared me, dared me I couldn't.'

'Did she have a baby?'

'Yeah.'

'Where is it?'

'With her mam.'

'Do you see it?'

'No.'

His lips move up to my neck, kissing, and he buries himself there. I think of Christopher Lee as Dracula, and I'm not scared.

'My mam won't let me see it,' he whispers. 'She says it ent mine. It's a boy and they call him Danny.' His breath is very hot as he opens his mouth, wide, and sucks my neck. Then his teeth bite, just a bit.

I feel like I did when Jamilah kissed me; I don't want him to stop. But I don't want him to put his willy in me and do it to me either. I don't want to be small with a big baby inside.

'I like you, Kate.'

'I know.'

'No, I mean I really like you. You're weird and everything and you're younger an me and you ain't got tits –'

'So?'

'You wanna be my girlfriend?'

'Maybe.'

He stops kissing and pulls me to him. His willy presses into my leg and it feels different; strong, but somehow nicer inside his pants. I hold it and he sighs.

It feels as warm as Grandpa's bull.

'Let's go to sleep, eh Kate?' he says. 'You comfy yet?'

'Yes. Thanks.'

He snores quickly and I'm hot, wrapped tight in the sleeping bag, my hand holding him still.

TELEGRAM TO IRIS HAPPY HAPPY FARM BOLDENHAM
HEREFORDSHIRE ENGLAND 6/19/1953

THEY DID IT STOP CANT BELIEVE STOP ONE MINUTE
BEFORE SUNDOWN FRIDAY STOP THE ROSENBERGS
EXECUTED STOP DONT WANT TO HEAR ABOUT YOUR
GODDAMN CORONATION STOP RITA

16

Joanne's the one with sandy hair, while Trish has *her* Barbara Streisand perm in black. They're Brian's older sisters, and Gran calls them *Jailbait*.

It's warm in their bedroom; warmer than Brian's hut last night.

He walked me back to his house this morning for tea and Weetabix, and now Mrs Ruck is calling Gran. I suppose everyone was having a freak out because I was gone, I'm sure Gran was even on the phone to Rita.

Brian's house smells of cooked chicken. It always does. This is made worse by the coal fires in every room. It's like being inside a Sunday Roast oven. The fires don't stop the mould though. Brian and I found mushrooms growing from the back of his telly once. He says my Grandpa should do their house up, seeing as it's his and all.

Trish is smoking a Silk Cut and blowing smoke-rings out the window. Joanne's painting her nails black and Brian and me are sitting on the floor listening to 'Too Much Too Young' by The Specials. Terry Hall is singing about population booms in his living room.

Brian holds my hand; in fact, he hasn't let go all morning and it's damp over mine. He told his sisters I'm his girlfriend. Trish ignored him and just went on about The Specials and Coventry and how that's where she and Joanne are going tonight.

'It's great. Everything's happening there. All the clubs. We'll get bludy murdered if Da found out. He reckons we're off to Cardiff to our nans.' Trish blows more smoke-rings out the window, her jaw gulping like a fish.

'Won't your gran tell your dad you're not with her?' I ask, shifting on the hard floor.

'Fuck off,' says Trish.

I'm just Miss Ladidah kid from up the road. Miss Ladidah who's going with their brother now so she can't be all that Ladidah after all.

'She ent got a phone, us neither, so how's he gonna find out then?'

'How are you getting there?'

'None a your bludy business.'

Brian kisses my hand and I frown. I don't like him this close in the daylight.

'Instead of the bus to Cardiff, we'll just get one to Coventry. Easy see.'

'Is there a bus there then?' I ask.

I'm spoiling their fun; their night chasing Black boys in Coventry. Anything to get Brian off me.

Joanne and Trish love Black boys. They love Neville and Lynval from The Specials and Rankin' Roger from The Beat, though Trish thinks he's too skinny. There's no one Black in Madness so they don't love them. I wonder if they love Mr Crabtree.

Trish and Joanne are going to Coventry to have Black babies.

'Dad'll just go fucking mad!' Joanne squeals.

I look out at my Grandpa's green fields. 'Can I come with you?' I ask them.

'Nuh. Fuck off.'

Trish stands up and starts stuffing clothes in a plastic bag. Joanne's grabbing the three fresh packets of fags stored under her bed.

'You two done it then?' she asks.

'Might have,' says Brian, and winks.

'No we haven't,' I say, and finally pull my hand out from his; it slips out like a wet fish.

'Well, you just watch it, Kate, dunt matter if you got the curse or not. Use a johnnie.'

'Yes, I know.'

'See ya!'

And like two rabbits into a hole, they shoot down the stairs, shouting, 'Da! Drop us at the coach station, Da. Gotta get to Nan's!'

Brian smiles. 'They're gonna get so bludy murdered!'

I get up and lie on Trish's bed. It smells of smoke and chicken. I want to go to sleep.

'You all right?' Brian tries to lie next to me.

'Yes, I'm fine, please bugger off.'

'Right-e-o,' he says. 'I'll get us some more tea eh? You have a nap,' and he runs down the stairs too. I can hear him fussing his mum in the kitchen ('No she dunt like that. No sugar, Mam. She dunt have sugar in her tea.')

I close my eyes and imagine Mrs Ruck's house filling with Black babies; they're spilling down the steps, giggling and gurgling, and outside her yard is filled with The Shahs and all their friends, killing sheep and wearing pretty saris. The Specials are there too, and Mrs Ruck is running about locking doors and toilets and cupboards, but it's no use. Even Kenny Rogers is singing 'A Message To You Rudy' on her wireless.

I hope Trish and Joanne get their wish this evening. I turn over and go to sleep.

'Wake up now, Katherine.'

I feel the mattress sag as someone heavy sits on it.

'Katherine. Your mother's in the car waiting.'

I open my eyes to Francis; his big blond bulk fills the small chickeny room. Mrs Ruck's behind him muttering, 'No trouble.

She can stay for her dinner, mind.' Mrs Ruck looks like a grey mole.

'Come on now, Kate.'

I try and get up, but I'm wobbly, the smell and the hot fires have drugged me.

'Let her sleep a bit more, poor mite,' says Mrs Ruck.

I fall back on the pillow, but Francis picks me up. It's nice and he carries me down the tight stairs. Francis smells of soap.

'She all right?' Brian asks. 'Where you taking her?'

Francis doesn't reply.

'I'll come and call tomorrow,' Brian shouts after me. 'We had fun didn't we, Kate?'

'Sh!' his mother bites.

It's freezing out in the Rucks' yard, and I'm shivering as Francis opens his car door.

'Where the hell have you been?' It's Mum and she twists round in the front seat. 'I'm talking to you, child. What the fuck do you think you're playing at?'

Francis starts up his Range Rover.

'I told you about hanging out with that boy.'

I sit up and see Brian and Mrs Ruck wave from their front door. Brian looks tall and flushed, and Mrs Ruck looks old; her hair greasy like Grandpa's, with two kirby grips each side of her forehead. I remember how she told me she 'smoked through her kiddies, to make em small. Cos small uns is easy to have, like.'

It hasn't worked with Brian.

'Where's Gran?' I ask.

'Your grandmother, apparently, has better things to think about than you. It seems your aunt Rita's coming for Christmas. She called last night, and she's bringing that ridiculous husband of hers.'

'Brilliant!'

Mum leans into the back seat. 'I don't think so,' she spits. 'You know your grandfather can't stand the woman, and neither can I.

It's typical of my mother to −'

'Calm down, Marlene,' Francis tries.

She turns on him. 'Don't you tell me to calm down.'

'I only meant −'

'Well, don't.'

'When did you miss me, Mum?' I cut in.

'What?'

'Yesterday, when did you miss me at the pub? Notice I'd gone, I mean.'

'Oh, don't be a bloody drama queen, Kate. We had Mrs Ruck's call this morning, didn't we? Now, I'm dropping you at the farm, we've got our own Christmas shopping to do, we've got our own bloody surprises.'

She's only been with Francis for twenty-four hours, and they're a 'we' already. Mum's always been quick with men; a bit like Gran is with a Dover Sole. It doesn't matter anyway; Rita's coming for Christmas and she'll make everything all right again.

'Are you buying a present for me, Mum?'

'No. You killed yours, remember?'

I lie down and think of what I should write in my Christmas card to Jamilah.

> Dear Jam,
> I'm sorry. I touched Brian's willy. But it was in his pants and I like kissing you best. See you in January. You can come up to my attic then. Have a Merry Christmas and A Happy New Year. My mad Auntie Rita's coming and I'm so excited!
> Lots of Love, Kate

10th August 1954

Dear Eva,

I don't like to think that you are still ill when I am getting better. Mummy's chicken soup helps so you must drink it, and let Millie rub that smelly yellow stuff on your chest. I can't remember much about being ill. The doctor told me that was a dellyearium from the newmonia. Hope you're not having one too. How is Auntie Mathilda? Is she better too? I saw some lovely bull finches out of Millies window today and Mr Millie has got extra coal in for me. Even though it's sunny I get cold, as I'm sure you do too. The doctor comes to see me every day, does he see you too? He's got cold hands, but he looks like James Mason in The Wicked Lady. I am making a dolly for you, with real marble eyes, so she can ride your rocking horse. I know you think you're too old for that, but I think you will like it. I am getting quite tired, so I shall give this to Millie to give to you. Please get better soon. It is very lonely in this sick bay (it is Millie's bedroom) but I can see Boldenham Green from her window and today it is cricket. They are running about. Someone I don't know just made lots of runs. I so wish I could join in but the doctor says no. Please give Mummy and Mathilda a kiss, and when you're better we'll go riding down to the river, and I'll watch you swim.

Your loving sister,
Marlene.

17

My electric hair has been brushed and I'm polishing Gran's silver Menora with Duraglit; she brought it down from the attic last night. I'm so excited Rita's going to be here, Millie says I'll rub the bludy plate off. She's on the brass because she won't touch the Menora. 'A bludy devilish thing,' she calls it.

Gran's already cleared a downstairs room for my one-legged aunt. There's an oxygen tank and a commode in there too as Rita's not well. Dr Croften's been here, organising, and Millie said they've all been working flat out, mind you, and she filled me in on the dramas.

1) Like how no one noticed I was gone, they were so busy.
2) And how Mum called Gran 'a murderer as that woman'll kill my father!'
3) Then Grandpa howled, 'Bloody women! Avast!' but put his socks on and that was a good sign as he hadn't done that on his own for two weeks.
4) And Bosum 8 had diarrhoea in the downstairs bathroom because the poor mite hadn't been out for days.

Now Millie is kneeling next to me, paper laid out for her brass, and continuing her list of ways I can die on a farm, 'for old times' sake', she said.

She's had a while since my birthday to come up with more.

'Well what about that anthrax and foot and mouth, then? Had

them in my day. And then there's them pigs, real vicious they are. I even heard a sheep done a man in, over Rhaeader way. They can turn, look you.' Millie sighs and glances out the window. 'You know what, Katherine?'

'What?'

'There's no snowdrops, lovie, cause they've all been drowned.' She gets on with a candlestick.

'Mil?'

'Yes?'

'What about pneumonia? That can kill you on a farm, can't it?'

She crosses herself, frowns, and changes the subject. 'You like that man your mother's with now then?'

'They've only been together two minutes.' I rub hard on the Menora.

'Yes, but they've known each other years, mind. She was engaged to his brother once, see.'

I look up.

'That's right, when she were eighteen. He got burnt up though, in the hop press – and that's another thing that can get you – took him almost a year to die and your poor mam was going to that hospital every day to see him. That was why she went the way she did I reckon. All that at that young age. Put her off. Still, it's nice to see them together, as that Francis always had a terrible crush on our Marlene. Specially after his brother died. Asked her out at the funeral. Imagine! Barefaced cheek, isn't it?'

Millie's great at filling in blanks. I smile and think of Francis's brother, with his black flaky skin, as ashed as Dad.

'And what you doing hanging about with that Brian now? I heard about you going off yesterday. Not that he's a bad lad, but he's older an you missy, and a sin is a sin, no matter what, mind you.'

'We didn't do anything, Millie. We didn't do *it* anyway. Honest.'

'Shocking!'

'Well, Mum didn't miss me did she?'

'You know he got that Sam Morris in trouble last year and that witch of a mother of his won't let him see the babbie?'

'Yeah. Something like that.'

'Well, let that be a lesson, lovie.'

'I've gone off him anyway.'

'And that's worse, leading him down the garden path.'

I try and change the subject this time. 'Where's Gran?'

'Diabetic jellies.' ('Di–a–be–tic' is a lot of work for Millie's sour and sweet voice to get out.)

'What?'

'For your auntie. She can't take no sugar can she, see, so your nan's getting all sorts.'

I think she means the liquorice.

'Then she's off to the airport to get her. All that way. London, isn't it? But it'll be right nice to see Rita, we get on, we do. Talked down the years on that telephone of your nan's. Your Rita's as straight as a die, mind you.' She spits on the brass. 'You know, I had a cousin once was diabetic. Poor man got fat then died. Cremated he was. We thought it was catching then, but that was years ago. You can't catch it now, isn't it?'

'I don't suppose so.' I'm rubbing the Menora hot. 'Millie?'

'Yes lovie.'

'Did you ever meet a woman called Mathilda?'

She looks up and quick as a snake says, 'What d'you want to know about her for?'

'Did she live here with Gran?'

'Don't nose in things that don't concern you.'

'But it does.'

'How's that then?'

'It just does.'

'Nosing more like. What's done is done and He With No Sin Shall Cast The First Stone. Now then, that's all the brass. Floors next I reckon. And my lips are sealed, as these bludy floors should be.'

A car is rumbling down our track, but it's not Gran's Peugeot. Millie clears away the newspapers and puts the brass on the dresser.

'You going to help? Keep you out of trouble it will.'

The garage doors open, feet shuffle, and I hear the hum of complaint coming from the kitchen.

'Kate? Are you here?' It's Mum.

I don't reply.

'Kate? For fuck's sake!'

'Oh, she's got a mouth on her that one,' says Millie, and it's then I hear another voice.

'Language! Marlene!'

I freeze because that voice isn't Grandpa's but at the same time it is, only worse.

It's Aunt Regina – 'Reggie' – Grandpa's twin.

'The goddamn Wicked Witch of the North, East, South and West,' Gran calls her.

So this is Mum's surprise. Two Aunts for Christmas. Checkmate.

I put the shiny Menora in pride of place in the middle of the dresser as my mother walks in.

'What are you doing with that?' she asks.

'Cleaning it.'

She snorts.

'Kate! Little darling!' I hear, and Aunt Reggie slips in front of Mum. Reggie is the ugliest person I know. She has long white hair in two plaits, and her face is so wrinkled you can't see her eyes. She's more bent over than Grandpa so she has to stare at the floor most of the time. Reggie had polio too. The only time you can look Reggie in the eye is when she's sitting down (and that's not a great thing as her eyes are bulging, watery green). Gran says she looks like a chameleon, and you can't trust her either. *Blends and attacks, that's your aunt Reggie.*

I think she looks half bird, half tortoise.

Reggie smells of cat piss and toffees.

'Look! You! Haven't grown. Pity. Hair's brushed. Good.'

Reggie sounds like a wartime telegram.

She opens her arms, but it's like she's trying to hug the parquet floor, so she turns to one side and her neck twists round like an owl's. I get a bit of wrinkly face. 'Come. Kate. Here!' she cries, and Millie backs soundlessly out of the room.

Reggie's put three baskets of her cats on the third floor, and two pink hams on the stove to boil. She's rearranged Grandpa, too.

Gran's not back from the diabetic jellies, or the airport.

The smell from the kitchen is making me gag. Reggie pulled off the thick ham skin in front of me and it sounded like a plaster coming off. I nearly threw up.

'Pity,' I heard her whisper to Mum. 'Kate's got it. In the blood. That woman's sort. Allergic to pork.'

'Well, I'm not,' Mum said and gobbled some ham skin.

'Good. A Happy. Through and through.'

'Are you glazing them, Reg?'

'Yes. Golden syrup. Treacle. Two tins. Brought with. Marvellous.' Reggie poured the syrup on the hams. 'Pork on the boil. Like camphor for fleas. Fumigation!' she laughed, but Mum frowned.

I don't know what my diabetic auntie's going to eat when she gets here, because treacley ham is definitely out. Rita's not a Church of England Chew like Gran, she's a real one; a Chew Chew.

I press my face up against the dining room's cold, dark window. It's almost half past five and I want Rita to be here now. I want it to be like the last Christmas I saw her; she'll make us laugh, talk about Dad, and tell me *everything*.

One of Reggie's cats snakes round my legs. It's fat and white, not like our wormy tortoiseshells. I tell it to bugger off, so it trots off and throws up ham skin in front of the lit coal fire.

'Sulking?'

I turn round, Reggie's staring down at her cat's vomit, but talking to me.

'No.'

'Upstairs. Have to organise. Come with.' She clicks her arthritic fingers.

'But I'm waiting for Gran.'

'Stuff. And nonsense.' She walks out, ignoring the cat puke, and I obey: Reggie doesn't give you any other choice.

She passes Grandpa's bedroom door and tut-tuts. 'Poor brother. Abandoned man. Wifely duties. Mine now.' Then she scurries up three flights of stairs, quick, her slacks buzzing like flies. It's amazing to see, and she's almost up on her third floor before I've left my grandmother's pink kingdom.

'Hurry. Ham crisping!'

'Coming.'

I think Reggie is a beetle, scurrying like that. Then again, I suppose chameleons zip up trees too.

Reggie has created a home in Samuel and Wilhomena's library. She's only been here half a day, but the put-me-up bed is made, the fire's going, and she's hung Indian cloth on the walls.

Gran must be right: a chameleon, slow in public, speedy when no one's watching.

'You like?'

'Yes, it's very cosy, Auntie.'

'Reggie's the name.'

'Sorry.'

'Oxfam connections,' she points at the hanging material. 'No traders. No child slaves. Good stuff.'

'Yes, it's very pretty.'

'Pretty! An art form!'

'I suppose so.'

'No suppose. Generations –'

A huge tabby jumps on Reggie's crooked back.

'Noodles. Off. Off!'

She's trying to reach it, but she's so bent over she can't. She turns in circles, the cat flat on her hump.

'Off! Damn it. Noodles!'

The cat starts kneading her lumpy back, purring. It's actually making bird noises, like the chirruping the nightjars make in our back field in August. Reggie tries twisting from side to side, as the cat stares at me with two big orange eyes. It's the biggest cat I've ever seen.

Reggie walks round the big library table, crying, 'Off! Off! Off!' but Noodles keeps purring. Reggie's tiring out.

'Can I help, Reg?'

'Please,' she gasps, and stands still.

Unfortunately, I don't know how. I can't lift the animal, it's almost as big as me. 'Er, Noodles, come on,' I tell it.

It just stares, making that funny sound.

'Come on cat, or I'll set Bosum on you.'

Reggie's whimpering.

One of her sticks is in the corner (she's got as many as Grandpa). It's a black one with a tiger tooth in amber on the top, and she calls it her talisman. I pick it up and poke the cat with the rubber end, and it plays with it like a rat's tail or a feather. Then suddenly, it leaps off Reggie, yowling. I turn and see a gingery farm cat hissing behind the library door. Noodles thunders down the stairs after our mongrel moggie, and I wonder if he'll sit on it too.

'Chair.'

'You okay? Reggie?'

'Chair.'

I pull a peeling leather thing out; there are scratch marks down it and the stuffing's hanging out.

'Oh. That. Noodles.'

'He's enormous.'

'Maine Coon.'

'Sorry?'

'Breed. Crossed the Atlantic. Caught rats in ships. During Slave Trade. Handy beggars. Huge. Likes small spaces.'

I don't quite see how Reggie's back is a small space, and I wonder if, in her flat in Aberystwyth, she's stuck like that for days; just standing there with a buggering big cat on her back. I wonder if she has to go out on the street and ask a passer-by for help.

'Kettle on. There.' Reggie points to the end of the library table. She's got everything here; teabags, milk, biccies. Even half a Victoria Sponge.

'Now. Katherine.'

'Yes.'

She taps a pile of books and letters in front of her. Her watery, green eyes sparkle, but not prettily. She brushes her white fringe away and applies some very metallic pearl lipstick.

'Now. Kate. Family. Family. All here.'

For a moment I panic that she's found Mathilda's letters, or maybe she's broken into Eva's Sanctuary. I wouldn't put that past my auntie Reg. Then I realise; anything to do with Gran isn't family at all. She's not a Happy, *by blood*.

'All here. This is *it*.' She taps the leathery books again, then the pile of crusty papers. Another of her cats (normal size) twirls round her skinny, polio legs.

'This. The project. The book.'

'Great.'

'All here.'

'Lovely.'

'All.'

She's bonkers, my aunt. Her lined face is flushed and her long, dirty nails touch the spines of each book.

'This. Your history. Kate. You *are* a Happy.'

'Well, a bit of –'

'All! All!'

She picks up a big volume and reads from it. It's all 'The

Honourable Happy did this, blah blah, did that, blah blah,' and I
wonder if it mentions Grandpa sinking his ships, and Mum running over my dad. I look round the library. I'd forgotten it was so
big, the shelves of books locked up behind iron grilles, like
they're precious. Maybe it's just so the cats don't pee on them.
There's a layer of dust everywhere, thick as gravy. Reggie fits in
up here.

'Family Tree. Think of the great Wilhomena. Samuel. And further
back. Ethelred The Unready. Edward The Confessor. Henry. Damned
Norman conquests. Nothing to do with us. Paying attention?'

'Yeah.'

'Yes. Say "yes". It's all here. For you. I am doing this for you.' She
gets up, very slowly, and circles the room. 'To save you. From that
damned. Yankee business.'

The kettle boils and I make tea. I want to say, 'Shut up you old
cow,' but instead I watch Reggie suck the red middles out of a plate
of Jammie Dodgers. She puts the soggy biscuit bits back, and my
skin prickles like it did in The Natural History Museum.

I suddenly know I don't want to be saved from the Yankee business, because it's the only thing I like.

'Are Samuel and Wilhomena here?' I ask her.

'Sometimes. Don't like my cats. I channel you know. Spirit
guide's a Masai Warrior. Glorious fellow. Samuel and Wilhomena
tell me all. Family matters.'

I wonder if they tell her about the Happy Home and their
locked-in-a-cupboard-mongey-son, Little Boy. Personally, I'd rather
hear about gefilte fish and sturgeons' eggs and the Atlantic lapping.
I nibble a corner of a Rich Tea biscuit.

It was Reggie who turned me off sewing. I made my own rag
dolls and I was good at it, then she came to stay and barked, 'Jewing
are we, Kate?' and took my needle and thread away.

'Katie? You up there, honey?'

'Gran!' I drop my Rich Tea on the floor and scarper.

'Katherine Happy!' Reggie shouts. 'Back here. Work to do. Family work!'

I jump down the three flights of stairs as quickly as Reggie scuttled up them. 'Gra-an!'

She's in the hall with a funny little man in thick glasses. He looks as bug-like as Reggie.

'This is your Uncle Zev, honey. Rita's in the car. She's tired, can you help us get her in? Is your friend here? Heathcliff?'

'Grandpa fired Brian, remember?'

'Oh, right.' Gran looks very tired.

'Hello, Uncle Zev,' I say to the bug man. He's bald but too weedy to be Mr Barlow.

'Sholem aleykhem, Katie.'

Gran looks at him like he's just said a bad word.

'Rita's told me plenty bout you,' he smiles and his teeth are so white they look false.

'D'you think you could find Heathcliff? Get him to come help?' asks Gran.

'What's the matter?'

'Oh nothing, honey. Just we need all the hands we can get. Where's Millie?'

'She went home.'

'Oh.' She points upstairs. 'That who I think it is?'

'Yes.'

'Who goddamned invited *her*?'

I shrug.

'Oh, I don't have to ask. Your mother I suppose. Thinks this is all some kinda joke. She'll soon see. There ain't nothing to laugh about here.' She takes Zev's hand. 'Life goes on, Katie, and we all suffer, remember that. Oh, and honey? Call Dr Croften. We need him.'

For A Little Angel, Gone but Fair
The Lord Hath Taken Thee to Share.
Eva Regina Mathilda Poppy Happy
July 28th 1944 – August 16th 1954
Taken From Us Too Soon.
She has Gone to Sleep in Jesus.

18

'You all right in there, Mrs?' Brian says.

Rita nods, eyes sleepy. I'm sitting in the driver's seat holding her squidgy hand while Brian is the other side, trying to get her out and into her wheelchair.

Gran's geese circle her car like Apaches, pecking at the paintwork.

There's much more of Rita than before, she can hardly fit in Gran's Peugeot. She isn't exactly fatter, she's looser, and she pours over the seats. Rita doesn't have a stick now, just a wheelchair, and she hasn't bothered strapping on her leg. It's in the boot; the red toenails chipped.

Dr Croften has given her some injections and now he's talking quietly to Gran, who's crying.

'Oh, my,' says Rita. 'So much trouble. I shouldn't be so much trouble, and look at you, little Katie. So cute!'

'Thanks Auntie. It really is lovely to see you again.'

'Sweetcakes.'

This is about the fiftieth time I've told her it's lovely to see her again, as I don't know what else to say. She keeps going to sleep and talking nonsense about pickles.

'Get the pickles from the barrel, Iry!' she was yelling when we first came out into the yard. 'Got more customers! More pickles, honey!'

We covered her in blankets, and then Dr Croften gave her some medicine. He said she was having a diabetic fit, and could die right here, and that it was a crime the air company let her fly. Both Gran and Zev started wailing then, and Zev cried, 'I couldn't stop her! Couldn't stop her!'

The doctor had to give him something, too, and now he's asleep in Gran's locked lounge.

Mum and Francis drove off when the doctor came, and Reggie and Grandpa are buried somewhere inside the farmhouse.

Brian's being great though.

'Come on then Mrs, one more go eh?' He pulls Rita's big arm, his foot up on the Peugeot for extra strength, and I push from the passenger seat.

'It ain't no use, sweetcakes.' Rita looks more alert.

'You've got to, Auntie,' I try. 'You really have got to.'

'I just —'

'Go on, please. Everyone is getting so upset. Then we can have a nice Christmas.'

Rita looks me in the eye, and smiles. 'You've grown up, haven't you, Katie?'

'I suppose.'

'Ain't no supposing about it. Come on then, let's get to work.' And Rita starts to sway from side to side, a bit like one of those big, strong walruses David Attenborough puts on the telly. 'C'mon little man, pull!'

And Brian does.

'Oh!' says Rita.

'You can do it, Mrs.'

'Oh!'

And like a cork, she's out. I notice her one foot is so tight in her shoe, it looks like rising dough. She wobbles for a moment, upright on one leg, then Brian pushes the wheelchair under her, and she plonks! into the seat. Rita's as white as one of Gran's geese now.

'There Mrs Bloomfield. Breathe.' Dr Croften's attached a little tank of oxygen to the back of the wheelchair, and he puts a mask on Rita's face.

'I ain't –' she pulls it off, 'a Bloomfield no more, I told you, it's Ichmann. Rita Ichmann, and proud.'

'Yes, quite. Now I think it best we call an ambulance, get you to hospital.'

'You just got me outta that thing and you wanna get me back in? No goddamn way. It's been a day I been travelling, getting to see my goddamn sister and if I die here right now that's the way I wanna go –'

'Yes, I'm sorry, Mrs Ichmann, if you could just calm down.'

'Calm down you say!'

'Reet, Reet honey, don't upset yourself, please,' Gran tries. 'Let's get you inside, huh? Isn't that right, doctor?' She smiles and takes the handles of the wheelchair; she tries to push her sister across the yard, but Rita's too heavy. Brian and the doctor help, and somehow they slide her through the muck and get her into the garage.

'This place ain't changed much,' Rita barks and her oxygen mask clouds. 'See you ain't tidied up then, Iry.'

Gran gives a nervous laugh. I notice she's not wearing pink; it's a dark purple.

Brian frowns, 'How we going to get her up them steps?'

'Where there's a will there's a way,' says Grandpa. He's standing on the top step, the kitchen door and his dressing gown open.

'Larry honey, get inside, you'll catch your death,' Gran tells him, then hisses, 'and make yourself decent.'

He ties his dressing gown belt, unfazed. 'Hello, Rita.'

'Hi there, Larry.'

'You haven't changed.'

She laughs. 'Oh yeah? Well, neither have you.'

They both smile.

It's weird Grandpa being nice to Rita and I wish Mum was here to see it.

'Right,' he says. 'Brian, you're the strongest, so take the top part. Doctor, you take the legs. Or, um, leg.'

'I ain't a piece of meat, Larry.'

'Well, well.'

Brian grips her under the arms and Rita counts with him, 'One, two, three. Ah!' she cries as she's moved. Gran pulls the empty wheelchair up to the kitchen first, and I run in underneath for the rest of my aunt.

But it's not funny anymore. Rita's making all the right noises, all the 'ohs!' and 'ahs!' as we struggle up the steps; I can even imagine her yelling 'My leg is popping out!' if she'd bothered to strap it on.

The thing is Rita looks scared. She stiffens what she can, and as we reach the kitchen threshold, she just breathes out when we lower her back into her wheelchair.

'There, you okay, honey?' says Gran.

Sweat runs down Rita's face, Gran wipes it off, and Dr Croften wheels her out. It takes a while to manoeuvre her, as the wheelchair almost doesn't fit; our doorframes are too small.

'I shoulda thought of that,' Gran says, tearful. Grandpa takes her hand, and they follow the doctor into a dark corridor.

'That your auntie then?' says Brian.

I give him a funny look. 'What do you think?'

'She's a big un.'

'Shut up, Brian.'

'Hey, I got your Christmas present, and your card, Kate. You'll like em, really you will.'

I'd forgotten it was nearly Christmas.

Brian kisses me full on the lips. 'Look, got to go, helping my dad now. We're selling Christmas trees. Getting them from the forest tonight, but don't tell your grandad.'

'I won't.'

'Hey, Joanne and Trish never did come back. Dad hit the roof, found out they weren't with our nan.'

'Oh.'

'I know. Fucking great, eh?'

He kisses me again and jumps down the garage steps. I stare back into the darkness that's just swallowed my aunt.

The Universal Home Guide

ETIQUETTE

1 CONVERSATION

NEW novels and sports are excellent topics. Never start by talking about yourself, your ailments or family history. Avoid saying unpleasant things about people who are not present. Religion is a subject that should never be discussed in good society. It is a matter on which some people find it extremely difficult to restrain their fervour when contrary opinions are expressed.

19

Rita and Reggie have been here a week and the sugar-free jellies never set. It's Christmas morning.

Auntie Rita doesn't talk much, just, 'Hiya, sweetcakes' and, 'So cold, going for a nap,' when she's already in bed. The wheelchair is folded up like a card table in her downstairs bedroom where the portable heater is permanently on. I sit with her every afternoon, and sweat. Millie sits with her too. Gran told me Rita is very ill and she has to go to the hospital a lot to get her kidneys cleaned, then I heard Mum say Rita's here to die and it's a pain in the arse.

Gran has spent the past week slaughtering geese for the neighbours and looking after Rita. She'll sit with me in Rita's bedroom with smears of blood and goose-down on her hands. That's probably where Gran is now; in the shed with her knife.

I'm alone in her bed. Reggie banged tins for the cats on the third floor hours ago (that's how she feeds them, she opens five tins, bangs them and pours it on the floor; the house stinks of cat piss *and* rotten Whiskas now).

I can hear noises from downstairs.

'Oh! Su–perb!' my mother cries.

'Lene!' says Grandpa.

'Lovely goose!' says Reggie.

I listen out for Gran, Rita and Zev, but hear nothing.

There's a full and lumpy pillowcase hanging from the bedpost.

I unhook it and empty the contents on Gran's pink satin duvet. This is my Christmas stocking, and Gran does it every year, except she's usually here to open it with me.

I look down at the bed. There's:

1) Oranges (Gran says they remind her of the war, which I think is odd).
2) A white rabbit's foot, which must be from Millie.
3) The *Beano* Annual 1981.
4) Two books and a polka-dot dress from Mum. One book is called *How to Care For Your Birds* (yeah, funny, Mum) and the other is *The Virgin and the Gypsy* (she's written 'if you really must' inside). The dress has a Biba label, it's one of her old ones.
5) A small bar of soap that says 'The Three Breezes, Torquay' from Reggie.
6) A book from Zev called *Got Questions? All You Want to Know About Moses, Aaron and Miriam For Ages 7–9*.
7) More *Spiderman* comics from Rita, and a colour programme called *The Famous Coney Island sideshow, 1969*. There's a dedication inside.

> *To darling Rita, The softest girl this side of the Union Line, love from your slap-happy boy, Jeremiah Seal-o.*

8) And at the very bottom of the pillowcase are two Christmas cards, one from Jamilah that just says 'Happy Xmas' and another with writing I don't recognise. I open it.

> Dear Kate,
> Wishing you lots of fun this Christmas and this is my address if you ever need to talk or anything.
> Lots of love Jeremy and Harry

I lie back on Gran's pillow and think of his ice-blue eyes. I can't remember where I put that purple stone.

'Come downstairs, darling, we're having champagne.' Mum's waltzed into Gran's bedroom. She's holding a glass of pink bubbles and looks pissed already.

'Get a move on sleepy head, Francis is here, isn't that lovely? Blew his own family out, spending the day with us, and he brought a case of *this*. You should have some. Put something nice on too, none of your tomboy rubbish, or that ghastly red uniform.' She grabs my hand and tries to pull me out of bed.

'All right Mum, calm down.'

'I–just–want–to–have–fun, so let's do it!' She twirls on the spot. She's wearing a bright, embroidered shawl and it drags on the floor.

'Francis bought me this. Isn't it divine? Spanish.'

Mum's voice is changing, she's trying to sound really posh. She stops twirling and stares at Gran's photo display of the dead Happy girls, then she drains her glass and walks out.

'Come along now, Kate, I want a proper daughter this Christmas!' she yells from the hall.

At least it's not freezing downstairs. Still, I've put a cardie over the thin, polka dot Biba dress, and rolled up the sleeves it's so big. I pass Rita's door, but don't knock; I'll let her sleep and find Gran first.

In the kitchen Aunt Reggie is stuffing a goose up the bum, but there's no Gran. Reggie's got one of Mum's tie-dyed kaftans on and she's puce with champagne; the drink is making her speak in proper sentences, though.

'My dear brother loves his goose. I expect your grandmama never learned to cook it, Katherine?'

'She's been killing them all week.'

'Not the same, dear Kate, not the same at all.'

'Well, she does know how to cook a goose, so there.'

'Not the Happy way.'

I don't bother to argue. Francis is pressing Mum against the Aga, as Bosum 8 and Jessie 13 run in. They pee in the same spot, up against the sink, and growl at Francis. Whenever she visits Reggie sets the dogs free, and they chase the cats, and crap all over the house.

'Where's Gran?' I ask.

'Bloody thing!' Grandpa barks. He's in his pantry, the door open, and he's trying to tune in a new radio.

'Darling, help my father, will you?' Mum untangles herself from Francis who goes in and kneels by Grandpa. I've decided Francis looks like a big baby rather than a toad.

'It's a Roberts Radio,' says Mum, 'top of the range, thought it was about time my father had something new.'

'Not that it bloody works, Lene,' Grandpa mumbles and Mum looks hurt.

'Where's Gran?'

'Do you have to wear that bloody woollen thing over the nice new dress I gave you, Kate?'

'It's not new.'

'There, my poor boys. My poor little loves,' Reggie murmurs and throws Bosum and Jessie a gooseneck. Reggie once told me her ambition is to open a donkey and dog home here at Happy Farm, called 'The Happy Hunting Ground'. Gran said over her dead body.

Reggie told me that when she went to Spain in 1975, she stopped a man whipping a donkey by whipping him instead, and she was put in prison for a month. She doesn't mind *eating* animals, though.

Or stuffing them.

'Where's Gran?' I ask again.

'Kate, this is for you.' Mum pulls out the biggest envelope I've ever seen from behind the fridge; it's up to her waist and has 'Kate' printed shakily on the front. 'Well? Open it.'

'Who's it from? You?'

'That common ghastly thing! I don't think so.'

I stare at it.

'Oh, for godsake, child, if you're not going to open it, I will, we want to know who it's from,' and she cuts through the top with a goose-greasy knife.

'Mum!'

She pulls out the big card. I blush and grab the thing. It's as big as me and there's a cartoon puppy on the front with its tongue hanging out.

'Oh look, Francis,' Mum cries, 'above that grotesque dog it says "From a Secret Admirer, Happy Christmas." Well, who's a little heart-breaker then, Kate. Taking after your mother, eh? Who is it from?'

Inside there's just a big

?

'Gosh, a mystery. Lucky you.' Mum looks jealous. 'Or maybe, Kate, the person who sent this can't write. Hope it's not from that awful boy.'

'Mum, where's Gran?'

'Off to the Infidels!' Reggie barks and gives the goose an extra big shove up the arse.

'Actually, they've gone to Cardiff,' Mum tells me.

'Though they did say they'd be back this evening,' Francis adds.

'But it's Christmas.'

'Don't mean a thing to them!' Reggie barks again, just like Grandpa.

'Yes it does, it's Rita's birthday.'

'Well, that's the thing, darling,' Mum pipes in, 'she wanted to go to a bloody synagogue. On Christmas Day I ask you! So Mother had to phone round. I think Rita was having a diabetic fit or some-thing. A derelict fit more like. Good god, she caused a scene. Never laid eyes on anything like it.'

'So they went?' I hide behind my enormous card.

'They left you that.' Mum points at a letter by the scraps bin. I snatch it from the potato peelings as Reggie threads a big needle and sews the goose's arse up.

'Well, what does it say?' Mum asks.

'None of your business.' I hop over the dog pee, walk down into the garage, and sit amongst the buckets of rags and bleach.

Dear Katie,

Sorry honey, Rita is a little agitated this morning so we're off to find spiritual succor I think (or ice-cream – unsure). She's not well at all. V. worried. Just need to get out of this goddamned Happy House. Too cold, right?

Chin up as your grandpa says. We'll be back before dark and we're taking you out tomorrow. Your mother wanted you for today. Hope you like my present. It's under the bed. We'll get you more presents in Cardiff.

Rita and Zev send hugs and love to my little girl,

Iris (Gran)

I listen to the hubbub from the kitchen.

'Larry! Top and tail my lad, top and tail, don't massacre them!'

'She always was the boss, my sister.'

'Oh, Aunt Reggie, you're a breath of fresh air. More champagne, Francis!'

I slip into my yellow wellies and walk out into the wet yard. Gran's car tracks aren't even in the slush. There's no trace of her at all. I do up my cardie.

'I bin waiting for you. Happy Christmas.' It's Brian, and he jumps off our stone wall.

'Thanks for the card.'

He smiles but doesn't say anything. Then he takes my hand, walks me round the house, and up the backyard to the hay barn. We sit down on a damp bale.

'Bludy freezing. I've bin waiting ages.'

'I haven't got you a card.'

'Dunt matter.'

I remember the Starsky and Hutch car. 'There's something inside though.'

'Here, Kate.' He hands me a rolled up bit of newspaper, and I hope it's not another penknife. I unwrap it and there's a pretty silver bracelet.

'Gosh. Thanks Brian.'

'I'll put it on.' He kisses me; no tongues, and slips it on my wrist. 'Where's your gran gone?'

'Cardiff.'

'Saw them go off.' He kisses my hair.

'Why do you like me, Brian?'

'What d'you mean?'

'Do you want to come for Christmas lunch?'

'Dunt think your mam'ud like that.'

'Sod her.'

He smiles and blows into his red hands as Bosum 8 and Jessie 13 run round the corner and into the cow field. It doesn't feel Christmasy at all; not without my gran.

I put the Menora in the middle of the table as the telephone rings.

'Kate,' Reggie shouts from the hall, 'your grandmother.' I leave Brian to lay up.

'Gran?'

'Hey, honey. Happy Christmas.'

'Are you on your way home?'

She breathes heavily.

'You're not coming back, are you? Oh Gra-an.'

'Don't be a baby, Kate. You're a grown-up now and I got a lot on my plate. But I love you and we'll be back tomorrow. Okay?'

'But it's Christmas.'

'Have you opened my present?'

'Not yet.'

'It's under the bed.'

'Yeah.'

'Don't sulk, Kate. Give me a break, huh?'

'All right.' I look out of the window, it's raining and I think of Mrs Crabtree and the Big C. 'Say Happy Christmas and Happy Birthday to Rita, Gran.'

'Sure.'

'When will you be back?'

'Tomorrow.'

'You're gone all night?'

'No whining, honey. Rita's not her best and we've booked into a Ramada. What's the big deal anyway? You got your mom.'

'Yeah, well, she can go to hell.'

'You don't mean that.'

'Look, bye Gran. I've got to help Brian —'

'Hi, sweetcakes.'

'Oh, hello Rita.'

'How you doing?'

'Okay.'

'Well, I'm pretty awful, thanks for asking. They gotta mini-bar here, though.'

'Mmm.'

'Look, don't blame your grandma, huh?'

'Okay. Happy Birthday.'

'Don't be sore, sweetcakes.'

'Look, I've got to go.'

'We love you.'

'Yeah, okay.'

'Bye, sweetcakes.'

'Bye.'

I put the phone down and listen to the tick-tock of the grandfather clock, Rita's croak of a voice still ringing in my ear.

I miss the pump of her oxygen.

The cackling laugh she still manages.

I go back to the dining room.

'These here candles won't fit,' says Brian. He's trying to force one into a thin arm of the Menora.

'But they have to, Brian.'

'Hey, dunt fret.'

Stupid big, English candles.

I go to the sideboard and pick up the bone-handle carving knife. 'Give them here.'

'You'll do yourself a damage.'

'No I won't. Are you going to help me?'

We stand over the family brass and shave down the ends of the candles until they're narrow enough.

Some are a bit wobbly in their holders; some are shorter than others where the carving knife worked too well, but the Menora looks pretty, lit at the centre of the laid table. I'm sure you're meant to say something holy over it so I try the Lord's Prayer.

'Our Father Who Art in Heaven. Hallowed —'

Brian stares at me.

'What the hell is that?' Reggie squeals as she walks in; she's twisted her head up, a gravy boat in her hand.

'That's Mrs Happy's candlestick,' says Brian.

'Well, get it off the table, boy. Now.'

'No,' I tell her.

'Well!'

'It's staying, Reggie, and you can like it or lump it.'

'Well!'

'It's Gran's!' I walk out to the kitchen and grab the peas. Grandpa's still fiddling with his radio and Mum and Francis are snogging amongst the wellies down in the garage.

'Well, I've never heard the like!' Reggie yells from the dining room.

This is going to be the worst Christmas, ever.

The goose is bones and Bosum's making his way through the untouched turkey. Reggie put the whole bird under the table for him; he's biting and growling and he'll be shitting up a storm later.

Jessie's tied up outside because he killed one of our farm cats.

It's actually warm in the dining room now. Francis is snoring in a torn leather armchair, Mum on his lap, her hands beneath her bum and on his crotch.

The thinned candles in Gran's Menora have burnt down and wax has dripped on the table.

'The thing with Ceylon,' says Reggie, 'is tea and young boys. Marvellous!'

Our Christmas lunch has been a voyage through Reggie's life: her childhood in India; a marriage in Kenya where she opened a safari lodge and met the Queen, and a divorce in Macau where she had clam and pork suppers with travelling fascists.

Now we're on Ceylon and she's missed out Aberystwyth.

'Actually, it's Sri Lanka,' says Francis, suddenly awake.

Brian's still at the table, holding his fork in a fist and eating with his mouth open.

'No matter. Manservant there. Faithful fellow. Head bitten off by a hyena.'

I don't think they have hyenas in Sri Lanka. Aunt Reggie on champagne is worse than Grandpa on sloe gin.

'And the Governor came. Official business. I strung a battered and skinned cat across his windshield. A protest. Terrible treatment of cats in Colombo. "Who did this?" The Governor asked. "My wife, Sir," said husband. "A strong woman! A powerful woman!" Governor replied. He knew the measure of me. Small man though. Mountbatten far more handsome.'

Bosum is throwing up under the table and Reggie homes in on me. I try and think of something else; like Jamilah.

'I was the English woman in Kenya to fight those rebels. Took things into my own hands —'

I wonder what Jam got for Christmas and if she's enjoying her turkey-Halal lunch.

'Little boy. Size of you. Fell for me. Sweet child. Only white woman he'd ever seen —'

I've been to Reggie's bedsit. She's got a little mattress and a map of the world on the wall. Her cupboards are filled with tinned peaches, cat food and Carnation milk. Grandpa has to give her money every month.

Gran says we should put Reggie in a glass cage and study her as a Fossil of England. I want to stuff her and stick her in the Unnatural History Museum.

'Once. I was a film star, you know. A poster girl for Franco's men —'

Her white hair's coming loose from her big plaits, and I wonder how old Reggie and Grandpa actually are. I've never dared ask, in case they blow away like powdery mummies as the numbers pass their lips.

'Had all manner of men after me —'

Suddenly Reggie reminds me of my mother. I don't want to ever end up like Reggie.

'What do you think? Boy? Can you see it?'

She's parading in front of Brian, head to one side, kicking her legs up (which isn't far) in a goose-step. Brian looks up, his mouth full of gravy and potato. I slip out of the room, and up the stairs.

'Some enchanted evening,' Reggie's singing below. 'Come boy, dance with me!'

It's freezing in Gran's room, and I crawl under her bed to find my present. It's huge and I tear off the wrapping.

It's a pink, leather photograph album and Gran's written this inside:

> For my honey, Katie Ichmann,
> For a new leaf and a new life,
> And turning it over.
> Love Gran.

I think I'll sleep under her springs tonight.

TELEGRAM TO MRS IRIS HAPPY THE HAPPY FARM BOLDENHAM
HEREFORDSHIRE ENGLAND
IO/5/I955

BROOKLYN DODGERS KINGS OF 55 WORLD SERIES STOP CRUSHED
YANKEES STOP HAD TO SEND THIS SO EXCITED ZEV TOO STOP
CALL YOU WHEN GET HOME STOP SAW DOC SAYS I GOT SUGAR
PROBLEMS BLAH BLAH BLAH
RITA
ZEV SAID I GOTTA PAY FOR THE BLAH BLAH BLAH AND WHAT A
WASTE SO AM PUTTING A GODDAMN PS

20

*I*t's New Year's Eve and the cows' breasts are tight as bubbles; blue veins mark them like Stan Ruck's tattoos.

I'm waiting in the back field for my mother. She wants to go for a walk and my mother doesn't walk. We haven't gone for a walk together since 1976.

A pylon buzzes above me.

Rita, Zev and Gran aren't back. Rita called me to say she wanted to spend a little longer at the Ramada with the mini-bar. She said if she dies she wants the contents of this mini-bar thrown on top of her, 'Like a goddarned Viking, sweetcakes.'

She also said she spoke to a Rabbi who made her feel better, so they're coming home tonight.

My nose is running and I feel like hugging a cow udder for warmth, but it's good to get out of the house because the dogs crapped so much over the holidays, it stinks. What with that, the cat pee, and the Whiskas, Grandpa had to get Millie in to help. Double time of course. Reggie slept through all the cleaning. 'Not well,' she said. 'Unable to assist. Apologies.'

Millie fumigated the ground floor with Jeyes Fluid, and Bosum 8 is tied up with Jessie 13, and all the other stuffed Jessies, in the shed.

The last time Mum wanted to go for a walk she took me to Regent's Park and told me we were leaving Dad for good.

I jump on the frozen ground as Grandpa's new bull calls from the barn. He got it for Christmas, from himself. Grandpa keeps this one inside, and it pushes its big, ringed snout above the open top of the stable door. The snout looks like a baby's bum.

Mum is walking across the yard in heels. She's got smarter since Francis appeared, and she doesn't swear so much. Smoke still follows her though, and so do Bosum and Jessie, as she's let them out of the shed. Every few paces, Bosum crouches for a crap; he's still got the runs.

'Darling!' she shouts and skids in her heels.

I wave and wait.

'Darling. There you are!'

I watch her stumble over the stile as Jessie barks at the cows. They ignore him; their boobs too tight to run. Bosum crouches again, but nothing comes out.

We start walking, Mum unsteady in her stupid shoes.

'What is it then?' I ask.

'Sorry?'

'You hate walking. What is it?'

She stops. 'God, you're so suspicious. I just wanted to spend some time with you. That's all.'

My chin's numb and Jessie's licking a frozen puddle.

'Poor bloody cows. Look at them,' Mum says.

'They'll be milked today, I expect.'

She stares at the herd. 'But they'll be in the same boat tomorrow. God, what a life. Churning milk in your breast. I remember that feeling with you –'

'Mum. Please.'

'Well, it's natural.'

'It's disgusting and anyway Gran said a Norland Nanny bottle-fed me while you went to the South of France.'

'I dried up. What do you expect?'

'Mum!'

'Bet these poor bitches wish they could dry up.'

A cow munches, jaw loose, her pink nose stained green.

'I doubt it, Mum, because then Stan would slaughter them.'

'Kate, do you have to use such, well, farmerish words.'

I climb over a gate. 'What do you want, Mum?'

'Hold on —' She's struggling over the bars, so I stand on a hard molehill. The dogs shoot past. Mum finally stumbles towards me.

'It's just, well, Francis and I. We're getting quite serious now.'

'Oh, please.'

'That's just the way I operate, Kate. All or nothing.'

'And?'

'Don't be like that. I want you to like him.'

'He doesn't bother me. You've had worse.'

'Well, your father wasn't a prize.'

'That's not who I'm talking about.' I jump off the molehill and kick a clump of white-frosted nettles. I'm talking about The Australian; The American; The Bloody Richman, Poorman, Beggarman, Thief. I'm talking about Antique Andy; The Waiter; The Ski-instructor; The Candlestick Maker.

'Look, he's asked me to move in with him. What do you think?'

'I don't care.'

'Don't be like that. We're off on holiday.'

'That's nice.'

'Yes, but we're leaving this evening. For New Year. We're skiing. He has friends in Gstaad.'

'Can't wait, Mum.' I know there isn't a ticket for me but I feel like winding her up anyway. I try and look upset. 'But hold on, I thought you came back to spend the New Year with me, that's what you told me on my birthday.'

'Did I?'

'Yes.'

'God, you do remember everything, don't you?'

'That's what children are for.' I smile and chase the dogs, and she has to shout after me.

'You've always been bright, Kate! Far cleverer than me! Your father was clever too! That was his downfall, too much brain!'

She looks small up by the gate, so I run back to her and wipe my nose. 'Did you love him, Mum?'

I watch her smoky breath in the cold.

'Who?'

'Dad.'

'Oh, not that old chestnut.' She throws her stub away, and takes out a green Sobranie. 'Of course I loved the bastard.'

I jump on the spot and realise my feet are tight in my wellies; they even hurt. I look down and the sleeves of my mac are just a little short. 'Can I have a fag, Mum?'

She looks at me. 'Only if you inhale. Properly.'

I choose a pink one and she lights it. It tastes disgusting, not like Brian's mostly-paper roll-ups. I cough and Mum laughs.

'It takes practice, Kate. Lots and lots of practice.'

'Do you miss him?' I ask her, taking a pink drag.

'Yes.'

'The night he died, Mum. Why did you come back?'

She looks shocked for a moment, and breathes funny like it's a blow to the chest. 'To tell you the truth, I thought he was going to kidnap you.'

'Dad?'

'Yes. He was very possessive, Kate, and he loved you. He really did. When he arrived out of the blue that night, your grandmother called me, straight away, and I drove down from London because I thought he was going to ride off with you into the sunset. And then it all went, well, horribly wrong.' She shakes herself like a dog getting rid of water. 'I wouldn't have minded if that was what you wanted, to live with your father, but –'

'But what?'

'Your dad. He wasn't stable, darling. Always threatening to top himself. I thought he'd hurt you. He was slightly bonkers, you know.'

'I don't remember him like that. He was never like that.'

Mum takes a long drag. 'Well, that's kids for you. They remember the best.'

I throw the pink Sobranie away. 'I can remember everything with *you*.'

Two crows are fighting a buzzard in the sky, cawing like a gargle of TCP. Mum watches them, and starts to say something, but she can't. I know she's crying, but just as quick she laughs, because Bosum's crouching in front of us, dragging his arse on the cold ground, straining; and all that's coming out is wind.

Aunt Rita is back in her boiling room, intact, and I'm sitting with her. She arrived after lunch, when Mum and Francis had left. I've watched *Digby the Biggest Dog in the World*, read *The Virgin and the Gypsy*, and Rita's gone back to sleep. It'll be the Big Ben bongs on the telly soon.

Gran, Grandpa and Reggie are asleep.

Rita's oxygen mask mists over. She has a machine that goes bleep now. The oxygen sounds like gas and her false leg is propped up in the corner; I've repainted the toenails, in her favourite red.

'Hey, sweetcakes.'

'Hello, Auntie.'

She takes off the mask, but doesn't sit up. 'How long have I been out?'

'Ages.'

'Is it the New Year?'

'Nope.'

'Good, ain't missed out. Where's the champagne?'

'I have some Lucozade and you've got sugar-free blackcurrant juice.'

'Wow, golly, woop-de-doo,' she does a sarcastic face. 'Everyone else asleep?'

'Yes.'

'Can't take the pace, huh?'

'I suppose.'

I pour out some saccharine cordial and help Rita to sit up. It's hard, bits of her slip through my fingers. This close she smells of pear drops. I like being in here with her though, it's peaceful.

'Well, Katie, it ain't as nice as the Ramada, that's for damn sure.'

'I missed you.'

She smoothes down her bedcover, hands puffed. 'You know what?'

'What?'

'After I go, you and Iris'll be the only Ichmanns left.'

'Am I an Ichmann?'

'Look at you, sure you are. A Lieberman too, you got my momma's eyes. Only Jew on our block with those blue eyes.'

'But I've got brown bits in the middle.'

'Just like Momma.'

'My mum's got them, so isn't she an Ichmann-Lieberman too?'

Rita ignores this. We watch the mute telly; it's a Clint Eastwood film and he's being washed by lots of women.

'You know, Katie? Me and Lula never could have children. That's why I flew all the way over here. Needed blood family, it's not the most important thing for nothing, right?'

'I suppose.'

Sometimes talking to Rita is like talking to Reggie.

'How long's Uncle Zev staying?' I ask. Zev gives Rita her injections because she can't reach herself any more. Rita says she's now as big as Fatima, The Biggest Girl at that Coney Island sideshow. 'Holy smoke she was fat, sweetcakes, she was awful fat. Took seven men to hug her. Made good money though, and she sure was a heartbreaker. A darned marriage wrecker, too.'

I don't want to inject Rita if Zev goes.

'Oh, he ain't staying long, Katie. Annoys me. We've been divorced twelve years and I never could shake him. You know he lives above me at home? Had the builders come in and make apartments, and who's my first rentor? Zev Bloomfield, that's who.' She laughs and wobbles and doesn't look annoyed at all. 'But you know, we had our time. That's for sure. He's a small man, but capable. Real capable. It's the quiet ones, ain't it, sweetcakes? You should find yourself a quiet one, a small guy just like that.'

I try and smile, but feel a bit sick.

'And boy he could do the craziest stuff. When the war was done, you know where we got hitched? You'll never believe this of your old auntie, sweetcakes, but we got hitched at the top of The Parachute Jump!' she gasps. 'You'd sit in a little swing and get lifted all the way up, and just hang there from the cables, ready to fall. Boy oh boy, what a view! You could see Manhattan!' Rita stares up at the farm ceiling like she can see the sky. She breathes deep. 'So, he had me up there in the wedding dress, and him in his top hat and tails, and the orchestra with clarinets and oboes. And the gal on the clarinet was sure a screamer, she yelled her lungs out! Oh, the crowds we got, you had to be there to believe them.' She coughs and I wish she'd speak slower. 'The Rabbi was with us too, he was a swell guy. It was a quick wham bam, no long ceremony, you got to be sure of that. The orchestra played, we said our stuff, then bang! down we went.' Her arms reach up, flesh swaying. 'We dropped from the tower on those metal cables all that way, until our little parachutes opened. And when we got to the bottom, we were man and wife. Zev said it was harder than jumping from a plane into enemy lines! I remember my darned dress flared, showed the world everything, Zev's hat went and we laughed all the way. Yeah, Zev Bloomfield had his day all right.'

I smile but don't know whether to believe her. I suppose it doesn't matter. She looks exhausted.

'And we all went to Child's Restaurant after. Gorgeous it was. Course your grandma wasn't there. She was here in cold, old England. That kinda spoilt my day.' Rita sighs, her loose bosom heaving. 'But anyways, Zev's gotta leave so I can put all you guys right.'

'What do you mean?'

Rita takes a gulp of air.

'Oh come on, honey. You're wrong, all of you, and someone's got to do something.'

I suppose she's got a point. 'How are you going to do it, Rita?'

'I'll figure it out,' she taps her nose with a fleshy hand. 'Hey, had any adventures while I've been gone?'

'Not really.'

'Hear you gotta boyfriend.'

'Not really. Rita?'

'Yes, sweetcakes?'

'My dad, did Gran ever say he was ill?'

'Sorry, honey?'

'I mean in the head. Mum told me he was bonkers. And it said in the newspaper, when he died.'

'Don't go over the old stuff, honey, there's so much new.'

'I know Grandpa can be bonkers, and Mum too. But I don't remember Dad being off his trolley.'

'Well, you just leave it like that. It's better that way, ain't it?'

I can't argue with that.

'So, Katie, last day of the year huh? How long we got?'

'It's just gone half past eleven.'

'D'you think I'll make it?'

'It's only half an hour. You might.'

She laughs. 'Well, that sounds just dandy. Listen, my eyes are hurting staring at that boy on the TV. Read me something, sweetcakes.'

I wonder if she'll like the flood bit from *The Virgin and The Gypsy*, but instead I pull out the scroll of letters I keep in the pocket of my dungarees (it's the only place Reggie won't look). I read one aloud.

Iris love,   21st July 1954

I'll be back Tuesday week. Your car a bloody godsend. I'll be home late as Mother's much worse and they say it's pneumonia and the hospital, but I wouldn't miss the girls' birthdays for the world, so I'm coming back, duck. I have some lovely pressies for them both.

The thing is, I never did see eye to eye with Mother in any case and don't think she likes me here. My little sister Betty is the golden girl and she wants to look after her till she gets better, so that's just fine with me. Is Larry due home soon? Must rush to the post, and see you Tuesday week.

Love to you all,
Mathilda

'Where did you find those, Katie?' Rita points at the roll of thin letters.

'In the attic.'

'She'll miss them, you know. You should put them back.'

'Just one more –'

'I know the story, sweetcakes. I know how it turns out.'

'How's that?'

'You're the detective.'

'What happened to Mathilda? Did she die too?'

Rita's eyes flutter like she's thinking real hard, but she doesn't answer my question. Instead she says, 'A goddamn little sleuth, you are, like that Basil Rathbone in the *Sherlock Holmes* movies – now there was a Jew if I ever saw one, goddarnit he was a handsome man. Oh, his voice! Make anyone melt.'

I think Rita might be having another fit; she gets one if she's too excited, because her sugars are all wrong.

'D'you want some more squash, Auntie?'

'No. Katie, listen, love is love and it can hit you any place, from any place. Don't matter bout anything else.' Rita looks at me. 'It hit you yet, sweetcakes?'

'I don't know.'

'Well, if you don't know, it ain't.'

I concentrate on Rita's oxygen. The noise is a steady gasp and it's keeping Rita alive, so I must watch it; I'm the only one here.

'Hey, sweetcakes, ever tell you I'm getting cremated? I just decided I want to be *portable*, you know? Your grandmother can take me wherever she pleases. Don't want to be buried in this goddamn cold and oity-toity English earth in any case, and the insurance won't cover me going home *intact*. Don't tell Zev, though, it's against everything, he'll go crazy.'

On cue, Zev pops his bald head round the door. 'Hey girls, vos hert zikh epes?'

I hardly understand what Zev says. Rita moans.

'Come on now, Reetie, time for your medicine.' Zev shuffles in, part bug, part hairless monkey, and I try and imagine him young, on top of Coney Island's Parachute Jump ready to say 'I do.' He pulls Rita's blankets down and her nightie up. I see the stub of her chicken wing-leg as he injects her with insulin.

'God should protect you, little girl,' he whispers, then tucks her in.

He's funny, Zev. When I sneeze he shouts 'tsu gezunt!' I asked Gran if he was a German and she said, certainly not.

'We watching the bongs, girlies? Always heard about them Big Ben bongs.' Zev changes the channel. 'You got resolutions, little Kate?' he asks. 'Me I gotta watch my cholesterol, right Reetie?'

'Zev, there ain't a thing wrong with you a good square meal won't fix.'

'Well, there's my feet. Pain something awful.'

I'm trying so hard to see him laugh up in the sky, in a top hat and tails. 'Listen!' I tell them, and Zev turns up the telly.

Big Ben bongs in Rita's little bedroom, in time with our grandfather clock in the hall, and I think about resolutions.

1) Make sure love hits me in a place like it did Auntie Rita.
2) Put Mathilda's letters back in Gran's piano stool.
3) Find out who Basil Rathbone is as I might get hit with love in that place.
4) Don't tell Zev about the cremation.

I watch Rita breathe; her cheeks puffed and cold as marshmallows. I don't think she'd make that Parachute Jump now.

'Happy New Year, sweetcakes,' she tells me.

'Happy New Year, Auntie.'

'Le'chaim!' says Zev and he holds Rita's hand.

December 14th 1958

Dear Diary
Saw the film 'Carve Her Name with Pride' with that cute Virginia
McKenna. The movie theater in Hereford's my favourite place now. I
seem to walk round for the longest time these days.

Think I met Violet Szabo at the Hereford May fair one summer years
back. Think one of Larry's pals introduced us at the coconut stall. I never
did nothing like her. Wish I knew French and could have been a spy in
the war. Wish I could have made donuts and been like Janet Fiorello.

Thirty-four now and Eva's been gone four years. Lene's a terror and
still at boarding school.

Think Larry's still too sick for me to leave him for good.

Spoke to Rita this morning and she said a young boy called Elvis
Presley just might cheer me up. Not sure but will keep eyes peeled.

21

Our house looks lonely but at least river water's creeping across the fields towards it. Grandpa dug a circular trench round the house years ago, and so before we flood, we moat. It's a warm day, almost spring, and if it wasn't for the floods there'd be daffodils and purple crocuses dotting Grandpa's Field of Bolden. As it is, we've got mud, medieval soldiers, and a camera crew from Japan.

We're standing in a line by the hedge, all in wellies. That's Gran, Brian, Jamilah and me. Grandpa's in his pickup by the gate; Rita is at home, oxygen pumping. She said she didn't want to get her wheels stuck in the mud. 'Don't want me in their battle, sweetcakes. They'd have to shoot me like some old heifer, and they didn't have guns then.' Gran says it's a miracle Rita's still alive. Mum says it's a curse.

Brian yells, 'You're going home in a St John ambulance!' at a medieval soldier, who flicks the V's.

'Well, that isn't very Ye Olde England, is it?' Gran whispers as she hands out fishpaste sandwiches to everyone but me. 'Do you eat these, Jamilah honey? Are they okay, for your religion? It's fish.'

'They're fine, Mrs Happy.' Jamilah's got a pretty, purple sari on beneath her Parka, she said she wanted to dress up, in case she got on Japanese telly. She crosses her eyes and sticks her tongue out as Gran turns to me. I laugh and take a sandwich.

'Put that back, Katie, none for you, I saw you have breakfast with your grandfather.'

'That was ages ago, Gran.'

'Don't be a fatty-fat.'

Once Gran's trudged across the mud to Grandpa by the gate, Jamilah gives me half a sandwich, so does Brian.

'She's mad your Gran,' Brian says.

'Okay-mad though,' Jam says through a mouthful of fishpaste, 'she's just got a thing about fat people.'

'What about Kate's auntie then, that Rita, she's so fat she dun want to get out of bed.'

'She's dying, Brian,' I tell him. 'Gran thinks it's okay to let yourself go when you're dying. She said she's going to choke on Tootsie Rolls when her time comes.'

'What's they when theys at home?' He stuffs a whole triangle of sandwich in his mouth. 'She's bludy bonkers your nan is.'

We watch Gran offer some soldiers fishpaste. She's got a tight pink dress on: she's got pink Wellington boots on too. She calls them galoshes.

'And she's always going on about her hips isn't she, Kate?' Jamilah looks snooty at me. 'She told me she was a Beauty Queen and that explains everything I reckon. Exploitation.'

Jamilah's moved on from oppression to exploitation, she's driving Gran mad and it's only Saturday. She's staying with me for the weekend because Mum didn't let me go to Gloucester in January as I went to school instead, back to Redbrook. It's okay. I don't have any friends, but I'm excellent at English, French and German (I haven't told Gran about the German), and crap at Maths and Physics. Mr Crabtree's giving me extra lessons about something he calls pie and The Laws of Gravity, which Mum says I've always had a bloody problem with.

At the other end of the field, soldiers sit on plastic chairs that sink with the weight of their chainmail suits. They're sipping tea out of polystyrene mugs, served by women in cone hats and velvet dresses who aren't muddy at all. One bloke falls right back and everyone laughs. I wonder if he'll rust, lying there. The soldiers are knackered because their armour is so heavy, and half of them can't even pick up the big swords.

'Get on with it!' Brian yells and me and Jamilah elbow him in the ribs. Brian has stopped writing me soppy cards and kissing me. The last time we went to our hut was just after the New Year.

Sometimes I miss it.

Grandpa told us he's getting a lot of money for this battle, otherwise he 'wouldn't entertain the bloody nips'. Mr Iwase, the Japanese man who kept ringing us, finally got his way. When he called for the twelfth time in one day, Grandpa said he was going to put all that slitty-eyed treachery behind him and allow the nips the Field of Bolden for a week. At a price. They're filming a Battle of Britain. This morning I asked Jamilah which one and she said; 'Which do you think, dimwit? It's the Battle of bloody Boldenham, haven't you read anything? When the English killed all the Welsh and *your* family were the English.'

'But we're Welsh, a bit.'

'Not then you weren't. You've been bastardised since.'

'What's that?'

It's really because of the wedding that Grandpa's doing this. That's Mum's wedding, not Lady Di's. Though it's ever since we watched Lady Di running away from cameras and blushing on the telly that Mum went blonde, got a Lady Di haircut, and threw her hippie dresses away. Not long after she started wearing high heels and frilly necked blouses, Francis proposed. Last week, when the Announcement of The Wedding was on the BBC (Lady Di's this time) with her looking all giggly in blue, Mum told Grandpa she wanted a big do just like that, as last time it was registry and she couldn't remember a thing about it.

'What, not even Dad?' I asked, and she ignored me.

Grandpa's sitting half in, half out of the front seat of his pickup; shooting stick at his side; twelve bore on the passenger seat. 'Can't ever trust them,' he told me as Gran spread fishpaste on Mother's Pride this morning, 'damned odd beggars the Japs, cruelty y'see, it runs in their veins. Abandon ship!' Gran yelled something about atom bombs at him then, and Grandpa told her that was a damned Yankee thing and nothing to do with the likes of him.

I wave at Grandpa and he salutes from the front seat. He's better now, and he's got his Naval uniform on. That's why he's sitting; he can't do up the trousers and if he stands, they fall down.

'Akshun!' Mr Iwase shouts; he doesn't seem to mind us all standing by the hedge.

Mr Iwase is a small man in a green cagoule, and he's got the hood up so I can't see much else of him. He's staying at Borders Gate and he told Gran he wanted to buy the gate, and where was it? Gran's trying to sell Mr Iwase our barns. He exports English things, like whole houses.

'Hey, we could sell him the goddamn farm, Grandpa and all,' she told Rita before we left.

'And that bull, sweetcakes, cos that thing keeps me up nights.'

'And what about Reggie? Hell, we should sell her on for a loss!'

Gran said Mr Iwase exports houses from Stratford-upon-Avon for rich people in Japan to live in, and that he'd told her he'd put in an offer of a million pounds for Anne Hathaway's cottage.

'Lucky girl, whoever she is,' said Rita.

'Yeah, bloody hell, Auntie, that's a lot.'

Gran laughed at us both. 'Oh, but just imagine the irony, Reet, Mr Iwase could be our ticket out of here. We could all go. You, me, and little Katie. Saved by the Japanese, huh?'

'Pearl Harbor,' said Rita, slowly.

'Hiroshima,' Gran said back, and they were quiet for a long time; there was just the hiss of Rita's oxygen.

The muddy soldiers have tossed their tea away, and now they're running shakily to the middle of the field. The cameraman puts up his hand and they all yell half-heartedly, then bash swords together in slow motion. Their steel helmets glint in the sun and the crowd of women in cone hats skip about. About ten of the soldiers are on horses, and they've got long hair and wear flags on their chests like aprons. Gran called them goddamn hippies, but they're professionals. Not *The Professionals*, as Jamilah pointed out to Brian when he got all excited, but a group who travel round the country fighting old battles and getting paid. The rest of the soldiers came from the pub. They're the Welsh and they have to die horribly.

A bay mare close to us rears up and squeals.

'Cruelty!' Gran yells, and tightens the pink headscarf under her chin.

I wonder if Mr Iwase is filming us: he doesn't seem that bothered. Jamilah's taken off her parka and she's waving in her purple sari. I keep quiet: I don't really want to end up in a Battle of Britain.

'Is Millie coming?' I ask Gran.

'Nope. Said she'd only come if the Welsh win. Any case, she's with Reet.'

'Watch out!' Jamilah pulls me back as a medieval soldier falls at my feet.

'You all right up there, love?' he asks from the ground.

'Yeah.'

'Help me up, then.'

We grab metally bits of him and after a lot of pushing and pulling he's on his knees and we're covered in mud. Jamilah looks really pissed off because her sari skirt's now brown.

'My mum's going to kill me!'

'Now you kiddies should all be a bit further back, eh? This is dangerous.' The soldier stands up, wobbly; sword in hand. 'It's man's work, eh precious?' and he winks at Jamilah.

'Stupid more like,' she says back at him, and the soldier slots his visor down and waddles off like a steel duck.

In the distance a horse goes up on its hind legs and a soldier falls off, while another one jumps on him and pretends to stab him with his sword.

'Cut!' Mr Iwase yells and we all clap. 'Good, good. Good film!' I haven't heard him say much else.

'Bludy hell, that was bludy fab that was, wan it, Kate?' Brian gasps, mouth open.

'Testosterone,' says Jamilah.

Brian frowns. 'What?'

'Testosterone. That's all this little show is about. Uncontrollable male urges.'

'If *you* say so, poncing round in your dress, but *I* reckon it's a good show.'

'And I suppose you enjoy fighting?'

'So?'

'I bet you even like boxing on the telly.'

I love the wrestling. Big Daddy and Giant Haystacks at half past four every Saturday. Rita and I watch it together; we're watching it this afternoon.

'Oh bugger off, you lezzie,' Brian says.

'Children, children,' says Gran, 'less of the politics. Look, here comes Marlene with the tea.'

Mum's driving her Spitfire into the field. Aunt Reggie's in the deep front seat; you can only see the top of her turtle-ish head. In seconds, Mum's stuck, mud flying from the back wheels. A group of soldiers slow motion run to her rescue.

'Damsel in distress, huh?' Gran mutters, and reties her headscarf so tight I think she's cut something off, because her face goes red. 'And she's got the goddamn chameleon. Look honey, I should go check on Rita, I hate leaving her.'

'She'll be fine, Gran.'

She looks at me, eyes full; 'You don't know that, Kate.'

'Millie's with her.'

I love my aunt Rita, but even she admits she's 'taking a darned eternity to die'. Zev's gone back to Brooklyn because his dry cleaning business, 'The Clean Sheet', was going under. He cried when he said goodbye to Rita, even though they're not married anymore. Rita told him she wasn't going back because there was no way in hell she was passing from this world into the next without her own blood at her side (and she meant me, Gran *and* Mum, I suppose). Zev got upset and more wrinkly at that.

'Stay Gran, please.'

She sighs. 'Okay, honey. For the floorshow at least.' She's watching my mother being carried across the field in the arms of a particularly big and steely soldier. Aunt Reggie's been left behind in the mud and she's waving like she's sinking.

'Could anyone? You there! Soldier! Come! Could you?' she cries.

I think the problem is, as usual, she can't lift up her head so it looks like she's having a good conversation with the ground. She circles her arms above her.

'Help! Men! Help!'

'Thinks she's a bloody helicopter,' Jam whispers. Jamilah can't stand Reggie because every time they meet in the house, Reggie goes on about India. 'My mum's from Pakistan,' Jam told me, 'and me and my dad and the rest of us are from bloody Gloucester.'

'Look at me, Kate, look at me!' Mum yells, and we can't help it. Jamilah rolls her eyes as I watch the big soldier carry Mum towards us like a Sindy doll.

'Oh, Sir lovely Knight, just put me down here. But watch the clothes.' Mum's got her 'twin-set and pearls' on; that's what Jam calls my mother's new Lady Di suits. 'And what is your name, kind sir?' she asks the sweaty soldier.

'Gerald.'

'Oh, how big and strong you are, Gerald.'

'Cheers love.'

She giggles beneath her new blonde fringe; it doesn't suit her at all. Mum's living with Francis in his gatehouse now and her engagement ring is blue with little white stones round it. Mum doesn't say 'fuck' anymore and she thinks tomato ketchup, brown sauce and council houses are common. She says Brian lives in a council house, even though it belongs to Grandpa. Brian told me he wished he did live in a council house, as at least then they'd have proper electric and heating.

'You got the biccies then?' Gerald asks.

Mum stops smiling. 'Oh. Yes. In the back seat of the car, three boxes of Rovers. Your catering people aren't very organised, you know. Forgetting the biscuits I mean.'

'They just got some funny Pot Noodles which don't taste like Pot Noodles. You got some cake in there too, darlin'?'

'You'll just have to check, won't you Gerald?' she taps him on a metal shoulder.

'Right you are. Cheers, Mrs Happy.'

'Marlene, please,' and she blows him a kiss.

'Oh give it a rest, Mum.'

'What darling?'

'Stop getting off with *everyone*.'

She giggles again, but it doesn't sound innocent and nice like Lady Di.

Four men in the middle of the battlefield are pouring something red over it.

'Hey, look at that, that's *blood* that is!' Brian yells, pointing.

Mum stares at him. 'What's he doing here?' she hisses.

'Free country, Mum.'

'Bloody ferret.'

We watch the field turn red as the blood runs through puddles and mixes with the mud. Jamilah's pulling a face and Brian's laughing at her.

'You still a veg-e-tarian?' he asks.

'Am now.'

'They got that from Dad this morning. It's from more than a couple of sheep, I reckon, Jam.'

'That's disgusting.'

Brian and Jamilah haven't got on for ages. Gran says they must be in love.

'Hey!' Mum shouts, because the camera crew are moving her Spitfire. 'Hey, watch it, arseholes!'

Mum can still be Mum when she wants to.

Once the sports car is out of the medieval battleground, Mr Iwase yells, 'Good! Good! Akshun!' and the soldiers are at it again, swords dragging, but now splashed red with blood. Jamilah and I have just read *Shirley* and *Carrie* (I'm still sticking to Charlotte Brontë and Stephen King) and Grandpa's field is how I imagined that pigs' blood at the prom at the end of *Carrie*.

'Come on, Gerald,' Mum shouts.

Gran looks really strangled by her pink scarf. 'I should check on Rita,' she says.

'Oh don't worry, Mother, she's probably dead.'

'Marlene!'

But before they can dive into their 'I wish Rita was dead'; 'Oh no you don't'; 'Oh yes I do' argument, I see Aunt Reggie turtling across the battlefield. I'd forgotten she was there and no one has spotted her; not even Mr Iwase and his cameraman. It's because she's a chameleon and she's blending. She's left her cane behind (it's sticking like a runner-bean pole out of the mud) and head down, she seems to be sliding undetected through the battling armies. Neither the Welsh nor the English notice her and the horses rear out of her way. That's like elephants being scared of mice: a sixth sense; a weird animal thing. Reggie's got bloody mud up to her hips now, but she's still moving forward through the soldiers. Millie would call it Moses Parting The Waves, and I want to tug Mum's sleeve, get her to help my turtle-aunt, but I'm held, spellbound by the way Reggie's magically avoiding every sword and falling soldier. I'm waiting for something to happen.

Then something does.

Grandpa spots her. And then over the yells and crashes of metal I hear him shout, 'Reg! Reg! Starboard old girl! Starboard!' He pounds on his pickup horn and we're all staring at him, wondering what the matter is. I look at Mr Iwase, but he's standing over his cameraman who's down in the mud filming a nasty fight between two soldiers. He doesn't seem to mind.

None of us say anything. This is because Grandpa has made the terrible mistake of getting out of his pickup, so now he's standing up, his undersized naval uniform trousers have fallen down. Grandpa's screaming, 'Reg! Reg old thing! Starboard!', his twelve bore cocked over his arm, his Captain's cap askew; in his underpants.

Grandpa's gone very red in the face, and Gran whispers, 'Oh, Larry.'

I'm the only one looking out for Reggie. She's still sliding through the fighting throng, except now she's trying the new starboard course towards her brother. I can hear her gravely voice cut in and out of the fighting, 'Blood-y Japs! Blood-y Welsh! Blood-y English!'

The fighting soldiers still don't notice her.

Then we all hear it, Grandpa's twelve bore shot (luckily) above our heads. My ears ring and Mr Iwase shouts, 'Cut! Cut noise! Noise!' He's looking over at Grandpa but he can't see him because Grandpa's fallen back in the mud, trousers down, gun up.

The soldiers go back to their plastic chairs as if nothing has happened. A few of them are staring at Grandpa though; a few of them are shaking their heads.

Reggie's left in the middle of the field, a muddy vole. She's dazed and doesn't move. The film crew and the soldiers get tea, the horses neigh, and it's only because Jamilah's mouth is still gaping open, and Gran and Mum have their heads down, that I know I'm not crazy and it was all real. Brian's gone. He's over with Grandpa, helping him up, holding up his splattered white trousers while they both struggle back into the pickup. Then, slowly and easily, the big soldier Gerald, Frankenstein-walks to the middle of the battlefield and picks Reggie up.

'One more, love!' he shouts at us, and we're all suddenly animated.

'Oh lovely, Gerald, thanks so much,' says Mum, squeakier than usual.

'Yes, you are real kind,' Gran pipes in.

'Where do you want her?'

'Oh, here is fine.'

'She all right?' He nods at Reggie, cradled in his arms like a baby alligator.

'Oh yes,' says Gran. 'Are you all done with the fighting now?'

'One more I think. Works with the blood don't it, the battle?'

'Definitely.'

'That'll look grand in a film that will.'

'Oh yes,' repeats Gran.

Gerald deposits Aunt Reggie in a white plastic chair next to Jamilah (who's still got her gob open). Now Reggie looks like Carrie, because her eyes are big and starey from a face caked in muddy blood. She's gazing out at the field and I wonder if she'll make it catch fire; I wonder if the Japanese film will burn up in the camera and the horses will spontaneously combust.

I hope Reggie doesn't go *all* Carrie on us later on, and crucify everyone with kitchen knives.

'You're catching flies, dear,' Gran says to Jamilah.

'Uh?'

'Your mouth, honey. Close it, there's a good girl.'

I look at Jam. It's the first time I've ever seen her look stupid. I suppose my family can do that to a person. Mum pulls out a flask from her Liberty bag, and gives Aunt Reggie a hot cup of tea.

'There you are, Reg, drink up.'

Gran is staring up at the sky. I hear the barking calls of geese and I look up to see them flying in a big, sharp arrow. Gran sighs.

'Fly home. Fly home to Jesus,' she says.

* * *

Brian cleaned Grandpa up back at the farm, and now they're at Borders Gate with Mr Iwase and the soldiers. Mr Iwase said he thought the big bang was 'English tractor, not Mr Happy gun', and laughed. Jam stayed at the pub, but I've come back to watch the wrestling with Rita. Jam said I was 'an exploited idiot.'

Rita's propped up in bed, oxygen mask on because she feels rotten today. Dr Croften still wants to put her in a hospital, but she's waiting for her diabetic coma for that, 'Then wheel me off, sweetcakes! I won't know no different!' Aunt Rita's gone yellow all over, also her white roots have grown through, and she's now got glasses so thick she doesn't look like Rita anymore. She says she's as puffed up as a puffer fish, and just as poisonous.

Her room smells of wee and boiled sweets, but I don't mind, I always sit with her after school. I try and spot her false leg, dusty in the corner, but it's dark in Rita's room. The curtains are drawn because she says light bothers her, though she's definitely not a vampire. Anyway, I don't believe in them anymore.

Rita's got a small fridge in here, full of her medicines, and she calls it her mini-bar.

'How was the battle?' she asks; her voice echoes behind her oxygen mask.

'Fun.'

'I wouldn't call it fun, Katie. Those poor horses.' Gran's in her pink leatherette chair by the window; she dragged it in from the hall one afternoon as she hardly uses the phone now. Gran spends most days with Rita and I've never seen her happier.

'You shoulda been on Foreo, Iris, all in armours, you'd a shown them a thing or two. Joan of Arc you woulda been.'

'I'm not having my poor horse involved in that nonsense, Rita, honey. And anyways, that Joan was French.'

'Oh pull that cork out of your ass, Iry.'

I laugh. Sometimes Rita can be very funny.

'Rita! Just cos you're ill, you think –'

'Listen,' Rita winks at me as Gran leans in closer. 'Iris, honey, you're about as uptight as that goddarned sister-in-law of yours, Reggie the chameleon. So take a chill pill.'

Gran looks shocked, 'And you, Rita Ichmann, sound like a hippie.'

'Well, a bit of that would do you some good. Didn't you have the revolution here? The Summer of Love? I know you've been stuck here since 1944, and I still can't figure how or why, but really. Get-with-the-program, Iris!'

'It was 1942.'

'Whatever. You always got to take things face value, Iry, like that snake-charmer gal, The Queen of Sheba —'

'You having a fit, Reet?'

Rita laughs, 'Don't be cheeky, you know who I'm talking about. Remember how you'd run down Surf Avenue to the Dreamland Circus Sideshow every day, just to see her?'

Gran looks a little red.

'Katie, she just couldn't believe this little gal could charm those big snakes. Dressed up like Sheba, all Egyptian she was, and I just said, "Iris, that gal's got ether in her pants, stuns those babies, then she can do what she wants with them." But oh, Iris here couldn't believe it, went every day after school to see Sheba the Snake Charmer. Didn't you, hon?'

'You sure do remember the oddest things, Rita Ichmann.'

'And ain't it just fun?'

They can go on like this for hours; teasing each other like puppies. Gran crosses her arms and sulks; Rita laughs.

'Still, Larry's got his heart in the right place, hasn't he, Iry? What I always said. That money you get from the Japanese'll come in useful for Marlene's wedding.'

I don't like to think of Mum and Francis as husband and wife; it's weird. Maybe Mum's shagging Gerald the soldier right now and it'll all be off. But then she'd go back to being a smelly mad hippie upstairs, so I suppose Francis isn't so bad. As long as I don't have to live with them and call him Dad. And I don't think I do. No one's asked.

The showdown between Big Daddy and Giant Haystacks has started on the telly. The ringmaster is talking into the long, dangly microphone.

'"An-dah, in the red cor-nah we have —"'

'Turn it up, sweetcakes.'

'It's almost full blast.'

'I want to hear the body slams. They're great. Oh! Go on Giant!' Rita waves her saggy arm in the air.

'You like him? Oh I hate him, Reet. I like Big Daddy I do.' Gran's stopped sulking; she never can keep that up with Rita.

'My dear and lovely sister, Big Daddy looks like a darned big baby.'

'Oh come on, Giant Haystacks is a hairy beast!'

'I know Iry, I kinda like them like that. Imagine, all that weight!'

'Sh! Not in front of the girl, Reet.'

'Oh, don't be so stuffy, you know all about that, doncha Katie? The birds and the bees and the shakey knees?'

I love it when Rita gets silly on her medicine; and it makes sense her liking Giant Haystacks after all those years with Zev. He can't weigh more than a flea.

I watch Big Daddy grip Giant Haystacks in an arm-behind-the-back manoeuvre. They grunt. Sweat flies from Haystacks's long black hair.

'Yeah, don't worry, Gran, I know about the facts of life.'

'Well, I didn't tell you.'

'Mum did. Ages ago.'

'Yeah, Marlene probably acted it out for you, huh, sweetcakes?'

'Ri-ta!' Gran looks shocked but I just laugh, because it's pretty true.

'Oh! The big baby's down! The big baby's down! What did I tell you, Iris? That's gotta hurt.'

Big Daddy's gone puce. Gran's frowning.

'Don't get too worked up, Reet, you're steaming up.' She takes a tissue and wipes the inside of Rita's oxygen mask.

'My, my, that Giant Haystacks is such a big man. Like the bikers we get in the summer in Coney, Iry, you remember them?'

'Not in my day, honey.'

'You know, the Hell's Angels. They'd come and cause a ruckus, but me and Lula knew how to handle them, before she went off with Frank the Salesman, a goy but what can you do,' she sighs. 'I'm the only sister was a real Jew y'know. Born a Jew, married a Jew, die a Jew.'

I listen to the hiss of her oxygen.

'Anyways, we had a couple of them Hell's Angels staying when me, Zev and Lula took in holiday boarders, sweetest men you could imagine. Real old-fashioned men. Smelt of oil and would do anything for a lady. Course they were too young for us, but we had our moments, me and Lula. That was the year Nixon was sworn in, and who woulda thought he'd come to that? Sending our boys off to fight in some goddarned jungle, sending them all to die, Iris.'

Gran is standing above her. 'Here Rita, take this, calm honey, calm –' She feeds her sister squash. It dribbles. 'There now, there, just sit back, there we go.' Gran smoothes down Rita's half red, half white hair, as Giant Haystacks sits on Big Daddy and the crowd squeal.

'You okay?' she asks.

'Hmmm.' Rita's eyelids flutter.

'There we go, honey, there we go.'

'Should I call the doctor, Gran?'

'No, sweetheart. It's okay, she'll come round in a minute. She just needs her jab is all.' Gran's an expert on Rita's rises and falls. She knows exactly what to do. She's read up on everything about diabetes, and she hardly ever leaves her. At nights she sleeps on the camp bed in here. It's only when Rita asks for privacy that she'll go.

Gran lifts up the blankets and injects her sister's little cut-off leg.

'You remember Jackie?' Rita murmurs.

'Who darlin'?'

'That beautiful Jackie. Brooklyn's king. The biggest hitter we ever saw. He'd set Ebbets Field alight, every game.'

'Sure, honey.'

'First Black man I ever loved.'

'I know.'

'Think we all did. Did you, Iry?'

'Course.'

'Even Mr Rogers. Member him? Terrible man. Hated us for being Jews. Hated everyone for not being him. But he loved Jackie.'

'You wrote me, I know.'

'But then they go and smash down the stadium.' Rita's crying now. She claws off her mask. 'Oh, can you believe it, Iris, they're bulldozing the stadium. Today! Building apartments and that's where cousin Lou is gonna live. Flatbush Apartments, on the ground of our beloved Ebbets Field, oh I can't bear it, Iry, I ain't gonna visit Lou, I ain't, you can't make me, not on the grave of our Jackie. Not on the graves of our very own Dodgers. I won't!'

'There, honey. I know. Take a little more.'

Rita sips again and her cheeks wobble, her chins are stained orange. I wonder what it would have been like looking after Dad, if he had just been hurt and bedridden. Would I have been as patient as Gran is with Rita if it was Dad blubbering from the bed?

'Sorry,' Rita says.

'Oh, sweetheart, you ain't got nothing to apologise for.'

'It's just –'

'Sh –'

'I'm sorry I came over, Iry. I shoulda stayed home. Oceanview Avenue. Zev'll be back there now and I'll never see it again.'

'Don't talk silly.'

'And putting you through all this.'

'Well, who else have I got?'

'If I'd a stayed at Oceanview Avenue, maybe you'd a come over.'

'Course I would.'

'I ain't so sure.'

'You should sleep, honey.'

'But would you, Iris? Would you have come over? I mean, you didn't go over for Lula and I just never did understand that.'

'Shh, honey.'

'Why?'

Gran's crying now. They do this a lot. 'Oh my little baby sis. It was timing. Everything was wrong. It was when Marlene had her troubles. And –'

'And what, Iry?'

'You know I've never been brave. I just can't –'

'I know.'

'Shall I call Dr Croften?' I ask them again.

Gran's still standing, smoothing down Rita's hair, she looks up and past me, at the telly. The ringmaster's counting Big Daddy out.

'"One-ah, two-ah, three-ah –"'

'No, sweetie. Let's sit with.' She turns back to Rita, 'We'll sit with it, okay?'

But Rita's eyes are closed.

I think I should reach out and hold Rita's big swollen hand, too; but I can't. I look at her hair instead. She looks like a ginger tabby with her white roots and pale orange ends. Rita has a hair appointment tomorrow. Gran's hairdresser Kirsty-Ann is coming in, specially, to give Rita her red back.

I wonder what Gran means about not being brave?

The door opens and it's Reggie, face to the floor and the mud cleaned off.

'Tea? Millie has it brewing.'

Gran looks up and smiles, which is odd; she never smiles at Reggie.

'Why Regina Happy, that would be lovely.'

Aunt Reggie turns to the side and pulls her face up. She gives Gran a very turtle-ish look. 'Right then. Tea all round.'

'No biscuits for me!' says Rita. 'Who won?'

We all look at the telly. Big Daddy's being carried off on a stretcher, moaning, and the ringmaster's trying to lift Giant Haystacks's arm up above his head in victory, but he can only get it as far as the huge man's waist. Giant Haystacks looks like he's doing, 'I'm a little teapot, short and stout, here's my handle, here's my spout'. Giant Haystacks looks like a headbanger.

'Oh goodie,' says Rita, eyes peering over her mask. 'When's the re-match?'

February 7th, 1964

Dearest Iry,

Thought I'd send this postcard. They're The Beatles
and I made Zev take me to John F. Kennedy Airport to
scream at them. I was with all the teenagers! Cheered
me up. Still sad about JFK so it was nice to laugh in his
airport. Zev calls me crazy, but I'm still a girl at heart.
Ask Lene if she likes them.

Love Reet

p.s Where the hell is Liver–pool? When you think of the
word, it isn't pretty, why'd someone go name a town that?

Mrs Iris Happy
The Happy Farm
Boldenham
Herefordshire
England

22

'Budge up.'

'Okay.' I pull back the covers and heat pours out.

'That mattress is bloody awful.'

Jamilah snuggles in next to me. She smells of curry even though we haven't had one.

'Your aunt okay now?'

'Not really. You got all that mud off you?'

'It wasn't on me, it was on my bloody sari – Mum's going to kill me when I get home.'

'You could soak it.'

'Yeah.'

Actually Jamilah's hair smells of vanilla.

'You should have come to the pub, Kate, it was fun. All them Japanese have gone though, your grandad said they were off to Stratford next.'

'Bugger.'

'What.'

'I bet he's not going to buy my gran's barns.'

'Who?'

'Mr Iwase. He was going to buy her barns and we were going to go to America.'

'Cool.' Jamilah fidgets. 'Anyway, all the soldiers were at the pub.'

'I know, you said.'

'And you wanted to watch wrestling, Kate, I don't know –'

'Rita enjoys it, and anyway I think she nearly died.'

'What?'

'It was weird. Did you have booze at the pub?'

'Just a sip of Brian's snakebite.'

'Did you get drunk?'

'Nah. What do you mean, your aunt nearly died?'

'She just had a turn, that's all.'

'She okay now?'

'Yeah, I said. Jam?'

'What.'

'At the pub, did Brian snog you?'

'No! Germs!'

'Gran says you both are in love.'

'We bloody well are not.'

'When are you going home, Jam?'

'Trying to get rid of me?'

'No.' I look over at Tatum in her crescent moon. I've replaced David Cassidy with Siouxie and The Banshees. 'It's just, I don't want you to go at all.'

'You're going to America though.'

'I'm not really. Gran always says that. She's been saying it for years but she'll never actually go.'

We curl in and whisper into each other's faces.

'When's your mum's wedding?'

'Don't know, don't care.'

'She's not mad anymore, is she?'

'No, but she's changed, took some pills. She's gone posh.'

'Yeah. She asked me to be a bridesmaid.'

'Jam, don't.'

'Why? You don't like that bloke she's going to marry?'

'He's all right, it's just, I don't want to be a bridesmaid and I don't want you to be a bridesmaid either. It's stupid.'

She snuggles closer. 'I saw Brian's sister Joanne at the pub. She's as big as a house, though she said she was only a few months gone. I think it's stupid getting pregnant when you're still at school. What she going to do about her exams?'

'I don't think they go to school much.'

'Like you?'

'I go now, anyway, that's different.'

'Why?'

'Just is, and I'm not thick.'

'Neither is Joanne.'

'Is she getting married?'

'Dunno. She told me her dad won't let the dad of her baby in the house. He's a Black man from Hereford.'

'That figures.'

'You sound like your gran you do. "That figures",' she giggles, 'Oh. You're American. You're American –' She tickles me.

'Get off.'

We're quiet for a while, me smelling her curry and vanilla scent. I listen for the hiss of Rita's oxygen two floors below, but can't hear a thing; just a funny beeping noise. Reggie's up above us, pattering from room to room.

'I hope your aunt Rita doesn't die when I'm here, Kate. I'd get the willies.'

'Yeah.'

Jamilla's eyes are bright in the moonlight and I like being in my bed with her.

'You know who my favourite singer is now?' she asks.

'Nope.'

'Toyah. She used to be fat and a punk but now she's all New Romanticy. She's got a lisp too.' Jamilah whisper-sings 'It's A Mystery' at me and I think back to the months before Christmas when Mum filled the house with her music at nights. I miss that. I miss 'My Sweet Lord'. It's been quiet since she left. I know she's leaving for good now, and she won't want me at Francis's gatehouse.

Sometimes it makes me sad, but not all the time.

'Kate?'

'Yeah.'

'Take your nightie off.'

'Why?'

'I'll take mine off too.'

We sit up in bed and peel off our nighties. Blue sparks crack in the dark and I lie back down. Jamilah's soft. I snuggle into her and touch her boob by mistake.

'Sorry.'

'That's okay.'

I go back and it feels so nice. Her breathing goes funny and I put my arm around her waist, because she's got one. Our chests touch, mine flat and cold, and her hands move up and down my back until I feel like I'm melting. I touch her whole bosom then, with the palm of my hand, and she lifts my chin up, and kisses me. It's more than the kiss in the graveyard with Brian watching. It's little kisses, and she tastes like metal.

'Does this make us lezzies?' I whisper.

She laughs.

'Does it?'

'I don't know. It's nice though. Do you like it?'

'Yeah.'

'Have you snogged a boy, Kate?'

'You know I have. Brian.'

'He doesn't count.'

'Have you?'

'Yes.'

'More than Brian?'

'Yes.'

'Did you like it?'

'I'm asking you!' and she pushes me out of the bed, like Mum did the night she came back.

I hang onto the candlewick cover and laugh. 'It was all tonguey with Brian!' I say and laugh again because I'm falling. Suddenly I land with a thud!

'Sh!'

'Sh!'

'We'll wake up Gran.'

'And your aunt Rita.'

'Never mind her, what about Reggie upstairs?'

'Oh, her, bloody hell, "I remember Indiah! Rah-rah-rah!" Oh god, Kate, she's awful!'

Jamilah's sitting up, naked. Her boobs are amazing, she looks so grown-up, like they're not her boobs at all.

'Quick, I can hear someone,' she whispers. 'Get in, Kate.'

'But!'

'Quick!'

I jump in and under the covers, and we listen to Reggie shuffle past my door. She takes ages and we're giggling so much I can't believe she doesn't hear us. Reggie's followed by lots of little pad-pad-pads and meows; the thumping is Noodles the big Maine Coon.

'What's she doing?'

'Oh, she always wanders about at night. It's to annoy us, Gran says, and she eats everything from the fridge.'

'Or gives it to those mingey cats of hers.'

'Probably.' I shiver.

'You cold?'

'A bit.'

Jamilah slides her hand under me and pulls me closer; she's really strong. She kisses my forehead, and I can feel her heart beat against my chest.

'Why do you like me, Jam?'

'We're friends aren't we?'

'Yeah. I mean, why do you like me like this?'

'Dunno. Why do you like me?'

'You're clever. And pretty.'

'No I'm not.'

The flat of her hand feels for my boob then, and it's like she knows what to do. Brian never does stuff like this. I've only got nipples but it still feels nice. I touch her boob, and we start all over again. Jamilah's kisses are soft as petals. Her thigh pushes between my legs and goes up, and her fanny brushes against my tummy.

'Ur –'

'What?'

'Nothing.'

'Don't you like that?'

'I don't know.'

She kisses me again, pulling me under her, climbing on top. She's not Giant Haystacks but now I know what Aunt Rita meant about the niceness of being crushed. I feel her flatten out against me and I wish I were bigger; I wish I was a proper grown-up girl like her.

When I'm with Brian, I never want to be grown-up.

Jamilah bites my neck and it doesn't scare me. I couldn't care less if she was a vampire. Even if she tap-tap-tapped on my window I'd let her in.

There's a knock at the door.

'Katie?'

'Quick, it's Gran!'

Jamilah jumps off me and dives under her sleeping bag, just as Gran opens the door.

'Katie?'

I pretend to be asleep. My cheeks are burning, my neck is wet, and I'm fizzy from being naked and Jamilah touching me all over.

'Kat-ie wake up, I need you.'

'What?'

'It's your aunt Rita. There's an ambulance coming and I've got to pack. Reggie's with her now, but she's useless, please honey. I need you.'

Jamilah sits up, sleeping bag pulled over her boobs. 'Mrs Happy, is everything all right?'

'Oh don't you worry, dear, it's just Kate I need, she can deal with her auntie, you go back to sleep.' Gran turns on the overhead light and everything's too bright.

I glance at Jamilah. She still looks beautiful.

'I'll expect you down, quick as a cat's whisker, I have to go dress.' Gran's always got her sayings wrong; she rushes out.

I pull the sheet up to my neck, too embarrassed to stand up naked in the light in front of Jamilah.

'Katie! Hurry up!' Gran shouts from the landing.

Jam's quiet.

Finally, I struggle out, the sheet covering some of me, and reach for my dungarees.

'Is she going to die?' Jam squeaks.

I look down at her; brown and naked by my bed. 'I don't know,' I tell her.

'I'm scared, Kate.'

'Don't be.'

'But I am.'

I'm not embarrassed anymore, and I walk over to her, squat by her mattress and kiss her on the lips. I don't mind touching Jamilah in the light; not like Brian. She smiles and lies back down.

'Could you turn the light off?'

'Sure. Go back to sleep.'

Reggie's fussing and her cats are everywhere; there are two kittens in the fruit bowl. Rita's sleeping, eyes fluttering, but the one machine she's hooked to is making a funny noise.

'I don't know. Dying people in the house. It's terrible. Shouldn't be allowed. A young girl like you. Going through something like this. Off Noodles, off!'

The big Maine Coon has jumped onto Rita's bed. Luckily it just landed on the space where Rita's leg should be.

'Out Noodles. And you Truly. And you Nettles. And you David.'

I turn to see the cat called David, a funny white thing with orange and brown splodges. It skits out of the room. Gran was right about animals with human names; it's just plain weird.

'Is her oxygen at the right level?' I ask.

'What, what? I don't know.'

'It's that gauge by you, Reggie, it should be about halfway, that means it's pumping properly.'

She twists her head to one side. 'Oh yes. Yes, that's fine. I suppose. I don't know. Who taught you all this?'

'Gran, and the District Nurse. I look after Rita when I come home from school so Gran can go out. You know that. You're upstairs.'

'Yes. But too busy. Too busy up there, my dear –'

'Why did you come downstairs, Reggie?'

'Hmmm?'

'Did you hear something? Rita's machine or Gran calling? It's just I didn't hear a thing.'

'Oh, no. No, that was little Daphne here,' she points at a very ugly black and white splodge cat on Gran's pink chair, 'she wanted to go out. I just passed your grandmother in the hall. Panicking. I calmed her down. Told her to call that nice doctor.'

I don't believe that for a second.

'And he told her to call an ambulance. Is she in one of those comathingamybobs?'

'I think so. Rita? Auntie Rita?'

'Best for things to take their course, Katie. Best for all of us. If she was one of my cats –'

I give Reggie a look, but don't bother to tell her off. Her head's so bent she's looks like she's praying.

I can hear the nar-nar, nar-nar of a distant ambulance. Rita must be really bad for Gran to have called them because they'll take her away. There's the sound of a car on the driveway before the ambulance arrives though. I peek out of Rita's curtained window and see Dr Croften's Audi.

My neck's still burning; still sticky wet. I must smell of vanilla now.

I watch Dr Croften get out by the yard light. Even in the middle of the night, he's smart looking. Rita's mask isn't clouding much and she's gone from yellow to white. I hold her hand; cold as usual, as Gran runs in with a pink suitcase. She holds it up.

'What do you think she'll need, Kate? How long should I pack for? Will this do?'

April 1st, 1966

Iry,

Joined the march with the Colombia College kids. Made banners and drove Zev's van into the city. The Evening News said there was 200,000 of us! Lindy next doors says I'm a bad wife but we got to fight this war any way we can, right? Poor kids. Zev says if wars good enough for him it's good enough for them. What a ga–ho–la. Whats Lene think? Where is she? Last I got a postcard from Tunis — where in the hell is that?

Love Reet.

p.s got a cockatiel, calling it Honeybunch.

Mrs Iris Happy
The Happy Farm
Boldenham
Herefordshire
England

23

In the hospital we've got a room to ourselves because Gran made a fuss. She said she wasn't having her sister dying with a bunch of goddamn English, so they gave us a room in isolation. They gave Gran a sedative too, I think it was Dr Croften who made them.

The pump of Rita's hospital oxygen sounds like Ivor the Engine: 'shhh-de-cut, shh-de-cut, shh-de-cut'. It's more efficient than the one at home, I suppose. She's hooked up to all sorts of bleepy machines, and what looks like a bag of water. Rita is still unconscious. It is a comathingamybob.

When Grandpa was on a ward here, they brought him a chair and closed the curtains when he wanted to go to for a wee; but Rita's got another bag for that and it's hanging from the side of the mattress; dark orange.

I haven't seen Ange, the nurse who sewed my knee up. That seems years ago now. I rest my foot on Rita's metal bed and touch my scar; it's soft and pink. This room smells like Ange though, like Jeyes Fluid. There's that extra taste of mince too.

Gran's sleeping on a bed opposite Rita, sedated and snoring. Dr Croften's off with the nurses, flashing his white teeth, and I'm thinking of Jamilah. The bedside light is on, and Rita's already got flowers; Gran yanked them out of the hospital garden when they told her her sister might not last the night. They're an odd mix of daffodil blooms, bulbs and soil.

'Swee –'

I turn to see Rita's eyes flutter.

'Rita –' but I've said her name too loudly and she jolts. 'Sorry,' I whisper.

'Sweetcakes?'

'Yes.'

Her eyes are crossed. Rita can't see much without her glasses.

'Do you need anything?'

'Wadder.'

I take her oxygen mask off and put a cup of water with a pink straw up to her mouth. She drains it like a horse.

'Feel dizzy.'

'You're in the hospital.'

'Not an idiot, honey.'

'I'd better put your mask back on, Auntie.'

'No –' she gulps a bit. 'Iris?'

'Look, she's right there on the bed. They gave her something to make her sleep, but I can wake her up if you like.'

'No.'

'But –'

'No.'

'Should I get a nurse?'

'No.'

She puts the mask back on herself and breathes deeply. She takes it off again. 'Sweetcakes. Look after her, right?'

'Who?'

'Iris.'

'Course.'

'You're the only one she's got.' Rita closes her eyes. 'Don't feel like dying.'

'Maybe you're not.'

'Feel goddamn awful.' She sniffs. 'Katie?'

'Yes.'

'I've left it to you.'

'What?'

'House. Everything.'

'What house?'

'4342 Oceanview Avenue –' gasp '– Coney Island. Goddamn, stupid.'

'I don't need a house.'

She lifts up one enormous arm and tries to pat me on the head. I have to lean in to it. Rita smells of talcum powder and TCP.

'Aw, don't cry, honey.'

I didn't know I was.

'Take her back.'

'Who?'

She opens her eyes and her face flushes; 'Get with the program, huh? Sleeping Beauty there –' gasp '– Iris, she's gotta go home.'

Rita's going white now. I hold her cold hand.

'Why didn't you leave the house to Gran, then?'

'Give her something to think about. Right?' She winks, eyes crossed. 'Hey, wipe those cheeks. Your grandpa says I've had –' gasp '– "a good innings". What in the hell is that?'

'Cricket.'

'What?'

'It's something in cricket.'

'Goddarned English crazies.'

'Auntie? What shall I do with a house?'

'Give your grandma her life back.'

'Go to America?'

'Yeah.'

'What about Mum? And Grandpa?'

'Don't spend long getting an answer, huh?'

'What about the dogs?'

'You're a silly!'

I try and laugh with her.

'More wadder.'

'Here you are.' And she sucks again. Her cheeks collapse in, crisp as paper. She lies back.

'My momma moved from the Lower East Side to Oceanview. Brighton Beach to one side. Coney to the other.' Rita taps my hand. 'She took in circus folk. A nickle a night. Went down to the beach where they all slept and took them in. Made good in the summer –' gasp '– and what summers they were.' Rita smiles, 'Cotton candy. Nathan's hotdogs. Folks thought it was dogmeat, we had so many strays –' gasp '– but we were glad of them. Needed the fleas, see. Show people, they'd pick them off the mutts and boil them up in a pan. And those that floated, well those guys made it to the Flea Circus. Real fighters. Performers. Like my doll of a man, Jeremiah. But –'

'Shh, Auntie.'

'But that's the past. It's all –' gasp '– all about you now, sweetcakes.'

'Okay.'

'You're the goddarned future.' Her eyes flutter and I move the mask back over her mouth.

'It's okay, Rita,' I tell her, copying Gran. 'It'll be okay. We'll sit this one out. Right?'

I'm waiting in the corridor, knackered because I've been here since yesterday. Gran is in with Rita. Grandpa came this morning and told me Jamilah's dad had picked her up. Millie came later, but Mum hasn't visited, she called the nurses' phone and told me I was an idiot for hanging round death; 'But you've always been a little *macabre*, haven't you, darling?'

It was that word again.

I had a bath in the hospital, and breakfast. I ate loads. I had toast and bacon and baked beans and a funny scrambled egg that was solid and white.

I can hear a bleep coming from Rita's room. The sister knocks and goes in.

Last night, curled next to Gran, listening to the puff and hiss of Rita's machines, I dreamt of 4342 Oceanview Avenue, and the waves splashing up against the stoop. Someone was yelling 'Flea Circus, Flea Circus, roll up!' and all the Bosums and all the Jessies ran into the house. Everything was black and white in my dream and I was in my dungarees, just like Addie Pray, with ribbons in my hair, while an old-fashioned car sat in our driveway. Gran was inside the car, hair curled, cooking pot-roasts and pot-luck, and making bombs for the war. She was covered in yellow. A gramophone played 'It's Only a Paper Moon' and Mathilda was waving from the attic window. She shouted down at us, 'All right, ducks?' but Gran wouldn't get out of the car. She kept muttering 'noodle kugel!' and 'rations!'

I remember standing there looking moody, like Addie, as the ocean pushed closer and closer.

They put Rita on a machine that goes through her throat. It looks like the cord you get on a newborn pup, but in the wrong place. It's because she can't breathe on her own. I haven't told Gran how Rita woke up and spoke to me; I'm not sure if she really did now.

'Kate? Kate Happy?'

'Yes.'

It's the sister. 'Would you like to say goodbye?'

'Sorry?'

'To your aunt? Would you like to say goodbye, dear?'

I say 'okay', but what I really want to ask is; where has she gone? I didn't see her hop past me on her one leg.

The sister smiles and puts an arm across my shoulders, guiding me into Rita's Jeyes Fluid and mince room. Gran is slumped over the bed, sobbing. The machine is doing a longer bleep. The sister switches the sound off.

'Gran?'

She looks up, 'Oh, honey!'

I stand at the end of the bed. I'm silent because I feel like my mum. In fact I can feel bits of my mother pinprick through me, pushing past my skin like the grubs in India Grandpa said hatch from your ankles. Because what I really want to say is, 'What's the surprise, Gran? We knew she was going to croak, didn't we?'

Rita's gone even looser; her flesh looks like it's trying to slip off, trying to escape.

'She was my baby sister!' Gran wails, and she pulls at her own pink blouse until the buttons fly off; she's ripped it under one arm. 'She was my little girl!'

Then, suddenly, she's calm. She stands up and smoothes down Rita's red and white hair. 'I'm sorry, honey, sorry Kirsty-Ann couldn't get to your hair in time. You would have looked so good with the wash-in and set she had planned.'

I hold onto the cold poles of the bed.

'Tell you what, we'll get her in later. That'll be nice, huh? You'll be a knockout, honey.' Gran looks up and walks towards me. 'Would you like to say goodbye to Reet?'

How? I think.

Byeeee.

See ya!

Ate logo! (as Mum said when she shagged a Brazilian)

À bientôt! (ditto, but with a Frenchman)

See you around, Lovely Rita Meter Maid (because that's what Dad called her).

I reach down and touch Rita's foot through the white sheet, and then I feel a bit sick. I can only cry when Rita talks to me, not when she's gone off like this.

'What are we going to do with her now, Gran?' I ask.

Gran frowns at me. Then she turns, swoops round the room, and starts to pack up Rita's things.

July 22nd, 1969

Honey,
A giant leap for mankind, right? What about
womankind! Ha Ha. A blast watching men on the moon
with you on the end of the line. So you're going to wait for
Lene to have the baby, then come home? You better. Call
Lula. She's not well. Zev and I are going to separate,
nothing you can say to change my mind, hon. Love to
Lene and Michael and Larry and can't wait for the baby!
love Rita
p.s it isn't so bad with one leg, don't worry, I'm
walking fine.

Mrs Iris Happy
The Happy Farm
Boldenham
Herefordshire
England

24

*G*ran and I have spent two days cooking very sweet cakes. There's Victoria sponge (17); fruit loaf (16); Marshmallow Surprise (1, because we're still not sure what the surprise is); coffee and fudge fingers (13); brandy snaps (loads) and 108 chocolate brownies.

We threw out all the saccharine jellies and the diabetic chocolate bars when we got back from the hospital. Gran said Rita would have wanted it this way.

Since Rita died Gran's been 'chipper' (that's what she calls it), but she's put sheets on all the mirrors (Grandpa keeps cutting himself shaving), she won't answer the phone, and the door to Rita's room is locked (we speed past it, and don't knock).

Mum hasn't come near us, she's been at Francis's gatehouse choosing wedding dresses, while Reggie's holed herself up on the third floor. They've ignored it all, but Grandpa hasn't. This morning he put his arm round Gran's shoulders and said, 'There, there, my love. You're a damned strong girl, you'll do it. Take a deep breath.'

He didn't explode in Naval-speak at all.

I still haven't told Gran about my talk with Rita and I don't think I will.

'What do you think, honey, too much?' Gran is holding a cream-piper above one of the Victoria sponges.

'Nah.'

'Okie-dokie,' and she squeezes thick sweet cream in swirls, before putting big strawberries and glacé cherries on top. I'm starving.

'What time is *it* happening, Gran?' I prefer not to say funeral.

'Twelve. They pick us up at twelve. They got Rita.'

'They' are the Mr Barlow-looking men with tall black hats, who, five years ago, cleaned up my daddy like they're cleaning up Rita now. Five years: that's a lot and a little time rolled into one. I wonder if they've got Rita's false leg, to put her back together again like Humpty Dumpty.

That's where Millie is, with the Mr Barlow funeral men. She insisted on making Rita up 'right tidy' herself 'for old times' sake'. And she dragged the hairdresser Kirsty-Ann with her, to set and colour Rita's two-toned hair. They came by earlier this morning to pick up Rita's best green dress and shoes, and Kirsty-Ann was shaking 'with the nerves'. Millie told her she'd pay her extra, and Gran gave them our biggest chocolate cake to put in the coffin with Reet. Kirsty-Ann went very white then and made a face like my Gran was bonkers. Gran told me that, sometimes, talking to Kirsty-Ann is like talking to a retard.

It's going to be a cremation, just like Rita said. There's not even going to be a vicar, or a Rabbi; just a cremation-person. Then Gran's bringing Rita back here.

'In an urn?'

'Yes, sweetie. She told me. That's how she wanted it.'

'Like Mum did with Dad?'

'Yup.'

'Are you going to put her in a mayonnaise jar?'

'No I am not. That's your goddamn mother.'

'Just asking.'

I gobble a strawberry as Gran mixes eggs, butter and sugar. There's sugar everywhere in our kitchen now; granules have spilled on the tabletops and the floor. 'Hey, we could do the shoe shuffle!' Gran said when we were mid-bake, and she did, across the sugar-sprinkled quarry tiles in her pink slippers.

It's like a sweet frost in our kitchen and I lick my lips. 'Gran?'

'Yes, honey.'

'When are we going?'

'I said, they'll be here at twelve.'

'No, I mean to America.'

She stops mixing and puts the bowl down. Gran's got butter on her cheek. 'I don't know what you mean, Katie.'

I take a deep breath. 'Don't you think Rita would want to go back to America? In her urn I mean? Zev would want her back.' I dip my finger in a swirl of sweet cream. 'And if we did go, we'd miss Mum's wedding.'

'Well, you wouldn't want that,' and Gran's back in motion, turning her wooden spoon.

'I would.'

'Oh, honey.'

'He's not my dad.'

'Does he want to be?'

She's right. Francis has never hugged me and said, 'I'm your daddy now, Katie-watey.'

'Are we ever going to America, Gran?'

'Sure we are.'

'You always say that and you've got all those envelopes of money up in the attic from all the Bosums, and everyone else says you're rich –'

'Well, everyone don't know squat.'

'Is it because you're scared? You said you were.'

She hits her wooden spoon on the tabletop. 'When? When did I ever say I was scared, Kate Happy?'

'When we watched the wrestling, after Mr Iwase did that battle, when we were watching the wrestling, you said –'

'I said, "I wasn't brave."'

'Same thing.'

'No, it is not. Katie, please don't hassle me, honey, not today. You are meddling in things that do not concern you, and we'll go to America. We'll go.'

'When?'

'Uch! God give me strength!'

'Pick a date.'

'That's silly.'

'No it's not.'

'Just give me some time, Katie, please. Thirty days at least.' Gran starts to count on her fingers. After a while she says; 'Okay. April 5th, how about that? Satisfied?'

I nod.

'Good. You're more like your goddamn mother than you know.'

'Does that mean we miss the wedding?'

'Oh, please gimme a break!' Gran pours a steaming cup of coffee from the permanent pot on the Aga, and sits down. Her eyes are red. I watch her swallow a big chocolate brownie down in one.

'I'm sorry,' I tell her.

'Have one of these Katie,' she mouths, chocolate-full, 'they're damn good.'

We polish off a whole plate and I run upstairs with chocolate on my hands. I haven't eaten so much in my life.

I was going to wear the same black dress I wore to Dad's funeral, but wonder of wonders, it doesn't fit. Gran gave me a dress of hers to try, and I grab it from the pink-quilted hanger and drop it over my head. It settles, nice and silky, and I stare at my reflection.

The dress is above my ankles, not dragging on the floor. I tie the belt. The shoulder pads make me look bigger, and I like that. I run out onto the landing, to the doorframe with my Buenos Notches, stand up against it and measure.

I've grown.

A whole hand.

Maybe I'm a vampire and I only grow when someone dies. I touch my neck and think of Jamilah.

'Katie, d'you want Rita's brooch?' Gran shouts up from her pink floor. 'It'll look cute.'

'Er, no thanks, you wear it.'

'You sure?'

'Yeah.'

I can't think about Rita right now. I don't want to wear her things. I'm thinking of Jamilah.

There was a note when I got back from the hospital, and the envelope had S.W.A.L.K. written on the back.

> Kate, (it said)
> I have to go. Dad's picking me up. Sorry. Your aunt Reggie said you'd probably be gone all day. Your grandpa and her are really weird. They stare at me. Can you come and stay? I'll miss you a lot as you're my best friend and I really like you. Listen to Toyah, she's really brilliant. When I have a kid, I'll call it that (if it's a girl). Hope your aunt got better and call me (not after 7 that's homework time). I'm going to see Breaking Glass with Najid at the Cannon tonight. Can't wait. S.W.A.L.K.
> Jamilah.

'Gran?' I call down.

'Yes, sweetcakes?' (She's using Rita's words now.)

'Do you have any shoes I can borrow? I've only got yellow wellies or sandals.'

'Okie-dokie.'

Gran sounds very odd today.

In my still-vanilla-smelling bedroom, I pull my hair out of my plaits and let it be electric. I think it's nice. Mum's left one of her red lipsticks on the dressing table and I dab it on and I rub a bit in my cheeks too. My head's buzzing with chocolate.

'Will these do, hon?' Gran walks in. 'Oh, my,' she says, and then circles me like I'm a horse at the Three Counties Show. After a moment she smiles and pulls my chin up. 'You look gorgeous, sweetcakes, but here −' she takes her hanky out and spits on it, 'I'd lose the lipstick. It *is* a funeral, you know. Not a damn hooley.'

I could say the same to her because my gran isn't wearing black, she's gone fuchsia and it makes my eyes smart. It's the loudest pink on the tightest two-piece I've ever seen, and it's all strapped to her small body.

I cross my legs in the back of the big black car because that's what ladies do (I've even got tights on; black and ribbed). There are two sets of seats here and they face each other, like on a train. Grandpa and Mr Crabtree are opposite me, and either side of Gran (each holding one of her hands). I can't believe Grandpa is letting another man touch my gran; he's even letting a man from Barbados touch her. I smile at Mr Crabtree and he nods; his hair and his beard are almost white now, but his glasses still go dark in the light. Grandpa seems calm. Maybe it's that too-calm.

I'm sandwiched between Millie and the hairdresser Kirsty-Ann, and we're following the hearse with the coffin in it. Kirsty-Ann's sniffling; she smells of marzipan-chemicals and her hair's so yellow it looks like a corn on the cob. She's telling us how she did Rita's hair.

'Oh, it was terrible. I had to close my eyes while Mil here told me what to do. But you know what, after a while it just seemed normal. Like any of my regular ladies. So I chatted to her, see. It was a new colour we got in too, aubergine, like that Kate Bush has. Looks lovely it does, Mrs Happy. Such a pity it's a cremation.'

Gran's not listening. Mr Crabtree is clasping her hand and tapping it up and down in his lap. I think my grandmother's finding it difficult to breathe in that fuchsia jacket and skirt.

'Nice day for it, mind you,' says Millie. She's staring straight ahead at Grandpa: I think it's Millie who's keeping him in check.

'Yes, Millie. You're right. Very right. It is,' Grandpa says.

We pass Beavan's Farm and the Barratt Estate; all built now, with cars already parked up identical driveways. Grandpa snorts, then winds down his window and yells, 'Ford bloody Granadas!'

'Larry —' Gran whispers.

It does look odd though; a field of houses in the middle of nowhere, like a field of cows. Grandpa's head is out the window now.

'Like the bloody Midlands! Ghastly new towns! Not the countryside anymore! Roundabouts! Flyovers!' He sits back, out of breath, and turns to Gran. 'Sorry old girl. Force of habit.'

We pass the Field of Bolden, all churned up and red from the battle.

'Did you get the cheque, Larry?' Gran asks.

'Certainly did.'

'Good, I'm glad. I know it wasn't easy.'

'It'll see Lene proud.'

'It sure will.'

Grandpa squeezes her hand and stares out at his field. Kirsty-Ann coughs into her hanky and Millie leans over me to whisper to her.

'This your first one, Kirsty, lovie?'

'What's that?'

'First funeral. First cre-ma-tion.'

I want Millie to say 'di-a-be-tic cre-ma-tion' in her sour and sweet Welsh voice.

'Yeah.'

'Dunt worry lovie, over in a minute. Just take a hanky. Extra you'll need. Specially after you met her this morning and all. It can be difficult up at the cremy, look you.' She sits back, handbag on her lap, ankles thick with stockings. 'I'm into my fifties now, with funerals,' she tells us all, 'This'll be my fifty-first mind you, and thirty-eighth, no ninth, at the cremy.'

The indicator tic-tic-tics, and we follow the slow hearse onto the main Hereford road. The crematorium is at the top of the hill, past the garden centre. This is where they burnt up Dad, and I'm sure there are flaky bits of us Happys all over this crematorium. I once read about, how, when they give you the ashes it's probably the ashes of a million other people, not just the loved one. So Dad's got loads of other people with him in his Hellmann's jar up in the attic, and Rita will have a whole party going on in her urn.

We park behind the hearse. The Mr Barlow-men get out, slow as moles above ground, and slide Rita's coffin out. It's very plain, almost like cardboard. They carry her on their shoulders, and the coffin looks so small, like she's shrunk since the hospital. Gran's already crying, she bobs from Mr Crabtree to Grandpa. Millie holds Kirsty-Ann's hand because she knows I'll be okay, and I watch the backs of Gran's heels walking into the big crematorium room. I watch her fuchsia, young girl's figure clash with the red carpet.

So the bombs fell and the boys were lost, and I met my darling Mat in Room 46. Oh, my darling. And why does Larry have to come home? Why, out of all those men on board was he saved?

I follow Gran in, and sit behind her.

Millie is solid as a pound cake on my one side, while Kirsty-Ann's wobbly on the other. A man stands up and speaks for a bit. He tells us how Rita loved her sisters and loved life and did a lot of good things, especially raising money for her local Little League baseball team in America. I wonder how he knows all this as we sing 'Land of Hope and Glory' (Rita loved it when Grandpa got drunk on sloe gin and sang that). No one gets up to say anything else; not even Gran. Then I hear a whirring sound and little red curtains at the end of the room open, like at the beginning of a play. It reminds me of the puppets' stage the Von Trapps have in *The Sound of Music*, with Julie Andrews singing about lonely goatherds and 'a-leyeo-a-leyeo-a-ley-oo-oo'.

Rita's coffin rolls in.

'That's it then. That's her done,' Millie whispers to Kirsty-Ann.

Millie's crying, though.

I loved my aunt Rita. I loved it when she called me 'sweetcakes'. I loved her leg popping out, and I wonder, if it's in the coffin with her, will it melt and cause a big splodge?

* * *

We're standing outside, waiting for Gran who's gone hysterical with Grandpa and Mr Crabtree. Kirsty-Ann's smoking a Silk Cut.

'You want one?' she asks.

'Okay.'

She lights it for me. I try and inhale because Rita must be in the air by now, and I'd rather breathe in Silk Cut than my great aunt.

'Oh, give me the creeps these places do,' Kirsty-Ann says. 'And I've had such a day of it. Never thought I'd touch a dead un, not a customer mind. But I know hairdressers who do that professional like.'

'Do what?'

'Dead bodies. Oh, I couldn't, not permanent. There's no chat.' She inhales. 'Now my mam went to a funeral last week, was her old boss, but they buried him, and I think that's kinder.'

'Probably.'

'All this burning. It's a bit savage, ent it?'

'Yeah.'

'What if they wake up?'

'Sorry?'

'What if they's not really dead and they wake up in all that fire? They'd reckon they was in hell, wouldn't they?'

I think I prefer Kirsty-Ann crying. 'Well, better than being buried alive,' I tell her.

'Oh, you give me the willies you do, girl.'

I take a drag and cough.

'You're very quiet about it though, didn't you like your aunt?'

'I've done it before.'

'What chu mean?'

'My dad, he died. They cremated him here.'

'Oh you poor thing,' she pauses, 'Your name's Kate Happy, ent it?'

I frown. 'Yes. Iris is my grandmother, I'm her granddaughter, remember?' (as Gran says, it is like talking to a goddamn retard.)

'I know all about you. Read about it in the paper. Bout your dad and all. Few years ago now, wanit?'

'Yes.'

'That was terrible, that was. Was it an accident, then?'

I look at the crematorium doors, praying for Millie; she's in the Ladies because her bladder's the devil.

'Your mum didn't go to prison, did she?'

'No.'

'Well, probably best, with you to look after.'

'Quite.'

'And you've turned out nice.'

'Thanks.'

''Spect you got a boyfriend?'

I flick my cigarette onto the mown grass, it lands in some daffodils. 'Have you been doing my gran's hair for long then, Kirsty-Ann?'

'Oh, just since Christmas, since Pierro was off sick with his veins. I had to take over, hold the reins your nan calls it. Oh, it's all reins and veins at The House of Pierro!' She takes a deep drag. 'She's nice your nan.'

'Yeah.'

'I could do something with your hair, mind. Get that frizz out and those knots. Get a bit of light in it too. Crimp it. That would be nice.'

I see the crematorium doors open. 'Millie, we're over here!' I yell.

She marches over, strong, 'Okay lovie, no need to broadcast.'

Millie looks like she's cleaned herself up; wiped her wet face and put it back on. She loved my aunt Rita too.

She opens a tin and offers us travel sweets.

'You got a nice spread at home then, Kate?' Kirsty-Ann asks.

'Cakes.'

'What?'

'Just cakes. It was Gran's idea.'

Millie giggles but Kirsty-Ann looks confused.

'My aunt was diabetic,' I tell her, but this information doesn't seem to help.

'Oh, that's good that is,' Millie says, 'Rita would a liked that. She'll be laughing up a storm.' She sighs and sucks a yellow sweet, hard, as we watch mown grass blow about on the crematorium lawns. 'Yes, she was a one that Rita, I remember your nan got the first telephone in Boldenham, 1945, and ever since, me and Rita'd be shouting things down that thing! I couldn't understand her and she couldn't understand me, but we got on like pikelets on a skillet.' Millie pauses. 'Well, here's to her, she loved the right things your auntie did,' and she lifts the tin of travel sweets like it's a glass of sherry. 'Here's to her. For old times' sake.'

I feel a tap on my shoulder.

'Kate, how are, child?'

It's Mr Crabtree. He doesn't say 'child' like my mum does; it's more gentle with no 'd' on the end.

'How's Gran?'

'Okay. Okay. She'll be right enough, soon enough.' It's only Mr Crabtree's creamy voice that keeps me interested in his maths. I remember I have homework for him, and hope he lets me off. 'Shall we all get into the car then, my dears?' he asks us and winks.

Millie calls Mr Crabtree 'a huge flirting foreign man'.

As we drive off I watch more mown grass swirl then twist high into the air in a long spiral. It's a mini-tornado.

We turn back onto the Hereford road and it's like nothing has happened; I'm still crushed between Kirsty-Ann and Millie, staring at the sandwich of Gran, Grandpa and Mr Crabtree. Except now, they can't hold her hands as she's holding Rita; that's Rita and the flakes of a million other people in a big, golden urn.

'And how's your homework coming along now, Kate?' Mr Crabtree smiles.

Bugger.

'I'll give you until Tuesday week, then we'll see what we can do, right? Two P.M. as usual? And, Katherine –.'

'Yeah.'

'Chocolate biscuits this time child, not Garibaldis. Your grandmother knows what I like.' He touches her arm and smiles.

'Aft!' Grandpa shouts, and Millie leans forward.

'As I said, nice day for it, right, Mr Happy?'

She never calls him Larry.

Gran starts singing to herself. It's 'Under The Boardwalk' because Rita loved that, and I try to picture Coney Island with its cotton candy and sideshows, and Oceanview Avenue that's mine now. I close my eyes; wanting my black and white dream to come back, except this time Rita will be there, waving from the attic window with Mathilda. I can hear her shout, 'Hey there, sweetcakes, I told you I'd come home!'

I open my eyes and the farmyard is filled with cars. Mum's Spitfire is here, and Francis's Range Rover.

In fact my mum and her intended are at the garage doors, waving. Mum is in a white, neck-ruffled blouse and a powder-blue cardy, pearls over the collar. Francis is in a black pinstripe suit. She has her arm through his.

'Oh Jesus H. Christ,' says Gran, 'it's fucking royalty.'

We all stare at her because none of us have ever heard Gran swear like *that*.

'Brownie or Victoria sponge, Millie?'

'Both. Don't look a gift horse in the mouth, isn't it?'

The cakes are going down well. Kirsty-Ann asked if the brownies were made by The Brownies, and weren't they clever at such a young age.

Retard.

Gran's bluebird lounge is filled, but dust covers the tabletops. No one seems to mind, apart from Francis's mother, who keeps wiping her index finger across surfaces and shaking her head, like in the Pledge ads. Silly cow. Gran lit a big candle for Rita and it's on the piano; she called it something in Chewish while Reggie looked daggers and told the vicar about her ailments and her vision of God in a really loud voice.

'Big man. Like my father. Commanded regiments. Before malaria. Terrible death. Cremation. Ganges. Not a religious man.'

I watch Rita's candle flutter, and I snake through people that she didn't know, and neither do I.

I'm wobbly in Gran's high heels.

In the kitchen, Mum's piling up same sized Victoria sponge sections onto a plate.

'You look ridiculous in those,' she says, pointing at my shoes with her knife, 'mutton dressed as lamb.'

'Well, you don't look so hot in your get up, Mom.'

'Talking Yank, are we?'

'Better than your yar-yar-yaring.'

'Don't start, Kate, my future in-laws are here and I want to make an impression.'

'Well, I'm sure you will.'

'Less of your lip.'

I cut the coffee cake and wonder if Francis's parents know about Trixie and the white Rolls-Royce. I wonder if Francis knows.

'Mum?'

'Yes.'

'Why are you being such a weirdo?'

'I certainly don't know what you mean.'

'Since Francis came along, you've gone all posh and boring.'

'Don't be ridiculous, Kate.'

'I think I preferred you mad.'

'I really do not know what you're talking about,' she repeats, carefully measuring out same-sized sections of the next cake.

I wonder if she's still on those pills. 'And why didn't you come to Rita's funeral?'

'Well it was hardly a proper ceremony, didn't even have a vicar.' She plays with the ruffles of her blouse and checks the flicks of her

Lady Di cut. 'And I don't know why your grandmother didn't get in a proper caterer. This sweet stuff is so common. I had one arranged, you know, wanted to try them out before our wedding. But no, she wanted to do it herself. I'm so embarrassed.'

'Mum you've gone really overboard with this Lady Di stuff. It's a bit stupid, isn't it?'

'Put the kettle on, Kate. Tea drinkers this lot. Ghastly.'

'I bet Lady Di isn't a snob,' I tell her. I want to rub my new posh mother in brown sauce and tomato ketchup *and* a council house. Gran says becoming a different person is just *her* way of coping. But coping with what? I think she's madder than she ever was.

I walk out with the coffee cake.

The lounge is hot and there's a smell of butter on the turn. Everyone has crumbs and icing on their lips. Grandpa's got crumbs and icing in his lap. I leave the cake on top of the piano by Rita's Chewish candle, and slip outside to the yard and Gran's stoop. I like sitting here. It's where I sat with Dad the night of the Eurovision, 1976. Five years ago: a little and a long time rolled into one.

There's more noise inside than there ever was when Rita was here; which is a shame, because Rita loved noise. I hug my knees as Grandpa's new bull moans, and I decide I like the feeling of tights.

'There you are,' says Gran. She walks down the stoop. She's got no shoes on and she looks older (though she's still in her tight fuchsia pink).

'Where have you been, Gran?'

'Packing Rita's stuff.'

'She hasn't got much here.'

'There's enough.'

For the first time today Gran undoes her jacket and seems to breathe. She sits down next to me on the cold stone, which is unusual; Gran's a stickler for chilblains and piles.

She's holding a gold cigarette case and she takes out a fag and lights it. I've never seen her smoke. She coughs.

'Found these in Eva's Sanctuary. I smoked when I was pregnant. Can you believe it? Thought it was good for me. We did in those days, oh the things we did!' She coughs again, 'Gee, these are some dry-assed cigarettes, near forty years old. Crazy huh?'

I suppose it is.

'None of them in there knew her, Katie,' she points at the dirty lounge window, then looks out at our shitty yard. 'Your daddy knew her.' Gran lets her head drop. 'Oh, it's too late for regrets, but —' she sighs '— to hell with it. To hell with it all.'

I wonder what Gran was doing in Eva's old room. I lean in to smell her breath because Gran's talking like she's drunk. 'You okay?' I ask.

She looks up. 'Oh, sure, honey. Sure. It just went so quickly, y'know. Just a moment ago I was at High School and riding The Wonder Wheel at Coney, then wham! That's it. Here I am. Nothing in between.' She runs her strong fingers through her black hair, and for the first time ever I see grey roots. 'Happy Time, huh?'

'Sorry, Gran?'

'Happy Time. That's what the Germans called it. Die Glückliche Zeit, spring of 1942, cos they sunk so many of our US ships, off our very own coast. We even had stuff wash up on Coney. Terrible stuff. Larry told me it was the reason he came over. To help us. Was the reason I met him, I suppose.'

'I didn't know you could speak German, Gran.'

'Why not? What my poppa's family spoke when they could. "To Happy Times!" was what Larry said. He thought it was fate, you see, being there and finding me. Maybe it was. What a ga-hoo-la.' She sniffs and throws the ancient cigarette into the yard. 'But I am still Iris Tallulah Veronica Miriam Ichmann. I still am, Katie.'

There's laughter from inside; it sounds like a cocktail party in the bluebird room.

'Honey?'

'Yes.'

'I found this.' Gran hands me an opened envelope. 'Read it,' she says.

Hey Iry, my big sis of a girl,   2.23 a.m. January 1st, 1981

I guess if you have this then things didn't turn out so great for me. No surprise though is it? It's New Year's and I've just had a lovely time with our little Katie. We watched the Big Ben bongs on the telly with Zev. She's a darling girl. Crazy as Paris but darling. We had a great talk. She knows more than you could ever imagine, Iry. She knows the lot.

I want you to know I love you and I forgive you (if there's anything to forgive anymore, I'm kind of hazy on the old stuff) and I hope you do me. I say that because I'm leaving it all to Katie see. I know you don't care about the money Iry, you never have, but I know you care about the place. I'm doing this cos I can't give you all that responsibility again, you deserve a rest, and I think Katie can take it. No, I know she can. You just follow her lead, right? She can take on all the memories of Oceanview Avenue, and more besides. That's her gift. I leave it up to her.

Hey, don't look so down, honey, it'll be fun and you know I could never resist a little fun. Right? Don't forget I'm watching you so don't go all damned religious on me either, honey. No tearing and shredding. Just the right stuff.

Get out of here, Iris. Before it's too late. Does it take me dying here to let you see?

You know what, give my love to Larry. He's a sweetheart really. And don't worry about Zev, I'm writing him myself. He has full residency at Oceanview Avenue, till he croaks. He never did get anything else from me in the divorce. Crafty huh?

Now listen, my lawyers in the city know it all. I've sorted it. Not so fat and useless in this bed, huh?

Night-night my big sister, and see you soon, and don't forget you got to take me back there. I fancy the sea. Remember the song? 'By the sea by the sea, by the beautiful sea, by the sea by the sea oh-how happy we'll be!' Some Like it Hot, my favourite movie. Tony Curtis, what a god! I'll miss him.

Your loving sis,

Rita.

p.s. hope you sniff this out, honey, it's the only goddamn place I can think of that Reggie won't get it.

Gran drags on another forty-year-old cigarette. It hisses and pops.

'I found it in her leg, honey. She'd hid the thing in the cupboard. It's hollow y'know.' Gran sighs. 'So, she left it all to you, Kate. Did you know about this?'

'Yes.'

She takes a deep drag and coughs, gasping.

'But it's not my fault, Gran, I didn't ask for the house. I don't want it, you have it. Rita was going on about me and the future and I didn't really understand a blinking word.'

'Don't be disrespectful, Kate. Do you want to live over there?'

'I don't know.'

'The molar coaster. That's what she called it.'

'What?'

'Reet. Called The Cyclone the molar coaster, cos when you looped the loop, your goddamn dentures fell out.' Gran smiles and puts her arm round me. 'Oh, sweetie.'

I think about America.

'If they'd let me off school, I suppose I could go, and I haven't been on an aeroplane for ages and it must take days to get out there too. Can we take the dogs?'

'You know? You're such a little kid sometimes. Think we all forget that.'

I watch her cry into her tight, fuchsia sleeve. It starts to rain, but we don't go in. There's too much cake in that lounge and people like me and my grandmother can't cope with that.

I am going on yacht probably.
Back to Northern Africa Tunis.
Shall return about 6th.
Photo for Kate while I am gone.
Nanny v. good and expensive pls make welcome.
All love,
Marlene

25

I can hear them below me.

'It has to be perfect, it just has to be!' Mum yells from my bed-room. 'We've only got five hours, Kirsty-Ann, so it better bloody well work. Get that arsing hairdryer out.'

Mum's dropping the Lady Di act today, and as soon as she gets the ring on her finger, I'm sure she'll start effing and blinding round Francis's gatehouse, permanently.

I'm sitting on the threshold of the attic. This is the only place I can think now. Everything's been so busy. So many people talking and wanting me to reply.

Dad is on the top step with me, and I've got the pink scrapbook Gran gave me for Christmas open on my lap. I'm sticking in my second clipping with Gloy Glue; it's over a month since Rita died.

The Hereford Times
1 April 1981

Captain Lawrence St John Happy and Mrs Iris Tallulah Veronica Miriam Ichmann-Happy of The Happy Farm, Boldenham, Herefordshire, announce the nuptials of their daughter Marlene Ginger Celia Martha Mathilda Happy-Mahoney, to Mr Francis James MacGregor Wyn-Franks Esq. son of The Honourable James McGregor Edward Wyn-Franks and Mrs Lettuce Mary-Jane Wyn-Franks (née Seedly-Pittel) of Ridgefield House, Sugwas. The service will take place at St Mary's Church, Boldenham, April 4th 1981 at 2.00pm.

So many names, they're like Crufts Champions. Gran insisted on the Ichmann. Reggie said the whole world will know about the Chewishness now.

I've got glue on my bridesmaid's slip.

'What do you think, Dad?' I ask him. 'Is it a good idea? Her doing it again?'

He's quiet; pissed off more like, left up in the attic for months. Though someone's been up here; someone's moved everything round. Gran's money has gone, and Eva's schoolbooks, even the old plane tickets to JFK.

'Marlene? Marlene dear, it's the florist,' Gran shouts up from her pink kingdom.

'Can't you deal with it, Mother? Can't you deal with just one little thing for me?'

'Got it, Lene!' Grandpa yells from his floor below. 'No panic. All done. Ahoy!'

Gran can't cope with much anymore, not since Rita. Grandpa looks out for her now. She only changed out of her fuchsia suit on Tuesday (it was an off-brown colour by then, and baggy she'd lost so much weight). That same day she put on proper shoes and make-up, packed two suitcases, took me to a photo booth, and told me not to smile too much. Gran wouldn't say what the pictures were for, but it was such a relief to see her lips bright red; her feet no longer dragging in slippers, I gave up asking. She keeps Rita's urn on her dressing table, next to the dead Happy girls in gilt frames. Zev's called on the telephone a couple of times, asking for Rita back. He told Gran that cremation was a sin, and she won't return his calls anymore.

I had a letter from a real American lawyer. They're different from English solicitors. Grandpa said they're mostly Chews and he dealt with it for me. 'Don't tell your mother about this though, it would break her heart.'

'Why?'

'Oh, family stuff, Katie, family stuff. Aft!' Grandpa is the only grown-up who's *dealing, coping*; all those words Mum and Gran say but can't use.

Rita's lawyer did everything for me, and Grandpa paid. He said he doesn't mind, as inheritance is an important thing.

'Watch it, Kirsty-Ann! That bloody well burns, I don't want to be bald on my sodding wedding day,' Mum shouts. Old Mum is definitely back. She'll be yelling 'arse-creeper' down the aisle.

I pick Dad up and shake his black soot. 'Do you want to come to the wedding, Dad? I could put a bit of you in my pocket?'

I knew he'd say no.

It's the Eurovision Song Contest tonight and it's a band called Bucks Fizz, which is champagne and orange juice. I think Mum's having her wedding on the same day on purpose. Gran told me to pull my head out of my ass and realise my mother just doesn't notice little things like that.

Little things.

'Kate? Where are you?' Jamilah is joining in with the yelling throng. She's so excited to be a bridesmaid it makes me laugh.

'Up here!'

'Where?'

'Above Reggie.'

On the cue of her name Reggie pops her head out of Samuel and Wilhomena's library, cats scatter. 'No time! Must work. Will be present at church!' then she slams the door.

Reggie hasn't finished her Happy Family Tree. She says she keeps finding 'things' that put her off, 'things that cloud, that darken the issue!' She told my grandmother we've mixed with the Welsh and *others*. Gran said, good thing too, give you some goddamn chins, and that was the first time I saw her perk up in ages.

'Kirsty-Ann? You up there, love?'

'Yes Mil, I'm in with Mrs Happy!'

'Which one?'

'Mrs Happy-Frankie-Wyney– the bride, Mil!'

'You got them hot rollers?'

'Aye.'

'Be right up.'

'It's not a free-for-all,' Mum cries, but Millie's walking up anyway, she never did listen to my mum.

This morning I overheard Kirsty-Ann talking to Millie in a dark corridor.

'D'you reckon she'll polish this one off like she did the last?' Kirsty-Ann asked.

'Oh no,' said Millie, 'last one she loved, look you.'

'Still, she could be one of those killers, those black widows what do in their husbands. For the money like.'

'Now you're being foolish, lovie. Our Marlene isn't as bad as everyone reckons.'

I liked Millie for saying that.

'What are you doing up here, Kate?' Jamilah's out of breath and her hairy top lip is wet.

'Nothing.'

'Well, do me up will you. Everyone else is going mad.'

She turns on the dark landing and I thread the little hooks up her back. It's nice to touch her again.

'Is your dress the same as mine, Kate?'

'Dunno.'

'You wearing make-up? I've got some black nail varnish. That would look brilliant.'

'Mum would have kittens.'

'Yeah, I know,' she smiles and sits down next to me. 'You like your new stepdad then?'

'Suppose.'

'You going to live with him and your mum?'

'Don't reckon.'

'Why?'

'They haven't asked.'

'Oh.'

'I don't mind.'

'Your mum's still gone weird then?'

'Yeah.'

Jamilah leans over, pulls my face to hers and kisses me, mouth open. She sticks in her tongue and smiles when she's finished.

'You don't mind, do you, Kate?'

'No.'

'I've been wanting to, for ages.'

'Me too.'

Her eyes are a lovely black.

'Is Brian coming?' she asks.

I pull my petticoat down over my knees and laugh, 'Yeah. Had to twist Mum's arm. He can only sit at the back of the church though.'

'My dad gets his meat from Gloucester now. He and Mr Ruck had a falling out. Did you listen to that Toyah tape I sent you?'

'Not yet.'

'It's ages old now. What's that?' She points at the jar.

'My dad.'

'What?'

'Bits of my dad.'

'What you going on about?'

'He was cremated.'

'Eh?'

'Burnt up.'

'And you got him in that jar?'

'Mum put him in.'

'But he saw us snog!'

'It's only his ashes.'

'That's terrible.'

We both stare at Dad.

'Doesn't look any different from the ash you get in a grate,' Jamilah says.

'I know.' I stand up and look down over the banisters; the drop still makes me queasy.

'You've got marks down your dress, Kate. Your mum's going to kill you.'

I think Mum's heard because she's yelling 'Kate! Ka-ate!' up the stairs.

'Ye-es!'

'Down here, child. Now.'

Jamilah rolls her eyes. I laugh and put Dad and my new scrapbook behind the attic door. As I follow Jamilah downstairs, I notice she's perfect and clean in white; not creased and mucky like me. We cover our noses as we pass Reggie's cat-pee library.

My room smells better, and worse, as Kirsty-Ann's shaking a tin of Gran's Elnet above Mum's head. Kirsty-Ann looks worried.

'Don't you fret, Mrs Happy. I know what I'm doing, it'll all come out right.'

'It's Happy-Mahoney you little witch and I'm going to be a Happy-Mahoney-Wyn-Franks so this better be perfect.'

Jamilah and I giggle from the threshold.

'What's your problem, arse-creepers?'

'Nothing.' I play with the mucky lace of my bridesmaid's slip. 'Just your new name. It's a bit of a mouthful, that's all.'

'It's history, darling. You wouldn't understand, and wipe that dirt off your bloody dress.'

I jump on the bed as Kirsty-Ann turns on a big silver hairdryer. Mum has to shout.

'Now! I want you two looking and behaving like innocents, not sluts!'

Kirsty-Ann puts the dryer under her arm and twists Mum's hair into big rollers.

'Jamilah, go and get the bridesmaids' flowers. Kate, stay!' Jamilah races out of the room like Mum really is Lady Di.

Kirsty-Ann unplugs the dryer and tries a smile. 'There we are. I'll leave you to set then, Mrs Happy-Mahoney-Wynkey-um –'

'Franks.'

'Franks. And I'll get on to your mam.'

'Don't forget whose wedding it is.'

'Oh no, course not, Mrs Happy-Mannyho –'

'Never mind, never mind. I wish to talk to my daughter, alone.'

I smile at Kirsty-Ann. Mum's not Lady Di, she's the bloody Queen of Sheba with ether down her pants. Kirsty-Ann looks stunned.

Mum gets up and closes the door. She looks funny in white underwear and I've never seen her hair in rollers in my life. She sits at the end of my bed.

'So, Kate, do you like Francis?'

'He's okay.'

'Just okay? Are you moving in with us?'

It doesn't sound like a request.

'It's up to me?'

'If you like.' I watch her hand tapping on her thigh.

'I'm close enough here at the farm, aren't I?'

'With your grandparents?'

'Yes.'

'You like it here, then?'

'Dunno.' I'm thinking 4342 Oceanview Avenue: Mum doesn't know Rita left it to me, yet.

'Oh god, you're not turning into a teenager, are you? When are you thirteen anyway?'

I count on my fingers. 'Nineteen months.' I'm getting better at maths. 'Rita told me thirteen's a batsmissedfor.'

'Don't talk rubbish, and don't be a clever cloggs.'

'Why do you want me to live with you anyway, Mum?'

'Because I am your mother.'

'So?'

'Don't be cheeky. Anyway we'll talk about it when you get back.'

'Get back from where?'

'Oh, never mind.' She leaps off the bed and yells down to Gran's floor, 'Kirsty-Ann! Up here, now! Let's get this show on the road! And do something about my daughter's damned hair. Iron it. Cut it. Anything!'

The church is so bright I can see everything. Flakes of white burst off the limewashed walls and every time Mum moves yellow pollen poufs out from her bouquet, like sherbet. As the dust dances, I sneeze and think of Zev's 'tsu gezunt!'

We're standing at the front; Mum and Francis in the middle and Jamilah and me to the side. We're doing that horse-smile thing; that bare your teeth to stop you looking bored thing. Francis looks like that anyway. He and Mum are standing on the same spot Dad once lay, horizontal, before they took him off to the cremy and burnt him up.

Brian's at the back; he was under the fanny-gargoyle when we marched Mum in. He said me and Jamilah looked 'blinking gorgeous' but I think he might be lying about me. Though my hair's pinned back, at least.

It took ages for Grandpa to walk Mum down the aisle as he's gone more shakey. Millie had to pound the organ pedals with 'Here Comes The Bride' four times.

Gran's in the first pew, in dull blue, because Mum said it was stupid for an old woman to wear pink and steal her day. I don't think Gran gives two hoots or a rat's ass what she wears anymore because her mother-of-the-bride two-piece is about four sizes too big. It looks like a sack and clashes with her red lipstick; but at least Kirsty-Ann got rid of her grey roots.

Francis's side of the church is filled with little men, partnered by big women wearing big hats. They all have very bad teeth, and moustaches. When they cough, they spray in the sunlight. Our Happy side is mostly Grandpa's friends from Borders Gate. Mum wouldn't invite anyone she used to know. 'The past is the past, darling. I'm different now,' she told me.

I listen to the vicar drone like the sun-woken wasps at the stained-glass windows. Weddings are more boring than funerals. I close my eyes.

The last wedding I was a bridesmaid at was some friend of Dad's when he and Mum still laughed and kissed each other and I was very small. We drove for ages with my white, ruffled dress on the back seat next to me. I remember touching it beneath its plastic cover and the surface was smooth as jelly.

'How long have we got to go?' I kept asking. 'How long is it till we get there?' It felt like we were driving to the end of the world, and Dad sang all the way.

'Three maids, a ri-i-i-i-sing!'

I still can't remember the rest of that song.

But when we did get there, and I stood in my itchy-white dress with a puffball bouquet on a ribbon, I screamed. I caused a scene. It was because I had to hold the pageboy's hand, and he was a boy who looked nice apart from his nose. This was disgusting and catching because just above his lip and hanging out of his nostrils were crusty scabs that bled when he talked.

Dad dragged me behind a bush. 'Don't be an idiot, Kate, it's not his fault.'

'Yes. Listen to your father. Poor kid. I doubt it's infectious,' Mum chimed in.

I blubbed even more, but I was made to hold the boy's hand, all the way down the aisle to an altar that was as stony and cold as the abattoir where Grandpa took his cows. I could feel my arm prickle with blisters, then one whole side of my body crust up with scabs.

So I threw up in front of the vicar and made the church stink.

Dad said I had ruined his friends' lives *forever*. That was the only time he hit me.

With my eyes still closed I listen to the rustle of this church; the silent pauses followed by the clutter of standing and coughing. It's like water; the push of waves kissing your toes, then the silent suck as it pulls back; again, and again. I think of the Coney Island Atlantic, lapping at Rita's stoop. Rita's lonely stoop. My stoop. I think of the three-storey wooden house, tall as a skyscraper, where all those people from another land lived like sardines, one on top of the other: Momma and Poppa Ichmann; Grandma and Pops Lieberman; Little Lula, Rita and Iry. I think of The Deli and the memory of vinegar; of the sideshow freaks and The Coney Island Carousel that is music for their, and now my dreams.

'I now pronounce you man and wife,' the vicar says, and I open my eyes to Mum and Francis snogging. Jamilah and I pull faces and laugh.

26

$\mathcal{G}$ran and me have left the party at Ridgefield, Francis's big place (or palace, Gran calls it). It's late; 'Late enough not to be missed,' Gran told me, 'and I need you to help me, Katie.'

She was very secretive.

We drive down our muddy track; me in my bridesmaid's dress stuffed in like egg-white froth, Gran in her dull blue mother-of-the-bride tent.

In the yard we jump over black puddles and I ruin my satin slippers. The farmhouse still looks like Thornfield, even with the uPVC sunlounge. Actually, it looks like a face; the garage doors are an open mouth; the windows are eyes. Jessie 13 leaps out of his barrel, and I jump.

Maybe I have been reading too much Stephen King.

'Down Jess!' Gran hisses and he whines.

She switches on the garage light and I follow her up kitchen steps that make me think of Rita. Reggie's cats pour out of the door, yowling.

'Oh wait for your goddamn mistress!' Gran spits, and they spit back.

Gran's perked up since this morning.

In the kitchen she takes a key out from her loose jacket pocket and marches down a beeswax and pee corridor to Grandpa's red front room. It's still freezing in here, and dark. The chaise-longue looks wet with damp and the Toby jugs are caked in dust. Gran speeds through, as it's a shortcut to the hall, where she jogs up to her pink floor like a young girl. I notice her pink chair is back by the black phone, but I'm not sure who Gran can call now. I lag behind her, careful not to slip on the reminder notes that still yell 'Gelatin!' from her stairs.

With the landing light on, pink dazzles. I sometimes forget how amazing her pink kingdom is. It's almost a lifetime's work. The first time Jamilah saw it, she said, 'Bloody hell, it's like being inside a stick of rock,' and she's right; because sometimes you do feel like licking the pink embossed wallpaper that shoots up from the candyfloss carpet, just like Hansel and Gretel once did. Over the past month Gran's painted the furniture in pink Dulux gloss. There's no more black oak and Reggie was livid, she said Gran has ruined the precious Happy family heirlooms forever.

I think I know why Gran's favourite colour is pink now; it's a relief, an antidote (I looked that up in Bosum's *Medical Dictionary*) to all the darkness in the rest of this farmhouse. Gran's floor *is* cheery, after all.

Instead of going into her bedroom, though, we're standing at the door of Eva's Sanctuary.

'Come with me,' she says, and I feel like Jane Eyre following Rochester into Bertha's den.

'What are you doing, Gran?'

'Something I should have done years ago,' she turns the key in the lock as I rustle in chiffon behind.

Gran switches on Eva's light.

It's not how I remember it at all; the room is smaller (adults say this about places they go back to and now I know what they mean). The huge pictures of Eva are actually just normal size and hanging from mould-spotted walls. Now I'd be too big for the rocking horse in the corner, and I remember it being enormous, with great flaring nostrils. Eva's dolls are still naked on top of it, though, looking creepy.

It smells of vinegar in here.

Gran's touching things. She's walking along the table by the rocking horse tapping each photograph album, each ornament. I don't remember Eva's room being littered with ornaments, and the Union Jacks that hang from the wardrobe doors don't ring any bells.

There's a coating on everything, thick and dark.

'Yes, honey, I know, but you said it would be *easy*.'

'Sorry, Gran?'

'Mm?'

Her eyes are glazed, so I don't bother asking who in the hell she's talking to.

'You know, Katie, I got this before I met your Grandpa.' She holds up an old-fashioned viewfinder, 'It was my treasure.'

Mum had one on the Bayswater Road, with loads of pictures of the South of France in it.

'Hold it up to the light, take a look, honey.'

I do, and I see London in the olden days. Ladies in bustles and lacy hats are pushing perambulators down the Strand. Gran changes the picture and I see a man with big sad eyes wearing a crown.

'I'd sit up in my room on Oceanview Avenue, just poring over these. Anything English, you see, Rita called it an obsession.'

I'm now looking at old planes in a black and white sky. It says, 'Our Men Fight the Hun!' beneath.

'Yup, I loved it all, the history of the kings and queens and the English movie stars. It was Momma's doing. Told me the story of the Carousel shipped all the way over from England, and how it sank just off Coney. She told me that story when I was nothing but a pinprick, she'd take me down to the beach and whisper tales of those Carousel horses. Said there was bluer than blue foals, silver stallions, and even a golden unicorn. And they all lived out there under the salty water. Told me about how they'd been crafted and conjured by Englishmen, just for us, and how they'd fought free of that ship and jumped into the ocean, whinnying. I'd dream about those horses under the waves galloping, just galloping. Brighter than bright. And I'd dream about England, too. The place where these magical creatures were born. Thought it had to be some kind of wonderland. But –' Gran snatches the viewfinder and chucks it in a half-full cardboard box; her eyes unglaze and she comes to life, 'but it's all just stories, honey. Now I'll have this, you grab anything. Anything. Then take it downstairs.'

'Where shall I put it?'

'In the backyard.'

'Why?'

'Don't ask questions, and don't trip on that goddamn stupid dress of yours.'

I pick up four photograph albums.

'Dump them right in the centre of the yard, to be safe, and come on back up to me, okay?'

'Yes, Gran.'

On my way down I hear Bosum whine from the bathroom.

It's chilly outside and my dress billows out like a sail as I drop my pile by the drain.

'Goddamn thing,' Gran mutters, she's behind me already; she must have flown down those stairs.

'What are we doing, Gran?'

'No time for questions. Come on and help me. Next lot,' she grabs my hand and pulls me inside. I'd forgotten how strong my grandmother is.

She jumps up the stairs.

'Don't dawdle!'

Back in Eva's Sanctuary Gran's pushing ornaments into another empty box. They smash.

'Gran, careful!'

'Good riddance.'

'What are they?'

'Knick-knacks. Worthless.'

I see a miniature double decker bus; a doll dressed up as a Pearly Queen, and lots of china with Union Jacks on.

'Stuff I collected. Would you believe it, got this in Coney.' She holds up a King George VI cup and it's the same man with the big sad eyes I saw in the viewfinder. 'Won this on the shooting gallery. Got me five English Kings in a row. But mostly me and Reet would order, from magazines, and once the war started, there was so much! English flags and plates, even table cloths and dresses. Look at this!' Gran holds up a tea towel with 'Ye Olde History of Englande' written on it. 'Oh my god. And this.' She sounds like a little girl. 'Oh, Reet sent me this, it was a joke. Quick, turn the light off, Katie.'

I'm suddenly worried; maybe Gran's going to have a séance.

'Now wait,' she commands in the darkness. 'There. Look.'

A greeny splodge-thing is glowing on the table, like a mini-Mr Barlow.

'Don't worry, honey. Look closer.'

I do.

'It's a glow in the dark Nativity set.' She laughs. 'Do you see? That's the Little Baby Jesus, there, and that's a, well, some kinda beast. A cow maybe. Oh, it still does it for me, Reet had such a sense of humour, she found it one day when she was delivering for Zev in Flatbush. Said she had to buy it for me seeing as I was converted and all. Oh, she had a funny bone, my sis.' Gran switches on the light and I'm glad. She picks up the Nativity set (which just looks like a plastic glob rather than a manger) and chucks it in the box too. 'Everything. Everything,' she mutters. 'No prisoners.'

She takes down the photographs of Eva without looking at them; glass smashes as she throws them into a box. I grab faded gymkhana rosettes, school certificates, and stop at a framed picture of Mathilda. It's one of those studio portraits and she looks quite pretty; her blue eyes tinted; her freckles washed out. She's got her lips closed so you can't see her overlapped teeth.

'Kate, I said don't dawdle.' Gran hands me the filled box. 'C'mon, chop, chop.'

My arms ache as she follows me down the stairs, and I wonder if Eurovision's started yet. I saw Bucks Fizz on *Blue Peter* in bright oranges and blues, the boys ripped the skirts off the girl singers. Every one of them had blonde streaks in their hair, even the boys, and Gran said they looked 'peachy American'.

The pile in the backyard is getting taller and I still don't know what Gran's going to do. She just throws her loads on top of my neat columns and more glass shatters. I want to stop and flick through an album to see Gran and Mathilda, and Eva and Mum, smiling on a pebble-beach (and was it Grandpa taking those pictures?). I want to read a few of Gran's old words.

So the bombs fell and the boys were lost, and I met my darling Mat in Room 46. Oh, my darling. Why does Larry have to come home? Why, out of all those men on board was he saved?

'Nearly done,' she says, as we jog back into the hall. I can feel patches of sweat under my arms. 'Just a few more trips, Katie.'

On the way up the stairs, I look up at our labyrinth of balcony rails that lead to the attic and see two faces peering over, with countless pairs of green eyes at their feet. It's Samuel and Wilhomena and they look like grey, olden-day photographs. I suppose they're worried, in case we come up two floors more, and throw them in the backyard too.

'Here we go, honey, keep up,' Gran passes me. She's got the rocking horse and she nods at a box on the top step. I catch my breath hop up the rest of the stairs and take a last glipse at Eva's Sanctuary.

It looks like an ordinary, empty damp room now. Nothing special. All that's left are the naked dolls. Gran's taken down all the pictures of Eva, and they've preserved lighter patches on the teddy-bear walls. Her Sanctuary has gone.

I feel a little scared.

'Okie-dokie. Up and at them.' Gran's on the threshold, her face wet with rushing, and her eyes a bit mad. She grabs the dolls and switches off the light. I pick up the last box and follow her down the stairs.

'What are you going to do?'

'Soon see, honey, soon see. Then we can get going, get out of this place.'

Sweat dries cold on my face as wind blows down the yard.

Foreo snorts, the bull moans, and Gran has disappeared into one of Grandpa's sheds. She comes out with a can of something.

'Don't look surprised, Katie. What did you expect?' She holds the can upside down, and splashes liquid on all the things we've dragged from Eva's room.

I think it's petrol.

'Gran?'

'Uh-hu?'

'Are you sure you want to?'

'Sure as I'll ever be, honey.' She doesn't seem sad, just determined.

I take a step back and watch as she lights a long Cooks match. She throws it on top of the dolls and their hair catches. Then blue fire blows up in a cloud. It smells of Bonfire Night, and chemicals. Things begin to melt. Black flakes twist in the air, and I look at my grandmother and she's laughing; like Bertha on the battlements.

'I never thought it could be so goddamn easy, honey! I just never thought!'

Glass cracks.

'You were right, Reet, honey,' she shouts at the darkness. 'You were goddamn right. Let go!' Her face looks orange in the light as smoke coughs round us. Then Gran's taking off the big blue jacket and skirt Mum made her wear and she throws them on, too. They land on the flaming rocking horse, like winter blankets. 'Hey, this is fun, right Katie?' she asks in her pink slip.

The fire will leave a mark. I watch laminate pages melt and words black over, and I wonder if I could do this to Dad; to my scrapbooks?

Then I remember something.

'Did you put Mathilda's letters in there?'

'You mean the ones you stole?'

'I only borrowed – how did you know?'

'I know more than you think. Those letters certainly had an effect on you, didn't they?'

'What do you mean?'

She smiles.

'Are they on there?'

'No doubt.' She looks glazed again.

'Gran?'

'Hmm.'

'What happened to Mathilda?'

'What do you mean?'

'Where is she?'

'She died, honey.'

'When?'

'A few days before Eva, in my bed. Pneumonia.'

'I thought –'

'Never mind, anyway, you better go say your goodbyes.'

'Who to?'

'To everyone, honey. April 5th tomorrow and we're going to America, like I said.'

'What?'

'You were the one made me pick a date. I got you a passport and a visa and I told your mom, she doesn't seem to mind.'

'But what about school?'

'You'll only be gone a while. Don't worry. I thought you'd be excited.'

'I am. I suppose. I just haven't packed.'

'You'll have time.' She pokes the dying fire with a stick. 'That's it then. Come on, let's go back to the party, otherwise Marlene will have a hissy-fit.'

'Aren't you going to get dressed?'

'Hmm?' Gran looks down at herself and laughs. 'Oh Jesus creepers! Gimme a minute, okay?'

I watch her skip off in sheer pink. Charred paper flutters about me, and I walk round the embers, hoping to save something, but it's all too late.

Gran's soon running back in her old favourite, the Jacqueline Kennedy Special. She takes my smokey hand and we walk to the car, stinking of bonfires. As we back down the drive, faster than Barry Sheen, she turns the radio on.

'And congratulations to Bucks Fizz in Dublin this evening, who did us proud with one hundred and thirty six points and first place at this year's Eurovision. Congratulations Bucks Fizz, and here's "Making Your Mind Up!"'

There's a band of old men playing trumpets in the ballroom. Mum told me it was 'ragtime' and it's an awful bloody racket. People are trailing about Ridgefield House, champagne glasses like jelly bowls in their hands. The women have little black cigarette holders, while the men are holding cigars and throwing back their heads going 'ah-ah-ah!'

I don't recognise anyone.

The last time I saw Jamilah, she was dancing to ragtime with Davey Prosser from Sugwas. I want to tell Jamilah the news about Bucks Fizz, and America. Brian's not here to tell.

I wander through rooms; it takes ages they're so big.

In the ballroom I trip on my egg-white dress as a waiter offers me a silverskin onion. Mum's dancing with an old man in the corner. I run to her and tug on her wedding dress.

'Fuck off,' she hisses.

'Mum.'

'I said, piss off.' She's definitely dropped the Lady Di act.

'Mum!'

She smiles at the old man and drags me to the other side of the room. 'What is it that couldn't wait? God, you smell like a bloody gypsy.'

'Thanks.'

'So what have you and the Yank been up to, to stink of smoke? Tying burning logs to my car?'

'No.'

'And what's that mud doing on your dress, I told you to keep smart. Look at your shoes! And your face is smudged.' She dips her fingers in her glass of champagne and washes my cheek off.

'Mu-um!'

'I don't want my new in-laws thinking I've got a slut for a sodding daughter. Have you talked to them?'

'No.'

'You should. They're *your* grandparents now.'

'They're not.'

'Yes they bloody well are and be thankful.' Mum's got blue mascara on. 'Darling, I have to change and give Francis his oats. Won't take long. You staying here? Where's your friend?'

'I don't know. Mum?'

'Not now, darling.'

'Why don't you mind?'

'Mind what?'

'Me and Gran. Going –'

'Look, I don't have time for your riddles,' and she rushes out of the ragtime room and up the huge swirling staircase of the Wyn-Franks's home, in a flurry of ivory-silk and puffed sleeves.

Not a tear in sight.

'Now, don't you look lafly,' a woman with a hairy top lip leers down at me. Some of the hairs are grey. 'You're Keet of course, Marlenah's gel.'

'S'ppose.'

'Adorable! You've pecked up the eggcent hare. How long have you been in the shire?'

I stare up at her.

'Most charming.' She clucks like a hen and walks off in tapestry-print.

I push some French doors, and wander out into the statued garden chewing a strand of my hair: Mum's right, I stink of smoke.

'Ja-mil-ah!' I yell, and a couple jump.

'Well, really!' the man says. 'It is *not* polite to shout, young lady.'

'Oh, sod off,' I tell him. I've had enough of my mother's Lady Di wedding.

'I *beg* your pardon.'

'You heard.'

'Well, I say!'

'You seen Jamilah round here? She's the other bridesmaid.'

'I really don't know who you mean.'

Down an avenue of trees, there are lit places in the huge Wyn-Franks's garden. They've got something called a ha-ha here, and a maze. I might get lost in the maze later and cause some bother.

I see Jamilah on a stone bench next to a stone dragon. She's snogging Davey Prosser, and they're making the same sound Gran does when she guts a goose. Davey's got his eyes open.

'What are you staring at?' he says.

'Your ugly mug', I tell him.

'Hi, Kate.' Jamilah pulls away and Davey stands up.

'Why are you snogging him, Jam?'

'Dunno.'

I sit down next to her, and Davey offers us a fag.

'Don't smoke,' we both say, and laugh. He shrugs his shoulders, lights up and walks off.

I kick my legs back and forth, cold. Jamilah blows into her hands.

'Should have brought my Parka.'

'Yeah.'

There's a huge oak to one side of us, half dead. It's got a big limb hanging off: it must have been hit by lightning.

I don't know how to tell her. I wonder if she'll cry and beg me to stay.

'Jam?'

'Uh-uh.'

I want her to sob, because Mum didn't. I hold her hand and squeeze it.

'Jam, I'm leaving.'

'Yeah, I'm getting a bored too. We going with your gran?'

'No, I mean I'm really going. To America.' I look into her eyes, to check for welling up, for an overflow. Maybe she'll whisper, 'after all tomorrow is another day!' or 'what light from yonder window breaks?' (because I'm doing *Romeo and Juliet* in school).

But all she says is, 'Oh, right.'

'I'm going tomorrow.'

'Brilliant.'

'Won't you miss me?'

'I suppose, but you can bring me something back.'

I look at her face; not flushed like Mr Rochester's cheeks in the moonlight; not calling me her bird, her sprite, her fairy. In fact she's smiling.

'I might be going for ever, Jamilah.'

'I'll come and visit then. It'll be brilliant. I've always wanted to go to America. Shall we go and nick some champagne?'

I don't move.

'Come on Kate, don't be moody. I'm sure you won't be gone for long, you have to go back to school, don't you? And I'll do a tape for you, with Hazel O'Connor and Toyah and Siouxie. It'll be great. Don't be a misery guts, let's get drunk.'

Jamilah kisses me, and then pulls me inside.

October 22nd, 1971

Iris,

Lula's funeral last Wednesday and I'm finding it difficult to write. She missed you there is all I can say, she missed you for two months at the hospital. You say Marlene's disappeared. No doubt a blessing in disguise. Please don't call me for a while. I'm real angry with you, Iris. Going to take time to forgive.

Your SISTER

Rita

Mrs Iris Happy
The Happy Farm
Boldenham
Herefordshire
England

27

'You still smell like a bloody gypsy, darling.'

'Thanks, Mum.'

'You're welcome.'

She and Francis have come to Heathrow with me and Gran because their honeymoon doesn't start for another week. It's salmon fishing in Canada. My mum *has* gone insane. On the drive up, though, she made sure I knew what a sacrifice it was, Francis taking us all this way, with a hangover.

Mum looks green beneath the airport strip-lights. A woman in a yellow sari cleans the floor round her.

'So, Kate, you'll be back in May, right?'

'That's what Gran says. I'll miss a bit of school.'

'Well, I'm sure you'll have a great time. I'll call when we return from our trip.'

Francis pitches in, 'Yes, we'll miss you, Kate. Your mother's quite worried about you, you know. Maybe we could pop down from Canada?'

'Don't talk rubbish, Francis, the child will be fine. But remember, darling, men after dark. Avoid them.'

'Yeah, and Moonies get you at airports with fudge.'

'What?'

'Never mind. We'll be fine, won't we, Gran?'

I turn round but Gran's gone. She's over with Grandpa on the red plastic airport seats. Her hand is on his thin polio leg and they're talking, faces close.

'Leaving an old man to fend for himself like that,' says Mum, 'what about her vows?'

'He's got you, Mum.'

'*I'll* be in Canada.'

Francis smiles at her, 'Come on now, darling, Reggie said they'd look after him while we're away. And Millie has her niece coming in.'

'Yes and that's the blind leading the sodding blind. Poor Daddy.' Mum starts to cry quietly.

I listen to the announcements; a woman's posh voice echoes in the huge terminal. Francis smiles at me.

'Now Kate, would you like some comics and sweets for the journey?' he asks.

'She'll throw up.'

'The *Beano*, the *Dandy* and *My Guy* please.'

'"Please-Thank-you, Francis,"' Mum looks daggers at me, and the departures board clatters. Francis runs off.

'Where's that funny friend of yours, Kate?'

'Which one?'

'The girl. Dark.'

'You know her name's Jamilah, Mum.' I frown. 'Anyway, her dad came by really early to pick her up.'

'Good.' Mum looks at her red nails, fingers spread. 'So, who knows, when you get back we could all move in together.'

'Yeah.'

'We'll discuss it later, then.'

'Right. Mum?'

'Yup.'

'On your passport, will you have to change your name? To Marlene Ginger Celia Martha Mathilda Happy-Mahoney Wyn-Franks?'

'Yes, what of it?'

'Will it fit?'

'Oh god, you *are* a teenager. Look, here comes your grandmother, you should go through.'

Gran's holding onto Grandpa, who shuffles across the lino floor, feeble. They pass the mopping cleaner.

'Okay, Pa?'

'Yes Marlene, don't fuss.'

Mum looks away.

'You look after yourself, Katie dear,' he says. 'Remember me to the old place, eh?'

'Sure.'

'Don't do anything I wouldn't do. Aft!'

'There, there Larry, calm down,' Gran pats his arm.

'Okay. I'm okay, Iris.' But he's not because he's crying; tears catch in his lined skin. 'Right. See you old girl.'

'Yes. Bye bye, Larry.'

For the first time I see my grandparents kiss. Grandpa leans forward and down, and Gran holds his big face in her hands.

'You've been a good man,' she tells him, and I turn my back; shy. Mum walks off.

Our flight is announced and Francis runs over from WH Smith with my comics. He hands me the bag, whispers, 'You'll be thankful for those Mars Bars. Don't tell your mother,' and winks.

I'm almost beginning to like Francis.

'Well, we got to go, goodbye.' Gran waves, even though everyone is inches away; she doesn't want a scene. 'Where's Millie?'

'In the loo, Gran.'

'Honey, go tell your auntie Millie to get a move on or she'll miss the plane.'

I run towards the Ladies, the WH Smith bag hitting against my leg. I expect Millie's in there praying. She's been praying all morning, because as she said in the car, 'A big hunk of metal like that going up in the sky just isn't right, mind you.'

She's coming with us though; she even gave her cat to Reggie to look after. Reggie's looking after the dogs, and Foreo too.

November 29th , 1975

Can't wait. Booked PanAm. What a price! Arrive
December 18th for your Christmas/my birthday. Can't
wait to see Lene and Michael and that little Kate. Got
so many photos but in the flesh is better. Call you later.
love Reet.

Mrs Iris Happy
The Happy Farm
Boldenham
Herefordshire
England

p.s Zev keeps muttering 'Mountain, Mohammed!
Mountain, Mohammed!' now Honeybunch started,
goddamit.

28

Everything is bigger here, apart from the sea. It doesn't look like an ocean at all, more like the flat blue carpet in Grandpa's hall. The sea in *The Love Boat* that's on the telly is powder blue and huge, and much better than the one past Oceanview Avenue. Gran says Brighton Beach and Coney aren't what they used to be, and what with the nuclear waste and the mess the junkies leave, it isn't safe to swim.

There's no Luna Park and Trips to The Moon: no Elephant Hotel or Flea Circus, but there are Projects, which Gran told me are council houses, only much, much bigger. The Cyclone molar coaster's hanging on for dear life, though, and Millie says that's a wonder in itself, as it's wooden.

We have new words here, there's *boardwalk, screendoor*, and *Lysol*. They have *fireflies, sharks* and *hypodermics* on the beach, where you can buy a plate of chips in the middle of the night, as long as you ask for *french fries*.

4342 Oceanview Avenue smells of *Pine Freshness* instead of Vim and Millie loves it. She told me she'd bathe in it if it didn't make her come up in a rash. Rita's house is bright and white, and I wish there were thicker curtains as the sun shines in so much. Vampires wouldn't stand a chance. The house smells better than beeswax and pee though, and Zev told me it's the cedar that gives the place that sweet scent.

Gran says everything is new here because we brought nothing

with us. 'We're starting fresh, honey.' The only things we made sure of were Aunt Rita and Dad. They were checked in as luggage. Gran calls us refugees, like those boat people on the telly. I even left *Jane Eyre* and *'Salem's Lot* at the farm, because I wasn't keen on Mr Barlow or Mad Bertha following me halfway across the world.

Though it wouldn't have mattered: there are enough odd people here to scare anyone.

I wipe sweat from my bare legs with a tissue, and try to breathe, but it's like swallowing hot wool. The boardwalk's crowded today. There are a bunch of kids with combs stuck in their hair doing funny dancing by the railings; one is spinning on his head. A man at The Pleasure Beach Beer and Clam Stall turns up Bruce Springsteen and the boys shout. Someone yells, 'Corndogs!' and I stand to one side; I'm waiting to go into The Sideshow Museum.

I've lost Millie.

The boardwalk is where old people walk on aluminium sticks, while young people get drunk (though Millie says it's more than the alcohol does that). Zev told me the young people here are Russian Babushkas, and the old people are Chews who speak a special language called Yiddish like him. He said he'd teach me that soon.

The sea's flat and dark as usual, the sand looks dirty and seagulls cackle. It was cold in April, now July heat sags me. Our visas have run out, so we might get shipped back anytime, Gran says.

'One ticket, please,' I ask the man in the booth, and hand him a damp dollar. I'm not waiting for Millie any more.

The man's badge says 'Hi! My Name is Fred!' and his thick glasses give him one eye bigger than the other. I push through a pair of black velvet curtains, and shiver, because inside the air conditioning is on freeze.

I've been waiting over three months for The Sideshow Museum to open. I've stared at its frontage, its bright paintings of The Crazy Tattooed Man and The Amazing Seal-o for so long I'm past goosebumps and butterflies. I can't believe I'll soon meet Jeremiah, though how I'll tell him about Rita, I don't know.

Inside it's dark as well as cold and my eyes and hot skin take time to adjust. I squint. This place is certainly not like The Natural History Museum, in fact, it's just a black room that smells of stale beer and underarm. 'Hello?' I say. 'Is Jeremiah here?'

But there's no one at all.

A few dim spotlights come on, and closest to me I see a sign: 'The Tallest Man In The World!'

For a moment I wonder if Norman the giant will jump from behind the shabby curtain, but all I can see is a black and white picture on a stand; it's of a very tall bloke in glasses next to a normal sized man.

I walk to the next spotlight.

This highlights a shop dummy, headless, with flaky Superman transfers stuck all over its body. He's called 'The Tattooed Beast of Borneo'.

'Oh, now that's a nice chill,' Millie comes in, pushing soft ice-cream into her clenched teeth. Millie sucks up ice-creams and snowcones all day. 'You all right, lovie?'

'This is bloody rubbish, Mil,' I tell her. 'Where are all the freak people? The real ones, I mean.'

'Shh. It's a museum. You've got to be quiet, look you.'

'It's a bloody swizz –'

'Dunt get upset now. I dunno, they probably died out, isn't it? Like the dodos.' Millie's in her navy wool dress and tan tights, she's dripping sweat; the heat means nothing to Mil when she wants to look her best.

'But Rita said she knew them all, said she saw them every summer.'

'C'mon now, time wasn't much to Rita, mind you, maybe it was years ago, she just got mixed up. Be nice Katherine, for old times' sake.' She nibbles on the wafer bit of her cone.

I fold my arms and sulk.

Because Gran hardly ventures out now, I go everywhere with Millie. It was July 4th, not long ago, when people had barbecues and fireworks like Guy Fawkes night, that Gran put on one of Rita's big floral print dresses and told us that from now on she's keeping to the house. Millie says she looks like a pea in a sheep's bladder in Rita's clothes, and that a man will soon cure her of all that grieving. Most days Gran sits at Rita's green formica table, licking honey from a spoon and asking, 'Shall we go back home, Katie?'

I know she doesn't want a reply.

She told me High School begins after something called Labor Day, and we have until then.

Funny-eyed Fred from the kiosk walks into the black room and coughs. He's actually quite young. His blond hair is in a ponytail and he looks up at the ceiling as he talks.

'The sideshow freaks of Coney Island were an Unnatural National Treasure.'

'That's good, mind.'

'No it's not, it's a swizz.'

'Shh —'

'Every summer they would come far and wide to share their Unnatural Wonders with us lesser mortals. Surf Avenue would teem with sideshows as people from all over the tri-state area stood in line for just a peek at these beauteous oddities. Take No Face here, as you ladies can see, a man with no face. Born with no eyes, no nose and just a toothless slit for a mouth, No Face was the talk of New York.'

Fred talks with a bored drawl, like he's chewing dough.

Noo Yarwk.

I stare at his long spider-fingers as he points out No Face in a photograph. Fred's got black nail varnish on, and he looks like he plucks his eyebrows.

'Here we have Baron Paucci, the smallest man in the world. And if you move along here, there are Chang and Eng, the most famous Siamese twins of them all.'

Millie nods, as if there's something to agree with.

'Now, for more history; pictoral and written —'

'What's that, Katherine?'

'Bits from the newspapers, and more bloody photos.'

'Oh.'

'— of the local boy, The Amazing Seal-o, now retired to Florida.'

'My auntie Rita was his girlfriend,' I shout, hand up like I'm back at school.

'Please don't interrupt the tour, Miss.' Fred won't look me in the eye.

'But she was, they fell in love, and she only had one leg.'

Fred ignores me. He stares at the ceiling and coughs again.

'And here we have Tors-o, Seal-o's rival, and more popular due to his lack of arms *and* legs.'

Millie follows Fred, sucking her soggy cone; I stay where I am and read Seal-o's display. There's a framed bit from the newspaper.

AN AMERICAN DREAM COMES TRUE

Born Jeremiah Albert Hopkins to a Jewish father and Cherokee Mother, Jeremiah became The Amazing Seal-o at an early age. His mother, who worked with Buffalo Bill Cody on his last Wild West Show, and his father, Bill Cody's accountant, were well versed in showmanship, and later toured with their infant son throughout the depression. Speaking to him at his luxury Condo, on Longboat Key, Florida, The Amazing Seal-o explains his colourful past. 'My poppa said, "There's always someone wanting to see a boy worse off than them, even in a depression." So we toured everywhere, and that's how we got through. I supported us all; Momma, Poppa, my five brothers and three sisters. It was a good family life, even then. And the war never came my way, on account of my arms, so life just went on. Three of my brothers died for this country and that just about broke Momma's heart. She did always say it was a blessing, me being born like this.'

Jeremiah is celebrating the recent launch of his fifth restaurant in the West Florida area, The Sealboy Special 5.

Above this there are lots of photos of him with his pretty mum and his handsome dad. Seal-o's handsome too, very. His skin is brown and his face is wide; cheeks packed. He's tall. In one picture he's smoking, hand up, so his arms couldn't have been that floppy and out of reach.

And that's when I spot the hair: red as tomato sauce.

Rita's standing on the boardwalk, on a bright Coney Island day, and she's dwarfed by Jeremiah he's so huge. She's got a lovely grin and his flippery arm is reaching almost across her shoulders; you can see the tips of it poking round. They look like the most opposites-attract couple in the world, far more than Gran and Grandpa; what with him and his dark hair down past his waist, and her with her red fuzz. Rita's leaning into him, in a lime green dress, and her false leg looks so convincing no one could ever tell. I look into Jeremiah's eyes; big and black, and they smile back at me.

Underneath the photograph is a little typed strip.

'JEREMIAH THE AMAZING SEAL-O AND FAN. CONEY ISLAND, SUMMER OF LOVE, 1969.'

That was the year I was born. The same year Rita was flippering and hopping around with Jeremiah.

'And here we have Minatura, the smallest woman in New York State,' says Fred.

Millie's still following him. They're buried deep in a black corner, so I lean in, kiss the picture of my aunt Rita and her one true love, cough, and tear the photograph off the display.

It burns in my pocket as I slip out through the cold velvet curtains and back into the woolly heat.

Serves Fred and the stupid Sideshow Museum right, I think.

I dodge people, then sit on the edge of the hot boardwalk. For fun I try to imagine *them all* inside that little cold room with Rita and Jeremiah. There'd be Reggie The Relic! Jamilah The Hairiest Girl in Hereford! Brian Feral Boy, Watch Him Growl! Grandpa The Matchstick Leg! Marlene The Lady Di Double! Francis, Mr Toad of Toadhall!

Roll up! Roll up!

And me; I don't know what I'd be, yet.

The boardwalk shakes with the weight of walking crowds, and the air is just that bit cooler sitting down here. The same someone yells 'Corn Dogs!' as the Astroland Fair jingles and jangles behind me.

I've had one postcard from Mum.

SweetFart,
Canada was bloody freezing but caught
a big fish, name of Francis. Ha ha ha!
Hope you're not getting too Yankee.
All Love,
Mum

Miss K Happy
4342 Oceanview Avenue
Coney Island
Brooklyn
New York
USA

Dear Mum and Francis, (I wrote back),

It's fun here and hope you are well. Kiss Bosum 8 and Jessie 13 for me, but don't bother with all the cats, you'll get worms. Hope you are well. I expect we will be back soon or you will come over here. Glad Canada was nice and you caught a fish (ha ha ha).

Lots of love,

Kate

The Cyclone starts up. It whirrs like the little conveyor belt in that crematorium place we took Rita, only much louder. People scream. Zev calls them howlers.

When I first got here, I'd lie next to Gran in Rita's old bed and listen out for the fair. For the longest time I heard nothing; just the hum of steel cables in the wind. So I'd slip out from the sheets and press my ear to the window screen. Then, when our street's air conditioners switched into gear, it began. *The Magic Roundabout* whine of rides, the crack and rumble of the Cyclone, that big thing on stilts, backed like a whippet, that rises and crashes like waves. Millie and I go on it all the time now, and she always takes her teeth out and pops them in her handbag first. She says the Cyclone and The Wonder Wheel aren't much better than the Hereford May Fair, *and* there's a man at the Clam Bar who looks just like Terry Jenkins, the Ledbury gypsy man.

Millie's homesick. She's started cooking lamb stews with the widow Zolensky who has our top floor: she told me it's the only meat sweet enough to cure her. I think Gran's homesick, too, but not for Happy Farm. Zev says it's for something that's gone and she can never have back. Before she locked herself up in Rita's bright apartment, she took me to Janet Fiorello's old house every day and told me again, and again, about Janet driving out to the troops with coffee and donuts during the war. There's a plaque on Janet's house, telling that same story. Food is very important over here.

I feel in my pocket for the photograph; still there, but instead I take out a postcard.

It's from Jamilah.

Kate,

I've had my exams. They were awful and I reckon I failed them all. I did R. E., English Lang, and Maths 'O' Level early. The rest were just end of year ones. Sorry I didn't write but you sound like you're having fun, better than us in France. We're in a bloody caravan in Normandy and Mum and Dad aren't speaking. It's raining and it's fucking awful!! I better put this in an envelope (so I can write over the other side) and so my dad doesn't read what I've written. Thanks for your telephone number but I don't think they'd let me call America.

Lots of love and see you soon now I'm running out of space.
Jamilah XXXX

p.s. you must be really homesick by now. See you soon, right? I miss STUFF with you.

I hate postcards from France.

'Mil!' I shout, because she's walked past me.

'Oh, there you are, lovie, we should keep together, look you.'

Millie's been listening to Mrs Zolensky and her stories about the rapist junkies of Coney Island.

'You set then, Katherine?'

I look up at the haze of heat and nod; Millie's streaked with sweat, and her new black hair's gone limp.

'We should go shopping for your nana mind, get some Royal things. Like scones.'

'Yeah.'

'Bit of a disappointment that museum place, isn't it?'

'Definitely.'

'Waste of money if you ask me.'

I tacked the picture of Rita and Jeremiah above my side of the bed and Gran said, even if I did steal it, it was ever so nice. 'They've come back home,' she whispered.

It's dark outside because it's really early morning, but our lights are on. I can smell Gran's lockshen pudding, and Mrs Zolensky's lamb stew cooking, and neither of those are great morning smells. The telly blares from Zev's apartment above. It's an English voice.

'This morning in London there isn't a scrap of pavement, an inch of road free. Here we have a city of high expectation, a country of high expectation, as we wait for one of the most momentous occasions this land has seen.'

From Rita's bed I stare up at the bright, white ceiling and breathe in the smell of cedar. We're almost at the end of the street here and I can hear cars speed on Ocean Parkway. I love the noise. This house is exactly as I saw it in my black and white dreams: sometimes I expect to see Rita and Mathilda wave at me from the top storey window.

Gran and I have Rita's apartment on the ground floor, and it's just how she left it. There's on orthopaedic bed that we share, with a plastic sheet that crackles. Hershey's Kisses are still hidden under Rita's cushions, and in between her floorboards. I hunt for them, and gobble them up, melted out of shape. I love Rita's apartment, because the walls are painted lime green, and it's full of noise.

'You want the Jello, Zev?' Mrs Zolensky yells down from her top floor.

'Better than that darned meat!'

'Okay, okay, so you don't like the meat. Meat is good. Good for small men like you.'

'Not at 4.30 a.m.'

'Uch! I can do nothing with you. Millie? You have meat with me?'

'Wouldn't say no, dearie.' Millie's voice is muffled because she lives in the basement. It's even bright down there.

'Zev, you got that machine working?' Gran joins in from our landing: Uncle Zev is on the first floor.

'Sure have, Iris.'

'What is it again?'

'VCR, I told you!'

I think we need an intercom in this house. Millie calls 4342 Oceanview Avenue 'The Funny Farm' instead of Happy Farm, but I think it's a bit more like The Waltons, except everyone shouts.

This house isn't as tall as a skyscraper, though, and the sea doesn't lap at the stoop; but it will do, for now.

'Iris, honey, you got my Sweet and Low?' Zev cries.

'Uh-hu.'

Gran calls Zev our security guard because every night at 11 p.m. prompt, he shuffles down the white-painted wooden stairs, closes the screen door and quadruple locks us all in with our *Pine Freshness*. 'Snug as a bug in a rug,' I think. Zev says it was Nixon's fault that Coney Island's gone to the dogs and Reagan ain't no better. 'Was just after Vietnam we had to go locking our doors at night. Free as birds before them hippies and vets,' he told me. 'Now we got the gangs and the junkies. Set fire to anything, those kids will.'

I still can't see how vets are dangerous; apart from the one that killed Honeybunch, Rita's cockatiel.

Gran pokes her head round our bedroom door. 'Wake up, sweetcakes, almost time.'

We're used to her using Rita's words now.

She's also swallowed up by one of Rita's big dresses, a yellow one with purple stars. Gran's excited, she's got her siren-red lipstick on.

Mrs Zolensky pops up behind her. 'Oh! I want to know the wedding dress, Irees! That pretty Lady Dee-ana, and what he wear?'

'Haven't the foggiest Mrs Z —'

'But you must know, you English, Irees.'

Everyone thinks this; it's strange. Poor Gran, she can never get it right, either side of the Atlantic.

'You want me to bring the tea up, Mrs Z?' she asks (Gran drinks tea with milk and honey now; no coffee).

'I help. But not milk, not milk in mine. You crazy with your milk, Irees.'

I get out of bed as they rummage through our cupboards full of Cheerios and Rocky Road cereal.

The last time I saw Gran so excited was before she holed herself up here. It was in June, and she took me to Manhattan for the day. We rode the subway across a big bridge, to where people live in lofts. We bought soft ice-cream in Washington Square Park and watched white girls with dreadlocks like Trixie dance to Bob Marley, while men said 'sensey, sensey' like they had a screw loose. Gran told me not to worry as she'd seen madder in Boldenham during the war.

There were black squirrels in Washington Square Park and Gran said New York University was a fine place to aim for.

After, we walked round a village, which wasn't like Boldenham at all: no red telephone or post box, just yellow taxis. Shops had pictures of Marilyn Monroe and a boy called James Dean in their windows. Gran said they'd been dead for ages and how life just never moves on. I bought black eyeshadow, black nail varnish and a green spiral earring, and Gran took me to The Empire State Building and gave me a King Kong pen. It was only on the way back to Coney Island that I remembered I don't have my ears pierced.

Manhattan is where Debbie Harry comes from, so I'm going to dye my hair like hers: with Millie's bleach, or maybe *Lysol*.

Still in my nightie, I walk up one flight to Zev's first floor apartment, and knock.

'Come in!' they all yell.

Zev has a huge sofa, and he's got Millie on one side and Mrs Zolensky on the other.

'Come sit, mayn kind,' he says.

Gran has her own chair and she's poured the tea, and ladled out noodle kugel and lamb stew. I snuggle next to Millie and pull a blanket over me. Streetlights still glare onto the Avenue outside, but it's getting light.

'Ew, get that goddarned stuff outta my face, Iris,' Zev cries at the lamb.

'Bit of nice lamb'll see you right, Mr Bloomfield.'

'Oh leave him be, Millie,' Gran tells her. 'You got that VCR thingy working, Zev?'

'Sure have.'

'You sure sure?'

'Said I was sure didn't I? Stop nudging, Iry.'

'Katie, wake up.'

'I'm not asleep.'

'Well, open your goddamned eyes.'

I do, because that's the first time my Gran has sounded like a Yank since we got here.

'And you should go dress up for this. Your mom'll be watching in England, you know.'

'So?'

'Now, sh!'

I watch the T.V. screen. It's daytime over there, and big crowds are waving plastic flags and wearing Union Jack hats, like other crowds did at the Jubilee. I remember getting a mug from school then. I look at bits of England on the American telly and wonder if Grandpa is watching at home and shouting 'Aft!' A few weeks ago he told me there were riots and now every city in England is on fire. But I can't see any scorch marks. We get letters from Grandpa every week. One for Gran and a separate one for me. I've come to look forward to his shaky writing.

Dearest Katie,

All fine here. Your mother and Francis doing well. She sends her love, I'm sure. Reggie still at it with cats and books upstairs and a new woman Mrs Phelps looking after me well. Brian turning out well. He asks to be reminded to you and to mention something called 'Ghost Town' by The Specials is at Number One. Whatever that means. As you know got Best In Show at Three Counties. Breeding going v.v.well on both counts. Bull and dog both up to scratch. Jessie 13 in house but lips sealed apropos Grandmother please. The dogs miss you, Crabtree over for poker Wednesday nights. Hope you will be coming *home* soon. Shan't go on.

Your Loving Grandfather

p.s. Found this pic. of us. Head chopped off. Amusing, no?

Gran also gets letters from Mr Crabtree, and she hides them. I've read them and he wants to come over to stay.

'Popcorn, Katie?' Gran asks, trying to wean me off anything more fattening; but I'm not tempted by lamb, or pudding.

I put the salty cardboard in my mouth.

'Not long now,' says Millie.

'What?' I ask through a stuffed mouth.

'They don't get married till later, honey. We've gotta go through all the guests first.'

'Gra–an!' I lie back. 'Wake me up when she's on.'

'Oh Katie, you'll miss all the good bits. Spoilsport.'

'And on this most momentous of occasions, the Royal party will ascend The Mall, where well-wishers have camped overnight –'

Millie pours out her precious supply of Harvey's Bristol Cream and I hear the chink! of glasses. The crowd in Trafalgar Square cheer at something, and I close my eyes to the sound of England in Zev Bloomfield's sitting room.

The first night we slept here, Gran told me about how the house used to be. How Rita, Lula and Iry had the top floor, Momma and Poppa Ichmann were below, while Grandma and Pops Lieberman were on the ground floor on account of their age. And then there was the Deli (four blocks down, and Sammy's Pizza now), as well as the basement, filled with barrels of pickles and pickled fish all the way from Europe. She told me how the house smelt of a salt that wasn't the sea.

Sometimes I think I can hear them; like I could hear Samuel and Wilhomena fight like cats above me at the farm.

'Ida! Some iced tea!' Pops says.

'On the porch!'

'Whadaya say?!'

My hairs stand on end at each shout and sometimes I try and bring back the silent buzz of Happy Farm; the still hang of Pledge in the air, just to make the Ichmanns and Liebermans quiet.

'Oh, look, sweetcakes, here she comes! Look at that carriage! Sweetcakes!'

Gran shakes me awake and I open my eyes to see Zev staring at my grandmother like he's just seen a ghost. What with the dress and the 'sweetcakes', Gran'll be getting the red hair-dye out soon.

Mrs Zolensky's all pink with the Harveys Bristol Cream and the lamb has all but disappeared. 'Oh gold. Is all gold? Poor horse pull all that?' she asks.

Millie fills her glass again, and the phone rings downstairs.

'Who in godsname is that?' Zev yells.

'No need to shout!'

'Iris, I will not be ordered about in my own house.'

'Hardly a house, this apartment.'

I slip off the big sofa and jump down the painted wood steps to our ground floor. I pick up the phone that hangs from Rita's wall, and twirl the long cord round my finger like American women do on the telly.

'Hi?'

'Hello Kate? Is that you?'

'Uh-hu.'

'My godfathers, you really have gone Yank.'

'Hi Mom.'

I'm doing it to annoy her now.

'So how are you, arse-creeper?'

'Fine.'

'Just fine? Miss me?'

'Suppose.'

'Are you watching it on the television? Isn't it just delightful?'

'Yes. We all are.'

'Well, Francis is out and your grandfather can't be bothered with stuff like this, but I – oh hold on –'

'Mum?'

I hear a crackle; our voices echo like Jessie's bark in his oil drum.

'Kate?'

'Yes.'

'Ah good, just needed to replenish. I tell you what, married life could make a wino out of the best of them. Ha!'

'Are you and Francis coming over to visit?'

'Maybe. Maybe. He's so busy with the estate.'

'Right. Have you seen Bosum? Is he okay?'

'Yes. Still firing.' I hear her glug and want to ask; is it red, white, whisky or gin? 'Oh, isn't this exciting, Kate. Watching this with your mama. Can you see the television?'

'Sure,' I lie.

'And such a lovely day too. Bloody hell!'

'What?'

'The dress! It's bloody enormous!'

'Yeah.'

'Oh what a pity, and it's so creased. Ha! Look at them trying to smooth it down, and that train! Je-sus, if I'd have had one of those they'd never fit me in that pissy little church.' She takes more glugs. 'Ah. Isn't that nice. Floating up the steps. Never thought I'd be into this stuff, Kate. Must be age.'

'Must be.'

'Less of your cheek, darling.'

'Sorry.'

'Oh, in she goes –'

'Yeah.'

'Do you like it over there, Kate?'

'I suppose.'

'Do you want to come home?'

'Gran keeps asking me that.'

'Well, you'll make your own mind up.'

'Probably. Mum?'

'Oh, isn't she lovely! Ya?'

'Are you pregnant?'

'What?'

'Just wondering.'

'Odd question.'

'Not really.'

'Well no, I'm not, who put that into your head, your grand-mother?'

'No.'

'Well, less with the fertile imagination. About all that's fertile too.'

'Okay. I don't need to know everything.'

'Well, you asked.'

'True.'

'Oh, isn't that a great shot. The aerial view. My god that train is long. Doesn't she look happy?'

'Yes.'

'She really does.' She glugs again. 'Anyway, sweetheart, shouldn't keep you, should I, darling?'

'No.'

'Take care.'

'I will.'

'And see you soon, one way or the other. Oh, Kate?'

'Yes?'

'You've got your father, haven't you? Just, I seem to have –'

'Yes. I've got him.'

'Thought you had. Anyway. Much love. Bye.'

There's a click and a hiss and nothing but the sound of Gran, Zev, Millie, and Mrs Zolensky 'oohing' and 'ahhing' above.

It's the night for it, Gran said. No one about and if there are, well who cares?

If there are you'll get mugged, said Zev, and worse besides. Gran shushed him.

We walk down the boardwalk ramp and into the dirty sand. I can feel the day's heat move through the wood to my sandals. It's hotter at nights and the air smells of Nathan's Famous hot-dogs and sweet garbage. I've put on black nail varnish, because it seemed the time for it. Gran is flapping about in one of Rita's numbers. It's a particularly striking one; salmon pink with big blue rabbit silhouettes. I don't know where Rita got her clothes. Gran's upset, because she still hasn't got one ounce bigger; not even her hips. The wind catches the dress every now and again, cracking it like a sheet.

They have big grasshoppers called cicadas here, and you can hear them on the beach. Gran says that's them rubbing their back legs together, that chirrup. It's the same noise as the nightjars Brian and I spied on in the back field on August nights. I close my eyes, but the air doesn't smell like the farm; there's just sugar from the fair and sewage from the sea.

I follow Gran over little mounds of sand. I hope we don't step on any hypodermics. Mrs Zolensky said they go right through your shoe, and then you become an addict, your teeth drop out, and you'll do anything for a dollar. I follow Gran all the way down to the tide; it's bright in the full moonlight.

'Here, honey,' she says, 'come.'

I walk to her and feel sea-scum kiss my feet like meringue. Gran licks her finger and holds it up.

'This'll do,' she says.

Lights flash in the sky, white and red, a plane coming in to land. There are more stars here because I can only remember The Plough at home. The moon shines on the sea and I think about Gran's English Carousel, the one her mum told her about, on this very beach on a night like this. The one that sunk out there, just off Coney. I wonder if the golden unicorns and bluer than blue foals are intact, if the silver stallions are still galloping under the water. Or if they've got eaten up by pollution and crabs.

'You ready?' she asks.

I nod, and hear her say her Our Father's as she unscrews the lid. I do the same with mine, and it's tight as hell. If I was back at Rita's I could run it under hot water; twist it with a towel.

It gives.

Gran's whispering gobbledegook now. Her Chew words she's never forgotten. They sound like the words Zev mutters when we have to sit in his apartment and have a Sabbath. Zev told me I can be a Chew, because I'm a girl.

There's the tiniest salt-shake sound as Gran lifts up Rita's urn and tips it into the night wind; then, I suppose, she's gone.

I lift up my dad, but don't say anything. There aren't many words. Perhaps I should sing 'Save Your Kisses for Me', but I don't want my gran to laugh. A dog barks from an apartment block balcony, and a man shouts in Russian.

I'm glad Dad's out of his poubelle in the South of France, and out of Gran's piano stool in the attic. And he'll be fine here, my dad, mixed with the calm sea and the dirty sand. I shake him.

'Kisses for me, save all your kiss-es for me. Bye-bye baby, bye-bye –' I sing, because Gran's muttering her gobbledegook again.

I'll keep the Hellmann's jar, though.

For old times' sake, as Millie says.

Dad can dissolve in the ocean now, he can get mixed up in the salt water that dances round that English Carousel. He can ride the underwater stallions like King Neptune himself.

ACKNOWLEDGEMENTS

A huge and boundless thank you to both Clare Reihill at Fourth Estate and Veronique Baxter at David Higham Associates. Also to the lovely Jessica Axe, Venetia Butterfield, Essie Cousins and Rosie Gailer at Harper Perennial. Grateful thanks to Louise Tucker, to Terence Caven for the design and patience, and to the AHRB for valued support.

Nothing is possible without mentors, so thank you to Paul Magrs, Kamau Brathwaite, Bernice Rubens, James Redmond and Colin Gray. Absolutely nothing is possible without friends, family or dogs, so thank you to Joan and Fritz, Bess, Squire, Chloe, Brumus and Effie, with love. Also to my other family, the McGoverns of Clonkeen Road, Bang-Bang.

For Laurence Oliver and Ugly Girl.

In memory of my grandparents and my uncle.

P.S.

Ideas &
features . . .

The Singing Gamekeeper

Eithne Farry interviews Tiffany Murray

❛ When I was six I wanted to be a rock 'n' roll singing gamekeeper. ❜

TIFFANY MURRAY is relaxing after bounding around a field with Ugly Girl. The girl in question is not a punk rock chick, with outdoor tendencies, although she does wear a dog collar. Ugly Girl is a lurcher, so named because she is, well, *ugly*. Tiffany explains: 'I saw the litter being born, and Ugly was the runt. She was the last out and the pigment hadn't quite kicked in, so she was the most unattractive pink thing you've ever seen.' Laurence, Tiffany's husband, just fell completely in love with the pup, 'because she was the under-dog, ha, ha'. Ugly Girl plays an important part in Tiffany's writing life. 'I walk her about five times a day, poor thing. That's how I write, I go off into the fields and narratives stream through my head. There's nothing like a bit of outdoor meditation. Writing to me is about observation, whether you are in an apple orchard or pushing through the crowds on Eighth Avenue.'

Manhattan is her 'ideal place in the world' (she lived there for eight years). 'It's full of stories. No matter how chi-chi or gentrified it gets, there's always something at the core of Manhattan that is immovable, it has such history, such voices to listen to.' She started writing *Happy Accidents* when she was living in New York and feeling homesick for Britain. 'I was heading for my thirties and getting very nostalgic for my Welsh border country childhood, so I started to write about that in a series of vignettes – probably because I was reading too much Jean Rhys at the time. Then when I came back home and the nostalgia for New York came to the fore, my New Yorker/Coney Island characters came to life in the book. They were the voices I then missed.'

Tiffany grew up in Herefordshire, and her burning ambition was to be a singing gamekeeper. 'I'm always desperately jealous of writers who knew that that was what they wanted to be from the age of six. When I was six I was best friends with the local gamekeeper's daughter, and because my father was in the music business and obsessed by Elvis Presley I used to go round singing Elvis songs while she hunted small animals.' Tiffany soon abandoned her *Lord of the Flies* phase, became a teenage vegetarian, and took up acting.

She went to London University and gained a first-class degree in English and drama while studying 'the acting part' at Central School of Speech and Drama. 'My class was in a shed out the back. Rufus Sewell was a contemporary, but he was on the proper acting course. We just did ten-minute extracts or those incredibly short Beckett plays, whereas they did Macbeth directed by Judi Dench.' Tiffany's favourite role was playing Winnie from Beckett's *Happy Days* at the Young Vic studio; her worst and last acting job was as a Victorian tour guide at the Museum of the Moving Image. 'I admire actors who have stuck to it, and obviously sometimes I wish I had, but I just couldn't cope with that kind of life – heading out for auditions and singing ▶

6 I'm always desperately jealous of writers who knew that that was what they wanted to be from the age of six. 9

LIFE
at a Glance

After a few years pursuing an acting career in London, Tiffany Murray moved to New York as a Fulbright scholar to study Caribbean and African Literature at New York University. Eight years of professional dog-walking and graduate studies later she backtracked to the University of East Anglia, completed the Fiction MA and PhD and taught creative writing there. She now lives in Herefordshire with Irish husband and lighting designer Laurence and Herefordian lurcher Ugly Girl. *Happy Accidents* is her first novel, and she co-edited *Pretext 8* with Helon Habila. Tiffany is currently completing her second novel, *Diamond Star Halo*.

The Singing Gamekeeper (continued)

◄ something awful from a musical you'd learnt the night before.' But her acting training has helped her with her writing career. 'I love monologues, first-person stories, and I'm quite good at plugging into the way people speak.' She muses, 'When I started I wrote in the third person, because I thought that was what a writer should do. I also concentrated on thick, image-laden prose, but it ended up being rather distant. I'd forgotten about character. So once I'd tuned into Kate's voice, and the sense of freedom that brought, well, it was liberating.'

Kate Happy's perspective on farm life is Gothic, visceral and based in reality. Tiffany explains: 'My grandparents' farm was like the farm in the book. The incident with the bull crushing the cow, that was real, my mother witnessed it. My grandfather was a gentle, lovely man, but farm life can be pretty harsh. There's no time to pussyfoot around.' Even the fictional ghosts have their counterpart in Tiffany's real world. 'I don't believe in ghosts as floaty white things, but there's certainly something there. When you walk through parts of our cottage you'll suddenly feel cold, and the lights will flicker off and on. It's been happening since I was a child. Perhaps it's bad wiring, but I don't think so.'

When Tiffany is working she needs silence and long walks. 'But music is incredibly important to the environment that I'm writing about,' she reveals. 'I always think about what I listened to back then or what would be playing at the time the story is set. There's always a musical collage accompanying the words.' Tiffany's father made a compilation

CD of all the songs mentioned in *Happy Accidents*, and played it at her launch party. 'It was great. It went from "Too Much Too Young" by The Specials to "Sheep May Safely Graze".' And she doesn't believe that you can write without reading at the same time. 'Before I set to work on this book, I compiled a reading list, and then went up to the attic and brought down all my favourite childhood books. It was literally *Jane Eyre* and *'Salem's Lot*. After all, this is a book about childhood, and the world you inhabit as a child is quite often made up of the books you read.'

'*'Salem's Lot*?'

'Well, both *'Salem's Lot* and *Jane Eyre* are about vampires – on a literal level Bertha is up in the attic, scared of the light and biting Richard Mason. She's a Caribbean souciant: a vampire. And as a child I loved to be scared. I used to sleepwalk. My mother was always finding me in the oddest of places: once I woke up bashing my head on the cold grey stone of a turret when I was staying with an uncle in Scotland. That was certainly odd. And memorable.'

Tiffany is hard at work on her second novel, *Diamond Star Halo*. It is set in the eighties again and it's about first love, the music business and life in a recording studio in Wales. Her bedside reading for this book? 'Jane Austen's *Persuasion*, Dodie Smith's *I Capture the Castle* and Pamela des Barres' groupie memoir *I'm with the Band*.' She's also in the throes of leaving Herefordshire for Dublin. 'I had my New York years, then I dragged Laurence to my home in the Herefordshire countryside and now we're ▶

❛ The world you inhabit as a child is quite often made up of the books you read. ❜

The Singing Gamekeeper (continued)

◀ going to Ireland, where his family are.' She thinks that her favourite ghosts will make the move with her, but is also looking forward to hearing new voices, new stories. 'I don't like to think of myself as purely British. I'd like to think of myself as a hopeful New Yorker, via Herefordshire, via Dublin.'

And Ugly Girl?

'Well, she's going to have to come too.' ■

❛ I'd like to think of myself as a hopeful New Yorker, via Herefordshire, via Dublin. ❜

Tiffany Murray's
Top Eleven Books

Jane Eyre
Charlotte Brontë

Brothers
Bernice Rubens

Persuasion
Jane Austen

After Leaving Mr Mackenzie
Jean Rhys

The Lone Ranger and Tonto Fistfight in Heaven
Sherman Alexie

One Hundred Years of Solitude
Gabriel García Márquez

In Youth is Pleasure
Denton Welch

Modern Love
Paul Magrs

Wuthering Heights
Emily Brontë

Beloved
Toni Morrison

Women in Love
D.H. Lawrence

Ghosts in Our Own Fictions

By Tiffany Murray

'WHERE DO THESE STORIES COME FROM?' someone asks from the stalls. That's simple, isn't it? Because you've got six basic choices:

It's imagination.

It happened to you.

It happened to someone.

It happened to everyone.

It was something your mother told you.

It's something you stole from somebody else.

So that's it, either 1), 2), 3), 4), 5) or 6). Right? The truth is, fiction is all of the above and then a little more. It's a slippery business talking about where stories come from, and trying to separate these things is like trying to separate the ingredients of soup. In the first instance let's accept that fiction is a sort of biography. We write lives. Whether it's mine, yours, theirs, ours or someone else's, that's what we do. We even use the biographer's tools: we sit in libraries and research, we pore over historical documents and look at people from the particular time and place we're interested in, so that we know how to paint them and to give them life. We know what they wore/wear, how they spoke/speak, and what they did/do on a Thursday morning. Though unfortunately for us and our sanity these 'people' now turn out to be characters. They are living and breathing for us but in truth they never existed, not really, not in real life. Did they?

Real life. Now there's a humdinger. Lived experience. Memoir. Autobiography! And yes,

I can feel the next question coming –

'So what's real in your book and what have you made up? That bit? Or what about that bit there? Did that really happen? I mean you grew up in Herefordshire, about 1980, didn't you?'

'Yes.'

'With your grandparents, on a farm?'

'Yes.'

'Wasn't your mother called Marlene?'

'Yes. Well, sort of.'

'What do you mean, "sort of"? Was she or wasn't she?'

'She was christened Marlene.'

'There, see, I knew it. That is your mother. Easy job, writing fiction. It's just copying what happened.'

'No, really it's not.'

'But you said –'

'The Marlene in my book isn't my mother. Look, ask her yourself, she'll tell you. Go on, Mum.'

'*Tell them what? What do they bloody want? Arse-creepers.*'

'Nothing, Mum. It doesn't matter.'

'*Tell them what, darling?*'

'That's it's not you, the mother in the book.'

'*Oh bloody hell, not that old chestnut.*'

'Tell them it's not you.'

'*Well, everybody thinks it is.*'

'But it's not. I should know.'

'*You used my bloody voice for her, though, didn't you, child? For that ghastly Marlene.*' ▶

Kate Happy's Top Eleven Tunes

'Save Your Kisses for Me'
The Brotherhood of Man

'Happy House'
Siouxsie and the Banshees

'Me and You and a Dog Named Boo'
Stonewall Jackson

'In the Ghetto'
Elvis Presley

'Life on Mars?'
David Bowie

'My Sweet Lord'
George Harrison

'Wouldn't It Be Nice'
The Beach Boys

'Runaway Boys'
Stray Cats

'Too Much Too Young'
The Specials

'Sunday Girl'
Blondie

'Stop the Cavalry'
Jona Lewie

Ghosts in our own fiction (continued)

◀ 'Yes, but it's such a great voice, Mum.'

'*Yes, well, that's years of boarding school and bolshiness. But what's all this about "arse-creeper"? I never say that.*'

'Yes you do, you just did.'

'*Really? How awful.*'

'Yeah.'

'*And I have to tell you, Tiff, that Marlene in your book, she's a complete bloody mess. Terrible woman.*'

'And that's why it's not you, Mum.'

'*Bloody right, because I was always there for you. Still am. God, you have to be when your only bloody child decides to be a writer aged –*'

'Shut up, Mum. Don't tell them how old I am.'

'*What did you want anyway?*'

'For you to tell them that you aren't Marlene.'

'*Oh God, I'm getting sick of this. Life's too short. Listen, just read the bloody book. Who cares who's who because quite honestly I gave up dividing reality and fantasy a long bloody time ago and about time everyone else did the same.*'

So you see, it's not that easy. There's little either/or, and that lovely line between imagination and *what actually happened* doesn't exist, not clearly. They bleed into one another until there's this thing that is so removed from that particular experience or that particular family myth (although at the same time it is the myth, re-camouflaged, re-structured) that the poor left-out-in-the-cold author can only bleat, 'What does this have to do with me? Because this was meant to be a version of my childhood, wasn't it?'

❛ It's a slippery business talking about where stories come from. ❜

Then you see yourself, a glimpse, nothing more. You're just a flash, a ghostly figure, and that's it. You've reduced yourself to a shimmer of your *real* self because the either/or divide has been smashed and imagination has taken over to miraculously transform you into a skinny child that doesn't eat. You're on the same farm but your grandmother is American, caring, and dressed in pink, and your grandfather is a mix of all the old men you've ever loved in your life. Your mother sounds the same, her voice I mean, and she's had the same *very bad* experiences, but this Marlene is sloppy and unsure of herself. She's definitely not the firm arm who brought you up. And the Japanese film crew and Aunt Rita with her one leg, Aunt Reggie too, they could never happen. Could they?

It's odd, being a ghost in your own text. The writer Jean Rhys pinpointed this eerie feeling perfectly in her last story in her last collection, the aptly named *Sleep It Off, Lady*. The story is called, 'I Used to Live Here Once', and, in barely one and a half pages a third-person narrator tells us that a woman (unknown) returns to her childhood home in the West Indies. She follows the familiar stepping stones across a river; walks up the badly widened road, to this house of memory. In the garden there are two white Creole children under a big mango tree, a boy and a girl. The woman talks to them, shyly. They do not respond. Finally the boy turns to her and looks straight through her with his 'grey eyes'. He says to his companion, 'Hasn't it gone cold all of a sudden. D'you notice? Let's go in.' It is at this point that the woman's arms fall to her ▶

Tiffany Murray's Reading List for Happy Accidents

Jane Eyre by Charlotte Brontë

'Salem's Lot by Stephen King

Wuthering Heights by Emily Brontë

The Water Babies by Charles Kingsley

A Selection of Nancy Drew Mysteries

The Virgin and the Gypsy by D.H. Lawrence

Stig of the Dump by Clive King

The Secret Garden by Frances Hodgson Burnett

Anne of Green Gables by L.M. Montgomery

Fattypuffs and Thinifers by André Maurois

Ghosts in our own fiction (continued)

◀ sides 'as she watched them running across the grass to the house. That was the first time she knew.'

What she knows is that she'll always be trapped; a ghost in her own fiction. ∎

If you loved this,
you'll like…

Oranges Are Not the Only Fruit by Jeanette Winterson

'Like most people I lived for a long time with my mother and father. My father liked to watch the wrestling, my mother liked to wrestle …' So begins Winterson's début, a furiously funny look at sex and religion in the North of England. Our heroine is an orphan who grows up in an evangelical household, happy to shake her tambourine for the Lord. But when she falls in love with a girl, all hell breaks loose in this idiosyncratic and sensitive novel.

Cold Comfort Farm by Stella Gibbons

When twenty-year-old Flora Poste is left orphaned by her impoverished family, the sophisticated young lady heads to Sussex to take refuge with her rural relatives on the ramshackle Cold Comfort Farm. The Starkadders are, frankly, bonkers. Flora has to cope with a herd of cattle (inventively named Graceless, Feckless and Aimless), primitive washing conditions and the eccentric notions of Doom, the aged matriarch, who has never recovered from the shock of seeing 'something nasty in the woodshed'. But Flora is unflappable and sets about restoring neatness and order to their messy lives in this deliciously funny parody of 'rural gloom' novels.

Behind the Scenes at the Museum by Kate Atkinson

In which Ruby Lennox breezily reveals the carefully hidden secrets of her quirky, ▶

If you loved this... *(continued)*

◀ quixotic family. Her parents own a pet shop, her dad George is a serial philanderer and her mum Bunty is lost is a world of bitter daydreams. Ruby manages to condense five generations of familial history into a series of sparkling footnotes and charming anecdotes, while coping with the foibles of her two older sisters. What was it that Philip Larkin said about families?

Sleeping Arrangements by Laura Shaine Cunningham

You'd expect Laura Shaine Cunningham to be a little on the flaky side. After all, she was brought up by her eccentric uncles – Len, a six-foot-six-inch private investigator, and Gabe, a religious librarian who wrote songs in his spare time – in a makeshift flat. She had her harum-scarum moments, running wild in the streets and parks of the Bronx with her best friend, the highly strung and wayward Diana. Instead she grew up to be funny and wise and steadfast, as this memoir so touchingly reveals.

The Ninth Life of Louis Drax by Liz Jensen

Louis Drax is accident prone, arsey and acerbic – the sort of kid who has a fondness for vampire bats, hamsters and rocket launchers and a scathing disdain for the 'blah blah blah' details of the adult world. Happily embracing his 'Disturbed Child' moniker, he sets about bringing a little mayhem into the lives of his beautiful mother and estranged father. Things get totally out of hand, however, on a family picnic in Provence when Louis falls from a cliff and ends up in a coma. In a series of eerie episodes the truth behind Louis's accident is slowly revealed – and it's very sinister indeed.

The Taxi Driver's Daughter *by Julia Darling*
Julia Darling writes about the worry and wonder of being fifteen – with a neat-freak sister, a mum who's been caught shoplifting and a boyfriend who's been expelled from school for bad behaviour. Add in an art project where a local tree gets decorated with beautiful shoes, illicit drinking, burglary and bullying and you'll understand why flame-haired heroine Caris wants 'to steal away into the night, wearing fine gloves and Italian shoes and ride to a place where she could be someone else'. ■

Find Out More

… about Tiffany and the Happys on Ms Murray's website, www.happyfarm.org, and www.laurenceoliverlighting.com.

Interested in the history of Coney Island? Click on www.coneyisland.com.

Thinking of visiting Herefordshire? Discover more about its history on www.smr.herefordshire.gov.uk.

For tourist information about the area, contact the Hereford Tourist Board, 1 King Street, Hereford, UR4 9BW. Tel. 01432 268 430 or email hereford@herefordshire.gov.uk. ∎